JOURNEY [illegible]

Before us was a mansion such as I had [illegible] before. It was stunningly beautiful, glowing with the rays of the setting sun shining on it. A profusion of flowers softened the lines of the house. It resembled a Greek temple with six columns at the front supporting the shingle roof soaring over its two stories. A small flight of stone steps led up to the front piazza.

A man stepped out of the shadow of one of the columns and started down the steps toward the carriage, followed by two uniformed blacks. His steel grey hair was clipped close to his head. His cheeks were like worn leather, lined and tanned by the sun.

'Welcome to Maddocks, Fleur.' I gazed down in terror at the cold grey eyes of the stranger standing with his arms outstretched toward me. His lips twisted into a warped smile.

'Welcome home, Fleur.'

Also by Richard Tresillian in Sphere Books:

THE BONDMASTER
BLOOD OF THE BONDMASTER
THE BONDMASTER BREED

Fleur

RICHARD TRESILLIAN

SPHERE BOOKS LIMITED
30–32 Gray's Inn Road, London WC1X 8JL

First published in Great Britain by
Arlington Books (Publishers) Ltd 1979

Published by Sphere Books Ltd 1981

TRADE
MARK

Set in Intertype Times

Printed in Canada

Blacks and whites were not free to love each other without considerable emotional confusion, marked in part by a self-contempt projected on to the other. The tragedy of miscegenation lay, not in its collapse into lust and sexual exploitation, but in the terrible pressure to deny the delight, affection and love that so often grew from tawdry beginnings. Whites as well as blacks found themselves tortured as well as degraded, but not always for the reasons they thought.

From *Roll, Jordan, Roll—The World The Slaves Made*
by Eugene D. Genovese,
Pantheon Books, New York, 1974

CONTENTS

Book One
FLIGHT FROM SAVANNAH
Fall, 1858

CHAPTER ONE

The squat ugly shadow moving across the tiny room, now expanding into threatening proportions, then flattening into sharp lines, seemed a portent of what the future held for me. I kept my eyes on the tightly clasped hands in my lap, trying to block out the grating voice, to fight back my scalding tears and stifle the sobs that seemed to clutch at my throat. I dared not show open defiance but neither would I show weakness in front of this man.

Captain Finney raged as he paced up and down, his heavy boots setting the floorboards trembling and the furniture skittering against the walls. He was a man below medium height but his bulbous body, his violent movements, and his loud coarse voice made him seem larger. His cheeks, scabrous beneath his patchy grey beard, ballooned out. His bandy legs spun him around just before he crashed into the secretary bookcase in the corner of the room. Air whooshed from between his bloated lips in an animalistic snort.

He halted abruptly and I could sense his glare but I

would not look up. He whipped around to roar at the third person in the room, an old black man cowering just inside the door.

'Damn yer guts and hide!'

The old man whimpered, 'It ain't my fault, sah. Dere ain't nobody left now 'cept me and young Missy.'

'Hold your tongue, boy, or I'll rip it out with me naked fingers.'

Trott, the Negro, swallowed and lapsed into an indignant silence. Captain Finney rolled on his short legs across to the window. The tall proud masts which were visible through the thick pane of glass, where the vessels were moored alongside the wharf, seemed to calm him a little.

'Thirty days it took me to sail here to Savannah! I'm bound to sail again as soon as me cargo's discharged.' He looked around the room scratching his beard. 'When did they die?'

' 'Bout three weeks ago, sah!' The old man drew himself straight, sensing the hurricane of the captain's wrath had blown itself out.

'Bloody flux!' snapped the captain. 'If it ain't pellagra at sea it's the bloody flux on shore. The nigras too.'

'Yassah. I's the only one livin'.'

'By Neptune's balls, this is a cussed business.' He tugged at his beard and his bloodshot eyes returned to me. 'What in hell's name am I to do with this wench?'

Trott crossed the floor to the couch where I sat and stood behind it, placing his hands on my shoulders. The old man had been with my mother since she was a child and he loved me like a second father. His protective gesture in the face of Captain Finney's wrath sent a warm glow of comfort through me.

'Yo' be dis chile's uncle, sah. Mistis Charlotte warn me to take care of her an' give her into yuh safe keeping.' Trott defiantly repeated the information which had originally sparked off the captain's anger. This time Captain Finney shook his head sadly but his concern seemed more for himself than me.

From the time my mother gasped her last breath, I

had been preparing myself for this encounter. Mother had died ten days before, a little more than a week after my father. She had nursed Daddy devotedly until he died and clung to him passionately even when the spasms of coughing had wracked his body and warned of his death, only turning away in despair when the black dregs oozed from between his lips.

Mother had always been stern. Sometimes she had even seemed a bit harsh. But beneath her forbidding exterior were tenderness and warmth. Hers had been the strength that steadied my dreamer father. She came from an old Savannah seafaring family and the ship chandlery had been her idea. She had enlarged it from a simple store to one of the finest on the waterfront. Now, with both her and my father dead, the chandlery was in the hands of creditors and I was alone in the world with only old Trott to care for me.

Captain Finney began pacing the floor again. 'What did Charlotte want me to do with this barnacle?' Undisguised contempt was in his voice.

He came close, the odour of stale tobacco and unwashed flesh nearly stifling me. I looked up and he must have sensed my disgust, for his manner became even more offensive.

He leered at Trott. 'Hah! I could sell her, of course! There's many a New Orleans whorehouse would prize a daisy wench like her.'

'Missy Fleur be yuh own flesh and blood, sah!' Poor Trott was so shocked the angry words came tumbling out without thought.

Captain Finney eyed him angrily. 'Watch yer mouth, boy. She's mine to do what I please with.'

For once Trott refused to be intimidated. 'I done serve Mistis Charlotte since she was a young lady, Cap'n Finney. I done bury yuh own mother and father too. Missy Fleur be yuh niece. She respec'ble.' His mouth snapped shut, his expression implying utter disapproval of the captain's words.

The captain shrugged and towered over me. 'Yer age?' The question barked like an order to a deck hand, left me speechless. I opened my mouth but my voice failed.

The captain swung toward Trott. 'How old be she, boy?'

Trott was thoughtful. 'She was sixteen only two months befuh de Mistis die, sah.'

A beam of triumph split the captain's face. 'Wenches her age are worth a fortune in Cuba or N'Orleans. She's hot enough, I'll vouch, behind those silky features.' A strange wheezing noise, which I assumed was intended as laughter, tumbled out of his mouth. He strode toward the dresser.

As he poured himself a brandy from the decanter, he seemed to relax and I saw my chance to escape. Raising my skirts, I leapt up and raced out of the parlour.

'Where yo' going wench?' I heard him yell. But I paid no attention. Running as fast as I could, I mounted the stairs and wrenched open the door of my room. My fingers worked at the latch, and I leaned against the door, burying my face in my arm, letting the tears come at last.

I could hear the captain in the vestibule below, 'Bah! ' he roared. 'I ain't got no time to chase milady in her chamber. Not now leastwise.' Then to Trott, 'Stay close to her, boy. I'm off to Pulaski House for a grog and to consider the matter.'

I waited until I heard the riverfront door shut. Two sailors who had been lounging opposite our house fell in beside the captain. The three of them swaggered up the wharfside. Then with a sigh of relief, I tiptoed to my bed and collapsed upon it burying my head in the pillow.

Dream and reverie blended into one, and my father's voice echoed in my mind like a sign from the past. 'Fleur! Fleur! Do let me in. I've written a new poem.'

I remembered how I had run to the door that day to embrace him. He was a slender, carefree man with a mane of dark hair that tumbled across his shoulders. He glanced at the book I had been reading and still held in my hand. It was a collection of Byron's poems he had given me for Christmas.

He glanced at the book and patted my arm, smiling. 'Fleur, listen to this. It's quite the best poem I've ever written.'

The resonant drawl of my father's voice wafted over me. I had read enough of poetry to know that his talent was a limited one, but the poem was filled with love and happiness. I found joy in listening to him read it.

'Why, Daddy, that's perfectly beautiful,' I told him. 'Mother will swoon with happiness when she hears it.'

He looked at me doubtfully. 'Perhaps,' he muttered. He added with a wry smile, 'Maybe these words will chase out the clatter of coins from her ears.'

That night as I lay half asleep on my bed I heard my mother's voice drifting across from her bedroom. As so often there was a rasp of irritation in her tones. 'Oh do leave me alone, Lennie. I'm so tired. I've been on my feet in the chandlery all day.'

Father's voice was ringed with complaint. 'These days you're always tired. Can you remember when I was courting you? We sat on the river's bank when the moon was high and I wooed you with my poems.'

Mother's voice was gentler. 'Oh Lennie, dear. Can't you see we must keep the chandlery open? I do so want Fleur to be a young lady of consequence.'

'I'm sorry, Charlotte. I wish I had the resources to close that wretched canvas and tallow shop and have you live like a princess.' I could hear Daddy cross the room to sit on the bed beside mother.

'But I like the chandlery, Lennie. It gives us a comfortable income. Besides, the sea is in my veins.'

'There's warm blood in my veins. The strength of a poet's passion. Oh Charlotte! All these years I've loved you.'

I heard her give a little cry then, a sob, and I pictured her in my father's arms in a passion that might lie dormant but could never die. The soft murmuring, the wordless sounds of love floated to me. I lay still, the blanket of the night over me and a sense of security bringing me peace.

The reverie was shattered and I was jolted back to the present by the slamming of the front door below. The gruff tones of Captain Finney filled the house. A squeal of girlish laughter made me realise the captain had brought a woman back with him.

The two of them mounted the stairs with uncertain steps, swaying against the balustrade, muttering obscenities, laughing drunkenly. They stopped outside my parents' chamber. He kicked the door open with a shout.

'Aha, wench! I'll shipwreck in your thighs tonight. And on a bed of feathers instead of a bunk board! Get in there, wench!'

I buried my head deeper in the pillow to keep out the sounds that followed but I was wretched at the thought of the captain disporting himself with some riverfront whore in the bed where my father and mother had died.

What could I do? There was only one person who might save me from Captain Finney. My father had a brother. I had never seen him but I had heard his name often. Uncle Leo! What would he be like? I imagined him as kind and gentle as Daddy. If I could only reach him, surely I would be safe.

CHAPTER TWO

I awoke when the sun was beginning to pour its misty light over the river. The cries of our neighbours' cockerels mingled with the early morning oaths of the sailors aboard the vessels moored at the waterfront. The creak of pulleys, the splash of slops being jettisoned overboard, and the burgeoning hubbub of the wharfside chased the hard-won sleep from me.

As Savannah stirred, my mind raced with excitement

at the thought of what I would have to do to save myself from Captain Finney's evil designs for my future.

I dressed carefully. My wardrobe was not elaborate. My dear mother's concern for her chandlery had made her somewhat neglectful of my needs and I had never seen fit to protest. I did not have friends to call on, preferring the company of Daddy's books to the bother of mixing with other children.

Of course, living on the very banks of the great river which linked Savannah with the whole world, I could not be ignorant of life outside the secure limits of my home. But to me that life seemed to abound with unnecessary trivialities which deprived one of the enjoyment of mental pleasures.

One of these pleasures was to sit on a bench under the live oaks, those evergreens of such exquisite beauty which grew in Emmet Park, and to watch the flow of the river into the gloomy mystery of the opposite lowlands slipping away to the sea. The bustling of the pompous cotton brokers on Factors Walk often intruded into my contemplation of this haunting riverscape. I resolved to hurry to Factors Walk that morning.

Factors Walk was the name given to the walkway before the battalion of five-storey red brick buildings marshalled along the riverfront. The lower floors of these buildings served as warehouses with access on to the river itself while the upper storeys housed the offices of the cotton brokers.

My mother delighted to tell me about Savannah's importance as the Queen City of the Cotton Kingdom. Factors Walk was Savannah's court. The ramps of the Walk were paved with cobblestones brought as ballast in the same ships which carried away the cotton to foreign markets. The beautiful retaining walls which prevented the riverfront bluff from erosion were made of the same ballast stones.

I scrambled quickly up the thirty steps that scaled the wall behind our home to bring me onto the Walk. I had managed to slip out of the house while Trott was shuffling around in the kitchen. Captain Finney was snoring in my parents' chamber. No one had observed me.

I made my way quickly to the park. The air in the shelter of the oak trees, was tingling with the freshness of the new day. I sat on my favourite bench and gazed around.

Usually, it would have been unthinkable for a young lady of a respectable family to venture on the Savannah streets alone. The city had been planned by its founder, the English General Oglethorpe, in neat streets and public squares. As the cotton industry and plantations grew, Savannah expanded and became the trade centre of the entire coastal area, shipping rice and lumber as well as the big money maker, cotton.

Commerce chased away the city's gentility and the waterfront became infested with cut-throats, thieves, vagabonds and whores. Because of this, whenever I ventured out of our house, I was always accompanied by Trott or by one of the black girls who served my mother. However the disease which had ravaged the gentry had devastated the rogues too. As a result, Savannah's streets were strangely quiet, and no one had the time to think ill of a young lady sitting alone in the park.

The cotton brokers and their staff arrived to open up their offices, the clerks scuttling over the iron walkways in a great hurry while the factors followed haughtily behind. Groups of rough-looking men began to lounge under the trees along the walk. I studied them curiously. Of course, I had often seen gangs of planters roaming the streets in search of diversion, but I had never considered them as being of importance to me. Now they were.

With their bady tailored frock coats and ill-fitting trousers, they seemed an inelegant lot. Scanning their tanned faces, I picked out one man who seemed older than the rest. His white hair fell in a mane about his shoulders and he clapped his arm around the shoulder of his companion with self-assured authority. His coat was dark green and his trousers a light gold. I perceived by instinct that he was a man who would be civil to a young lady. I ventured toward the group of which he was the centre.

'Sir, sir!' I cried edging closer. None of the planters took any notice.

'Sir!' I sidled around the back of the group and put my hand out and touched the elbow of the man I had chosen to help me. He swerved around, leaving the group, but he was frowning and obviously thought I was approaching him for no good purpose.

I felt like crying but I managed to say, 'I need help, sir.'

'Money? A young lady like you accosting respectable planters on the streets! What has Savannah come to!'

'No, not money, sir. You misjudge me. My parents have recently died. My uncle, Captain Finney, intends to send me away.' I bit my lip, unable to explain Captain Finney's purpose.

The old man placed his hand on my shoulder. 'I see you're unhappy child. What do you think I can do?'

His touch made me feel stronger. I managed a weak smile. 'I have another uncle, sir. He doesn't know my parents are dead. I want to send him a message. Will you help me?'

The man hesitated. 'Why don't you ask your Captain Finney to do that?'

I gasped. 'Not Captain Finney! I must escape from him. I don't want to go away on his ship, sir. His intentions, sir!'

The man grinned broadly. 'You're an attractive lass.'

'My other uncle is Leo Singer of Caxton County. I want to inform him of my plight so he will send for me.'

'Singer!' The man exclaimed in surprise, dropping his hand from my shoulder. 'By old Horny, are you Singer's lass?'

'Lennie Singer was my father. He was a poet.'

'Indeed? Well, I had no idea Leo had a niece!' The old man was chuckling. 'What a dark horse he is!'

'Do you know my uncle?' I asked eagerly.

'My neighbour,' the man replied. 'It's Paxton County, Miss, not Caxton. Leo Singer owns half of it and I own the rest. You want me to take him a message?'

'Oh yes, oh yes, sir. Please tell him my parents died in the sickness and that I'm in danger of being taken away from Savannah by Captain Finney. I fear for my virtue, sir.'

'Hah!' The old man snorted. 'Do you indeed? That's a serious business, Miss. I don't know what Leo Singer will say to that. But I'll tell him. I'll give him your message.' He turned his back on me quickly when one of the factors waddled over to the group and the planters began to harangue him.

I felt he did not believe me and tears began to prick my eyes.

'I found yo' at las'!' Trott's words exploded in my ear. He gripped my hand roughly and tugged me away. 'A right scare yo' gib me. Cap'n Finney say he gwine lambaste me from de Harbour Light to Forsyt' Park if I don' fin' you'.'

I began to sob. Trott urged me away from the planters in great haste. He hurried me down the slope to the riverfront and along the wharf. I was too startled to protest; my thoughts dwelt only on the old planter, wondering if he would take my message to Uncle Leo.

Captain Finney's swollen features were puce with rage when he saw me being escorted along the waterfront by Trott. He pulled me into the house with such force that I tumbled on the doorstep and cried out. None of the throng of sailors, street vendors and merchants who jostled one another on the wharf paid any attention.

'I'll give yer something to bawl about, Miss!' shouted the captain, hastening me along the hallway and up the stairs. 'Yer'll not slip away from me ag'en!'

'You're hurting my wrist!' I shrilled, more with surprise at his handling of me than pain.

'I should beat your backside with my hands, that will give yer hurt to shout.' He pushed open the door of my chamber and thrust me in. I ran over to my bed and fell against it, slipping down onto my knees and covering my eyes with my hands. I felt wretched.

'Hah! Now yer feel sorry for yer morning walk, eh? Where were yer bound for, gal?' Captain Finney's bulbous figure seemed to fill the doorway. I glanced at him between my fingers then shielded my eyes again quickly.

'No answer, eh? I'd clap yer in irons if I had yer on board, me gal! Where was she, boy?'

'She be on Factors Walk, sah!' Trott stammered.

'Factors Walk!' Captain Finney looked puzzled. 'She ain't got no cotton to sell.'

'I was trying to send a message to my Uncle Leo,' I blurted out. 'He wouldn't treat me like this!'

'Don't be so sure, young Miss!' Captain Finney chuckled mirthlessly. 'I know about yer Uncle Leo. He'd as soon send for yer as he would for the bloody flux itself.'

I was puzzled. 'You're just saying that to keep me. Uncle Leo will want me to join his own family when he learns I am alone here.'

'Now what gave yer that idea!' His chuckle changed to a menacing guffaw. 'Yer Uncle Leo ain't got no family and he ain't likely to have one neither.'

Captain Finney's roar of mocking laughter made me wince. He slammed the door shut on my hopes and turned the key. I heard him berating Trott as he descended the stairs. 'Yer good for nothing nigra! I'm keeping this key in my pocket, boy. She won't be skulkin' in the city again, running wild like a hussy.'

I got up from the floor and ran over to the door. It was firmly locked and refused to yield. 'Let me out!' I screamed. 'Let me out!'

There was no response from Captain Finney. I glanced around the room. Not even when I was a child had I been locked in like this. Now I was utterly powerless.

I crossed over to the window, my head cast down in despair. I was in the habit of sitting by the window whenever I came up to my room to read. Books were such a joy to me but this morning I could get no comfort from them. How would the stories I read compare with the dreadful situation I was in, a prisoner in my own room at the mercy of my uncle's whim?

I raised my eyes and gazed out on to the wharf. The masts of the ships bobbed gently in the flow of the river. Teams of brawny men, their shirts open to their waists, scurried across the wharf loading the ships with bales of cotton. The sun was high, sending a sheen of heat glimmering over the dark water. I opened the window hastily, wondering if it would be possible for me to climb down the side of the house to the wharf.

The noisy shouts and cries of the crowds swarming along the riverfront swelled up to the room. I put out my head and looked down. The red brick of our house was smooth and afforded no hand hold. It would be impossible for me to descend and I shuddered at the thought of it.

Captain Finney suddenly emerged from the front door of the house. He had his hat perched on his head at a jaunty angle and began to stroll along the wharf as though he owned it. The crowd parted before him.

I watched two sailors follow him closely as he progressed up the lane leading to Bay Street and disappeared around the corner.

'Trott! Trott!' I shouted with delight when the old Negro stepped out of the house and looked up at my window. 'Oh Trott, please help me.'

'Ain't nothing I can do, Missy. De Cap'n say he gwine settle some affairs den he gwine take yo' away.'

'Let me out, Trott.'

'I don' hab no key, Miss. Cap'n done tell me he gwine open de door hisself when I totes up yuh dinner.'

My heart was racing and my throat was dry. I fell back on my bed. Trott could not help me, I realised. But I could not, must not, accept defeat.

CHAPTER THREE

'Lor, Missy, yo' ain't et yuh dinner.' These were Trott's first words when he unlocked the door to my chamber.

I was sitting in my chair by the window where I had a view of the whole length of the wharf up to the harbour light and miles beyond to the open sea.

Trott seemed miffed at my silence. He shook his head, mumbling, and shuffled to the door bearing the tray. As the door swung open, I stepped around it to slip under Trott's arm. To my surprise there was a body blocking my way. I gasped and stepped back into the room. Captain Finney followed me inside, pushing Trott out into the hall.

Somehow he did not seem as menacing as I had remembered him, and there was something like a smile twisting his bloated lips.

'I doubt yer know, wench, the trouble ye've cost me. I've a cargo on board and I'm ready to sail. It's only out of respeck for yer mother I'm tryin' to treat yer right. I could haul yer on board and sell yer at the next port.'

'Why don't you let me go?' I cried.

'Mebbe I will, mebbe I will.' For the first time I noticed a crumpled envelope in his fist. He said, 'Looks to me like yer was smarter than I thought. Looks like mebbe yer settled everything for yer self.'

'Whatever do you mean?'

'Yer have yer wish, young Miss.' He moved close to me and put out his arms as though to embrace me. In alarm, I edged toward the window and stood deliberately with a chair between us.

'What wish?'

'Yer Uncle Leo in Paxton County.' He waved the letter in my face. 'Yer planter friend met him on the road yesterday and gave him a report of yer parents' demise. He has sent a man to escort yer to Maddocks.'

'Maddocks?'

'His plantation, Fleur. He wants yer to live at Maddocks with him!'

Was there ever a girl so transported with delight as I was when I heard Captain Finney's words! I quite forgot to wonder if he was duping me for some cruel reason of his own. Instead I danced around the room, and when Trott pushed his head through the door, I embraced him and pulled him in.

'Is the man here? What am I to do? I have no carriage dress to wear for a long journey. Oh Trott! Oh Trott! '

Captain Finney snorted with disgust at my foolishness and turned on his heel. 'I'm to meet the man at the Pulaski House this evening,' he said, waving the letter at me from the doorway. 'Ye'll have to prepare yerself. Take all yer belongings, for I am to close up this house and sail this very night.'

'What about Trott?' I asked. 'Can he come with me?'

Captain Finney glanced with a sneer of contempt at the old man. 'He wouldn't last a day on board my ship! I've no use for him. I doubt he'll take kindly to plantation life, but he is yer'n if yer want 'im.'

'Yes, yes.' I clapped my hands together. Trott was old and stubborn but if he came with me I wouldn't feel such a stranger at this place called 'Maddocks.' I savoured the name of the plantation. It sounded very grand.

'Trott, I have simply nothing to wear! '

'Yo' hab dresses in plenty, Missy. On a plantation folks ain' concern 'bou' fashion like in Sabannah. Folks lib in a rough manner, Missy.' Trott sounded unhappy.

'Why, I declare you're vexed, Trott! '

'Me, Missy? No! I be t'inkin' what me folk in Sabannah gwine say when I does tell dem I gwine back county. We gwine stay at dis "Maddocks" fuh long, Missy?'

'How do I know, Trott? You should be pleased! Don't you realise that Captain Finney would have sold you along with this house if I hadn't asked for you?'

I was rummaging through my meagre collection of dresses as I spoke, lifting them out of the wardrobe and spreading them on my bed. 'What shall I wear, Trott?' He looked at me blankly. 'Oh, never mind. We don't have much time to prepare.'

I heard the front door of the house bang to a close. I ran to the window and peered out. Captain Finney was striding along the wharf accompanied by the two swarthy sailors who followed him every where.

'Quickly, Trott,' I said. 'Follow him at once.'

'Who, Missy?' His face screwed up with consternation at my request.

'Captain Finney. See where he is going.'

'He be gwine to Pulaski House, Missy. De Cap'n be partial to his rum, Missy.'

'Trott, follow him. I want to know what manner of man he meets. Who is the one who will escort us to "Maddocks"? See if he is old or young, dark or fair. Don't linger, Trott. I'm depending on you to hurry back with some report.'

Trott pursed his lips with resentment at my request. He hesitated at the doorway.

'Fie, Trott! ' I said, trying another tactic. 'Don't you want to know with whom we are going? What if he's a rich gentleman with his own carriage? Wouldn't that be something to flaunt before the eyes of Bay Street? Run now and find out quickly. Be discreet! '

The idea of Trott running was laughable but I had no time to consider it as such. I was in a frantic state trying to make my preparations.

By the time I sat, exhausted, on my bed and surveyed my efforts, the sun had set. Lanterns bobbed on the ships at wharfside and already the night was ringing with the curses of drunken seamen trying to board their vessels in the dark.

Where, I wondered, was Trott? Well, I was not going to wait for him to return, I decided, making my way down the stairs to the tiny kitchen at the back of the house. I had not eaten for two days!

Midnight had just passed when Trott burst through the front door. He paused in the gloom of the hallway; I could hear his heavy breathing while his eyes grew accustomed to the dark. I had lit no lamp and had been lying on the couch in the parlour alternately dozing and fuming at his lateness.

'Missy! ' Trott sounded worried.

'I'm here, Trott. Where have you been? I've waited hours and hours.'

Something about Trott's manner as he blundered into the parlour sent a flicker of foreboding through me. He stood fidgeting, a darker shadow in the centre of the room.

I rose to my feet and peered at him suspiciously.

'Well, where is Captain Finney?'

'He at Pulaski House, Missy.'

'Has something happened, Trott?'

'Yes, Missy!' He was panting, his face dramatic with the excitement of calamity.

I sat down again and stared into the blackness of the tiny room. The raucous shouts of sailors passing along the wharf disrupted my attempt to remain calm. 'Light a candle, Trott.' I ordered. He responded clumsily, finally placing a light on the table.

'Very well, tell me what happened.'

Trott rolled his eyes, took a deep breath, and began to recount what had occurred since he left the house to follow Captain Finney.

The captain had sauntered along the cobbled streets to Pulaski House, the largest hotel in the city. He was greeted there by Captain Wiltberger and the two men fell upon each other with great good humour. Captain Wiltberger had been a packet captain before he quit the water and became a boniface. He was reputed to be the finest innkeeper in Savannah, and his hotel bar was the gathering place for the convivially inclined. He stocked the best of liquors, domestic and imported, to satisfy the most critical of connoisseurs. I had often heard mother speak of the bar as the rendezvous of the leading young men of the country from Savannah to the Florida line.

Peter Wiltberger guffawed happily as Captain Finney demanded rum. 'Sounds like it's a dry ship that yer skippers.'

'Bah!' Finney snatched the heavy cut-glass tumbler from the server, then drained the contents down his throat. He prodded Wiltberger in his stomach. 'Yer forget what the sea is like, Peter, with yer dandified life ashore.'

Wiltberger swept his fat arm around the bar room in an expansive gesture to indicate the young bloods squatting at tables rattling dice and noisily drinking.

'The life of a gentleman has more profit, Finney. Why, my house is full! The steamboat from Charleston just put in. New Englanders clamouring for warm water to bathe, lawyers wanting dinner, and cotton planters bursting to spend their wealth.' The innkeeper's heavy frame shook with merriment.

'It ain't no life for a real man.'

'That's yer view, Finney!'

'Where's the challenge? Where's the sou'-wester blowin' up a storm an' yer three days out of port? The only excitement yer get here is when yer cook burns yer shrimp gumbo!' Finney thrust his glass out for a refill.

The pounding of hooves and the clatter of a carriage driven on by the excited whoops of a young man interrupted them. The bar room doors opened directly onto the street. The two men hurried over, staring in amazement at what they saw.

A young man with the reins of a horse in his hands was perched on a little box gig racing down the narrow sidewalk toward the inn. Women and children screamed for their lives and jumped off the sidewalk into the middle of the sandy streets. Two police officers galloped along behind the man trying to catch him.

'By old Horny!' roared Captain Finney. 'The buck's crazy!'

'He's on a bust,' chuckled Wiltberger. 'See, he's cut off the axle-tree on the gig and brought the wheels close up to the body of the carriage so it can pass on the sidewalk. He has a long purse, I'll be bound.'

'He's coming here!' Captain Finney tugged in alarm at the sleeve of his host.

For a large man, Wiltberger moved nimbly. One moment he was arrogantly surveying the frightened women in the street; the next, he was pinioned against the wall as the horse and carriage charged through the wide barroom doors. Trott, who was squatting on his hams on the sidewalk, dived into the dust as the wheels of the carriage swept past him. He saw Captain Finney stumble backward and crash into a group of card players.

The young man in the gig chortled with delight when he saw Captain Wiltberger's eyes popping out of his fat face in fear. He hung onto the horse's reins and the animal reared up over the stricken barkeeper while the drinkers in the saloon scrambled for safety. The man took out his pistol and discharged it in the direction of the captain. The bullet entered the wall just above his head. Shouting and laughing, the young man whirled his horse before he could be seized by the bridge, turned about and dashed into the street again.

The police were blocking his path. They cornered the horse and seized the young man. Inside the bar room the patrons picked themselves up off the floor and dusted themselves down, calling for more whiskey and laughing among themselves. The police led the rowdy back into the bar.

'What the devil, sir!' Captain Wiltberger drew himself up pompously in an effort to restore his pride.

The young man ignored him. 'What a rollicking bust!' he exclaimed.

'Yer'll pay me five hundred dollars, sir, for the damage,' Wiltberger thundered angrily.

'Cheap enough! I've had a good frolic.' The young man drew a fistful of notes from the deep pocket of his coat and thrust the bills at the innkeeper, detaching some for the police. Trott, from his position on the sidewalk, eyed the money as Captain Finney clapped his hand on the man's shoulder.

'A fine scrape, sir. Would yer care for a measure of rum?'

'Whiskey, Captain,' smiled the man, accepting the congratulations of others in the bar before joining Captain Finney at a vacant table.

'Ye've got a fine spirit, sir!' Trott squatted against the wall of the hotel below the open window, so that he could hear what Captain Finney was saying above the braying of the drinkers in the bar.

'Spirit, you call it?' laughed the man, sipping his whiskey. 'Thought I'd have me a frolic before I go home. To the back part of the state,' he added, grinning apologetically. 'I came to Savannah to collect the money for the cotton crop my father sent to the factors.' He paused, draining the whiskey. 'And to escort a young lady.'

'A young lady?' Captain Finney's eyes bulged. 'Yer ain't the one!' he uttered in surprise.

'What do you mean, sir?' The young man snapped his head back arrogantly. 'Are you suggesting I'm not capable of escorting a lady?'

'No, no!' Captain Finney was taken aback. 'I've heard planters are a rough and ready lot. We don't do things like that in Savannah, sir. A gentleman has more finesse.'

'To hell with your finesse!' The rowdy jumped up from the table, pushing the edge of it against Captain Finney's bulging stomach. 'I'll have no more of your company, sir!'

Captain Finney's face coloured quickly at the insult. 'Yer damn well will, mah boy!' he spluttered. 'Yer know who I am?'

'I neither know nor care,' the young man muttered, stalking away.

'Stay, boy!' Captain Finney roared. 'What's the name of the chit ye're seeking? Fleur Singer?'

The man stopped suddenly, spilling the drinks of those who were following him. He pushed his way through them and strode back to the table. He rested his fists on the top and glared at the Captain. 'You Finney?' he demanded sourly.

'I'm Captain Finney to yer, boy, if yer please!'

'I don't please! Where's your niece?'

'In good time, boy.'

'I ain't your boy, Finney, no more than you're mah captain. Leo Singer of Maddocks has commanded me to escort his niece from Savannah. You must release her to me!' The young man lowered his head until he was eye-to-eye with Finney.

'Release? Release? What words are these? She's not my prisoner. I beg of yer, boy, calm yer passion and sit here like a gentleman so we can discuss it.'

'Gentleman!' The young man tossed his head back shaking the dark waves of his hair in derision. He spat deliberately at the captain's boot. 'Does a gentleman plan to ship a young girl with him? Does a gentleman harbour such evil intentions that a young girl is driven to run to a stranger and plead for help? What good fortune Fleur Singer spoke to my own father on Factors Walk and not a "gentleman" such as yourself!'

The man's sneer of contempt was too much for Captain Finney. His rage, quivering under the surface of his good manners, erupted swiftly. He lashed out with the back of his hand and slapped the fellow across his cheek. 'How dare yer insult me, boy!'

The man's face reddened quickly under the force of the captain's blow. His eyes narrowed and his mouth tightened. He pressed his face close to the captain's. 'Is it so you treat your niece, Finney? Well you've picked the wrong man in me, you fat sea slug.'

Captain Finney choked and his face puffed up with the wrath for which he was famous along the Savannah waterfront. 'Yer a damned raw-headed tit-suckler, boy,' he snorted, clenching his fists. 'I'll mash yer bones to gristle!'

The young man snickered insolently under the captain's nose. 'Although you're an old bag of wind, Finney, I'll thank you to withdraw your remarks or I'll be obliged to ask you to direct your friend to act in conjunction with mine.'

Captain Finney gaped at the young man in astonishment. Pulaski House was renowned for the duels hatched behind its brick walls, and by tradition, no man challenged in the House could refuse with his honour intact.

'The impudence!' Finney spluttered. 'Wiltberger, do you hear this snipper-snapper? He challenged me!'

The innkeeper was silent, comparing the financial merits of lending support to his old seamate or to the wealthy young blade. He smiled in the neutral manner of innkeepers whose only concern is profit.

'Forsooth!' Captain Finney spat in his excitement. He leaped to his feet and glared at the crowd of drinkers who had been watching the exchange. 'I'll thank yer fer a second, sirs!'

The two seamen who had followed the captain moved forward to pull the young man away from the table. Captain Finney waved them back. 'This is a matter of honour,' he growled. 'This pup would be strung to the mast and lashed within an inch of his life if he was on my ship!'

'And if you were on my plantation, Finney, I'd do the same to you.'

The captain was speechless. Some of the drinkers in the crowd jeered him.

'Come on,' cried the young man impatiently. 'A second to assist this sea slug to his destiny!'

Two men detached themselves from the drinkers standing around the brelin table. One was a youth and obviously acquainted with the young man for he gave him an encouraging pat on the shoulder. The other, an older man with a black frock coat and a limp, looked like a clerk.

'Johnson!' exclaimed the captain, gasping for breath. 'Demand a full retraction and apology from this *gentleman* here, or in lieu of that an immediate meeting with such weapons as he might select.'

Captain Finney's lip curled now that he had delivered the challenge in the time-honoured fashion of the Savannah *code duelo*. He had no doubt that the young man, his back county bravado cowed by Savannah tradition, would apologise.

The clerk Johnson conferred with the young man's second. Captain Finney returned to his seat, snapping his fingers for another measure of rum. The young man spoke airily to his own second who returned to Johnson. Both seconds shrugged their shoulders eloquently. Dueling was a regular occurrence in the city.

'He is resolved to fight you, Cap'n,' reported Johnson. 'He told me to ask Cap'n Wiltberger for pistols for two and,' Johnson smiled apologetically, 'a coffin for one.'

'Where shall it be? Across the river? Scrivens Ferry?'

'Here, Cap'n.'

'Here?'

'Yes, Cap'n. At this table.'

Captain Finney raised his eye as the young man drew back his chair and sat opposite him. A brace of dueling pistols were produced from the back of the bar. The two seconds examined them carefully. They were the old-style, smooth-bore pistols with caliber for a one-fourth-ounce ball.

Gradually, the revelers in the bar quieted down as the word passed around them that a duel was about to be fought. Trott, his ears straining while he crouched in his listening place below the window, coughed with excitement.

Captain Finney glared murderously at the young man who dared to make him look foolish among his own kind. 'I now demand, boy, in the presence of these gentlemen, all of whom are yer betters, that yer will publicly retract the malicious slanders yer have uttered, seriously affecting my reputation as an honourable seafaring man and a gentleman.'

Trott grinned to himself at the captain's flowing speech. He expected the young man to take this chance to escape from what would be certain death.

'No! ' The man spat whiskey on the table so it splashed Captain Finney's face. He laughed. 'I came to this city for a frolic, and by God, I'm having one. You're a dishonest villain, sir, and I will never perjure myself to save your reputation! ' The crowd murmured.

'What's more, my fat Finney, when I dispatch you, I'll rescue that niece of yours so she'll no longer be subjected to you an' your kind who slither along the Savannah river like eels poisoning the virtue of young maidens.'

A shout went up from the crowd.

'You want to know the name of the "boy" who is going to kill you, Savannah eel? Jem Hayard! Say it, so you die with my name on your tongue, Finney! '

Captain Finney cursed, flicking his fingers at Johnson. 'Say yer prayers, pup. Ye'll rescue no one, not even yer pride when I'm done with yer! Johnson, let's get on with it.'

'Here is the table! ' The young man stared boldly into the captain's eye. 'I will sit on one side and you on the other. Each will have his pistol in readiness for use. You will hold one end of this handkerchief with your left hand, and I the other end. At the signal from the second, pistols will be raised and fired.'

Captain Finney gasped. 'That's not a duel, that's murder.'

'You ain't refusin'?' Hayard asked mockingly.

The captain drew back his shoulders, brushing his hair away from his brow. He sneered at Hayard and raised his arm to stab his fingers in the young man's chest. 'Yer won't be the first man I've killed, boy!'

Johnson placed the pistols quickly on the table. Both men grasped them, flexing their fingers and cocking back the firing pieces. The young man's second placed the handkerchief in the left hand of both of them.

Captain Finney and Jem Hayard drew back from each other until the handkerchief stretched tautly between them. A hush descended on the crowd. Trott raised his head above the windowsill and peered at the duelists as they rested their pistols on the table.

'Are you ready?' asked Johnson.

The two men nodded.

'I will say fire and count one, two, three, stop. You must fire before I say stop and no one shall fire afterward.'

A wry smile crossed Hayard's face.

'Get on with it!' shouted Captain Finney.

'You sure are in a pother to leave this world, Captain Slug!' Hayard sneered.

A tense silence gripped Pulaski House. Trott's eyes bulged when he found himself staring at the muzzles of the pistols.

'Fire – !'

On the word 'Fire,' Jem Hayard grabbed his pistol from the table top. He threw himself off the chair, pulling the trigger before he reached the floor.

'What happened?' I clutched Trott's arm, crying with excitement.

'De bullet lodged in de cap'n's t'roat, Missy Fleur,' Trott trembled, ending his account with a sigh.

'Is he dead?' My voice was a whisper. The candle on top of the table was almost spent.

'Yes, Missy,' Trott beamed sadly. 'De cap'n die awash wid blood, Missy. He stain de floor ob Pulask' House wid he life.'

'What happened to the young man? To Jem Hayard?'

'He run, Missy. De cap'n's shipmates turn on him like dey gwine kill him. He lit out ob de bar room mo' fas' dan a bolt o' lightnin'. He jump on a horse he see in de street an' he gone tearin' down Bay Street in a whoosh ob dust. He ain' deber comin' back to Sabannah in a hurry, dat fuh sure.'

Trott paused and put his hands on his hips, watching me as I gazed at the flickering candle. 'Missy, what yo' gwine do now?' he demanded plaintively.

'Trott!' I exclaimed in anguish. 'Don't you realise the danger I'm in? Captain Finney's shipmates will be coming for me. From what you say, his crew know the young man had come to take me to Maddocks. They'll come here and take me for themselves.'

'Oh yes, Missy. Yo' be right. De cap'n mate an' all de crew gwine be seekin' yo' fuh sure. Dey ain' gwine take de cap'n's deat' widout recompense!'

CHAPTER FOUR

While we talked the candle had burned low in its sconce and its wavering flame left the room in near-darkness. I directed Trott to light a fresh candle, but as he reached into the cabinet where they were kept, I heard a scraping noise at the front door.

'Don't light it, Trott,' I whispered. I beckoned and he crept up to the window beside me. A man stood in front of the barred door of the house. While we watched, he pressed hard against the door with his shoulder. There was a slight creaking sound, but that was all.

He turned and muttered a few words to a second man who was lounging nearby.I could scarcely discern their figures, yet I felt sure they were the two sailors who had followed Captain Finney everywhere.

I slid the window open silently and I could distinguish a few of their words. 'Best wait for the rest of 'em. We'll get the wench out of 'ere fast.'

Trott was restless beside me. I tugged at his sleeve, drawing him back in the room. 'Trott, we've got to get away. But where? All my family's friends are dead. Anyway I can't stay here long. The house and the chandlery are sold. We must escape now while we can. Oh Trott, help me find a place to hide.'

Before Trott could answer, I left him and started toward the stairs.

Trott reached out a shaky hand. 'Where yo' gwine, Missy?'

'To my chamber, Trott. I have some gold pieces mother gave me. They'll pay our passage. You'll carry my luggage.'

'No Missy. Dere ain' no time!'

Trott was right. I raced upstairs, took my reticule and ran back down again, scarcely aware of what I was doing. The night was as dark as a tar barrel when I slipped out of the house with the old servant close behind me. I gripped his hand tightly.

We hurried along the sidewalk, dodging into the shadows between the lighted windows of the houses so no one would see us. Suddenly there was a sound of banging behind us. I dared not look back.

'Open up in there, I say!' a voice called gruffly. 'Are you sure this is the cap'n's house?' someone else asked.

Trott pulled me into a narrow alley which led between two huge warehouses.

'Where are we going?' I whispered in protest. 'We could walk more quickly along the wharf front.'

'No Missy,' Trott was brusque. 'If we be seen we be lost.'

'Those seamen don't know what I look like. We're safer now that we've left the house.'

'Is true, Missy, but dey gwine know yo' is yo' cuz dere ain' no oder young buckree missy roamin' de streets ob Sabannah at night.' Trott's tone indicated that he expected me to hold my tongue and concentrate on following him along the dark alley without falling down.

'I'm tired of running like this, Trott.' I tried to tug my hand out of his. 'I must know where we're going.'

'Shush, Missy!'

He suddenly jerked me out of the alley into a narrow lane which ran parallel to the river. There was an awful stench here and my feet squelched in the soft mud. I kept on stumbling against Trott, my face rasping against the coarse material of his coat. My feet were cold with the wet mud clinging to my shoes. I was panting so much, I had no breath to spare when Trott stopped in front of a wooden door and tapped gently on it.

It was minutes before a voice answered. 'Who dere?' the voice rasped suddenly through a crack in the door, making my heart jump with fright.

Trott put his mouth to the crack and whispered quickly in the Geechee dialect. A bolt drew back and the door opened slightly. Trott thrust me rudely through the gap and into the shack.

A woman held a candle briefly in my face and spoke angrily to Trott. She was an old black woman with a line of warts across her sunken cheek. She wore a flimsy pink gown and a pink turban over her coiled hair.

While Trott whispered apologetically, I glanced around the shack, grasping his hand for protection. The room, I realised, was the entire house. Trott pulled me into a corner and crouched beside me on the hard mud. Meanwhile the woman who had admitted us lowered herself painfully on a torn and filthy blanket and blew out the candle.

Despite the squalor of the shack I felt I was temporarily safe here, and I was grateful to Trott. I sat beside him with my head resting against his shoulder and soon was asleep. Several times I was awakened and once I whimpered as a rat scurried across my legs. Trott put his arm about me and drew me closer as though I were a child, holding me until I slept again.

Finally I opened my eyes and saw the shafts of daylight driving through the cracks in the boards. I roused Trott who went to the river and brought me back a basin of water to bathe my face and hands. The old woman squatted beside me with a cup of coffee, but she rose quickly and went outside before I had a chance to thank her. I never saw her again.

When I walked out of the lane and into Bay Street with Trott, I realised his plan had been right. Here in the daylight, we were no more than a young white lady and her servant out for a stroll. There were so many people thronging the sidewalk, our only danger of discovery was if we met any neighbours who knew us. On every side there was talk of the duel at the Pulaski House the previous night. Jem Hayard and his 'frolics' were the sensation of the morning.

Neither Trott nor I had been out of Savannah before. I sent him to enquire from his acquaintances about a carriage to take us to Paxton County while I admired the stores along Bay Street. He soon returned but his news was disturbing.

'A nigra from de back country say dere be a county like dat nort' ob de capital.'

'That's a long way, Trott. How de we get there?'

'Dey say a carriage be leavin' fuh Milledgeville in an hour, Missy.'

I felt excited. 'Then we must hurry. We mustn't miss it.'

Trott hung his head uncertainly. 'De trouble is, Missy, it be waitin' fuh passengers right by de Pulaski House.'

Trott followed nervously one step behind me as I walked up to the man who was checking the harnesses of the horses tied to the coach. I was careful to approach across the sand of the street so that the carriage itself obscured me from the view of anyone watching from the bar room.

I spoke quickly to the driver and paid for my passage to Milledgeville. Trott was to ride on the roof.

'May I board now?' I asked, stepping to the door which opened onto the road.

'Nay, Miss,' said the driver. 'You can wait with the other passengers in the inn.'

'Oh sir,' I smiled demurely, letting my eyes meet his. 'My mother would be mortified if she knew I had entered Pulaski House. I hear there was a dreadful duel there only last night.'

The driver chuckled, slapping the flank of one of the horses, and opened the carriage door for me. 'Very well, Miss. You make yourself comfortable. For meself, I need a whiskey before we set out!'

The other passengers climbed into the coach soon after. I kept myself pressed into the far corner of the carriage, hoping no one would see me from outside. Trott sat humbly on the sidewalk, blending in with those who were watching the loading and preparations for the coach's departure.

From the corner of my eye I glimpsed Captain Wiltberger at the door of the carriage. He was holding the gloved hand of an elegantly begowned lady who smiled condescendingly as he kissed it.

I glanced at Trott. His face was grey with fear and he was trying to hide behind the others in the crowd.

At last, the coachman climbed aboard. He shouted to Trott to jump onto the roof. Captain Wiltberger glared at him suspiciously.

'Hey, boy!' he called as Trott scrambled up. 'Whose darkie are you?'

'Me, sah?'

'There ain't no other darkie here, is there, boy? Who is yer master?'

Trott, I prayed, for once in your life, please lie properly. I scarcely dared to breathe.

'Mah marster, sah?' Trott mumbled as though he was completely stupid.

'It's awright, cap'n,' I heard the driver say. 'His mistress is inside.'

I breathed with relief when the wheels of the carriage began to turn and the coach jumped forward. Glancing quickly out of the side of the coach, I saw Captain Wiltberger speak to the men standing with him.

Suddenly, the captain clapped his hand to his head. I could almost read his lips.

'Now I remember who that darkie is!' he seemed to be saying. 'That's the boy attending Captain Finney's niece!'

CHAPTER FIVE

The sun was already scorching the day dry as the carriage bumped out of the city. At first, the lurching barely bothered me. I glanced several times out of the coach to see if Finney's men were following us. They were not. Perhaps I was foolish to be so worried.

The coach jolted over a rough patch of road and had all of us inside clasping one another for support. A jolly lady sitting next to me began to ask me questions. I realised it would be useless to lie. In the small exclusive Savannah society, everybody knew of everybody else. I told her who I was and where I was going. The only thing I did not say was that I was travelling alone because the young man called Jem Hayard who had been sent for me had shot Captain Finney.

'Lor' love! You have a long journey ahead of you. Paxton County is quite some miles north of Milledgeville, between there and Atlanta.'

'Oh dear, I understood I could get a carriage from Milledgeville.'

'I dare say you can, child. But who is this uncle you're bound for in Paxton County?'

I frowned. The lady was probably well meaning but I was not accustomed to being asked so many questions by strangers. 'Mister Leo Singer, ma'am, of Maddocks.'

My companion's eyes widened and her brows arched. She opened her mouth as though about to speak, then coughed, choking back the words.

I tilted back my chin, determined not to be put out

by her manner. 'Do you know him?'

The woman smiled, but something hard remained in her eyes. 'Who would have thought Leo Singer had a niece as pretty as you, my dear? He does know you're coming, doesn't he?'

'Oh yes. He sent a letter for me.'

'Wonders will never cease!'

'Why do you say that?'

'Oh, it's none of my business, I'm sure, my dear. For twenty-five years Leo Singer has lived at Maddocks. It's one of the best plantations in the county. But he's never married, my dear. They say in Milledgeville that Leo Singer, eh, well . . .' The woman watched me sorrowfully. 'It's only what I've heard, you understand. They say he doesn't want a woman on the place.'

I was conscious of the lady's eyes searching my face to see how I would react. Her information meant nothing to me. Uncle Leo was my father's brother. He would be handsome and kind just like Daddy and very soon I would be with him. I yawned, quickly shielding my mouth with my hand so as not to give offence.

'You poor child,' the woman beside me soothed. 'You must try to sleep. We have a long journey.' She placed her arm around my shoulder and drew me toward her. Gratefully, I nestled my head close to her large bosom. Soon, in spite of the swaying and heaving of our conveyance, I was asleep.

I slept the whole morning. When the coach stopped at an inn for dinner. I ate sparingly and made sure that Trott was fed. He grumbled good-naturedly about the discomfort of his perch on the roof, but there was nothing that could be done about it. The afternoon passed much as the morning had. I snuggled in the corner with my head lolling on my neighbour's shoulder while I dozed.

A shout, and a jolt which pitched me out of my seat and into the lap of the gentleman sitting opposite, rudely wakened me. The coach stopped abruptly, veering over at a precarious angle. There was confusion while the passengers thrashed around and tried to right themselves. The door was pulled open, and the coachman's gruff voice told us to descend.

'The axle is broken,' he announced curtly. 'Can't go no farther in this carriage.'

His news was greeted by a wail of consternation. I slipped quickly to the ground and looked about me.

It was growing dark. The rough road was in the middle of a pine forest, and trees stretched without a break into the gloom. A thicket of evergreen shrubs draped with garlands of wild jasmine broke the dreariness of the countless pine shafts. I breathed deeply to take in the warm fragrance of the pines and flowers which wafted around us.

'We must fin' shelter, Missy!' Trott's dark shape loomed beside me and he whispered urgently in my ear. 'De buckree tars know we aboard his contraption!' He kicked the splayed-out wheel of the coach and added ruefully, 'Mah joints fair shook apart wid de rattlin' ob dis cart.'

'Surely you're mistaken, Trott. None of Captain Finney's men will come after us now. They could have stopped us long ago.'

'No,' Trott insisted. 'De night is de time dey gwine strike.'

I stepped away from the others and smoothed down my dress. My fellow passengers were still absorbed in disentangling themselves from the coach, clucking and wailing at the inconvenience. Trott held his bundle and my reticule over his shoulder and I followed him a few paces so that we were isolated by the darkness. I drew my mantle around me for comfort.

'Where shall we go, Trott?'

'I don't know, Missy.'

Trott's uncertainty gave me fresh determination. 'We shall walk.'

'We ain' got no lantern, Missy!' Trott wailed, lumbering after me as I set off up the road in the direction the coach had been travelling. 'We ain' gwine walk far in de darkness, Missy Fleur.'

'Why ever not? If anyone is chasing us, we must find

shelter.' I stepped out along the track, steeling myself to appear bolder than I was feeling.

Trott stumbled along behind me. After about a mile, he drew up beside me and touched my arm.

'What is it, Trott?'

'I see a light, Missy. Dere near de groun'.'

I blinked and peered between the pine shafts. About a hundred yards from the road, someone had made a camp and lit a fire.

'Trott,' I spoke softly, 'go and find out who it is.'

He put my reticule down firmly on the road. 'Missy, I'd rather stay wid yo'.'

'One of us must go. If you don't, I will.'

Trott moved away reluctantly, peering back at me until he was lost in the darkness. While I waited, I listened for sounds of pursuit. The quiet was almost eerie.

The night hung around my shoulders like my mantle. I hugged my arms around my body to ward off the cold which was beginning to creep beneath my clothes. I stepped off the road and looked with longing toward the subdued blaze of the fire. A twig cracked.

'Trott?' I whispered urgently as a prickle of fear scratched across my chest.

'Oh Missy,' he croaked, groping his way to my side. 'It ain' safe here 'tall.'

I reached out my hand and drew him close. 'Tell me what isn't safe.'

'It be a coffle, Missy. Dere be a passel of nigras 'roun' dat fire an' de drivers, Missy. Wid long whips! An' de nigras all in chains.' Trott was trembling.

'Halloo!' From behind us on the track came a loud commotion. I clutched Trott in panic. He listened briefly.

'Dey comin' fuh us, Missy. Wid a horse.'

'Fleur! Fleur!'

It was a man's voice! A peal of gruff laughter was borne to us on the night breeze.

The clouds parted and the stars cut an uneven light through the boughs of the pine trees above our heads. I pulled Trott off the road and into the forest, ignoring the briars which caught at my dress. I dragged him along behind me, groping with my free hand to prevent branches snapping in my face.

'Where we gwine, Missy?'

'You hid me last night, Trott. I'm going to hide us tonight.'

'Oh no, Missy!' He stopped suddenly and refused to budge even though I pulled his arm with all my strength.

'Ah ain' gwine in dere, Missy. Dem people could be nigra stealers.'

While I pulled and Trott resisted, the horse was galloping closer, the rider shouting my name with reckless familiarity. I knew it was one of Finney's men. When I heard the horse reined to a halt near our hiding place, I sank to the ground, pulling Trott down with me. I clung to him, scarcely daring to breathe. My pursuer had seen the glow of the fire.

He plunged his horse into the forest passing only inches from us. Trott moaned. Fortunately, the noise was drowned by the cries from the slave camp when the pursuer rode into the coffle firing his pistol in the air.

I raised my head to peer through the bushes. The rider fired again but this time there was an answering crack, higher-pitched and whirring. It came from a whip that twisted like a snake around the intruder's wrist. The pistol dropped from his grasp. He gave a scream in which agony and outrage were combined.

'Give me back my pistol, sir.'

A husky voice rose above the shouting of the slaves. 'Ah ain't takin' no orders from a whelp like yo'. What's yo' business, young 'un?'

The heavy figure standing spraddle-legged in front of the fire, stroked the shaft of a long bullwhip.

The man whom I now recognised as Captain Finney's mate glanced around the table, studying the faces of the slaves illuminated by the fire. 'I'm looking for a white girl,' he shouted, guiding his horse out of the range of the whip. 'She's travelling this road alone with an old nigra. Have you seen her?'

'No!' The husky voice was adamant and unfriendly.

'If you do, I'd be obliged to you to hold her. I'll pay well.'

'And yo'll ride out of my camp, now!' growled the slave driver.

'My pistol?'

The whip cracked once more, falling inches from the shoulder of a tall black who stood near the rider. The Negro handed the sailor the pistol and backed away rapidly. I heard the whip lash out again over the horse's flank. It snorted and bolted out of the clearing with its rider struggling to hold the reins. The figure outlined by the wood fire laughed raucously.

I waited until my pursuer was on the trail and I could hear the horse galloping off before I stood up.

A twig snapped behind me and I put my arm out thinking to grasp Trott. Suddenly a hand gripped my shoulder and another clamped over my mouth. I felt myself falling backward. I kicked and twisted but I was powerless. I was being dragged into the pine glade.

'A busy night, Brutus.'

I heard the dry chuckle as my captor flung me at the feet of the slave driver. I stared at the muddied riding boots only inches from my mouth.

'Let's see yer face, gal,' the voice was curiously soft.

I looked up slowly, puzzled by the tones. My gaze crept along the rough breeches, observing the wide hips of the person towering over me. The long brown coat was open at the waist revealing a vest which covered swelling breasts. I could not conceal my surprise.

'Ah'm Ma Drax,' said the slave driver, smiling and extending a hand to me. 'Here, let me help yo' to yer feet. Ah don't suppose yo' are gonna run?'

I took the callused hand proffered to me and eased myself to a standing position, staring at the woman all the while. She had close-cropped hair under a man's cap which completed her masculine appearance. Even her voice and stance were those of a man.

'No,' I shook my head bitterly, tears stinging my eyes. 'I won't run. But please don't give me to that man.'

'Hah! Ah'll see about that!' Ma Drax slapped her whip against her thigh. She looked at the Negro who had caught me.

'She hab one nigra, Ma. He old. Wort' 'bout four hundred dollars.'

'Yer nigra?' Ma Drax looked at me again, her face expressionless. I nodded, too confused to speak.

'House nigra, ah 'spect, Brutus.'

'He don' look like no house nigra. Too dang crusty.'

Ma Drax glanced in Trott's direction. He was lying on the ground by the fire, quivering with fear. The black faces of the slaves chained to each other in the coffle regarded him impassively. They were guarded by a white boy.

'He ain't no bush nigra. That's fer sure.' Ma Drax chuckled. 'Don' matter, chain him with the others, Wayne.' The boy stood up lazily.

'No! You can't chain Trott!' I protested shrilly. 'He's not a slave.'

'He's yer nigra, ain't he?' Ma Drax snapped off a plug of tobacco and began to chew. 'If he's yer nigra, he ain't free and if he ain't free, he's a slave. Brutus, mah driver, values him at four hundred dollars.'

Ma Drax hawked and a stream of spittle sizzled in the fire. 'What yo' value yer freedom at, gal?'

'My freedom?'

'Yo' act surprised. I can call that sailor back and turn yo' over to him.'

'You wouldn't,' I gasped, covering my face so this monstrous woman would not see my panic.

'Hah! Ma Drax does what she wants. What yo' say? Yer freedom for yer nigra!' she prodded me with the handle of the whip, grinning.

'No!' I almost shouted the word.

'Well, at least yer got guts, gal.' She crouched down in front of me, pulling me roughly against her and rubbing her lips against my cheek.

'My! Yer a pretty chit to be sure.' She squeezed my breast, ignoring my scream of pain.

I spluttered as her foul breath blew into my face.

Her eyes gleamed in the firelight as she turned toward Brutus.

'Yo' caught me a dainty wench, Brutus.'

Brutus flashed a grin and pushed Trott over to the white boy guarding the slave gang. I looked at the boy for help but he turned his head away quickly.

Ma Drax settled herself against the trunk of a tree and dragged me down with her. She made me sit at her feet and studied my face carefully. 'Yo' don' have to be scared of Ma Drax, chicken,' she rasped. 'Not if yo' do like ah tell you!

'A soul needs a nice body like yo' to keep her warm on a night like this, eh?' she prodded me between my legs with her whip handle. I brushed it away quickly, feeling the shame flooding into my face.

'Oh such a pretty blush! Yo've quite captivated me, gal.' Ma Drax pressed me still closer, throwing her arm around my shoulder. I saw the pasty complexion of her face and the wattles of loose flesh under her chin.

Despite all my efforts I could no longer hold back my tears. Ma Drax let me cry, patting my hair tenderly, rubbing her fingers soothingly down my shoulders and breasts. Regardless of my revulsion at this woman, I felt a certain degree of safety with her.

Her lips hovered over my cheeks while she whispered words of comfort. I was exhausted. Her harsh voice changed to soothing tones and I felt myself drifting into sleep.

'De buckra comin' back!' It was Brutus, crashing into the glade and standing in front of Ma Drax. She pushed me aside with a scowl and stood up.

'Yo' gwine gib her back?' Brutus queried. 'De man hab plenty dollars.'

Ma Drax glanced down where I was stretched out under the pine tree. I pleaded silently with my eyes and she clicked her tongue crossly.

'Take the wench into the forest, Brutus. Stay with her 'til the tar goes.'

'The nigra?'

'He's chained, ain't he? The sailor won't recognise

him in the dark. Quick, take the gal.'

Brutus bent down and picked me up, holding me with ease in his huge arms. I wrapped my arm around his neck to keep my head from falling backward.

'Brutus,' Ma Drax chuckled, 'she's a pretty wench. I doubt a man's ever broke her in.'

Brutus grinned evilly. 'Ah know what to do, Ma Drax. We ain't gwine make no noise.'

His chuckle made me shiver, and I tried to arch my body away from him. In the light of the fire I saw the white youth who was guarding the coffle of slaves stare hard and long at Brutus. He scratched his tousled hair thoughtfully as Brutus ran with me into the pine trees.

CHAPTER SIX

The sound of horses crashing through the undergrowth swelled through the night air. The slaves began to wail. Brutus dodged swiftly into the depths of the pine forest ignoring the commotion. My concern that I might be found by Finney's men made me cling to him without daring to look back. Brutus had his arms firmly around my body and his face close to mine but I was too worried at being discovered to give him much thought.

Brutus paused, cocked his head to listen, and dropped to his knees. I struggled to get my feet on the ground but he pushed me down on the pine needles, held his finger to his lips to warn me to make no noise and nodded his head in apparent satisfaction when I lay motionless. He removed his arm from under my legs but kept his other arm around my shoulders. He beamed at me, pressing me close to him.

'So yer back, sailor?' Ma Drax's scornful shout echoed through the trees to us and made Brutus jerk away from me. He peered anxiously through the pines to the fire. I raised my head until I could see Ma Drax standing with her legs astride and her back to the flames. The intruders were out of sight and in the darkness at the edge of the glade. The slaves in the coffle were moaning restlessly. No one spoke.

Brutus faced me, his dark eyes glinting hungrily. I drew away from him but he eased himself on the ground and pulled me across his thighs. I gasped.

'Yo' mek one soun'. Missy, an' dem tars gwine take yo'!' His huge hand curled around my hip, pinning me to him.

Ma Drax's mannish voice broke the tension. 'We ain't got no gal here, mates, so yo' kin get!' She spat angrily into the flames.

I breathed more evenly now I knew Ma Drax would not betray me. Although he was keeping close guard on me, Brutus was watching Ma Drax intently. I suddenly realised then he was the only black who wasn't chained. His body felt alert, as though he was ready to leap into the clearing if anything happened to his mistress.

'If she's not here, you don't mind us taking a look around, do you?'

There were three of them. I recognised two as the men who guarded Captain Finney in Savannah and their leader was the captain's mate. They rode their horses in a circle around Ma Drax. She glared at them.

'Boys, yo' don't belong here. Ah'll give yo' ten seconds to get out where yo' came from or ah goin' to lash yo' to shreds with this whip.' She brandished the long bullwhip in the mate's face.

'They'll kill her!' I whispered to Brutus.

'No, gal.' He pressed my face against his chest to silence me so I did not see what happened next. The air was filled with curses, the snapping of the whip and Ma Drax's demented laughter. There was a shot and the pounding of hooves as the intruders' horses bolted out of the forest.

'It's black flesh ah deal in not white!' Ma Drax bellowed after the fleeing men. 'Yer gal ain't here!'

'Thank the Lord they've gone!' I whispered, wriggling to free myself of Brutus' grip.

'Aye!' Brutus flashed his white teeth in a twisted smile. 'Why yo' fidgetin' so? We got us a little pleasurin' to do.' He lay back on the pine needles and wrapped his huge hands around my hips and pulled me on top of him. I was trapped, pinioned to his body.

He stifled my scream by cupping his mouth over mine. I gagged and pulled my face away quickly as he rolled over. He kept his hold but changed his position so that he was lying across me instead of under me. His weight knocked the breath from my body.

He pawed at my legs, clumsily trying to ease my dress up to my thighs. I squirmed in terror underneath him but it was no use. His massive body crushed me into the pine needles covering the forest floor.

I paused in my struggle. 'Brutus!' I hissed into his ear. 'I have gold.'

His hand, working up my thigh, stopped. He peered into my face. 'Where?'

'In my reticule. I left it by the road. Let me go and I'll give it to you.'

He snorted, droplets of spittle from his mouth cascading onto my cheeks and lips. 'When ah done plug yo', gal, den ah gwine tek de gol'.' His hand wormed its way to the top of my leg.

'Ma Drax!' I cried in panic.

Brutus was too quick for me. His hand clamped over my mouth again before my voice could be heard. I began to choke, my chest swelling up as I heaved under his hand and thrashed my legs, beating my fists on his back and trying to throw him off.

There was a flash and a clap like thunder which resounded in my ears and left me deafened. The grip on my face relaxed and I was able to breathe again. Brutus lay on me, stilled by the noise. I expected him to leap off and defend himself but instead his hand slid away from my mouth and his body twitched. Suddenly he gurgled and, as I raised my head, his great bulk slid off me. He was dead.

I wriggled away from the body as quickly as I could. Someone stood over me in the darkness.

'Get up quickly, Miss. We must run!'

The voice that spoke to me out of the darkness was young and quavering.

'You're not Ma Drax!'

'No, I ain't. Come on!' The stranger bent down and grasped me by the shoulder. I twisted away from him and scrambled to my feet.

'Who are you?'

'This ain't the time for talk. She'll be here in a second. Take my hand.'

I brushed my torn dress down from my thighs, blushing in the darkness. 'You saved me!'

'I ain't saved you yet, Missy. Come!' The man's young voice cracked with panic. He grabbed my hand. 'Here she comes. Get down!'

Suddenly I found myself sprawled out on the ground again.

Someone was blundering through the trees toward us. My rescuer stood above me, eyeing the darkness carefully. I watched him hold his pistol straight out in front of him, take aim and fire. I screamed and covered my ears as the night exploded into tiny stars.

The man crouched down in front of me, breathing heavily, straining his ears to listen.

'Yo' shot me, Wayne!' Ma Drax's voice called from the clump of trees ten feet away. 'Help me, boy.'

'Get up, Missy!' My rescuer dragged me to my feet and pulled me by my hand.

'Where are we going? Ma Drax is hurt.'

'So she says. Come on, Missy. Don't you know what will happen to you if she gets hold of you?' He tugged my arms again and I followed a few steps deeper into the forest.

'What about Trott?' I cried.

'I loosed him already.'

This time I followed the youth, dodging with him around the trees and fighting my way through the bramble patches. He paused after a few minutes to listen.

'Is there any one following us?'

'Do be silent, Missy. I can't hear if you talk!'

My cheeks coloured at the boy's reprimand. He may have rescued me, I decided, but he was not going to boss me.

'Where are we going?' I panted after we had run for a few more minutes.

'Too much talk, Missy!'

I stopped. 'It may be too much for you. I want to know who you are. Where's Trott? I'm not going further until you tell me!'

I could see the youth in the vague light from the moon filtering through the edge of the forest. We were by the road, about a mile up, I judged, from the place where I had left my reticule. The youth was listening carefully. His tousled, dirty hair flopped on his brow and he looked like a ragamuffin in torn breeches and a shirt with ripped sleeves and no buttons. He was only a little taller than me and skinny. He flapped his hand at me trying to wave me into silence.

'I won't be quiet!' I said. 'Who are you?'

The boy's face darkened and his shoulders rose and fell as he sighed heavily. 'I'm Wayne, Missy. Now please be quiet. I want to hear if they are following us.'

'Who?'

'The men who were looking for you.' He held up his finger for silence again and stared out along the blackness of the road. Whether I trusted Wayne or not, I had no alternative but to do what he told me. His appearance did not inspire confidence; his face was grimy, his arms and legs bled from scratches from the brambles, and his scrawny frame showed little sign of strength.

'There's someone coming!' he hissed, pushing me back into the shelter of the bushes.

I listened carefully. 'I can't hear anything.'

'Quiet!'

I sniffed and sank down beside a tree trunk. Wayne crept away from me. I had been listening for the sound of horses galloping along the track. The night was silent. When I touched my face, my cheek was scratched where a thorn had grazed it. I looked in amazement at my hands and arms, scarred and bleeding from my flight through the trees and bushes. I probably looked as dishevelled as Wayne.

I listened for him now, wondering if he had abandoned me. I heard a stifled cry, a scuffle, then silence. Wayne! I wanted to shout. I began to tremble. There was a crackle of twigs by my side and I jumped to my feet.

'Hush, Missy!'

'Oh Wayne! I was so frightened!'

'Don't you ever do what you're told?' Wayne sounded exasperated. I peered eagerly in the darkness to see his face. Suddenly I realised there was someone behind him. The figure stepped forward.

'I scared yo' be dead, Missy Fleur.'

'Trott!'

'Hush!'

'Are we in danger still, Wayne?' I whispered contritely. 'I'm so glad you found Trott.'

'He was heading north like I told him.' Wayne sniffed. 'If those sailors have given up searching for you, you'll be in no more danger than any young lady alone in the pine barrens at night.'

'De men dey ridin' back to Sabannah,' Trott said.

'How do you know?' Wayne's voice was curt as though he was reluctant to believe Trott.

'Cuz I he'ah dem say so. An' dey ain' here, is dey?' Trott eased himself against the tree beside me. I put my hand in his.

'I never thought I'd see you again Trott.'

'Most like yo' wouldn't Missy. I ain' no bush nigra. It be dis buckree what found me. What we gwine do, now?'

'Where's my reticule, Trott? I have gold in it.'

'Bless me, Missy. I ain' know.'

'But you must. You left it beside the road when we had to hide in the forest.'

'Maybe I done dat, Missy Fleur. I don' remember.'

Wayne crouched in front of us. We were hidden in a clearing. The moon was faint and, by staying among the trees, we could avoid being seen from the road. Wayne looked around and then spoke to us, his thin voice hard and serious.

'Missy, we can stay here till daybreak. Trott can go and look for your reticule in the morning and then we can walk to Milledgeville.'

'Stay here?' I looked around the glade. 'In the open?'

'If we do stay, there's the risk of Ma Drax finding us in the morning, or those sailors you are running from finding you.'

'I'm not running from them. I'm going to my uncle's. Those men are from Captain Finney's ship. They want to take me away with them.'

Wayne scowled in the moonlight. 'If we wait until daybreak, you may get your gold but you'll lose your liberty. We must move tonight, now. We'll be safe if we can reach Milledgeville before dawn.'

I studied Wayne. Perhaps his face, under the pine and out of the shadowy light which enclosed us, was good-looking. He was watching me with that hard stare I had noticed when I first saw him in Ma Drax's camp.

'Well?'

'I don't know. I don't know anybody in Milledgeville.'

'Hah! I do.' He stood up and held out his hand for me. 'Come on. If we start now, we can be in Milledgeville in a few hours. We'll walk along the road and hide in the bushes beside it if anyone comes.' He gave a thin laugh. 'You're lucky. If anyone sees you now, Fleur, they'll take you for a gypsy instead of a lady.'

'Fleur? You called me Fleur.' I took his hand and let him help me to my feet.

'It's your name, isn't it?'

'Yes. But – '

'But nothing, Fleur. I'm not your slave and I'm not your servant.' His tone chilled. 'Now are you going to walk along the highway or shall I leave you here with only Trott's protection?'

'I'll walk,' I said stepping up the bank onto the road. 'But you'll have to help us. We've never been out in the country before.'

'What! And I've been in Savannah so many times.'

'With Ma Drax?'

'Oh no, when I had things to do.'

'Is Ma Drax your mother? Why did you kill her?' We were walking on the road side by side while Trott followed a few paces behind.

'By old Horny! That's a jest for you! Ma Drax ain't never had the pleasure of motherhood, I can assure you. I didn't kill her.'

'You fired your pistol at her.'

'Aye.' He seemed sad. 'It was her'n anyway.' He tapped the pistol tucked into his belt. 'Ma Drax ain't gonna die that easy. I wounded her, that's all. She'll be stomping along this road by daybreak rounding up her nigras. I loosed them all.'

'Will she look for you?' I stumbled as I spoke. He took my elbow roughly and urged me to keep walking.

'You ain't told me your story yet, my young Miss. What's a city lady like you doing on the road at night?'

I told him briefly what had happened during the previous days. Something about his manner made me want to trust him even though I wondered if he intended to turn me over to my uncle and then claim a reward for having saved me. My suspicions were confirmed when he demanded my uncle's name.

'Not Leo Singer of Maddocks!' He stopped in his tracks. Trott, wandering forward like a blind man, bumped into him in the dark.

Wayne ignored Trott, gesturing with his head for us to resume walking. 'He is one of the wealthiest planters this side of Atlanta,' he mused. 'Is he expecting you?'

'The man who shot Captain Finney was the one he sent to meet me.'

'Was he now? Well, there's fortune for me! I lose my share of a coffle and I've gained old Singer's niece.' Wayne's voice warmed. 'I'll see you get there safely, Missy Fleur.'

'I'm "Missy" now that you know who I am?' I observed tartly.

'I'm not proud, Fleur, when it suits my purpose. A man must survive. What was the name of the man your uncle sent to meet you? One of the Paxton blades I suppose.'

'I believe his name is Jem Hayard.'

Wayne gasped. 'Jem Hayard!' He released my arm and slapped his brow with the palm of his hand.

'Whatever is wrong!'

'Jem Hayard! Of all the bucks in Georgee I pick to tangle with, I have to choose Jem!'

'You know him?' I was intrigued.

'Who doesn't? He's the wildest, hottest, stupidest cuss a man ever saw. He has a fist for a brain and a purse for a heart. When he can't punch his way out of trouble, he buys his way free. Oh he's a reckless one, is Jem Hayard.'

'You sound like you admire him.'

'Perhaps I do. His family despairs of him, but he's popular with his kind. No traditions tie him down. I've seen him on his busts in Milledgeville when the politicians are in town. He stops their pompousness you can be sure. Jem Hayard ain't afraid of no one.'

'Then why did he run away and leave me?'

'I doubt that he did. He would have come for you in his own good time. Still, he seems an odd escort for Leo Singer to light on.'

'Is he not to be trusted?'

'Women don't trust themselves with him, Fleur.' Wayne peered at me in the faint dawn glow. 'You can feel fortunate you have found me to escort you instead of Jem.'

We rounded a bend in the road and saw the ring of houses outlined in the distance marking the outskirts of Milledgeville, the state's capital. I pondered my escort's remark. A gentleman of good breeding as headstrong as Jem Hayard would surely be preferable to the wise scoundrel who stalked at my side.

CHAPTER SEVEN

We stumbled into Milledgeville like the survivors of a shipwreck. My thin shoes were nearly worn to shreds but the numbness in my feet prevented me from feeling the pain of every step. My gown was in tatters, my hair dusty and dishevelled and my bonnet askew. I clung to our escort more to keep on my feet than through any desire for his close company; he looked as impoverished as a beggar. Poor Trott, with a covering of grime on his dark suit and a few buttons missing, was the most respectable of the three of us.

Fortunately we arrived in the town before dawn broke and the cocks crowed to rouse the populace. It was such a grand place! Savannah was a city of beauty and tradition, but Milledgeville was a modern marvel with streets a hundred feet wide. Its houses were large porticoed mansions, not the dull stone dwellings of Savannah.

'Wayne, how can we find help here?' I squeezed my escort's elbow in alarm at the sight of the imposing white-walled buildings looming out of the predawn darkness. 'It's lovely, but so intimidating.'

In answer, Wayne led us off the main thoroughfare and into a side street. He guided us down a narrow lane leading off this street, between some smaller houses, and then into a passageway obscured by the shrubs that grew lushly on either side. We arrived at the door of a shack very much like the one Trott had taken me to in Savannah. My heart sank, but Wayne was cheerful.

'I wonder if you'll feel any more at ease here, Fleur?' Wayne rapped on the door. 'At least you can rest safely. No one will find us, if anyone is still looking.'

The door swung open and a girl peered out, sleep souring her eyes. She was about my age with dull hair and a face drawn with hunger. She clasped a torn blanket around her shoulders. She glanced at us without enthusiasm, opened the door wide enough for us to enter, then closed it quickly behind us.

'What, no word of greeting, Fleta?' Wayne released

my elbow and put his arms around the girl. For a moment she remained rigid, her eyes flickering back and forth between us. Then suddenly she smiled and threw her arms about him. 'Welcome home, Wayne.'

Her gesture embarrassed me and I looked around the cabin. The room was sparsely furnished and the only other occupant besides the girl who had admitted us was an old lady who half-sat upon a tumble-down bed. She stared about her in the dimness of the dawn light.

Wayne knelt down beside her and held both her hands. 'How are you, Gran? It's Wayne.'

The old lady's voice was tremulous, scarcely audible. 'It's been a long time, Wayne. Are you in trouble?'

'Now what trouble would I be in, Gran?' He caressed the old lady's cheek gently, and now I realised she was blind. He said. 'I have two friends with me. We've been walking all night. May we rest here for a few hours?'

'Rest, of course. But there's naught else we can offer. We have no food here.'

I slumped down on an old rocking chair and Trott lowered himself to the floor, his feet stretched out in front of him. Sleep was tugging at my eyes. I tried to smile at Fleta but I was already nodding off.

When I awoke, the air in the tiny cabin was stifling. I stared around me in dismay. There were no windows to open to admit air and the door was firmly closed. I was alone, lying on the floor although I could not remember moving from the chair. My body ached as though every limb had been stretched and trampled on. The soles of my feet burned. I sat up, a feeling of despair welling through my heart.

The door was pulled open and Wayne stepped in. He laughed when he saw me. I pouted, ashamed at the way I looked and annoyed at him for his good humour. It was the first time I had seen him as more than a shadowy figure. He must have bathed, for his tousled fair hair had been slicked down and parted across his forehead and his pale features shone. He was dressed tolerably well in the clothes of a journeyman. He squatted on the floor opposite me and handed me a package.

'Fleta will bring you a bath,' he said gaily. 'There is a travelling gown in this package. I hope it's your size.'

'Where did you get it?'

'No, Fleur, it's no time for questions. Your smile is enough to show me I did right.'

'But where are we, Wayne? Whose cabin is this? What is Fleta to you?'

Wayne stood up and slapped his brow. 'Was there ever such a girl as you!' He stared at me with a half-serious look. 'Do I detect a note of interest, Fleur? What is Fleta to me, you ask? Does her relationship to me give you concern, Fleur?'

'What nonsense!' I retorted quickly, feeling my face begin to colour. 'I am feeling so hot in here,' I added fanning myself with my hand. 'I'm quite flushed with the heat.'

Wayne grinned knowingly. 'Fleta's my sister and the old lady is my grandmother. This cabin belongs to Mistress Richard McAllister Orme whose daughter's dress you have in your hand. She gave it to Fleta, who is her maid, and who is passing it on to you so that you may look like a Savnnah belle again!'

'It's lovely,' I gasped when I held the gown in my hands.

'After you've dressed, we shall be on our way to Maddocks. You can't appear before your uncle as you are now. He would denounce you as an impostor and that would never do. Oh no. I'm looking forward to making your uncle's acquaintance, Fleur, and you shall introduce me.'

Wayne paused by the door. His twinkling blue eyes revealed a softer heart than his tough attitude implied. It occurred to me that he was a clever but impoverished youth who might take any opportunity to improve himself at the expense of others. The cool way he had dispatched Brutus and fired at Ma Drax showed that he could strike out without compassion when he was aroused.

I was glad when Wayne bowed mockingly and with a laugh stepped back through the doorway, leaving the door ajar for Fleta to enter a few moments later with a canister of water from the nearby stream. I reached for her hand and tried to thank her but she flushed and retreated. Maybe the dress lying on the chair had been stolen. She might be ashamed.

After I had bathed, dressed in the gown, which fitted me perfectly, and eaten from a charcoal-grimed dish of ham and eggs, I felt quite recovered. I was certain, however, that I would be unable to walk. My shoes were in pieces and my feet a mass of blisters. I stepped experimentally to the door hoping to get some fresh air. Wayne rushed through the shrubbery and hustled me back inside.

'What's wrong Wayne? Are Captain Finney's men in the town?'

'No, Fleur. Those sea monsters have doubtless fled back to their ship. But Jem Hayard is here.'

'Here?' I caught my breath.

'Yes, indeed. Here in this very compound! He's calling on Mistress McAllister Orme's daughter at this minute. I observed him when I was seeking a carriage to take us to Maddocks.'

'He's friendly to your patron's daughter?'

'I have no patron, Fleur. And Jem Hayard, I can vouch, is friendly to every gentleman's daughter, and they to him.'

'Hah!' I sniffed disdainfully. 'If Jem Hayard had paid better attention to his responsibilities, I would have been at Maddocks last night instead of blistering my feet on the road to Milledgeville.'

'Your eyes dance with fire when you're scornful, Fleur.'

Wayne's soft tone took me by surprise. He was barring the exit from the shack, a look of dejection on his face.

'Why, Wayne, what's wrong?'

'I thought you'd forgotten me. You seem so inspired by Jem Hayard's proximity to us.'

'I shan't forget you were my rescuer, Wayne. But if Jem Hayard is here, why not deliver me to him?'

'Ho!' Wayne sidled inside the cabin. 'You don't know Jem Hayard, Fleur. He's not likely to do anything you bid him. Anyway, I can't take you to him in Mistress McAllister Orme's house while you are wearing her daughter's discarded dress!'

There was a sharp bang on the door which surprised us both. 'Who's there?' Wayne demanded.

'Trott,' was the solemn reply. 'I hab news of Marster Hayard fuh Missy Fleur.'

'We know already, Trott,' I told him when he stepped through the door. 'Jem Hayard is here. Wayne has seen him.'

'Has he, Missy?' Trott's eyes brightened. 'I don't know what he see but I done speak wid de gen'leman.' Trott bowed his head to avoid the low ceiling of the shack.

'You spoke to him!' Wayne flushed with anger. 'You had no right to speak to him. You don't even know him.'

I smiled to myself behind my hand. Trott was watching me. I said, 'I don't know if what you did was right or wrong until you tell me what you and Jem Hayard said.'

'I was standin' at de corner ob Washington an' Liberty Streets, Missy, obserbin' de commerce ob de town. It be mighty busy, an' a passin' nigra inform me dat de legislators fuh de whole state be legislatin' in dis bery town.'

'Yes, yes, Trott. Go on!' I snapped impatiently.

Trott pursed his lips in annoyance at my interruption. 'I was obserbin' de town when Marster Jem Hayard drive up in his carriage. "Hey nigra" he say to me, "go'n' find me a paper." I turn an' look an' tell he I serb no one but mah mistress.

' "Oh ho!" say he. "An' who is de mistress ob such a sour nigra?"

' "Mistress Fleur Singer," say I.

' "Fleur Singer! She's here?" say he.

' "Not far distant, sah." Wid dat, de young buckree glance 'round quickly like he scare' someone will oberhear an' he takes mah arm an' bids me to tell yo' how d'ye do an' he begs yo' to attend de hotel dis afternoon for he to drive yo' to Maddocks!'

Trott beamed at me when he finished his account. Wayne sat on the chair, his arms spread in resignation at the long narrative.

'Dam'me. It ain't right! I'm the one who rescued you and I'm the one should deliver you to Maddocks.'

I was touched by Wayne's disappointment. 'Wayne, you can still come with us. I'll tell my uncle what you did to save me.'

'Hah! You don't know what Jem Hayard will have to say about that. He is a scheming bounder as well as a ladies' man.'

The more I heard of Jem Hayard the more perplexed I became, and intrigued, too. People spoke ill of him but always with a certain respect, even with envy. One thing seemed certain. He was no ordinary man, tied down by the petty conventions of society. He was wild and free like my father's idol, Lord Byron. Perhaps he could set me free too, I thought. At least he would be no drab commonplace creature but a person who would offer me a change.

I was nervous when I entered the parlour of the hotel where the public table was set out for dinner. Trott escorted me. There was a young man sitting at the table by himself, an empty plate pushed forward in front of him, a glass clasped in his hand. Jem Hayard raised his head, tossed his long black locks quizzically and flashed a wide warm smile. I stared at him in bewilderment. In appearance at least he was all that I had hoped for and much more. I forgot all the evil I had heard of him. This man was like none other. No wonder he was envied; I felt the quickening of my heart and gripped Trott's arm for support.

His dark brown eyes glimmered under the longest lashes I had ever seen. His tousled black hair hung loosely over his forehead. His jaw jutted confidently in my direction. His smile was wide with apparent pleasure.

'You must be Fleur!' he cried, rising quickly. 'I had no idea! What a beauty!'

I lowered my head so he would not see the blush stealing over my features.

'Come, Fleur, come and sit with me.'

I hesitated before sitting on the bench he indicated. He gazed at me with a great show of amazement and then dropped down beside me.

'No one prepared me for this, Fleur. I shall have words with your uncle. He was quite inadequate in his description of you. You are exquisite!'

I did not know where to look or what to do with my hands. Wayne rescued me by sitting himself on the opposite side of the table.

'Jem Hayard!' Wayne bobbed his head in greeting.

'Yes, boy?' Jem spoke brusquely without turning his head.

'Wayne is my escort, Mister Hayard.' I managed to say, feeling like a tongue-tied child. 'Without him I would have been ravaged and murdered.'

'What?' Jem glanced at Wayne, smiled sympathetically at me, then turned back again to Wayne. 'I know yo' boy, don't I?'

'If you choose to, Jem Hayard. I have spreed with you in Milledgeville, Atlanta and Savannah.'

'Aye, I do remember. You have some training as a blacksmith don't you, boy?'

'The name is Wayne Carter, Jem Hayard. Not boy.'

'Wayne rescued me and is escorting me to Maddocks, Mister Hayard.' I hastened to speak as Wayne's nostrils flared angrily.

Jem's fine brow furrowed with concern. 'Rescued? From what? From a gang of compatriots of this ruffian?'

I quickly outlined what had happened the night before, concluding with the stipulation Wayne had made me promise to make. 'So you see, Wayne must escort me to Maddocks himself so that he can acquaint my uncle with what he did for me. I'm sure Uncle Leo will be grateful.'

'Grateful, be damned!' Jem Hayard leapt from his chair, almost upsetting me on the bench. He strode from one end of the empty parlour to the other while I glanced in alarm at Trott.

'Oh Trott, what have I said?'

'I don' know, Missy but he be no gen'leman.'

Jem must have heard for he swung around and glared at Trott. 'I suppose this ornery nigra plans to go to Maddocks too!'

'Of course. Trott was given to me by my mother before she died. It is my duty to see that no harm comes to him.'

Jem glared from Trott to Wayne and back again.

'Is there anything wrong, Mister Hayard?' I asked. I was puzzled at the change in his personality, but he looked as handsome when angered as he did when calm. 'I understand that my uncle has a large plantation. He surely cannot expect me to arrive unattended.'

Jem resumed his seat, grinning ruefully. 'You must forgive me, Fleur.' He bent forward so that his dark eyes were staring into mine. His hand patted mine softly before I could remove it from the table top.

'I wonder if you and I, and Wayne here, might enter into a pact?' Jem murmured.

'A pact?'

'Yes, a small thing of no consequence. To humour your uncle. He is a busy man and hates to be disturbed by trivialities.'

'What is this pact?' Wayne's voice was sharp with suspicion.

'Wayne, you can accompany Fleur to Maddocks and receive your reward for defending Fleur's honour. Why not? Maybe you can stay at the plantation, I'm sure there is need for a blacksmith of your skills.'

'The pact?'

'Yes, Wayne, the pact. One of secrecy. Fleur, would you and Wayne agree not to tell your uncle that I neglected to meet you in Savannah? He would be offended. You see, he made me vow to meet you and well, I was unable to do so. I would not like him to know that.'

Jem's eyes probed mine anxiously. I turned my head to Wayne.

'You'll use your influence with Fleur's uncle on my behalf?' Wayne demanded.

'Of course.'

'Then it's agreed. Not so, Fleur?'

I looked from one to the other uncertainly.

'I'm not asking you to lie, Fleur.' Jem smiled at me with a sophistication which made me feel I was his ally. 'Only to keep a secret.'

I shrugged my shoulders. 'I really don't see that it's important, but if that's what you wish, Mister Hayard –'

'Call me Jem, Fleur!'

He reached for my hand and squeezed it. I felt the flush across my cheeks again and the heavy throbbing of my heart. Try as I would, I could not deny my growing infatuation with Jem's good looks and the charm he possessed when he wished to use it.

A carriage was readied for us under Jem's instructions. Wayne and I travelled inside the coach while Trott rode in front with the driver. Jem told us he had some business to attend to and would meet us on the road. I had no doubt that he would. He was superbly built and I was sure he could ride faster on a horse than our slow lumbering carriage could travel.

I stared out of the window. It seemed to me that the farther we travelled on the Atlanta road, the rougher grew the people, the countryside, and the road itself.

Except for my thoughts of Jem Hayard, I would have wept when I recalled the comfortable house I had left behind and the courtly manners of Savannah. In the cottonlands I saw slaves treated like animals, almost naked, being herded in gangs by red-necked white men armed with pistols and whips.

Nightfall was nearly on us when Trott shouted with obvious relief from the coachman's box that the driver said we were approaching Maddocks. I looked out from my side of the carriage but all I could see were flat plantation lands stretching into the dusk with an occasional group of blacks waving at us.

I looked at Wayne, who appeared downcast.

'Please Wayne, don't be unhappy. It makes me sad too.' His face lit up and I added, 'There, your eyes sparkle when you're pleased.'

He grinned. 'It's not difficult to be happy when I look at you, Fleur. It's your heart that my eye can't see.'

'Whatever do you mean?'

'Nothing.' He took my hand in his and squeezed it.

'No, Wayne.' I withdrew my hand slowly.

'Last night I held you in my arms.'

'Last night we were in danger.'

'Yes.' He sounded doubtful.

'What worries you, Wayne? We aren't in danger now. We're near Maddocks.'

'I'm puzzled about Jem, Fleur. Why should he want us to keep it a secret that he didn't meet you in Savannah? What would have happened if we arrived at your uncle's without him? There's some mystery afoot, Fleur. I know Jem Hayard.'

'Jem?' I caught my breath at the mention of his name. Wayne noticed and regarded me with a perplexed expression. I spoke quickly to divert his thoughts. 'I'm sure he's only embarrassed because it was you who saved me. It can't be very nice for Jem Hayard to discover someone has bettered him.'

'Mebbe you're right! Jem sure ain't pleased when po' white trash like me saves his hide!'

Jem was waiting for us at a junction in the track a few miles later. I noticed immediately that he had changed the brightly coloured livery he had been wearing in Milledgeville for the planter's habit of linen coat and pants. He was hatless and his black locks flopped on his brow when he bowed his head in greeting. Sitting confidently atop his roan horse he seemed even more debonair than I remembered.

There was a black youth astride a pony at Jem's side, and he touched his woolly crown respectfully at me, flashing a broad grin at Wayne but ignoring Trott.

Jem jumped in the carriage with us, leaving his escort to lead his horse. He began chatting enthusiastically. I watched, fascinated by the glint in his dark eyes.

'Fleur!' Jem caught up my hand before I could withdraw it. 'I arrived an hour ago, I've been to Maddocks, and your Uncle Leo is expecting you!'

'What did my uncle say?'

Jem ignored my question. 'Aren't you excited, Fleur? Only a few more miles and you'll be home.'

Home. I turned my head away. Jem's servant was watching me through the window. I glanced beyond him at the dreary landscape. It duplicated the flat lands we had driven through for hours. I couldn't picture this place as my home. I turned back to Jem.

'Do you live here too?'

Jem erupted in laughter, patting my hand with pleasure. 'No, no, Fleur! Not at Maddocks. I'm a creature that can't be tamed. My father's plantation is nearby but I live where I choose.'

'Oh!'

'Disappointed, Fleur? Ah yes, that charming blush! Fear not, Fleur, I'll call at Maddocks often now I know those lonely walls hide such as you.'

I was stricken by Jem's comment on my blushing. He seemed to delight in taunting me, but his eyes were kind when I met his gaze. He said, 'It's a new life for you, Fleur. You'll love Maddocks.' He added as though to reassure me, 'We'll see each other often.'

I was too confused to think more about Jem's words. His voice seemed to hold some hidden promise, but at the back of my mind, I heard the nagging warning about Jem's renowned hot temper and the cruel streak which was reputed to lie behind his silken laughter.

The coach turned off the road into the driveway of a plantation.

'Here's Maddocks!' grinned Jem. 'You're home at last. Remember our pact!'

I looked at him with misgiving. Wayne was right. There was some mystery behind this, I was sure. The coach jolted around a bend in the trail. I glanced out of the window and my worry changed to amazement.

Before us was a mansion such as I had never seen

before. It was stunningly beautiful, glowing with the rays of the setting sun shining on it. A profusion of flowers softened the lines of the house. It resembled a Greek temple with six columns at the front supporting the shingle roof soaring over its two storeys. A small flight of stone steps led up to the front piazza.

A man stepped out of the shadow of one of the columns and started down the stairs towards the carriage, followed by two uniformed blacks. His steel grey hair was clipped close to his head. His cheeks were like worn leather, lined and tanned by the sun. He had a broad hinge of a nose and his hooded grey eyes were partly concealed by the crows' feet in which they were set. His straight mouth was a hard red slit.

'Oh, no!' I murmured, shaking my head. This man could not be my uncle. He was stern and regal, tall and hard, without the gentle warmth of my father.

'Welcome to Maddocks, Fleur.' The voice was crisp and solid, with a touch of the theatrical. One of the blacks flung open the carriage door. I gazed down in terror at the cold grey eyes of the stranger standing with his arms outstretched toward me.

'Welcome to Maddocks,' he repeated. But this time warmth had crept into his voice and crinkles gave life to his eyes. I jumped down and his arms circled around me. His lips brushed the top of my head.

'Welcome home, Fleur!'

CHAPTER EIGHT

'Isn't she a perfect surprise, Leo!' Jem immediately took charge of the situation. He jumped down beside me. 'I knew you would be captivated by her from the very first moment!'

Leo Singer removed one arm from me and placed it affectionately around Jem's shoulder but Jem brushed it off quickly and turned to me. He said, 'Fleur is tired after such a long journey and she's had some terrible experiences.'

'Who's this?' Leo Singer's sharp tone made me look around. Wayne was behind us.

Jem shrugged his shoulders. 'A boy Fleur picked up on the way.'

'He's Wayne Carter,' I said defiantly. 'Without Wayne I would never have got here.'

Jem nodded impatiently. 'Yes, Fleur. Leo, I will tell you about our adventures,' he focused his dark eyes on my uncle and grinned with a meaning I did not understand. 'Later!'

Leo Singer cocked his head and gave a smile which softened his face.

'This is my servant, Trott,' I said, determined not to let Jem Hayard intimidate me.

Leo Singer gave a quick glance at Trott and then beckoned for Jem and me to follow him up the steps.

'What about Wayne?' I whispered in Jem's ear when I realised he was not with us.

'He can't enter into Maddocks, not the house anyway!' Jem snapped. 'He'll bed down in the stables or somewhere.'

'You're angry I spoke about him?'

'No, I'm not.'

'Will you get him a position here? I'd like him to stay if he wants to.'

'Of course.'

'What's that? What's that?' Leo Singer spun around. 'What are you two whispering about?'

'I'll tell you later Leo.' Jem winked and gestured at a dozen or so blacks who had gathered around the porch and doorway, making them an excuse to postpone discussion of the topic.

At a command from Uncle Leo, the blacks fell back. They regrouped themselves along the edge of the piazza, leaning against the columns, gaping at me out of the darkness.

A Negro woman stood at the carved oak door opening into the house, barring our way. She was an impressive woman of uncertain age, tall and long-limbed. A bright yellow turban hid her hair and she wore her long dress with an air of authority. She was straight backed and slender, her brown face curved with wrinkles when she beamed.

'Lor', dis Missy is de mos' pretty gal ah eber seen, sah!' she exclaimed, extending her hands towards me in spontaneous welcome. 'Come, Missy, come and say how d'ye do to Mammy Mable.'

I glanced at Mr Singer, wondering if I would be offending him. He nodded his head and urged me forward. The woman put her arms around me and embraced me fondly.

'Chil'!' she exclaimed releasing me and staring into my face, her own eyes warm and friendly. 'Yo' look scare to deat'. Ah declah, Marse Leo, dis chil' plumb tucker out. Maylou,' she commanded, her voice suddenly imperious, 'run up stairs dis minute an' 'ten' de chil' in her chamber.'

A young black girl detached herself from the others and smilingly took my hand, leading me towards the steps of the piazza.

'Marse Leo, yo' gwin leab yuh pretty niece wid Mammy Mable tonight. She wore out wid trab'lin'. She need sleep bad.'

Marse Leo – as Mammy Mable called him – looked uncertain. Then he nodded assent and Jem flashed me a gentle smile, then followed Leo Singer through one of the doors which lined the oak panelled hallway.

Mammy Mable clucked, and steered Maylou and me inside the house and up the magnificent staircase. The ponderous mahogany furniture which crammed the hall and the heady scent of verbena which pervaded the corridors overwhelmed me. A lamp was burning in every corner and there was an atmosphere of serenity in the house. It warmed me and made me wonder if, perhaps, I really had found a home at Maddocks.

Uncle Leo seemed even less forbidding the next day. I had rested long and dreamlessly after Mammy Mable fussed me to sleep in a beautiful chamber with silk and velvet hangings. Maylou, who had been appointed my maid by Mammy Mable, slept in the chamber on a trundle bed which she pulled out from under the old tester bed which was mine.

Uncle Leo received me in his library. The room was cool and dimly lit as the jalousies were closed. He sat at his plantation desk, a mahogany table piled high with papers. Mammy Mable ushered me into a walnut wing chair with scrolled arms and diamond shaped feet. While I sat on the edge of the chair waiting for Uncle Leo to stop scratching in a ledger, I studied the walls. Three sides were lined with bookcases, containing tomes many of which were bound in rare leather. My eyes lit on a yellowed globe of the world on an ornately carved teak-wood stand. As I rose to examine it, Uncle Leo sighed and laid down his pen.

He smiled wanly. 'I enjoy reading, Fleur.' He sounded apologetic. 'It helps fill the hours of loneliness.'

Mammy Mable snorted as she hovered by the door and Uncle Leo rounded on her quickly. 'Mammy Mable, you had Fleur to yourself last night; now for goodness sake leave us alone!' Swinging back in his chair to face me, he spoke good-naturedly.

'Mammy Mable believes she owns me and all of us at Maddocks, Fleur, so you'll have to accustom yourself to her ways. Now, what do you think of my library?'

'Daddy loved books, too.' I looked at Uncle Leo, trying to pinpoint the resemblance between him and father.

'I know, I know, Fleur. While I built up Maddocks, Lennie was trying to create a beauty all his own.'

I found Uncle Leo's manner unsettling, sometimes so cold, at other times richly sympathetic. He was dressed in the formal manner of the gentlemen planters I had seen visiting Savannah. He gave the appearance of a man who tolerated no nonsense from his slaves or companions. In spite of the soothing tone of his voice, I hung my head to avoid the piercing gaze of his eyes.

'Your father and I were never close, Fleur. He led his own life and I led mine. He asked for no help from me and I gave none.'

The sad way he spoke made me raise my head. He was frowning, trying to explain something which he seemed to find difficult.

'I'm not used to the ways of young ladies, Fleur. You might find me a little strange at times. That's the way I am. Don't look for your father in me, Fleur. I can never replace him. I'm your uncle, and you're welcome here because you're my niece. Do you believe that?'

'I think so.'

'You have a doubt?'

'Everything is so different here. I've lived in the city all my life and now I'm in the country. I am used to having blacks around me, of course, but not hundreds like you have here. And the house, I never imagined anything so big and grand.'

He pulled his chair close to mine and leaned forward. 'Do you like Maddocks?' he asked anxiously.

'Oh yes, Uncle. It's the loveliest house I've ever seen. Everything is so beautiful!'

'You've no idea how delighted I am to hear you say it.' He almost smiled. 'It's the pride of the county, Fleur. Much better than Hayard's Hall.'

'What's Hayard's Hall?'

'Bless me,' he snorted. 'That's Granger Hayard's place. Jem's father. He's our neighbour.'

My heart quickened at the mention of Jem. 'Where is Jem?' I asked with a carefully casual air, for I wondered if he was still at Maddocks or had gone to his home.

My uncle's mouth becme a thin straight line. 'Why are you so interested in him?'

My lips trembled. 'I'm sorry, Uncle Leo, I didn't mean to upset you. He was such an engaging companion. I just wondered if I would see him again. This is all very strange for me.' I gestured helplessly.

'Oh!' Uncle Leo saw the contrition in my eyes. 'You're not upsetting me at all! Jem lives here, there, and everywhere. I've no idea where he is now.' He waved his hand to dismiss the subject.

I was appalled. 'But isn't he the heir to his father's property?'

Uncle looked startled. 'No, Jem's not the heir, though

why it concerns you, I don't know! He has an elder brother called Forest. Since you ask so much about him, Fleur, tell me what do you think of Jem Hayard?'

I stared at my uncle when he leaned forward again to face me. 'I barely know him.' I blushed. 'What should I think? He's a charming young man, I suppose.'

'You rode here from Savannah with him. You have surely formed some impression.'

I was silent.

Uncle seemed embarrassed. 'Jem is, well, I'm very fond of Jem. He's like a son to me, you might say, Fleur. He's hot-blooded, I know, but he's a young man of character. Good-looking, don't you find?'

I sat in confusion on the hard chair and wondered what I was supposed to say. Uncle was stroking his chin. 'Did Jem tell you about Wayne?' I asked.

The name apparently meant nothing to him.

'Wayne, the boy who came with us.'

'Oh yes, yes. I'll take him on in the forge. He can watch the blacks there, save the overseer some work.'

'Thank you.' My smile seemed to reassure him. 'I'm sure I'm going to like it here, Uncle, once I understand plantation life. If Jem is like a son to you, I'm sure I'll be seeing him often. And Wayne too. I won't be lonely and Maddocks is such a lovely house. Did you build it yourself?'

I was right to steer Uncle away from a subject which caused him concern. He began to speak with eloquence about Maddocks and how, twenty-five years before, he had ridden into Paxton County and decided to settle.

'I have no wife, nor children, Fleur, so all I have worked for over the years is mine. Twenty-five years ago, when I bought this plantation, I realised there was enough land here to grow cotton indefinitely and never exhaust the soil. So I decided to stay.'

The door to the parlour suddenly swung open and a finely featured Negro boy about my age stepped in. He was wearing breeches and stockings and a white silk shirt which contrasted with the glowing ebony of his skin. He held a silver tray in his hand and balanced on it were two cut-glass crystal tumblers containing a creamy liquid. Without waiting for a sign from Uncle, he proffered the tray to me. I took one of the glasses and returned the boy's friendly smile.

'Egg nog,' exclaimed Uncle taking his own glass. 'Close the door when you go, Garland,' he cautioned the youth as he slipped from the room.

'Not many planters take pride in possessing a fine house, Fleur.' Uncle's voice was serious. 'They pride themselves on the number of slaves they own. Well, I sold fifty of mine, Fleur, to build this house. That's a fortune to families around here. Only the Hayards have so many slaves they could sell dozens without noticing.'

He stood up and strolled across to the window which looked out on to the piazza. I followed him, holding my glass in my hand.

'Maddocks was built by my slaves, Fleur. I have the best Negro folk any southern man could wish for.' He gestured through the window.

'Those columns, they're called Doric columns, Fleur. From the Greek.'

I gazed at the fluted pillars which rose straight up to the roof guarding the piazza like sentinels. The piazza itself stretched the full length of the front of the house with a tiny balcony hanging over the front door. A grove of gigantic live oaks shaded the colonnade and hid it from the road. The long drive curved around the grove onto the flagged courtyard in front of the piazza and disappeared through a profusion of venerable magnolias back to the road.

There was a peaceful stillness about the scene, a sense of permanence as though Maddocks would survive forever no matter what happened in the outside world.

Uncle Leo pointed to the purple of the climbing wisteria and the streamers of grey Spanish moss twining through the branches of the live oaks. 'Next year those fields beyond the trees will be bursting with cotton.' He spun around from the window and beckoned me to follow him.

'When I was building this house, Fleur, I let the

foundations settle for a year before adding the rest of the structure. I lived with the slaves then, in their quarters. That's why none of my columns are cracked. Does this bore you?'

'Oh no, Uncle. It's very strange. I've never seen a house like this in the whole of Savannah.'

'Of course not. It takes time to build a great house like this, Fleur. Why, when the timbers were cut, I had to soak them in the mill pond for twelve months so they wouldn't shrink!'

He stamped his foot to draw my attention to the snugly-fitting floorboards of the library. His apparent nervousness at my company was forgotten and he guided me eagerly through the house. The library opened into the gentlemen's parlour which led into the hallway.

There was a parlour for ladies with a door opening off the hall. This gave access to the sewing room in the opposite corner of the house. From the sewing room, where my uncle said I would spend my time, we passed into the main drawing room and then across the hall to the dining room. This was the largest room in the house, with a high ceiling, hand-carved furniture, and a marble mantle over the gigantic fireplace.

My eyes widened when I tried to take in all the elaborate beauty in which this old man lived. He had created a house that was part of him, which seemed stern and correct but gave the impression of warmth and security. The boy who brought the egg nog for us stood at the doorway when we returned to the library. The maids dusting and the sound of Mammy Mable bustling through the house shouting orders suggested a casual intimacy between Uncle Leo and his slaves.

I tried to tell Uncle Leo as much but he protested his sense of isolation and friendlessness.

'How can you be lonely when everyone here admires you so much?'

'Lonely?' An odd expression of defiance filled his eyes. 'Yes, I guess I am. One needs one's own people. There's no one here with whom I can discourse, or even play a game of chess.' His eyes lit up hopefully. 'Can you play chess?'

'Yes, Daddy taught me.'

'Sometime soon we must have a game.'

I had a sudden insight into my uncle's character. For all his tough mannerisms, he must have been more used to dealing with black than with white people. He was ill at ease with someone like me.

I hesitated. 'May I ask you a question? It's a personal one.'

'You may ask – I'm not bound to answer.'

'Uncle, why have you never married?' Having asked the question, I added quickly, 'This lovely house is only missing a mistress to make it perfect. And children.'

It seemed that the old man's tanned cheeks reddened as I spoke. 'Some men don't marry, Fleur.' He sighed. 'And some men do. It's as simple as that. And as for children, Fleur, think what they would do to my treasures.' He pointed toward the ornaments lining his shelves. He was silent for a moment, then added, 'Fleur, it's you who will be the female presence you say my beloved Maddocks needs.'

Abruptly, he turned to read something on his desk, and I sensed that my interview was over. When I turned to go, Mammy Mable bustled into the library and escorted me out.

'Wha' for yo' upset Marse Leo?' the old slave queried when we were in the hall.

'I didn't upset him!'

'No? Well why yo' ax why he ain' marriaged. Yo' be mighty forward to come here from Savannah an' ax de Marster dat.'

'I'm sorry. I didn't mean to give offence.'

Mammy Mable watched me, pursed her lips and then drew me close to her, nestling my head to her bosom.

'Dat's a'right, chil'. Ah be surprise' Marse Leo took to yo' so quick.' She walked resolutely through the rooms of the house, cradling me to her.

CHAPTER NINE

The days moved slowly at Maddocks. There was so much activity on the plantation, I rarely saw Uncle Leo except at a distance. Wayne, too, was fully occupied and seemed to have little time for my company. At times, when he passed across the courtyard on his way from one task to another, I would wave to him from the window of the sewing room. He would glance at the library to see if my uncle was watching before returning my greeting. I longed to talk to him.

Trott, too, was busy. Uncle Leo took him into his house as his steward, a position which Trott deemed to be worthy of his status. I laughed when I saw him in the breeches, cummerbund and frilled silk shirt which was the dress for the houseboys at Maddocks.

'Now yo' see me dress proper to serb a gen'leman, Missy Fleur,' Trott stated proudly. 'Marse Leo hab mo' respeck fuh his people dan de buckrees in Savannah.' He closed the sewing room door and sat down on one of the straight back chairs. 'I sure yo' don' min' if I rest mah feet, Missy.'

'No, Trott.' I laughed.

Obviously Trott had something on his mind but it was useless to try to hurry him. He scratched his head and shifted uncomfortably in his chair. 'Dat Mammy Mable, she a real lady. Ain' not'in' in dis plantation she don' know. She say yo' spen' too much ob yuh time in dis room readin' yuh books an' sewin', Missy.'

'You talk about me with Mammy Mable, Trott?'

'Of course, Missy. When we alone.'

I sighed. 'I suppose I do feel lonely, Trott. At home in Savannah, it never bothered me. There was always so much happening on the waterfront. Somehow the books I have don't comfort me enough. I don't even see Wayne.'

Trott straightened his back and frowned with disapproval.

'Fuhgit dat Wayne, Missy Fleur. Yuh uncle tol'

Wayne to stay 'way from de house. Marse Jem mo' like de comp'ny fuh yo'.'

I wondered how Trott had read my thoughts. I was longing to see Jem, but he had never called since delivering me to Maddocks. I scolded Trott quickly to stop him getting ideas. 'You sound as though you're matchmaking, Trott! All I need is someone young to spend some time with. I'll ask Uncle Leo if our neighbours have daughter of my own age I can visit.'

A few days passed before I had a chance to speak to Uncle Leo. He was always too occupied for me to disturb him. His library opened directly on the piazza and, on occasions, I glimpsed him striding across the desk and down the steps intent on his plantation business. He was never alone. Sometimes it was the black youth, Garland, who accompanied him, or a burly man who Mammy Mable said was the head driver. I was perplexed by his attitude towarde me after we seemed to have reached such an understanding in our first interview. One afternoon I quizzed Mammy Mable about it.

'Lor', Missy!' she told me while I dutifully stitched my sampler in the sewing room as dusk descended. 'Dat his way. When he ain' ridin' round' de plantation chivvying de nigras, he be readin' in de lib'ry. Marse Leo ain' got no taste fuh comp'ny an' he not strong on small talk. Don't fret, Missy.'

'I believe, Mammy Mable' – I said, determined to jolt her complacency – 'that my uncle doesn't care to have me here because he doesn't like women.'

There was a silence in the room, broken only by a quick hiss while Mammy Mable sucked in her breath and stared at me.

'Indeed?'

The low-pitched voice surprised us both. Uncle Leo stepped out of the shadows gathered around the doorway. He sat down on the couch, stretched out his legs and crossed them. He dismissed Mammy Mable with a wave of his hand. She was reluctant to go and scowled at me when she backed out of the room, leaving the door ajar. I could see one of the housemaids lighting candles in the hall.

'You're very perceptive, Fleur. Does my dislike of women disturb you?' He sounded strained.

'No, Uncle.' I shrugged my shoulders.

'You must forgive me, Fleur. In the same way that you are adjusting to a new circumstance with your parents dead, I have to accustom myself to having a young niece in the house.'

'I so seldom see you. Or anyone!'

'Ah, I understand. A pretty girl like you craves attention, I'm sure.'

I blushed. 'That wasn't what I meant. But it does get rather lonely at times.'

Uncle Leo looked at me carefully stroking his chin while he considered my words. 'Don't you enjoy your reading?'

'Oh, I do. I love my books and I know I'm fortunate having yours to browse through when I wish.'

'Good. It's important that you learn so that when you get married, your husband won't have a giddy miss to share his life with.'

It was my turn to stare at him. 'I . . . I . . . I've never thought of marriage.'

'Of course not, Fleur. I hadn't expected that you would, but one should prepare, don't you think?' He uncrossed his legs, and leaned back on the couch.

'Paxton County is made up of large plantations like this one, Fleur. We have few near neighbours and none at all with daughters your age. Jem Hayard is the person nearest to you in years, I believe. He's twenty-one now.' Uncle smiled as though sharing a secret with me. 'Perhaps you would like Jem to call on you, Fleur? He's a scamp but he can behave like a gentleman.'

Uncle's words threw me into confusion. I sat staring into the gloom of the room after my uncle had gone until the maid came in with the candles. I realised I knew little of Jem Hayard but gossip. Was he really an irresponsible philanderer? He was such an attractive, exciting young man, just like the heroes of the novels I read. And he was only five years older than I! I gazed at the candle flame, picturing Jem's rugged, laughing face, and sighed.

That night, Uncle Leo asked me to eat with him instead of in my chamber. I was nervous as I faced him in the great dining room, the whole length of the polished mahogany table separating us. We ate in silence. I nibbled at slices of baked ham and left a portion of egg on my plate to be polite. Uncle Leo, too, ate sparingly. Although he said nothing, I was aware that he was studying my manners and features.

Gradually, it occurred to me that I was being put through some kind of test. When he had finished eating and the ever-present servants flocked around the table to clear it, Uncle took me by my elbow and steered me across the hall to the main parlour. A bright log fire burned in the red-brick fireplace. The room was cozy with its carved mahogany and rosewood furniture and its paintings in gilt frames hanging on the walls.

My uncle announced his intention of playing chess, and Garland carried in the chess table and placed it in front of us.

After a few desultory remarks we played in silence, each of us concentrating on the game. I was no expert but my father had taught me the rudiments of the game with meticulous care and, even though I went down to defeat in the end, I felt that I had conducted myself well. Uncle Leo expressed appreciation of my skill and, as he cleared the board, he said, 'I think you have something on your mind, Fleur. You're not altogether content here at Maddocks. Can you tell me about it?'

I hesitated. 'I don't wish to be any trouble but I would like to go out on occasion. Why, I've never even been to Paxton.'

'What's a girl of sixteen going to do in Paxton? You'll have the crackers sniffing around like randy pups.'

He smiled to ease the harshness of his words but nevertheless I was hurt. 'Surely I could walk around the plantation sometimes?'

He seemed absorbed in thought. 'Can you ride? I'll

not have you walking in the cotton fields. The nigras seize on any excuse to abandon their work. They'll be all over you with their cajolery if they see you walking among them. When you're on a horse you can keep them off.'

'Couldn't I learn to ride, Uncle?' I gazed directly into his eyes and watched the fierceness dissolve.

He looked thoughtful for a while. 'Yes, Fleur, you may learn to ride. I'll arrange it soon.'

My riding lessons were formal occasions. A riding habit was made up for me in a sombre grey material which made me yearn for clothes of a brighter shade. Mammy Mable chose my clothes according to what she described as 'princ'pals ob gen'le folk.' This was her excuse for the dowdiness of my wardrobe and her insistence that I have a chaperone.

I overheard Mammy Mable and my uncle discussing who could be my chaperone while I sat on the piazza one afternoon reading Walter Scott.

'She mus' have a chaperone, Marse Leo,' Mammy Mable insisted. 'Yo' hab to git anoder buckree lady.'

I could tell by Uncle's tone that he was exasperated. 'Mammy,' he said, 'where are we going to find such a lady? It's impossible! Fleur will have to have a black. The groom is old and harmless but I need a young one I can trust.'

'We don' hab no nigra gal can ride.' Mammy Mable sounded as though she was sulking.

'Who said a gal? A trusty buck would do.'

'A buck!' I was puzzled by the anguish in Mammy's voice.

'Yes, what's wrong? A boy.'

'A boy to chaperone Missy Fleur? It ain' decent.'

Uncle chuckled. 'What about that son of yours?'

The air wheezed out of Mammy's lungs. 'Garland?' she whispered, apparently mollified.

I pricked up my ears at the name. I had not realised that the boy who usually attended Uncle was Mammy's son. It had never occurred to me that Mammy had children of her own.

'Garland will be all right, Mammy. He's not so old he'll get frisky and he knows what I'll do to him if he does. Everyone here knows he's your son. None of them are going to trouble Fleur while he's with her.'

I picked up my Walter Scott and stared hard at the pages open in front of me. Nothing penetrated my brain but the thought that at last I was to be allowed to ride even if I could not escape having a chaperone.

CHAPTER TEN

The riding lessons were a great success. Hannibal – the old groom – was a patient teacher and took his duties seriously. He was a huge man, but his manner was so gentle that never once did I know a moment of fear, neither from him nor from the horse. At first, Uncle Leo watched dourly from the piazza when I trotted across the courtyard trying to accustom myself to controlling the living animal beneath me. Hannibal always rode at my side with the boy, Garland, close behind.

No sooner had I gained confidence on the horse than I concerned myself less with technique and more with Maddocks. The beauty of the house itself was stunning. With the afternoon sun striking the piazza, the columns and the white clapboard of the house seemed to vibrate. In spite of its grandeur, the mansion blended naturally with the landscape, the columns matching the tall pine trees, and the flowers and shrubs edging the piazza with colour.

I had fallen in love with Maddocks the first moment I saw the house and now, as I grew familiar with its mysteries, my affection deepened. I felt safe at Maddocks. The house had an air of calm authority which neither the elements nor man could upset.

'Dey say,' Garland confided to me one day as we rode up the long driveway with the house visible in front of us through the branches of the moss-hung oaks and magnolias. 'Dey say dat Maddocks was built wid Marse Leo's spirit.'

'Whatever do you mean?'

During the days I had ridden with Hannibal and Garland an easy relationship had developed between us. Being a house slave, Garland was bolder than Hannibal and, since I showed no objection, he delighted in telling me about the plantation. Hannibal, however, preserved a respectful silence and confided his comments to riding tips.

'Is what de people say, Missy Fleur,' Garland grinned. 'Marse Leo take t'ree years to build Maddocks. He work along side de slaves de whole time. Dey say he build de house wid love.'

I felt Garland's eyes on me as I gazed at the house. I knew what the boy meant.

'It's like the house is his son?'

'Yas, Missy.' Garland's face clouded with doubt and I wondered why the pleasant mood between us had suddenly become tense.

I watched him carefully. He was a dark copper colour in the sunlight and his skin shone as though polished. His face was almost handsome with a pleasing smile, quite a thin nose and eyes which were an impenetrable black. He claimed to be only two years older than I, but his body burst with the strength and energy of a fighter, muscles bulging under his shirt. He was much sharper than a field hand.

'Have you always lived in the house, Garland?'

Garland relaxed, turning to smile at me again. 'Yas Missy. Maddocks is my home.'

'But where do you sleep?'

'In de yard, Missy.'

'With the dogs?'

He laughed. 'In de cabin fuh Mammy Mable behind de kitchen.'

I nodded my head. It was unlikely that my uncle would permit his slaves to sleep in the house unless they were attending someone. My maid slept in my chamber but I had no idea who slept in my uncle's room, which was at the opposite side of the house. Another thought struck me.

'Is Mammy Mable really your mother?'

'Yas, Missy,' Garland laughed. 'An' Rollo's ma brudder.'

'Rollo, who's he?' I really knew so little about my uncle's people.

'He de black-skinned boy dat work in de kitchen.'

I smoothed back my hair as it drifted across my face and tried to picture the boy in my mind.

Garland must have sensed my perplexity for he added, 'We don' hab de same sire, Missy Fleur.'

'Oh!' I was shocked. 'Do you mean Mammy Mable had *two* husbands?'

'Not two alone,' Hannibal interrupted without sensing how scandalised I was.

'Hush yuh tongue,' snapped Garland. Then he smiled at me. 'Hannibal don' un'stan' white folks.'

'Dat ain' true, Garland! Ah be groom to Marse Leo all dese years. Marse Jem trust me wid he horse when he come in de night. Ah know white folks, ah does.'

'Marse Jem!' I echoed. 'Does Jem Hayard come here at night? I've never seen him.' We had reached the stables at the back of the house and I halted my horse.

'Yo' be 'sleep, when he come, Missy Fleur.' Hannibal grinned proudly at Garland now that he had asserted himself.

'Missy Fleur ain' concern wid yuh tittle-tattle,' cried Garland. He swung out of his saddle and held up his hand to help me from mine. Hannibal was holding my horse's head.

I walked around the side of the house with Garland two steps behind me. As we came up to the cobbled courtyard he stepped to my side.

'Missy Fleur?'

'Yes?' I was still puzzling over the remarks about Jem's visits at night. Why hadn't he asked to see me when he was here?

'Please, Missy. Please don' tell Marse Leo anything

'bou' wha' Hannibal say!' Garland's jet-black gaze bored into my eyes.

'Whyever not, Garland?' He frowned unhappily. 'Oh very well then, if it will get you into trouble, I'll say nothing.'

'Thank you, Miss Fleur!' He bowed his head and raised it smiling. 'You are very considerate,' he said in carefully articulated English.

Two nights after this strange conversation with Garland, when the moon was throwing a bright mantle over the cotton fields, a noise in the courtyard below my window awakened me. I suppose I had been listening for the sound since Hannibal's remark. I had still not seen Jem Hayard since the day of my arrival and my curiosity was aroused as to why he came at night to see Uncle Leo and why it had been kept secret from me.

I rose quickly and tiptoed across the floor praying that the boards would not creak and wake up Maylou. I need not have worried. Maylou was sleeping soundly on her pallet. I peered through the window.

The piazza was directly underneath my chamber and I was sure I heard the sound of someone striding across it into the library. I gasped. Lit up by the brightness of the moon, a man was gently leading a horse away from the piazza. It was Hannibal, taking the horse to hide it in the stables.

I had to know if the visitor really was Jem Hayard. I turned away from the window, recalling Jem's handsome face and dark eyes. I could not forget him even though he had never called on me and seemed to be a worthless young man. I was determined at least to look at him again and perhaps I would be able to straighten out my thoughts about him.

I crept across the chamber to the door and eased myself out although I was clad only in my nightdress and cap. A candle flickered in its glass sconce in the hall and I descended swiftly down the stairs to its welcoming glow. The house was silent and I prayed that no one was awake to surprise me.

I caught my breath in fear. A body was lying in the hall across the front door. It was Rollo, Mammy Mable's kitchen boy. I was paralysed at the foot of the steps wondering what to do when suddenly the body heaved, rolled over with a grunt and began to snore softly. Rollo, I realised with relief, was not dead but only an inefficient watchman.I edged past him into the smoking room.

The room was in darkness but there was a thin line of light under the door which led into the library. I put out my hands to feel my way across the darkened room, sliding them along the back of the couch very slowly, hoping my foot would not tip over a spittoon or any object that might be in the way. I reached the opposite wall without any disturbance and crouched down to listen.

'You don't show me much consideration, Jem! I've been waiting two weeks for you.' Uncle Leo's voice was resentful.

'So what?' Jem's arrogant drawl sliced through the air so clearly that I might have been in the same room.

'Jem, I missed you.'

'I had to go to Atlanta.'

'You always have to go somewhere, Jem. Couldn't you spend some time here with me for a change?'

'I'll try.'

'You don't sound very convincing. Why is it always you who makes these trips? What about your brother Forest, can't he go?'

Jem snorted with disgust. 'You know Pa wants him at home. He's the eldest and since Maxine lit off with her Republican he ain't letting him out of his sight. But he don't worry about me.'

'I do, Jem.' Uncle Leo's voice had grown soft but in it was a hint of desperation.

In the silence of the library I heard the floorboards creak as someone moved.

'What are you doing?' Jem spoke with sudden sharpness. 'Take your hands off me!'

'Please, please!' my uncle was plaintive. There was

another creak from the floor. 'See, I'm at your feet. Let me remove your boots.'

'No!'

'Jem, please. Why do you make me suffer so much.'

'Suffer? What about me? I suffer in terror every day that someone will find out about this –' His voice trailed off with disgust.

'Why did you come here then?' Uncle Leo retorted.

'To see if you've made the arrangements yet. How is Fleur?'

Jem's question surprised me. Why was he concerned about me?

'I'll tell you. Later.'

There was a sound of a slap then a book fell to the floor with a thud. My uncle moaned softly.

Jem laughed. 'I told you no, Leo! '

There was a sigh from Uncle. 'Fleur's young, Jem. But I'll keep my promise, I swear.' Uncle's whining voice changed to a sob. 'But remember, keep yours, please.'

'Have you changed your will?'

'It's taken care of, Jem.'

'Can I trust you?'

'My God, Jem!' Uncle sounded desperate. 'I should be asking you that!'

There were sounds, whispers, murmurs, the creak of the couch. I could not picture what was happening but I felt that it must be something ugly and I could not move for fear I might be discovered.

Then Jem's voice came through clearly again. 'Wait, Leo! You can wait, can't you? Soon I'll be here all the time.'

'I long for that day.'

'Well, it's up to you to arrange it then.'

A noise behind me made me stir. Someone was crouching at my side, holding his finger to his mouth in a gesture of silence. In the flickering light from the library door, I made out Garland's profile. He was frowning ferociously and tapped me hard on my shoulder, beckoning me to follow him.

I stood up and was amazed when his hand clamped hard around my wrist. His eyes stared me into silence and I followed him meekly out of the room to the hall. He closed the door behind him and waved at me to go upstairs.

I looked down the hall to the front door. Rollo had gone. 'What – ?'

'Shush, Missy!' Garland hissed. 'Go back to your chamber.'

'No!' I said crossly. 'I'm not taking orders from you!'

'You don't want your uncle to know you were spying on him, do you?'

'No.' I was sullen. 'But you shouldn't order me about like that.'

'It's for your own good, Miss Fleur. Forget what you heard.'

I glanced at Garland in amazement. 'You're speaking correct English! Who taught you to speak like that?'

'It ain' no concern ob yor'n, Missy.' Garland scowled and slipped back into the patois of a house slave. 'Please go to yuh chamber, Missy.'

I glared at him and sat down on the stairs. 'I will when you tell me what's going on here. What does Jem want from my uncle? Did you hear him? What did he mean about Maddocks? What are they doing in the library?'

Garland frowned. 'Missy, I don' know 'bou' dat. Marse Leo be a good marster. We don' ax no questions, an' yo' bes' do the same. Now, be yo' gwine back to bed, Missy, or does I call Mammy Mable?'

There was a noise from the library and I rose quickly and flounced up the stairs. 'I'll see you tomorrow!' I said, trying to make it sound like a threat.

'Yes, Miss Fleur.' Garland bowed his head like a willing slave but his reply scorched my ears with its arrogance.

Maylou was still asleep on her pallet when I entered my chamber. I kicked the trundle bed with my bare foot, more from frustration than rage. The maid stirred, blinking her eyes open. Outside the house, the moon was directly above my window. Its glow settled on the room.

Maylou was about my own age. She smiled a lot and barely seemed to understand me, sometimes treating me like a stranger from another country. But she was efficient, if slow, and brushed my hair and filled my bath each morning. She sat up now in her bed and gazed at me, her face contorted with alarm.

'Yo' be a'right, Missy?'

'Oh yes, Maylou.'

'Yo' was out, Missy?' She looked perplexed.

'Yes.' I walked over to the window. Hannibal had brought Jem's horse back to the courtyard and was standing beside it, patting its neck and whispering into its ear.

'Come here, Maylou.'

The girl padded obediently to my side.

'Do you know whose horse that is?'

Maylou rolled her eyes so that the whites seemed enormous. 'Oh no, Missy.' She stepped backward. 'Yo' ought to be in bed, Missy Fleur,' she pleaded. 'Yo' gwine get de moon in yuh head if yo' gaze at it too long.'

I smiled for the first time that night. Maybe I was going a little mad, I thought. It was all beyond me. I allowed Maylou to take my hand and lead me back to the bed. I lay down on it, surprised at how relaxing it was.

Maylou pulled up the covers, snuggling herself down in the bed beside me. Her arms crept around my shoulder and she hugged me close to her, stroking my hair.

I smiled again. Maylou was kind. I closed my eyes but the voices of Jem Hayard and my uncle kept intruding into my mind, even after sleep had come.

CHAPTER ELEVEN

The forge where Wayne worked was close to the stable. Sometimes when I passed the smithy at the end of my riding lesson, I would glance inside. Wayne, his shirt stripped off revealing his tough, sinewy torso, was usually darting about chivvying his workmen while the fire from the forge blazed behind him. I was curious to know how he had settled down to plantation life. The next afternoon, when Garland helped me from my horse at the end of my lesson, I suggested a walk to the smithy.

'Wha' fuh, Missy?' Garland looked askance.

'Why not, Garland?' I drew myself up to my full height. Of course, I was still several inches shorter than Garland, but I made certain he saw my determination. 'You don't have to accompany me. I can take care of myself. After all, it was Wayne who brought me here, so I'm in no danger from him!'

I hastily spun away from Garland and raced off as fast as my full-skirted riding habit would allow.

Wayne looked up in amazement when I stepped inside his door.

'How dark it is in here,' I murmured as his helpers stood back for Wayne to walk over to me.

'Fleur!' he grinned. 'I thought you had forgotten me. Life at Maddocks suits you. You look such a lady!'

'And you are such a blacksmith!' I touched his naked shoulder. 'I declare this work is putting flesh on your frame.'

'You mock me, Fleur.'

'No.' I was touched by his forlorn expression. 'Won't you step outside? Let's sit somewhere and talk.'

'Aye!' He grinned and shouted something at one of the men who handed him a shirt. He pulled it over his head and stepped through the door with a sigh. 'I figured your uncle don't like you speaking to me.' He nodded his head in the direction of Garland, who was at my elbow.

'Garland goes everywhere with me, Wayne. He isn't here to stop me speaking to you, or to anybody else.'

'That so, Garland?' Wayne winked.

'Ah does what Marse Leo tell me, Marse Wayne.'

I glanced first at Wayne and then at Garland. Wayne's face was bright and his eyes danced. Garland's was expressionless. 'You can wait for us here, Garland. I'll walk a short way with Master Wayne.'

'Oh no, Missy. Marse Leo say – '

'You see, Fleur! There's no way you can outwit him. Let him follow you if he must.'

I was startled by Wayne's outburst. 'Are you chiding him for being a slave?'

'No, Fleur. Forget what I say. Sometimes it riles me to see what these people let your uncle do to them. I got no respect for anyone who accepts his lot without protest.'

'Isn't that dangerous talk? Uncle Leo would dismiss you if he heard you speak so! You must be careful, Wayne.'

'Really! You urge me to control my tongue. Why, Fleur, why? So I may remain at Maddocks, no better than a slave myself? I only stay here to be near you, Fleur, to see that all goes well for you.'

I blushed, straightening my bonnet nervously. Garland coughed at my elbow. 'We bes' not stay too long, Missy. Marse Leo get heated if we be late.'

'Yes, yes,' I snapped. 'If you're no better than a slave, Wayne, look at me. Garland is forever telling me what to do and what not to do. I suppose I'm a slave too, to my uncle's orders.'

We were sauntering along the trail from the stables to the overseer's compound where, I knew, Wayne lived. There was a track through the pine trees to the left and Wayne guided me down it. 'This will take us behind the house, Fleur, by the kitchen. Right, Garland?'

Yas, sah.' Garland nodded his head dourly.

The trees laid shadows on the narrow track and provided relief from the winter sun. My cambric chemisette was moist under my basque. 'The climate is much pleasanter in Savannah,' I observed to Wayne.

'Would you like to return?'

'I can't return, Wayne, I'm obliged to my uncle. You can, though. You don't have to stay here, and certainly not on my account.'

Wayne looked crestfallen. 'I hoped you might want me to remain.'

I laughed. 'Bless me, whatever next? Of course it's nice to know you're here and that you fare well but otherwise Wayne — '

We were in sight of the house now and Mammy Mable was visible in a doorway. I increased my pace and Wayne dropped behind at the sight of her. Garland gave a sigh of relief as he caught up with me. There was reproach in his manner but I held my head high to discourage him from uttering it.

I avoided Wayne during the next few days, embarrassed by him and his feelings for me. I was pleased when Uncle Leo agreed to let me accompany him to Paxton to visit Mistress Dundy, the seamstress, to order summer dresses. Once again, there was the problem of who would chaperone me as I shopped.

There being no obvious solution, it was decided that Garland should escort me. He, at least, had suitable clothes and shoes, whereas the females in the house had only their calico house dresses. Uncle Leo was to be attended by Trott, and Hannibal was to take us in the carriage with Rollo as the footman.

We would have looked a pretentious party in Savannah but in the tiny town of Paxton it was expected that a planter of the wealth and status of Uncle Leo should conduct himself according to county tradition. To have done less would have been considered scandalous and disgraceful to the families of the neighbouring plantations, so my uncle claimed to his slaves.

'A planter's people,' Uncle Leo explained as we jogged along the narrow cart tracks to Paxton, 'expect a certain standard of behaviour from their master. Most of my adult slaves have been at Maddocks since we built the house. They are proud of me and look up to me. It's the same at Hayard Hall and all the plantations in the county. If we keep our standards, they will keep theirs, Fleur.' I agreed meekly, but I was not so young and uninformed that I did not have doubts.

Paxton was the county town. I was amazed at the number of people who walked the sandy road between the clapboard houses. Some women were dressed stylishly in gowns and bonnets while their men folk strode along in polished boots and smart topcoats. Many of them waved cheerily as we trotted along the main street. They called out greetings to Uncle Leo and me. Other whites were slouching in the shade of trees or sitting in sulky groups leaning idly against walls, and I asked Uncle Leo who they were.

'Lickspittles and crackers!' he retorted angrily.

'What are they?'

'The lickspittles got no slaves at all but they hire plantation nigras to work their scraps of land and imagine themselves as good as planters. The crackers are poor whites, Fleur. They are lazy, rude, and good for nothing. They won't work because they say work is for the nigras.'

I could not understand Uncle Leo's anger at these unfortunate people, many of whom were more poorly dressed than the slaves at Maddocks. For the moment, though, my mind was filled with the excitement of my first shopping spree since I had left Savannah. We halted outside Mistress Dundy's home in a narrow side street off the town's square. She was a small, plump, pleasant woman who took both my hands as she escorted me into her parlour.

Garland waited patiently outside the dressmaker's house, while Uncle Leo, having given him precise instructions concerning me, drove off in the carriage with Trott, Hannibal, and Rollo.

I lost track of time talking to Mistress Dundy. Actually, it was she who talked while I chose my cloth and she measured me. All too soon, I heard Garland inquiring for me in the entrance hall.

'Is it time to go, Garland?' I left the parlour and went into the hall.

'Missy Fleur, Marse Leo pass 'roun' de square. We mus' be leavin' now 'less we keep he waitin'.'

Mrs Dundy clapped her hands. 'Oh, I really shouldn't have talked so much, Fleur. It was such a pleasure seeing you at last. The whole of Paxton has been talking about you since you arrived at Maddocks. I didn't mean to delay you, I'm sure.' She ushered me through the door, flapping and clucking like a mother hen.

'Uncle Leo knows I was choosing dresses,' I complained as Garland and I walked along the hard red mud of the side street. 'That's not something that can be done in a hurry.'

Garland did not reply. He was eyeing the group of idlers ahead of us at the court house steps.

Garland coughed, stepping forward in a protective manner. 'Missy Fleur. If yo' be so good as to walk 'roun' de square instead of t'rough it, we ain' gwine pass dem men.'

'Fiddlesticks, Garland!' I exclaimed peevishly, 'If I want to walk across the square I shall. Why, it's perfectly lovely.'

Without looking back to see if he was following me, I chose a path through the square, which would take me directly past the court house.

There were five men there. One was sprawled out across the steps. The other four were sitting and regarding me sullenly from under lowered eyelids. I was appalled by their appearance. Their clothes were ragged and their complexions were red and mottled, flushed more by whiskey than by the sun.

'Cock-a-doodle-doo!'

I faltered when I heard the sound and glanced directly at the band of idlers. One had his hands to his lips and was crowing dementedly while his three companions nodded their heads in derision.

I quickened my pace but soon I realised that Garland was the primary object of their ridicule.

'Where y'll gwine, boy?'

'See the fine nigra with his dainty Miss.'
'Ain' y'all hot in them clothes, nigra?'
'Cock-a-doodle-doo!'

Their coarse shouts shocked me. Poor Garland! He held his head high with his eyes staring straight in front of him, but I saw him bite his lower lip as he pretended not to notice the cat-calls.

'I declare – !' I began.

'No, Miss Fleur!' Garland was beside me, touching his hand gently on my elbow. 'Don't let them anger you. That's what they want. Walk on like a lady!'

'Cock-a-doodle-do! Cock-a-doodle-doo!'

The stupid crowing of the fair-haired youth goaded me beyond discretion. 'Stop that silly noise!' I shouted, stamping my foot with rage. 'You sound like a perfect fool.'

'A perfect fool!' One of the men mimicked, and the others took the words up in a drunken chorus.

'Come, Miss Fleur,' Garland hissed.

I was about to walk on as Garland urged when I observed something familiar about the fifth young lout who was rousing himself slowly, shaking his head to clear the effect of a drunken sleep.

'Jem Hayard!' I gasped.

He opened his eyes and stared, no doubt bewildered by the sight of me and Garland at the foot of the steps while his cronies honked and hooted with ridicule.

'Shut up!' Jem's voice cut through their row with the authority of a bullwhip.

The crackers immediately fell silent, fidgeting uncomfortably on the step while Jem stood up. He brushed at his trousers, straightened his coat and strolled down the steps toward me.

'Fleur!' His face creased with pleasure and he held out his hands.

I was so angry I forgot myself. 'What are you doing with that poor white trash, Jem Hayard?'

'Ho ho!' Jem chortled. 'Fleur has found her tongue at last, has she? And why should it concern you with whom I associate?'

I stepped away from Jem's outstretched hands but I

was maddened into replying.

'It's no concern of mine, Jem Hayard, but I refuse to have a pack of lazy good-for-nothings insult me.'

Jem's smile spread across his handsome face. 'I'm relieved to see the combined efforts of your uncle and Mammy Mable haven't quelled your adventurous spirit, Fleur. Won't you take my arm? If your watchdog will permit, of course?' He grinned at Garland whose only reaction was a slight tightening of his mouth. Although I knew it was the wrong thing to do, I slipped my arm under Jem's elbow.

'I'm always coming to your rescue, Fleur.' His dark eyes probed my face as we continued across the square. The idlers muttered sullenly to themselves.

'For the second time you have saved me from a situation that you yourself created!' I corrected him tartly. 'Are those men friends of yours?'

Jem's voice sounded mocking. 'More acquaintances than friends. Don't you know about Jem Hayard? I carouse with everyone, Fleur, I'm not inclined to allow myself to be bound by the traditions of Southern plantocracy.'

'Plantocracy traditions?' Jem's closeness had made me bolder instead of intimidating me into the respectful silence which Southern men were said to expect from young ladies.

'The kind of rules which my parents and your uncle are governed by.'

'Is there something wrong with such rules?'

'So many questions for a young lady!' Jem grinned down at me, his dark eyes seeming to laugh. 'The plantocracy control Paxton County, Fleur. Have you ever wondered why your uncle hasn't taken you to visit your neighbours? No? Then your head is lighter than I thought.' He paused thoughtfully. 'It's because your uncle had to make sure that you wouldn't do anything to disgrace him. That you would conduct yourself according to his standards. I'm only allowed the latitude I have because I'm a wayward son. No one expects me to be anything but worthless!'

I glanced at his firm jaw and his straight nose outlined

in profile. I swallowed, remembering the excitement I had known when I first saw that face. I tightened my grip on his arm, warming with pleasure as though he had told me a secret.

Ahead of us, at the other side of the square, Uncle Leo was being helped into the carriage by Rollo.

Jem patted my hand. 'You must go home now, Fleur. Your uncle will start shrieking at you if you keep him waiting.'

I was puzzled by the mockery in Jem's voice. 'You're laughing at him?'

Jem raised his eyebrows. 'Am I, Fleur? Well, he is a bit of an old maid, don't you think?'

I frowned, trying to understand the point behind his remark. 'He's been very good to me.'

'Oh, I don't doubt it. Fleur. He would have me to answer to if he were not.'

'You? What do you mean?'

'What do I mean? Fleur, I delivered you to him, did I not? Were he not good to you I would be obliged to undeliver you quite smartly.'

Uncle had seen us now and glowered while we crossed the main street to the side of the carriage.

I spoke before he could. 'Jem rescued me from the attentions of some drunken men, Uncle. They were very rude and were ridiculing Garland.'

'She doesn't tell you I was consorting with them,' Jem laughed boldly.

'I expect no better from you, Jem.' Uncle's voice had an embittered edge to it. He glanced briefly at me then turned back to speak to Jem while Garland and Rollo assisted me into the coach beside him.

'I've been hoping you would come to Maddocks, Jem.'

'I was not so inclined.'

Jem's deliberate insolence puzzled me. He seemed to dare Uncle Leo to reprimand him. Uncle shrugged his shoulders wearily.

Jem was standing carelessly beside the carriage, his coat bedraggled and his hair blowing wildly across his face. He looked like a gypsy, and his eyes glinted with some private mirth as he addressed me.

'Fleur, you must persuade your uncle that he is very selfish to keep you to himself at Maddocks. The time has come for you to visit your neighbours. Don't forget us at Hayard's Hall, Fleur. My parents would like to meet you!'

Uncle Leo heaved his shoulders in a sigh and waved Hannibal to proceed. The carriage lurched forward. Jem was left standing in the centre of the road staring after me, nodding his head as though he had reached some decision which gave him enormous satisfaction.

I glanced at my uncle and was dismayed at the overwhelming sadness that made his face look crumpled and defeated.

CHAPTER TWELVE

Maylou was sullen when she helped me dress the next morning. I studied her reflection carefully while I sat in front of the glass and she brushed my hair. Her eyes, normally bright, were clouded with reproach. The handle of the brush suddenly banged against my ear, causing me to cry out.

'I declare, Maylou, you did that on purpose!'

'Oh, no, Missy!'

'Of course not. I'm sorry.' I said contritely, reaching for the girl's hand. But her face remained unsmiling and she snatched her hand away. She remined silent, pouting, and I was glad when she had finished. She left the room quickly and I could hear the heavy slap of her feet on the stairs. Obviously something was wrong with Maylou. I must speak to Mammy Mable to see if I could help her.

I listened for a time to the morning sounds of Maddocks and then decided to read for a while before going downstairs. Perhaps an hour had passed when the door burst open and Mammy Mable strode into the room. I looked in surprise at her stern visage.

'Maylou been sassin' yo', Missy?'

'No. Of course not.' I came quickly to the girl's defence. 'But she did seem distraught. Is anything wrong?'

'She ain' nowhere 'round where she belong. I scare' for Maylou, I 'fraid she plannin' to 'scape.'

'Escape!' I echoed. 'Why should she do that?'

'Eber since Maylou done tek up wid one o' dem no-good blacks at Hayard's Hall, all she t'ink ob is freedom. But ain' no freedom if dey hab to run de res' ob dey lives.'

She smacked shut her lips and stared at me. 'Dere, ah be sufferin' wid worryment. Ah sayin' t'ings bes' unsaid, Missy Fleur. Tek no notice ob me.'

The old woman frowned and left the chamber before I could question her further. It had never occurred to me that the Maddocks slaves were not content. Of course, I had read about insurrections and the quarrels between the slave states of the South and the free states of the North. But all that was so remote; it surely had nothing to do with Maddocks.

I left my book on my dressing table and wandered along the hall to a far wing of the house. Here a window gave a view of the cotton fields stretching as far as I could see. A gang of slaves were working in the nearest field. I watched them with curiosity, realising with a sense of guilt that I had never given much real thought to them before.

After dinner, which I ate alone as Uncle Leo was in the fields, I decided to take a ride. I wanted to talk to the slaves to see for myself what they thought of life at Maddocks. Were they treated so badly? I really had no idea.

Garland had my horse ready for me when I strolled over to the stables. He nodded politely and assisted me to mount. We set off down the trail to the overseer's house.

'You seem awfully quiet today, Garland.' I teased him when I realised he was not in his usual good humour.

'Yas, Missy.'

The angry tone of his voice made me turn my head. I watched him sharply. 'Is something wrong?'

'No, Missy Fleur. Ain' nutin' wrong.' He answered curtly, as though mocking me with his servile slave way of speaking.

I shrugged my shoulders and tapped the horse into a canter.

'Missy Fleur?' Garland's tone changed and I slowed down.

'Yes?'

'Do you really wish to ride this path, Miss Fleur?'

'Hah! Now you are speaking intelligibly, why shouldn't I ride down here, Garland?' I glanced along the trail. 'This will take us to the overseer's house and I'm going to ride beyond the house to the creek.'

'We can ride to the creek by the other road, Miss Fleur.' Garland pointed behind him to the main driveway.

'I'm aware of that, Garland.' I urged the horse forward.

'Yes, Miss.'

I was sure I heard Garland sigh but his face was impenetrable when I glanced back at him. He stared straight ahead and rode his horse with a casual grace.

We were close to the overseer's house when I heard the sound of people running. I turned to Garland, my eyebrow raised in query.

'We can still pass by the main drive, Miss Fleur,' he said softly.

'Why, what is it?'

'Nothing of interest to you, Miss Fleur.'

We rounded the curve in the trail where I saw dozens of slaves rushing pell mell down the path from their quarters. The drivers jogged along behind them, shouting urgently. The slaves were turning off the trail into the yard, bumping into one another in their hurry to escape the drivers' whips.

'Something must be wrong, Garland.' His eyes avoided mine. 'I'll go and see.'

'Do you really want to, Miss?' Garland trotted up to

my side and used the handle of his riding whip to prod the slaves out of my way.

'Of course, Garland. Why are all these people milling around?'

We reached the yard in front of the overseer's house. On one side was the long low building in which the tools and cotton seed were stored. Opposite were the barns where cotton was packed in bales, and the gin house. Another building, for the whites who worked on the plantation, enclosed the rectangular yard on its fourth side. This compound was located close to the slave quarters and not far from the creek which divided the Maddocks plantation in two.

The slaves were being herded into the yard by the drivers and bookkeepers. I saw a humpbacked man, Algernon Ferret, who was the overseer, standing in the centre of the yard with his hands on his hips. His thin-faced wife, Julie, was watching from the window of their house. She clutched one of her sickly red children in her arms. The others, five boys and two girls dressed in torn smocks like the slaves, slouched on the veranda.

I reined in my horse and paused in the shade from the roof of the gin house. Garland handed me my parasol which I opened while studying the hundreds of slaves filling the yard. Many of them were wailing with fear. I was amazed. This was the first time I had ever seen so many of them together. They looked miserable, ill-fed, weary, and dejected.

Some of them wore torn smocks of worn osnaburgh, others had patched breech clothes, and some of the women had their heads wrapped in faded kerchiefs. They were a sorrowful sight and I wondered how my uncle, who prided himself on the beautiful objects he kept in his house, could allow such misery to exist on his plantation.

'What's this about, Garland?' I demanded.

None of the white men grouped in the centre of the turbulent mob seemed aware of my presence. They were scowling with anger and I looked in vain for a friendly face.

Garland didn't answer me. He was obviously distressed by my presence in the compound. However, some streak of obstinacy required me to stay.

I gripped the shaft of my parasol and was grateful for the security afforded by the wall of the gin house when the slaves pressed around us. Garland was at my side, using his horse to shield me and to keep the desperate blacks from unseating me.

There was a flurry when the door of the storehouse was flung open. A fat, bald-headed white man emerged at the head of a small contingent of slaves. In the middle of them all walked Maylou.

Maylou's hands were bound behind her back and the links of a chain were wrapped around her wrists. The slave who walked behind her prodded her with a stick, holding the end of the chain firmly in his left hand.

'Whatever is Maylou doing there? Mammy Mable told me she ran away. Did they catch her?'

Garland stared at me in dismay. His mouth was working but he did not speak. The slaves in the yard jostled and screamed while Maylou was prodded onto a wooden dais in the centre of the yard by the bare-chested black guardian who escorted her.

There was a scaffold on the dais with its cross piece about seven feet high and parallel to the floor of the platform. There was a pulley on this cross piece and the Negro with Maylou pulled the rope threaded through this pulley and tied it to Maylou's wrists. He released her wrists from the chains when they were bound with the pulley and began to tug on the rope.

Maylou's eyes popped as though they would fall from her head. She looked at a huge black woman with a red bandanna who had mounted the dais beside her and opened her mouth to speak. The wailing of the crowd drowned her words. The huge woman struck her a vicious blow across her face and she fell silent. Her arms were now raised above her head. I noticed the patches of perspiration which stained her gown under her arms.

The black man standing at the side of the scaffold held the rope in his hands and glanced at the white men in front of the platform. The fat, bald-headed man nodded. The Negro pulled on the rope until Maylou's arms were stretched tightly above her head.

She screamed with pain. The Negro pulled again and Maylou was lifted off the floor of the dais. She extended her legs so that the tips of her toes still touched the floor but the white man signalled for her to be lifted higher. With her feet clear of the floor, Maylou spun when the Negro prodded her with his stick.

The Negro turned to the white man and beamed proudly. The man climbed onto the platform, helped up by the woman in the bandanna. She said something to him. The man nodded. She turned to face the crowd. As soon as she began to speak, the slaves whimpered into silence.

'Dis house nigra been cuttin' up,' the woman shrieked, globs of spittle frothing at the corners of her mouth. 'She be Missy Fleur's own nigra an' she done get bigged by a nigra from Hayard's Hall. She done try to run.' Her face was contorted with some cruel passion as she glared at the slaves in front of her. Not a soul raised his eyes to defy her.

The white man on the platform scowled. He reached into the leather sack at his feet and produced a paddle of hard leather with holes drilled into the blade. He swiped the air casually with the paddle and the slaves flinched. He spoke to his Negro assistant who stepped forward and placed his hand on the bodice of Maylou's gown. It was a pretty gown, a bright green with lace trimmings, one which I had given her myself.

The Negro tugged at the bodice with one hand, holding Maylou steady with the other to stop her spinning. The bodice ripped and the Negro pulled the dress off, slicing at the sleeves so that Maylou spun completely naked in front of the slaves.

I clutched my mouth with my hand to stop myself from screaming. Maylou's body was extended from the pulley to the ground, her breasts stretched over her bones.

The Negro prodded her roughly with his stick, jamming it between her legs, I shuddered.

The white man stepped forward, brushing the Negro aside. Although he was bald and fat, he was strong and his massive frame shook as he brought down the paddle onto Maylou's spinning body with a sickening blow. Maylou shrieked with pain and the crowd of slaves moaned in sympathy.

The white man moved with an agility surprising in a person of his bulk. His arm rose and fell so quickly, it was impossible to count the number of times the paddle sliced into Maylou. The holes in it pocked her skin with blood which dripped down her body onto the floor of the dais.

Maylou's screaming stopped. Every face rose to watch her. She gasped, lifted her knees to her chest and uttered a cry which chilled all of us with its anguish. Blood spurted from between her legs and a glob of flesh plopped to the floor. Maylou fainted. The white man flicked the bloody mess off the dais with his foot and resumed his beating.

I gagged and turned away. Garland caught me or I would have fallen. I stared at him and his young black face stared back at me.

'Why?' I breathed.

'You should answer that question for me.'

I frowned. 'Does this often happen?'

'Of course. We are slaves, not children in Sunday school.'

I could say no more. The world seemed to tilt around me at a crazy angle. Then an arm enveloped me and held me close. Somehow Mammy Mable had found her way to me. Her old lined face was filled with an ineffable sorrow and the dark eyes reflected a grief too deep for tears. She folded me against her breasts and I surrendered myself to her, letting her lead me back to Maddocks.

CHAPTER THIRTEEN

In the following days, I took great pains to avoid Uncle Leo. I could not believe he had ordered Maylou's flogging, but at best, he had taken no measures to prevent such an act of savagery. I stayed in my room much of the time, taking great comfort in Mammy Mable's ministrations. At other times I went riding with Garland.

Garland seemed to understand my mood. He did not try to bully me into a good humour, but carried out his job of accompanying me with silent respect. He answered willingly when I spoke to him but otherwise never intruded upon my sombre thoughts. He showed me trails I had not noticed before, leading me through the cotton fields busy with slaves, and along the shaded banks of the creek.

Whenever we passed a slave gang, Garland bade me ride on without stopping. I was in no mood to disagree with him for I had decided that the way to shut out of my mind the cruelty of Uncle's slave breakers was to pretend that the white men who worked on the plantation did not exist. When one saluted me, I rode past with my head in the air.

Garland was confounded by what he saw as my bad manners but he said nothing, bowing his own head respectfully to the white people we passed. Of course, it was not long before word reached my uncle about my outrageous conduct and I was summoned to the library.

Uncle Leo, as usual, looked the part of the prosperous plantocrat. Standing before him while he sat coolly in his chair facing his desk, I could not help wondering about the relationship between him and Jem. I frowned. There was Jem again, slipping into my thoughts with the persistence of a mosquito.

'Yes, Fleur, you may well frown. What's this I hear?' Uncle Leo picked up a note from his desk. 'You appear to have snubbed Mistress Ferret, Carlyle the bookkeeper and Mister Goodpaster. All for no reason. What do you say?' His steel grey eyes stared sternly. I blushed, lowering my head.

'Come now, Fleur. It doesn't pay to be rude to our white people. Some of them are very sensitive, you know, especially Mistress Ferret. Very much given to gossip, these people.'

'What do you mean?'

'Sit down, child.' He sounded exasperated. 'You know very well what I mean, and now I hear you are giving yourself airs and graces and ignoring those upon whom Maddocks is dependent.'

'I'm ashamed to know those people, Uncle.'

'Good Lord! Whatever for?'

'They treat your blacks worse than animals.'

'Ah, hah! So that's the reason for this contrariness?' Uncle left his desk and sat himself down on the couch by my side.

'Slaves have to be treated in a certain way to keep them working. That's why I have Algernon Ferret and Calvin Goodpaster. To see that the work is done.'

He patted my arm. 'You are young and city bred so I don't expect you to understand. Anyway, the slaves are the overseer's concern, not yours.'

I quailed before Uncle's hard eyes and indignant voice, and I murmured, 'I'm sorry for offending you and I promise to be nice to the overseers.'

'Of course, Fleur, I knew you would.' Uncle coughed. 'There is another matter, too, Fleur. I don't think you should go riding alone with Garland any more.'

'Whyever not!'

'Garland is, well, growing older, you know, and so are you.'

I was close to tears.

'Garland is like a friend to me. He's perfectly proper. Why do you want to stop me riding with him? It isn't fair.'

'Now don't cry, Fleur, please!' Uncle Leo's voice rose in panic. 'You must not look on Garland as your friend. He is a Maddocks slave, nothing more.'

Uncle patted my hand anxiously but when the tears started to stream down my face, he jumped up and hurried over to the door, calling for Mammy Mable. She must have been hovering near at hand because she entered immediately. A brown-skinned woman followed her. I was so surprised at the sight of a stranger in the house that I forgot my tears.

'Poor Missy Fleur!' the woman uttered, stepping over to the couch and sitting down beside me. She embraced me to her bosom and patted my shoulder sympathetically. She smelt of verbena and I felt oddly comforted by her presence.

I removed myself from her embrace, brushed back my hair from my face where it was caught in my tears, and studied her.

She was only a few years older than I but the travelling gown she wore gave the impression of greater age. She was of high colour with a peach-shaded complexion and a crest of jet-black hair piled high over her forehead.

'Honey, yo' sure are de pretties' young lady ah evah seen! Yo' an' me gwine had de happies' times togeder!'

I looked at Uncle Leo for some explanation. He in turn glanced at Mammy Mable.

'Ladybelle is yuh new maid, Missy Fleur,' Mammy Mable announced, her voice gentle.

Again I glanced at Uncle Leo. He coughed. 'Ladybelle has been lent to us by Mister Granger Hayard, Fleur. She was maid and companion to his daughter, Maxine.'

I stared at the woman sitting beside me. Maxine was Jem's sister. Why had her maid come to Maddocks?

'Where is Maxine now?' I asked.

There was a sudden air of uneasiness in the room. Ladybelle took my hand in hers and urged me up from the couch.

'Missy Maxine gone 'way an' leab me, honey. Ah'm sure glad she do dat else ah not hab de priv'lege ob servin' y'all.' Ladybelle beamed at me, her eyes sparkling.

Her good humour was infectious and I could not help smiling back.

'See, Missy Fleur, yuh tears all gone! Come, honey, why don' we go to yuh chamber for some young lady talk, eh?' Ladybelle hugged me, laughing merrily. I let her lead me out of the library and up the stairs.

Ladybelle was ecstatic when she saw my wardrobe and the new summer dresses Mistress Dundy had made for me. 'Honey, wid yuh figure an' yuh eyes yo' gwine hab ebery tomcat in de county ahowlin' aftah yo'!'

'What do you mean, Ladybelle?' I smiled in spite of my alarm at her brashness. 'I never leave Maddocks, so who is going to see me?'

'At yuh comin'-out one day, yo' be so pretty, yo' can hab any man in dis county, Missy Fleur. Ah gwine teach yo' how to fix it so dose buckrees gwine do anyt'in' yo' ax dem. Den you' gwine pick de bes' one to marriage wid an' gib yuh uncle a son to 'herit de plantation.'

I studied Ladybelle's face intently. Something about her expression made me pull my hands out of her grasp.

'Who's been filling your head with such nonsense?' I asked.

Immediately Ladybelle's confidence collapsed. 'Dat ain't nonsense,' she whined.

I broke away from her and stalked across to the window overlooking the lawns of Maddocks. I heard her rise but at the same time the door opened. Mammy Mable stepped just inside. I rushed over into her arms. Her body grew stiff as I pressed my lips against her soft cheek and she held me close. She was staring at Ladybelle, a hard, defiant quality in her eyes.

'Wha' yo' do to upset Miss Fleur?' she demanded.

'Nutin', nutin',' Ladybelle replied and looked at me with a conspiratorial gaze, as if trying to ally herself with me against Mammy Mable.

As Ladybelle settled into the household her attitude puzzled me more and more. She was polite to Mammy Mable but there was an obvious vein of hostility between them. She treated Uncle Leo with the same cool correctness with which he addressed her. I was the only person at Maddocks to whom she showed anything more than the usual emotions expected from a servant.

I became embarrassed at times by the intensity of her apparent affection. She liked to cuddle up to me and to touch me. When I took a bath a week after she came to Maddocks, she showed a delight in my body as if I were a lamb she was preparing to display at a county fair. I gathered the impression she was acting under orders. But whose orders? I could not imagine until one Sunday when Uncle Leo took me on a visit to Hayard's Hall. We arrived in mid-afternoon.

Granger Hayard and his wife Felicity welcomed us at the top of the grand steps which swept up to the classically columned porch. I was introduced to Forest and his fiancée, Miss Vain, and then Jem offered me his arm to escort me into the house. Uncle Leo followed with Mrs. Granger. Ladybelle, who was attending me, dallied on the porch.

Jem hurried me along and soon the rest were left behind.

'Where are we going?' I asked.

'For a walk!'

'But your parents. I must pay my respects.'

'Time enough for that. Come!'

It was impossible to resist his grip. I glanced back at my uncle who was standing gallantly by Mistress Hayard as she sat down. He nodded his head in consent, which puzzled me. Uncle had given me explicit instructions on how to behave. Yet now he appeared to be ignoring his own caution about good manners by letting Jem take me off before the normal courtesies were exchanged.

'Talk to me!'

Jem's curt command cut into my thinking. 'What?' I stammered.

'There is no point in walking in silence, Fleur. Surely you have something to say?'

'I don't believe I'm very practiced in small talk.'

'Ho! Ho! Doesn't my company inspire you?'

I was riled by Jem's behaviour. 'Mister Hayard,' I snapped crossly, 'I find you boorish! Please let me return to the parlour so that I can be well mannered in front of your parents and your brother and Miss Vain and not prejudice my place in society because of your churlishness.'

Jem released my wrist and stared at me. This time I did not lower my eyes but looked directly into his. I believed I saw a flicker of respect before he broke into a guffaw and slapped his thigh.

'Dam'me, Fleur! No wench has ever told me that.'

'I'm not a wench!'

'Don't be silly, Fleur. All ladies are wenches when they meet the right man.'

'Are you suggesting you're the man to make me a wench, Jem Hayard?' I bridled, blushing furiously. 'It will take more of a man than you! Now escort me back into the house this instant. You are making me ashamed with your donkey braying.'

Jem's chuckle suddenly ceased. His eyes seemed to pierce me and I swear I would have stumbled if his arm had not suddenly snaked around my waist. I did not know whether I should try to remove it or pretend not to notice. My cheeks reddened. I was sure he could feel the violent throbbing of my heart.

'Hah! For a moment I thought you were serious!'

'I am serious, Jem,' I whispered. 'Why do you tease me? I'm not a little girl.'

Jem's eyes softened when I raised my head to gaze at him. His whole face mellowed and I wondered if, under the bravado of his cavalier personality, he felt as insecure and uncertain as I did. He squeezed my waist tenderely then withdrew his arm, offering me his elbow. I curled my hand under it and we began to saunter around the flower garden.

Jem seemed suddenly eager to talk and just listening pleased me. He spoke of the plantation, the slaves, his childhood, even the flowers in the garden. After a while, conversation seemed unnecessary and we walked together in silence.

I squeezed his arm to assure myself he was still there. When I raised my face he was looking down at me, his lip quivering and his hard dark eyes moist with desire. I parted my lips to protest. His face drew closer to mine.

'Missy Fleur! Missy Fleur! Yuh Uncle Leo be callin'.'

Ladybelle's shrill voice snapped the spell between us.

Jem jerked his head back, his eyes angry. 'Dam' the wench!' he muttered.

He guided me back toward the house and I tried to get my features under control but I could do nothing about my emotions. I had almost been kissed by the man I dreamed about. Like it or not, I knew I was falling in love.

'Yo look like yo've caught de sun, Missy Fleur,' Ladybelle muttered. 'Yo' does be so red.'

'Shut up, bitch. And leave Miss Fleur alone.'

'Jem!' I pressed his arm. 'She meant no harm.'

'No harm! Fleur, you don't know Ladybelle. She's got a tongue like a snake. It's a family trait. On the bad side of course. Not like Forest.' Jem nodded with his head to where his brother Forest and Miss Vain were conversing on the piazza.

'Forest takes after my mother. So damned respectable, you'd think he was campaigning for sainthood. He'll not even think of kissing Miss Vain until he's wed her!'

'Jem, what are you talking about? How can Ladybelle have any traits from your family?'

The way Jem glanced at me, he had already forgotten what he had said. 'Ladybelle,' I prompted him.

'Oh, her. She's one of Pa's nigra gets. Got her mother's beauty though.'

I stopped at the foot of the steps onto the piazza. 'She's your half-sister?'

'You didn't know?'

'I had no idea.'

Jem shrugged his shoulders. 'I'd hate to guess how many outside gets Pa has. And to look at him now, you'd think he was more virtuous than a passel of virgins. Come on, let's go and be polite with my parents if that's what you want.'

'Wait a minute, Jem.' I held onto his coat sleeve. 'Tell me something about Ladybelle.'

Jem's good humour vanished. He glanced at me suspiciously. 'What?'

'Did you arrange for her to come to Maddocks?'

The tension in Jem's face eased. 'My, you are smart under those ringlets! Yes, what of it? I heard you needed a new maid. She was available. Your uncle is renting her from Pa.'

'Did you ask her to spy on me?'

Jem burst into laughter again, pulling me onto the piazza. 'Now that's a silly notion for such a clever girl!' he said, leading me into the parlour to join his parents.

Granger Hayard was a man about my uncle's age. Unlike Uncle Leo who affected a dress style more suited for the elegance of northern cities, Granger Hayard dressed in the rugged manner of a hard-working planter. His personality matched his appearance. He was bluff and laughed a lot, obviously enjoying himself as a hearty man of the world. His appraisal of me, when I sat opposite him beside his wife, had a hint of lechery in it. There was no mistaking that he was Jem's father.

Felicity Hayard was such a contrast to her husbnd, it would have been difficult for a stranger to imagine them living together as man and wife. She was frail and twittered like a hummingbird. Forest, their eldest son, clearly took after her. But I was surprised to see when Mrs. Hayard turned to stare at me, that Jem had taken his hard, passionate eyes from her, not from his father.

Jem was ill at ease in his parents' presence, and they seemed equally disturbed by him. Uncle Leo fluttered his hands and tried to make small talk with Mrs. Hayard but I could see the visit was not a success. Forest declined to join us, keeping his head low as he conversed with Miss Vain.

Soon the polite conversation withered. Jem escorted me to the carriage, winked at Uncle Leo and then sauntered off without any formal farewell. It scarcely seemed possible that he had actually behaved with any tenderness toward me earlier.

Uncle Leo was silent until we reached the entrance to our drive. 'Do you like Maddocks, Fleur?' he asked suddenly, breaking into my thoughts about Jem.

'Oh, Uncle, of course I do.'

'Yes, I thought so. I'm pleased about that. And what do you think of Jem Hayard? You find him an impossible rascal, don't you?'

I gaped at Uncle Leo, uncertain how to answer. 'He's

somethlng of a puzzle,' I managed to stutter, grateful that the shadows in the carriage as dusk descended prevented Uncle from seeing my features.

Uncle Leo looked at me sharply. 'He has fine points, Fleur.'

'I'm sure he has.'

'Good.' Uncle lapsed into silence as the carriage drew up in front of the house. Trott hastened down the steps, but Garland reached the carriage before him and held open the door. Uncle put his hand on mine when I moved to descend from the carriage.

'It's all arranged, Fleur,' Uncle said quietly. 'You are to marry Jem Hayard next month. Before Christmas.'

CHAPTER FOURTEEN

Garland caught me in his arms when I fainted. I felt myself falling and then there was a blissful feeling of floating. The firm hands which clutched me gave me support I did not want to abandon. I kept my eyes tightly closed while Garland lifted me in his arms and carried me into the house.

Uncle Leo was talking mournfully in the background and Trott's frantic bass voice called to Mammy Mable to bring a snifter of brandy. I breathed in, dreamily feeling myself being lowered, gently and lovingly, on a couch. Mammy Mable unfastened my dress and loosened my stays, murmuring soothing words as she did so.

Ladybelle fluttered about, getting in Mammy Mable's way until the older woman turned on her and ordered her from the room.

I felt Garland's palm behind my back as he urged me into a sitting position. He was holding the snifter to my lips. I opened my eyes slowly.

Garland's face was level with mine. His eyes mirrored deep concern and his proud face was creased with worry.

He beamed when he saw me stir.

'Yo' no' takin' de brandy, Missy Fleur?' he asked anxiously.

I opened my mouth to protest. He tilted the glass against my lips and poured. The brandy tasted tart on my tongue.

'Swallow,' he commanded in his soft voice.

I grimaced as the liquid tore past my throat and swept strength back into me. Mammy Mable decided Garland should take me upstairs, and she walked beside him as he carried me to my chamber.

It was night when I awoke. The curtains of my bed were open and a candle burned in its bulbous glass shade in the corner of the chamber. Even as I stared out at the moon suspended over the boughs of the live oaks of the lawn, Ladybelle's face appeared in front of me. She lowered her head closer to mine and plumped the pillows.

'What ails yo', Missy? Yo' done look bright enough sparkin' with Jem dis aft'noon.'

The moon quivered before my eyes. Jem. I passed my tongue nervously over my lips. Jem. Jem. What was I supposed to do?

'Ladybelle, did you hear what Uncle Leo told me?' I whispered.

'Ah don' listen to buckra talk dat don' concern me.' Ladybelle stood up and sniffed with disdain. 'Ain' no swoonin' business, nohow!'

'So you did hear?'

'Say what yo' like. Yo' done swoon an' preten' you' surprise'. Yo' don' fool me.'

I pulled myself up to a sitting position and glared at Ladybelle. 'How can you say such a thing? I have no reason to fool anyone.'

'Missy Fleur, yo' mean yo' ain' know yuh uncle and Jem plannin' fuh yo' to marriage wid him? Dat why yo' topple from de carriage like a sack ob turnips?' Ladybelle flapped her hands and sat down quickly on the bed beside me. 'How yo' don' know? Ah t'ink yo' know dat since Jem first bring yo' to Maddocks.'

I folded Ladybelle's hand in mine wondering what was to come. 'Why do you say that?'

'Lor', honey, cuz it de trut'. Dat why yuh Uncle Leo sen' Jem to Savannah fuh yo'. He wan' Jem to marry yo' bad, but ain' no one know why he take such a shine to de boy. Jem a wild one, Missy.'

I looked at Ladybelle, quite unable to speak. Yes, he was a wild one, but I thought I had seen tenderness and loneliness in those dark eyes when he looked at me that afternoon. Jem needed a love as strong as his own to satisfy him. At least that was what I wanted to think.

'Honey!' Ladybelle's husky voice called me back to the present. 'Don' yo' wan' marry, Jem?' Her profile outlined against the haze of the moonglow resembled Jem's. Her laugh was his. 'Yo' does be for'nate dat yo' get a buckree so young and handsome, Missy Fleur. Some plantation ladies 'blige to marriage wid ol' men what can't mount a horse jus' fuh de sake ob de plantocracy. Leastwise Jem gwine be one real husban' for yo'!'

I fell back on the bed and sank my face into the pillow. I felt ashamed! Surely love wasn't like this? The thought of marrying Jem thrilled me but Ladybelle's coarse words dashed romance from my mind. I remembered the day at the inn in Milledgeville when I had first seen Jem and his smile swept through my fears to my heart. Perhaps I had loved him since then.

Yes, I would marry Jem, but what troubled me was that Ladybelle made me realise that since my arrival at Maddocks, I had become like the Maddocks slaves. I was not free to do what I wished. I was a puppet in a scheme devised by Uncle Leo and Jem. Why?

The night I had heard Jem and Uncle Leo talking in the library returned to my mind. Now the conversation had a meaning. Uncle Leo was using me, and Jem, to ensure he would have an heir for Maddocks.

I rubbed my face into the pillow until Ladybelle, with an exaggerated sigh, got up from the bed and stalked over to her pallet. Her rude muttering encouraged my decision. Maybe it *was* part of someone else's plan, but I would be a good wife to Jem and bear him children to inherit Maddocks. I loved him and would be the Mistress of Maddocks to make him proud. And I would, at last, be able to live an adult life of my own.

The days before my wedding were filled with activity from the moment I descended in the morning until I returned wearily to my chamber at night. Because he was a bachelor, it seemed that all the ladies in the county wanted to assist Uncle Leo. He was content to let them do so. Jem's mother rode over in the Hayard carriage every day to supervise the volunteers and every day the ladies' parlour was packed with earnest women, anxious to help in the preparations and perhaps to engage in gossip.

Once, when other thoughts were filling my head and I entered the parlour quite without remembering the presence of the county ladies, an abrupt hush descended on the room. The high-pitched drone of Mrs. Runacres was the only voice not muted because her head was turned away from the door and she had not seen me enter.

'My dear,' she was saying, 'such a perfect alliance, Hayard plantation and Maddocks. It's only the people who aren't matched.' When no one tittered, Mrs. Runacres glanced around in surprise.

I caught her eye and smiled, choosing to ignore the remark. 'I'm sorry,' I murmured. 'I forgot you were all here. It's so kind of you to help.' I backed out of the door and closed it gently as the strident tones of Mrs. Runacres cut through the babble of voices.

'You might have told me she was there, the poor thing – '

The kitchen at the back of the house was in an uproar. Mammy Mable brought in women from the quarters to help bake the cakes and sweetmeats and prepare all the dishes needed for the wedding. Trott was appointed vintner and became more grand each day, his face aglow as testimony to the quality of the wines he felt obliged to sample.

All day long, carriages and wagons clattered up to

the house with loads of provisions for the feast which would follow the wedding. Garland had been put in charge of these supplies which probably accounted for his serious countenance whenever I saw him. Rollo was schooling a band of sable-skinned youths to be stewards and footmen while Mammy Mable endeavoured to instruct a group of inexperienced girls to be extra chamber maids.

The house was in perpetual commotion. Uncle Leo tried to find a haven in his library, but all the problems were brought to him to solve. He was telling me about the six hundred guests who had been invited when Algernon Ferret, the overseer, and Calvin Goodpaster came to see him.

Algernon Ferret was an ugly man, as sharp and as thin as a scythe. He was unable to stand straight because of a stoop which, for the slaves, must have added to the ferocity of his appearance. He was a wisp of a man, but he was an expert in the area of cotton, and Uncle Leo admitted that without him Maddocks might have foundered long ago.

Uncle received Ferret warmly and urged him to be seated. He did not extend the same courtesy to Calvin Goodpaster whom he merely acknowledged with a crisp nod of his head. Uncle Leo once told me that Goodpaster was a necessary evil on a plantation of this size. Ferret was not a strong man and could not lash the slaves himself. That was Goodpaster's job, although officially he was known as a bookkeeper.

I regarded the burly man with his bright red skin, wondering how he could ill-treat people and have no evil etched into his face to show for it. He looked quite jolly.

'Beg pardon for the disturbance, Mister Singer.' Ferret spoke with an ingratiating whine. 'It's the wedding, sir.'

Uncle Leo raised his eyes to the ceiling.

'I know you're busy, sir, an' I hope you'll forgive me for the intrusion.'

Calvin Goodpaster, standing behind Ferret, smacked his lips together impatiently. It was obvious that he wanted to speak but deference to Uncle Leo restrained him while Ferret struggled to bring out what was on his mind.

'We've had a good season, sir,' Ferret continued. 'The cotton sold well an' the nigras ain't done too bad. If it was in your mind to give them a little spree, sir, on the occasion of the wedding, it wouldn't meet no objection from me, sir.'

Uncle Leo nodded his head, obviously relieved. 'You know it's not my practice to interfere with you and the field nigras, Ferret. A spree eh?' he bit his thumbnail thoughtfully.

'Beggin' yo' pardon, sir.' The deep voice of Calvin Goodpaster forced my uncle to raise his head and look at him with reluctance. Goodpaster wiped his huge hand across his brow, over the shiny red bald patch and into the tufts of sandy hair at the back of his head.

'It don't seem right to me, sir. I told Ferret and he said come and talk it over with you, sir. Nigras ain't entitled to no privilege, sir. There's corn shuckin' which they take for a spree and it will soon be Christmas, sir. The nigras get too much spreeing already. It makes them contrary to handle.'

Uncle Leo did not like Goodpaster but he could see his point. He looked back at Ferret.

'Makes no neverminds, Mister Singer.' Ferret shrugged his shoulders. 'Them nigras are going to spree when they see all the white folks here whether we permit 'em or not. But give 'em that privilege, sir, and they'll recognize their new master and mistress properly.'

Goodpaster scowled. 'It don't do no good to be slack with nigras, Ferret. Not with all these damn yankee abolitionists 'round.'

Uncle Leo looked down at his hands and his voice was slow. 'Goodpaster is right, I'm sure, but Fleur is like my own daughter. I would like the slaves to celebrate too.'

'Then that's the way we'll do it, Mister Singer.' Ferret rose quickly, as relieved as Uncle that the interview was over. 'I'll make the arrangements.'

'Oh yes, please do. And Goodpaster, if any of the

people try to malinger the next day, I'm sure you'll know how to deal with them.'

Goodpaster's scowl showed his contempt for Uncle's compromise. I pitied the poor slaves who celebrated too much and fell foul of him.

The wedding day dawned as brightly as could be hoped. Ladybelle and I chatted gaily while she helped me dress. I was to be married at Maddocks by a clergyman from Milledgeville. All the arrangements had been made by the committee of ladies from the ladies' parlour.

I did not see Jem during the weeks leading up to the wedding but that seemed to surprise none of the cabal. Indeed, not one of those formidable ladies even inquired about him. I put this down not so much to their bad manners as their irritating familiarity with Jem's conduct. Everyone seemed to know more about my husband-to-be than I did.

For nights I had grown steadily more anxious. Having accepted my destiny as Jem's wife, I grew concerned about his nonappearance. What if he jilted me? Uncle and I would be the laughing stock of the county. He hardly knew me, I reasoned, why should he really care to have me for his wife? Did he love me? He had never told me so. The more days that slipped by without my seeing Jem, the more exasperated I became and perversely the more I longed for him.

Ladybelle was no comfort. All she could say was that he had 'plenty farewells to make.' The implication was that he was travelling the length and breadth of Georgia bidding his numerous female acquaintances *adieu.* It was very hard to bear.

Now it was my wedding day. I stood at the window dressed in my petticoats and sighed. I knew in my heart that Jem was not going to come. It was a wicked joke he had played on Uncle Leo, getting his revenge for something Uncle had done to him. I would never marry now. The gorgeous gown which Mistress Dundy had made for me lay out on my bed. The yard below was thronged with people and I could hear the murmur and commotion as they trouped in and out of the house.

Then, above the sound of the wedding crowd, there was the noise of a man's boots clomping up the stairs. I gasped a sigh of relief. 'It's Jem!'

Ladybelle and I waited for the door to burst open, but the footsteps stomped past, followed by the more sedate footfall of my uncle. A door banged.

'He in de guest room,' Ladybelle whispered. 'He preparin' heself.'

I frowned, straining to hear their voices. The guest room was next to mine and I recognised Uncle Leo's hesitant tones. He was growing agitated. Jem's chuckle cut him short, reverberating through the partition separating Jem's room from mine. The sound made me feel weak with relief and a wave of love for Jem surged through me.

'Is this the way to treat me, Jem?' Uncle's complaining voice burst into my thoughts. 'You haven't been here for so long, and I've been waiting.'

'Why?' Jem's tone was arrogant and weary.

'You know, Jem, I don't have to tell you.'

'Well, I've banned that.'

Uncle Leo gave a strangled cry.

'Damn you, Leo! Was any old maid as bad as you?' Jem flopped down onto the bed. The door linking our two chambers was ajar. Ladybelle watched silently as I crept over to it.

'But you promised!' Uncle's tone was tremulous. 'I've let you have everything you asked for. You should treat me better than this!'

'Leave me alone, Leo. I've ridden all night to get here in time. I'm going to marry her as agreed. Now let me sleep for half an hour.'

'You've no consideration for anyone but yourself, Jem Hayard. How do you think I felt waiting in the library for you to come? Night after night!'

'You shouldn't have waited. Now for God's sake, leave me be.'

'Oh Jem!' There was a rustling sound.

'Take ya' hand off me!' Jem's irritation made his

voice loud and rough, and his exaggerated accent indicated he had been drinking.

I glanced at Ladybelle. She shrugged and sat down in front of my mirror and began to brush out her hair.

'Jem, I thought when I consented to you marrying Fleur – '

'I told you to keep ya' goddam paws to ya'self!' Jem's voice tightened into a snarl of rage.

'Jem,' Uncle Leo insisted. 'Why are you so heartless? Don't you ever think of how I feel? You can have Fleur. One day Maddocks will be yours. But what do you do for me? You know how I feel about you. Come, Jem, come, won't you?'

There was a snort of disgust followed by a few seconds of silence, then a slap echoed through the room and a gasping choking sob from Uncle Leo.

'Yo' need it so bad, why don't yo' find ya'self a nigra, Leo?' Jem growled. 'Yo' get plenty of 'em here.'

'A nigra!'

'Sure. He'll have to do what yo' want. Yo' can lash him if he don't.' Jem's laughter was cruel.

Uncle Leo's voice changed, became harshly defiant. 'Maybe you're right, Jem. If that's the way you want it. I'll see what I can do. Maybe I can get along without you.'

CHAPTER FIFTEEN

Mammy Mable thrust herself into my chamber. She was an astonishing sight, swathed from top to toe in an excess of brilliant colour. Frills, flounces and ribbons enveloped her in bold patterns and she was crowned with a multicoloured bandanna that was a final touch to her flashing attire. Beads and baubles tinkled and clattered when she crossed the floor and stood in front of me, her hands jammed in mock anger through the band of her fanciful little apron.

'Is yo' gwine get marriaged today or not, Missy Fleur?' Mammy scolded, unable to keep the crinkles of laughter from around her eyes or the good nature from her voice. 'Ah declah yo' ain' even dress! Missy, yo' get yuhself on yuh feet. Ah ain' havin' no Missy o' mine disgracin' Maddocks by bein' mopish fuh she marri-age.'

I was in a state of confusion while Mammy and Lady-belle fussed around me. I could not understand what I had heard. Yet Jem was here, my own exciting Jem, and I was soon to be his bride. I was beyond worry now.

Mammy stood away from me to survey her work. 'Nuh yo' really look somet'in',' she crowed.

Her pride was infectious and I twirled around in front of the mirror. The dress was a perfect fit with my narrow waist exquisitely revealed by the elaborate full-ness of the white skirt alive with flounces and frills at my ankles. My dark hair glistened and I felt radiant. The doubt in my mind had vanished in the glow of their admiration.

'Now, Missy Fleur, yo' be fit to be a bride an' Mistress ob Maddocks.'

The door to my chamber was pushed open slowly and we all turned to see Garland standing in the doorway looking very self-conscious in his blue coat with bright buttons in the latest fashion. In his white Marseilles vest, with a gold chain fastened across his bosom and white pantaloons and polished boots, he might have been the bridegroom.

'Garland! If all my attendants look like you today, I declare I shall not recognise one of them.'

'Yas, Missy,' he smiled but could not conceal the sadness lingering in his eyes. 'Marse Leo sen' me to escort yo' downstairs, Missy.'

I gasped. 'Has the time come?'

Garland nodded his head.

'Where is Master Jem?'

'Rollo an' Trott 'tend to Marse Jem, Missy. Yo' go wid Garland.' Mammy Mable bustled me to the door-way. I held onto her, kissing her cheek, then glanced briefly around my boudoir. When I returned I would be

Mrs. Jem Hayard, Mistress of Maddocks.

My gown rustled along the polished boards of the floor as I followed Garland. At the top of the stairs he turned to gaze at me. He opened his mouth to speak but closed it quickly. His eyes seemed to seek some kind of reassurance in my own. I smiled at him, not understanding. His mouth twitched and he swung away from me to lead me down the stairs to the waiting throng.

With people pressing around on all sides murmuring compliments. I peered anxiously through the crowd for a sight of Jem. He was nowhere around. I had to wait until, in a blur of excitement, I stood in front of the Reverend from Milledgeville and he prepared to read the marriage vows. Then Jem came to my side. I glanced at him shyly. He was everything I remembered although his locks were dishevelled and his rugged face was drawn with fatigue.

Jem winked at me while the Reverend droned the service. Did he have no respect? But he was there! My nervousness passed and my heart pounded with joy at being his bride.

The formality of the wedding celebration quickly degenerated into a typical Georgia bash. Clinging to Jem's arm I drifted through the garrulous guests, listening to them but not understanding a word. Jem cracked jokes and laughed uproariously while I blushed.

Jem was outrageously handsome. His reputation as a devilish young man lent him a fascination which seemed to intrigue every girl there. His eyes flashed roguishly and he laughed with delight. Beside him, I felt demure and innocent, nervous yet proud that Jem was my husband and the centre of such attention. I clutched him possessively, twining my arm around his waist.

'Ah, Fleur,' he whispered in my ear, setting my neck atingle. 'I am yours now, and you are mine. Tonight shall see us bound together.'

My blush deepened. For Jem to speak of such things on the piazza of our house with hundreds of wedding guests about us filled me with embarrassment. I glanced around anxiously.

'Don't worry about them, Fleur. I'd carry you upstairs to your boudoir now but I feel I owe some respect to the whiskey your uncle's provided for us!' He raised his glass and bent down to kiss me.

'Jem,' I pleaded withdrawing my arm. 'Have consideration, I beg you.'

He smiled warmly. 'My sweetest little Fleur! You're a planter's wife now, married to the most irresponsible bounder in the county. You are my wife, Fleur. Consideration be damned!'

There was a murmur of interest from the guests gathered near us.

'I feel the taste for a bust, Fleur. It's not every day a man willingly slips into marriage, nor often a man has such a beautiful bride.'

Jem detached himself from me and pushed his way through the crowd, snatched a drink off the tray balanced on Rollo's hand and scuttled down the steps of the piazza. Two elegantly dressed young blades joined him, clapping him on the shoulders. A ribald shout arose from the three of them as they sauntered arm-in-arm away from the house.

'Plotting some devilment, I shouldn't wonder. And on your wedding day!'

The voice took me by surprise. I spun around. 'Wayne! I scarcely recognised you.'

Wayne had made a token effort to spruce himself up for the wedding. His unruly blonde hair had been combed and slicked back from his forehead. He wore an ill-fitting coat of inferior brocade and trousers which were patched at the knees. I was assailed by a feeling of guilt when I realised I had not seen him for weeks.

'It's the best I could find,' he said, grinning ruefully. 'I aimed to have a whiskey on your happiness, Fleur.'

'I'm Mistress Hayard now, you know.' I wanted it to sound like a joke but Wayne gazed at me sadly.

'Aye, I suppose so.' He scratched his head upsetting the careful arrangement of his hair. 'You really married him.'

'You sound surprised.'

'I believed you had more sense, Fleur.'

I looked around quickly to see if anyone was listening. The guests were intent on enjoying themselves, but I drew back against a column at the edge of the piazza so we would not be overheard. 'Do you mean to insult me, Wayne?'

'No, Fleur, never that.' He sipped the remains of the whiskey in his glass and flung the tumbler out into the drive with disgust. 'I ain't got no taste to enjoy myself, Fleur. You know what Jem is like. I told you that, the day I met you. I never dreamed that you would actually marry him.'

'Why shouldn't I, Wayne? He'll be a very good husband, I'm sure.'

'You are sure? Huh, it still puzzles me. Of course, I knew you could never think of me that way, Fleur. I never dared hope. But of all people to lose you to, why did you have to pick Jem? He's not courted you. You don't even know him.'

I was close to tears. 'Wayne, please. I'm very fond of you. Please don't spoil my happiness.'

'No Fleur. I don't want to do that. You have everything you want now. I suppose I should be happy too.'

He gestured at the garden and the plantation stretching out in front of us in the rich glow of the dying sun. He swept his hand around to embrace the vast cotton fields and the dozens of slaves squatting in the shade of the oak trees as they watched the guests. He inclined his chin upwards to include the columns and the piazza and the large airy rooms of Maddocks. He grinned ruefully.

'I gave up my freedom for you, Fleur. Maybe you've given up yours too.' He shrugged his shoulders and stepped away from me.

'Where are you going?' I gasped, conscious of being left alone.

He looked startled. 'I didn't think that would worry you.'

'Of course it does. I know I haven't seen you often, Wayne. My Uncle, you see . . .' My voice tailed off.

'You will stay at Maddocks, won't you?'

'Oh aye, I'll stay, Fleur. Fixin' tools and shoein' horses ain't too demandin' and the Maddocks nigras are obligin' boys. I have a wench cooks me vittles and there's whiskey when I want it. I ain't leavin' Maddocks because you've married Jem. No, I'm stayin'. I just don't want to see you hurt.'

Wayne's words filled me with despair. I looked around the crowd for Jem.

'Jem's gone, Fleur. He'll come to you when he's ready. Don't take any notice of me. I've already said too much, I'm sure. You've made your choice, Fleur, and I'll stand by you. When you need a friend, I'll be here.' Wayne smiled forlornly and shook his head.

I was stunned, but before I could speak, Mrs. Runacres swooped down on me and caught my hand. With a withering look at Wayne she bustled me off the piazza and into the ladies' parlour where Mrs. Hayard and the wedding committee sat waiting.

There were so many people to speak to, I had little opportunity to fret at Jem's long absence from my side. Of course, heads bobbed and tongues wagged, delighting in the latest scandal. About another bridegroom the gossip would have been repeated with relish but somehow Jem's reputation caused the wedding guests to expect some such outrage.

After a while, I could stand it no longer and made my excuses. I hurried up the stairs to my chamber. The celebration had tired me more than I realised. I entered my room with relief. Now I was Mrs. Hayard, I thought glumly, but where was my Mister? Even Wayne seemed to know Jem's habits better than I. Was I destined to be governed by Jem's passing whims?

I sat on my couch and sniffed, feeling sorry for myself. There was a thud on the floor. I straightened up and listened carefully. Someone was moving in Uncle Leo's room.

I rose and left my chamber to cross the passageway to his door. I had not seen Uncle Leo before I came upstairs. I resolved to see him now and find out what arrangement he had entered into with Jem. I had to know!

'Uncle Leo,' I called softly. The light of a candle flickered through the gap under the door. There was no reply. I pushed on the door and it swung open.

Uncle Leo was stretched out naked on his bed. A black man, his body like an ebony cloak, was mounted on the reclining white form.

I screamed.

The black man leapt away from Uncle as though a whip had lashed his buttocks and stared at me like a cornered stallion.

I screamed again.

The black rushed to the open window and jumped. He plunged over the balustrade and crashed down to the guests dancing in the piazza below.

I looked at Uncle Leo. He was writhing in agony. His cold grey eyes swelled as I stared. His mouth fell open and his tongue ballooned out. He clawed limply at his chest.

'Fleur – ' he gurgled. His body arched and air rattled out of his mouth.

He was dead.

CHAPTER SIXTEEN

'Fleur, what's wrong? Why did you scream?'

Wayne was at my side. He put his arms around my shoulders. I trembled with shock as I gaped into the chamber where Uncle Leo's body lay twisted across his bed. Despair swept through me, and a quick fear that now Uncle was dead I had no one to turn to. I burst into tears, covering my eyes with my kerchief.

Garland stepped up beside Wayne. He glanced quickly into the chamber and closed Uncle's door. The stairs had filled with people attracted by my screams.

'Where's Jem?' Wayne asked fiercely.

'He gone by de quartahs, Marse Wayne.' Garland's voice was stern, but I drew comfort from his presence.

'Send a boy to call him.'

'I have.'

Wayne stared at Garland for a second then turned back to me. My shoulders were heaving with my sobs but Wayne's efficiency and Garland's coolness helped me more than the caterwauling of Mrs. Runacres, who had rushed to my side to embrace me. I gulped, trying to suppress my anguish so that I could think sensibly.

I dabbed my eyes dry and pulled myself away from Mrs. Runacres. 'Ask these people to go downstairs, Wayne,' I ordered, my voice firm. 'No strangers, please. They may all be Uncle's friends, but this is a family matter.'

Wayne smiled at me as though he was proud. 'You'll do,' he said. 'I believe you really will.' He began to usher the spectators back to the rooms below. 'It's all right, folks. Please leave Mistress Fleur alone. It's a shock. We'll tell you what happened as soon as we know.' With Garland's help he cleared the stairs of the white people, but the blacks hovered around me.

'Missy Fleur, yo' be sure Marse Leo don' need help?' Trott's concerned voice brought me back to the present.

'No, Trott. No one can help him now.'

I looked at Garland in despair. 'Where is Master Jem, Garland? He should be here!'

'He'll come, Miss Fleur. You can go if you wish,' he whispered softly so the other slaves could not hear him. 'I'll guard Marse Leo's door and Ladybelle will come to you.'

I tried to express my gratitude to Garland with my eyes for I was too wretched to speak more. I shook my head: I must wait for Jem.

He came before long, although that vigil outside Uncle's door seemed to last an eternity. There was a commotion among the crowd grouped in the entrance hall, then Jem pushed through and bounded up the stairs. My heart lurched with joy at the sight of him.

His hair was damp and straggly. He had discarded his coat and his shirt was open to the wist. He emerged through the throng and rushed to me.

'By the devil, is it true?' he shouted.

'Yes, Jem, Uncle's – ' I put out my hands to grasp him but he brushed me aside and flung open the door of the chamber before I could finish speaking. Garland followed him quickly and the slaves crowded forward. Wayne barked at them until they stepped back murmuring resentfully. I gazed at Jem, longing to race across the floor and fling myself into his arms for comfort.

Jem bent over Uncle and prodded his sunken cheek with a finger. He scowled and swept his eyes down the length of Uncle's body. He muttered crossly under his breath and took hold of Uncle's legs and straightened them out. He picked up the bed sheet and threw it roughly over him. His face was fierce with anger when he turned on Garland watching him from the foot of the bed.

'You saw what happened, boy?'

'Nossah.' Garland seemed pained by Jem's indifference to Uncle's death.

Jem glanced at me in the doorway. 'You?'

I nodded my head, unable to speak. Wayne was by my side.

'Fleur saw it, Jem.'

Jem glanced at Wayne. 'And you? What did you see?'

'What does it matter, Jem? Fleur's uncle is dead. Your wife, Jem – she's distressed.'

'Hah! What about me?' Jem left the bed and strode over to the window. He leaned out. The naked body of the Negro still lay on the floor of the piazza below. His neck had been broken and he lay in a crumpled mass. At the far end of the piazza a horror-struck pack of twittering ladies and their pompous husbands kept their faces averted from the ugly sight.

'By the devil!' growled Jem. 'Is my wedding day to be remembered for this scandal?' He spun around to face me. 'Your dam' uncle! What happened to him, Fleur?'

'Uncle Leo, – ' I stammered, forcing myself back into the room. 'I think . . . he . . . had a heart attack. He saw me and then – . . . I came to thank him, for the wedding, for – '

I couldn't go on. I ran over to Jem and held my arms out to him. He glowered when I rested my head on his chest. I wanted to feel his arms encircling me, to comfort me. Instead, his finger gripped my chin and forced my head back until I was staring up into his raging dark eyes.

'Yes, Fleur? What did you see?' His eyes raked my face. I trembled. 'Tell me! What did you see?' he demanded, gripping my jaw.

'Jem, you're hurting me!' His eyes bored into mine, cowering me into submission. I lowered my eyelashes and sighed. 'Nothing, Jem. Nothing.'

Jem nodded approvingly and released me. I touched my chin where his fingers had bruised me and watched as he leaned out of the window again.

'Leo Singer is dead,' he shouted. 'The wedding is over.' A buzz of consternation rose from the crowd on the piazza.

'Singer died of a heart attack.' Jem spoke defiantly as though daring any one to question him. 'He was thrashing that nigra there when the boy tried to escape. He attacked Singer and the old man's heart gave out. My wife, Fleur, saw it all.' Jem looked mournful for the crowd then pulled back his head quickly from the window.

'That will have to stop their dam' gossip.' He called to Ladybelle. 'Take Miss Fleur to her room.'

Ladybelle stepped forward and slipped her arm around my waist. Wayne and Garland stood aside. I covered my eyes with my hands and allowed myself to be led away.

I lay on my bed while Ladybelle administered *sal volatile*. I was nauseated. If Ladybelle had not blathered so much, I would have fallen asleep. Instead, I closed my eyes and ignored her, listening to the wailing of the slaves and pondering the meaning of what I had seen. It was too much to comprehend.

How could I explain the way Jem had acted? Had he been too upset by Uncle's death to spare a thought for me? He had tried to save Uncle's memory from scandal. Was he considering the reputation of his wife? Did his harshness cover that?

I was his wife. The thought made me gasp. At least Uncle had lived to see our marriage even though he would never know the heir he wanted me to bear for Maddocks.

I opened my eyes to look around the room. Ladybelle must have slipped outside. I was alone. The house seemed to rumble with activity as the guests departed. I imagined I could hear the walls sighing with relief when they had gone. The house wanted to be left alone with its grief, too.

I twisted in my bed. When would Jem come to me? Of course, I knew he would be busy seeing off the guests and arranging for Mammy Mable and the women to wash and lay out Uncle's body.

I wished he would hurry. Had any bride, I wondered, been so wretched on her wedding night? I yearned with a desperation rooted deep inside me for Jem to enter my room, to hold me in his arms and to comfort me. I was no longer nervous about being his bride; I needed him by my side now that I was completely alone.

'My husband!' I breathed the magic words to myself. They sounded strange, conjuring up a vision of a tall, handsome man with a charming manner, and effortless authority. Jem was strong, his lithe body and long limbs moulded by a youth of diligent work on his father's plantation. His features were breathtaking, from the firm cut of his jaws and his classically straight nose to the sardonic curl of his lips and the glint of his dark eyes. His black, wavy hair crowned a face sometimes alive with laughter, at other times blooming with passion.

Of course, Jem had his wild, reckless side, but that, I believed, was natural in a bachelor with his strong personality. As a husband, Jem's undisciplined qualities would surely disappear. It was that way in every book I had read, I assured myself, drifting gently into sleep, exhausted by the long wait for Jem.

Suddenly, there was someone in the chamber. I roused in confusion, my mind struggling to understand the meaning of the man's voice. He was addressing Ladybelle. I opened my eyes and gazed at the tall figure of Jem standing by the door, peering across the room. I shivered. He had come.

'Ladybelle, I ain't aimin' to give you a performance. You can search Fleur's sheet for blood in the morning. Now git!' Jem stuck his foot under Ladybelle where she lay on her pallet and rolled her onto the floor.

'Oh, Jem!' Ladybelle's squeal of reproach changed to one of wanton laughter when Jem bent down and put his hands on her. 'Fleur gwine hear yo'!'

'Then don't make no noise!'

There was a giggle from Ladybelle, suddenly stilled. I twisted in the bed to see what had happened. Jem was kneeling on the floor, his eyes glinting with excitement. He smiled warmly at Ladybelle.

'It's dam' pleasin' for you that I'm here, Ladybelle. A wench like you was going to waste in this monastery. I'll be pleasurin' you soon enough. But not now.' He laughed. 'It's my wife's good fortune tonight.'

Jem stood up and turned toward my bed. I lay back on the pillows and pretended to be asleep. I could sense his gaze while he studied me as though he had never seen me before. He cleared his throat arrogantly and spat on to the floor. I winced.

I peeped up at the two of them. Ladybelle stood in front of him. He put an arm around her, squeezing a breast. He twirled her about and slapped his hand across her buttock.

'Git out, wench! How many times must I tell you?'

Ladybelle giggled and flounced across the floor to the door which she deliberately left ajar, Jem stepped over to it and closed it firmly, fastening the latch from the inside and drawing the bolt across the top.

He was bare-chested with a crucifix of black hair growing across his chest. The tail of hair narrowed between his nipples down to his navel. More hair, silken with his sweat, flared up from the waistband of his trousers over the hard flesh of his stomach.

In the wan light filtering through the window, Jem's body was magnified. I swallowed nervously at the sight of his muscular arms, broad shoulders and heavy thighs. He strode over to the bed.

'Are you sleepin', Fleur?' he asked gruffly.

I shook my head.

'Are you scared?'

'No.' My voice was a whisper. Why, I wanted to ask, had he dallied with Ladybelle? Were all plantation men this way? Jem towered over me, his face a brutal mask.

He drew the curtain around the fourposter, and I was enclosed in the confines of the bed with him. In the darkness, I could no longer see him. There was pressure on the mattress beside me as he lay down. I trembled, waiting for his hands to reach out and hold me. I was desperate to be comforted and reassured that, in spite of what I had seen and heard about him, Jem was my own loving husbnd.

'You're a sweet wench, Fleur.' His arm curled around my neck and pulled me roughly toward him.

I quivered with shame. This was not the feeling of passion I expected. 'Wench?' I protested. 'I'm not a wench!'

His lips crushed my protest, bruising my cheek and covering my open mouth. I wriggled at the violence of his embrace but Jem's body pressed me down on the mattress. Already his hands were tearing at the bed covers. I tried to escape him but the more I squirmed the more ardent he became. His mouth was devouring me, his tongue lodged deep between my lips. I could not breathe.

I beat at his shoulders with my fists. Jem arched his back and wrested the bed sheet away from me. He rubbed his hard body against mine, pulling his tongue from my mouth and brushing his lips against my face.

'Jem!' I spluttered, gulping for breath. My hands clawed at his shoulders.

'Fleur. At last!' He raised his body from mine and

fumbled with his hand. I felt his fingers on my ankle, tearing at the lace hem of my night dress. My heart raced. I was shocked and confused. I wanted gentleness and compassion but Jem was pounding me as though meting out a punishment.

I cried silently and dug my fingers into the loose hair at the back of his neck.

He was frantic, gnawing at my neck, at my breasts, at my stomach. I writhed with shame under the bite of his hungry lips on my body.

Suddenly, Jem slipped his hand under my waist and arched me up in the bed, ripping my night dress completely away from me. I quivered, utterly naked under him. His head swooped down and his hair brushed across my bosom. I shrieked in protest but his lips sank lower and lower and plunged into the soft down which crowned my maidenhood.

I shuddered as a spasm shook through me, followed by another and another. Jem's firm hands gripped my waist and clutched me closer.

Perhaps I swooned. Jem was on top of me, his lips biting mine, his arms gripping me. He shouted frightful words into my ear. I tore my fingers down his shoulders, feeling his flesh lodging in my long nails. Jem's hand reached down and spread my legs.

Jem drove himself at me. His lips held mine fast, staunching my screams. I felt him enter me viciously with a slash of agony that pierced my body. I pulled my face away from him, rolling my head from side to side across the pillow. I screamed at the tearing pain, beating my fists against his body, praying for him to stop.

Jem fought back. His mouth snapped onto mine, following me as I tried to throw him off. He drove further inside until I could feel him swelling within me. I was beaten. My fingers sank into his back, the blood trickling around my nails.

I gasped, my whole body aching from his onslaught. Jem owned me now. I was his wife. He rolled off me and I stared, unmoving, at the ceiling. My dreams were shattered. I had sacrificed myself to Jem but where was the pleasure a bride was supposed to feel? My body throbbed with pain and I felt only a numbing unhappiness. I waited for Jem's hand to hold mine and for him to utter tender words to comfort me.

'Well, Singer didn't sell me a pig in a poke, that's for sure.' Jem growled. 'You were a tight little virgin right enough. And look, my shoulder's scratched to pieces.'

I twisted around in dismay, utterly unable to speak. My silence seemed to worry him.

'Hey, Fleur!' At last his hand slipped over to comfort me. 'I reckon old Singer did me a favour.' He squeezed me roughly. 'Any other hot-blooded Southern planter with you for a niece would have tried the goods for himself. Not your uncle, eh?' He twisted my nipple in his fingers. 'I'm pleased that he preferred boys!'

Jem rolled over in the bed and the mattress bounced as he got out.

'Where are you going?' I asked torn between bewilderment and relief.

'Lord, Fleur! You ain't stop asking questions yet! To my bed, of course.'

'Bed?'

'You surely don't expect me to sleep here with you, do you? My chamber's next door, Fleur. I'll come to you again, when I feel like a bit of wifely loving.' He must have heard me sob. 'Oh, don't worry about me, Fleur. I won't pester you overmuch. Just enough to get us a son, that's all.' He flung open the curtain and groped under the bed for his boots.

'You know, Fleur?' he said, unaware of my despair, 'maybe your uncle did right to die today. I can take over Maddocks now without having to go through years of waiting. He said he would give me Maddocks when I married you. Maddocks was your dowry.'

'No!'

'You didn't know? I thought the old nance told you.' He gloated down at me. 'Leo said it's written in his will so you'll hear for yourself when the lawyer comes from Milledgeville.' Jem chuckled dryly.

'Pa always said I was worthless but he'll change his tune now. I've got Maddocks, a better house and plantation than Pa's own, and I've got you. What a fortune, eh?'

He cast his eye around the room. 'Of course, this house is too gloomy. Old Leo was a stick-in-the-mud, whatever his passions. I'll soon change Maddocks, Fleur. I'll tear down some walls, put up more columns, make the house lively so my cronies and their wenches can sport here. Hah! Maddocks will become famous throughout the state for my hospitality.'

Jem glanced at me and snorted disdainfully. 'Pah! You lie there like you're ailing. I tell you, marriage with me will make something of you. No more blushing and simpering like a love-sick spinster. You can play host to the brightest crowd of young blades in Georgia.'

Jem nodded his head. 'You'll see, Fleur. Now Maddocks is mine, your life here will change!' He picked up his boots and headed for the door which linked his chamber with mine. 'I must sleep. I'm off to Milledgeville tomorrow.'

'But, but, Uncle's funeral—' I managed to gasp.

'You can attend that, Fleur. That's a wife's job. I've got to go and bring that lawyer. I want to know what amount of cash old Singer left me. What I have to do to Maddocks will cost a lot.'

He stepped into his chamber and closed the door behind him without a further thought for me. I bit my lip until I drew blood. The pain made me resolute. Maddocks could not be Jem's! Uncle loved Maddocks and so did I. Maddocks must not be changed! I swore an oath to myself as the tears welled up in my eyes. Jem could do what he liked to me, but not to Maddocks. I would fight him with any means at my disposal. Even my life.

Book Two

'MADDOCKS IS MINE'

Winter 1858–Fall 1859

CHAPTER SEVENTEEN

Maddocks, always a beautiful but a sombre house, seemed sad and lonely without Uncle Leo. Before, there had been the clump of his boots on the hall floor, the echo of his full-voiced commands, and the creak of his door opening onto the piazza. Now only the hushed droning of the slaves showed Maddocks was alive. When a window clattered, the whole house reverberated in surprise. If a visitor stomped onto the piazza and shouted for Trott, the house seemed to shudder in alarm at the intrusion, doors banging of their own accord and floor-boards squeaking.

The corridors at night were mournful in the darkness, full shadows filling the corners with sorrow. Slaves no longer lurked behind doors and in the dimly lit passages to overhear Uncle's conversations. At night, they crept to their cabins in the kitchen compound, leaving only a boy to sleep across the front door and Ladybelle to keep me company in my chamber.

I did not mind the loneliness. Instead, I drew comfort from being able to share my sorrow with the very house which Uncle had created. It seemed that the dark corridors and the fine rooms of Maddocks were Uncle Leo. He was dead and had been buried with appropriate respect by the wedding guests in a plot behind the house the day after the wedding, but while Maddocks stood as he had built it, Uncle was still present.

Since Jem had ridden off after our wedding night, I had plenty of opportunity to consider his changed personality and his curious remarks about his plans. Even now, as I paced the corridors, my full skirt sibilant in the stillness of the night and my candle flickering in the sighs of the wind, I was afraid for Maddocks.

'I shall not let him change you!' I breathed silently to the rooms and the walls. 'Uncle loved you as you are, and I do too!'

I made an inspection of the house with Mammy Mable. We began downstairs with its paintings and draperies and the comfortable parlour resplendent with an enormous fireplace and ponderous furniture. The ladies' parlour and sewing room were charming and feminine while the smoking room opposite and the library bore the distinctive stamp of a man's touch.

'We must not change a thing!' I told Mammy Mable as she bustled me through the rooms.

'Ah, Mistis! Wait till yo' hab chil'ren. De house gwine come alive den.'

'It's not dead now, Mammy. It's such a peaceful place, absolutely none of the events of the outside world can penetrate here. It's like a fortress.'

Mammy Mable looked at me gently, hesitated as though about to speak, then shrugged her shoulders and brusquely led me upstairs. There was one guest chamber at the rear of the house, as well as the room appropriated by Jem which was linked to my own chamber, and Uncle Leo's quarters. I peered into Uncle Leo's chamber.

'Oh Mammy,' I cried. 'Why are all the windows closed? The room smells of death!'

'Why we open dem, Mistis? De marster gone now.'

'Of course you must open them. The *house* isn't dead.

Maddocks must breathe!' Somewhere, a door clicked shut as though the house approved of what I said. 'Mammy, you must not let the house maids neglect their duties,' I reprimanded her. 'Every day they must clean this room, and the whole house, just as if Uncle were alive. Maddocks isn't dead, I tell you, it lives.'

Mammy Mable leaned on the balustrade, her face puckered, her eyes tired. 'Ah lub Maddocks same as yo', Missy. But I ain' know who gwine keep de house and de plantation 'live. Yo' be a city lady and yuh husban' got no use but fuh wenchin' and spreein' from here to Sabannah.'

'Mammy Mable!' I said indignantly, for despite everything I felt called upon to defend my husband. 'You have no right to say such thing.'

For once the old woman held her ground. 'Ah done speak mah piece, Mistis. Widou' no man to 'tend to de cotton, dis house gwine die like yo' an' me.'

'That's nonsense,' I sputtered. But a cold finger of fear seemed to trace its way along my spine.

'Nonsense, yo' say? Where de money does come from widou' cotton, Mistis?' We were standing at the head of the stairs. I gripped the banister railing and tried to find an answer. There was silence. Maddocks, too, I thought, was waiting for my reply.

'Maddocks will survive, Mammy. I may be from Savannah but I love Maddocks and the plantation. I'm not going to go back. Maddocks is my home now.'

'Dem's fine words, Mistis!' Mammy Mable brushed past me and began to descend the stairs. 'Yo' ain' de problem! Wha' 'bout yuh husband, Marster Jem Hayard? Only one night we see ob him!'

'Mammy Mable!' The harsh note in my voice made the old slave pause in her descent. She gripped the banister and stared at me, the defiance draining out of her eyes. I turned away from her and scurried back up the stairs. Ladybelle was not in my chamber. I threw myself down on the couch by the window, pressed my hands to my eyes and wept.

I knew Mammy Mable was right. Jem's behaviour in

riding off and leaving me alone was unconscionable. When I awakened the day after the wedding and Ladybelle told me Jem had departed, I was swamped with despair. The tears I shed at the funeral that day were not all for Uncle Leo. Some were for myself. At the very moment I needed the strength of my husband, he had abandoned me. He had been gone for ten days now. I could not run a plantation, nor even the household, alone.

It was minutes before I was aware of someone in the rooms. Maddocks told me by the sudden crack of a floorboard. I uncovered my eyes and peered at the doorway. A pair of troubled eyes, as black as midnight, stared back. A dark figure hovered here, clutching the door jamb uncertainly.

'Mistress Fleur?' Garland's voice was doubtful. 'I beg excuse.'

I hurriedly dabbed at my tears with a lace handkerchief.

'I knocked, Mistis,' he grinned apologetically, 'but you ain't hear me. You was crying.' He stepped forward into the room and stopped, as though seeking permission to enter farther.

I shrugged off my despair and faced him squarely. 'What is it?'

Garland raised his hand and wiped his brow. He fidgeted as though searching for the right words. He was dressed smartly in clean white pants and a frilled shirt with a large cummerbund at his waist. Uncle Leo had always seen that his house slaves were well dressed, and Garland had not slackened with his master's death. He moved into the centre of the room, making the dainty chairs and tables of my boudoir look quite fragile.

I raised my eyes to his. 'Speak up,' I said. 'What do you want?' His Adam's apple bobbed up and down while he swallowed nervously. 'You aren't normally afraid to speak, Garland,' I chided him impatiently.

'Mistis Fleur –' he began, swallowed and started again. 'Mistis Fleur, I know yo' be feelin' 'sad cuz Marse Leo die and Marse Jem go way.'

'How do you know my feelings, Garland?'

'It be natural, Mistis. 'Specially when yo' be so sensitive.'

'Indeed?' Although I tried to sound calm, inside I was quivering. When Garland looked at me with his sombre, mysterious eyes, I felt strangely powerless. There was a knowledge in Garland's glance which made me feel that not even my thoughts were private.

'Yuh husband, Marse Jem, he comin' here in a few days.'

'How do you know that?'

Garland shrugged his broad shoulders. 'I know, Mistis.'

'Where is he?'

'In Milledgeville, Mistis.'

'Oh!' I was relieved.

'Yes, Mistis Fleur. He comin' back.' Garland's tone made me look at his face again. Was there a hint in his voice that he knew I had my doubts about Jem? He gave me a warm smile, which was oddly reassuring.

'It's kind of you to tell me Garland.'

'Yas, Mistis.' His tone slipped back into servility as I turned away from him to gaze out of the window. His reply arrested me and I twisted back in time to catch a glimmer of uncertainty in his eyes.

'Garland, what's wrong?'

He looked startled by my challenge.

'Mistress Fleur. We, I mean I, some of us want you to know that we have confidence in your concern for Maddocks.'

I was alarmed by Garland's intensity, his slide into speech so unlike his usual slave patois. He stepped over to the couch and gestured with his hand as he spoke.

'We know it's not easy for you here, Miss Fleur. Times are changing.'

'Really?' I listened carefully. Garland had obviously made an important decision and was determined to make me understand.

'Not only at Maddocks, Miss. State is setting against State over slavery. Some planters in the county are taking terrible steps against their black folk. Marse Leo was strict but he was regular and just. We hope you'll be the same, and Master Jem too.'

Garland stared down at where I was sitting nervously on the couch. I felt very small in front of him and he seemed to be aware of it. A strand of hair fell across my face when I raised my eyes. I brushed it away quickly. To my amazement, Garland sighed and spun away, stepping hastily over to the door.

'Garland!' I cried to prevent his leaving so soon.

'Yas, Mistis?' His face was cracked with concern.

'If I tell my husband what you've told me, would it be bad for you?'

'Yas, Mistis.' His features rapidly tightened into the expressionless mask of a house slave.

'Then I won't tell him, Garland. Thank you.'

He nodded wisely and slipped from the room.

The knowledge that Jem would soon be returning to Maddocks restored my confidence. Perhaps when Jem was back, he would settle down to married life and be a loving husband. I resolved to take interest in the plantation so that we would have something to share between us. I resumed my rides around the plantation, accompanied by Ladybelle and Garland.

After one such ride, when the morning air was crisp with winter, I dismissed Garland and Ladybelle so that I could stroll up to the house from the stables alone. I wanted to think. My path took me past the forge and my reverie was suddenly shattered by a familiar voice calling my name.

'Do you choose to ignore me, Fleur?'

I looked around as the speaker caught up with me. 'Wayne! I'm sorry. My mind was quite on other things.'

'As yes, no doubt! May I walk with you?'

'You were never in the habit of asking my permission before.'

'Well, you are my mistress now, Fleur!'

Wayne's bright face forced me to smile. 'You seem happy enough, Wayne,' I laughed.

'Enough? No, Fleur, not me.'

'Why not, pray?'

'Pray is something we might all have to do before long, Fleur.'

'What do you mean?' I looked at him idly as we strolled together along the path to the house. My ride filled me with a warm glow but I held my cloak close around me to prevent the cold from penetrating. Wayne wore a coarse jacket over his old pants and leather apron. His breath escaped in tiny puffs into the cold air as he spoke.

'There's things afoot, Fleur. Is Jem coming back soon?'

'Any day now.'

'Good.' Wayne fell silent.

'What things, Wayne? You can tell me.'

'Aye, Fleur, maybe I can. I don't want to worry you for nothing but seeing as you're involved, maybe I'd better speak out.'

'Me? Involved?' I smiled with disbelief.

'It happened last night, Fleur,' he spoke rapidly, taking no notice of my scorn. 'I was sharing a whiskey with Ferret and Goodpaster. I loathe their ignorant company but who else is there to talk to?'

I continued walking, crossing the courtyard with my head bent low so I could hear Wayne.

'We were talking about Jem, Fleur. Ferret said he hopes Jem doesn't interfere with the cotton. "If he keeps out of that, I'll still give him a nice profit every season, like I did for Mister Leo," Ferret boasted. And Goodpaster laughed and said, "And leave the nigras for me".'

We reached the steps to the piazza. I paused on the bottom step and looked down at Wayne. His bright eyes glinted at me expectantly. 'You want to tell me the story in full, don't you Wayne?'

'Of course, Fleur. You ain't gonna' know unless I do.'

'Very well,' I smiled. 'Come into the parlour. There's a fire there. We'll sit and chat though goodness knows what the gossips will say.'

'Do you care?' Wayne laughed, leaping up the steps by my side.

'No, I don't believe I do.'

Trott loomed before us at the front door. Ladybelle hovered behind him to take my cloak. 'Trott, bring a whiskey for Mister Wayne if you please.'

Trott looked doubtful but shuffled off without a word.

We settled ourselves before the fire in the parlour. Wayne sipped at the whiskey Trott brought him and studied me. 'You know, Fleur, it suits you being the mistress of Maddocks. I like it!'

His eyes twinkled then suddenly he became serious. He leaned forward. 'You must be careful, Fleur.' To explain what he meant, Wayne recounted what had happened the night before.

The Maddocks slaves were housed in cabins built around a large mud square east of Ferret's cottage. A short path through the trees led to this shanty village. The cabins were made of hewn post oak covered with cypress shingles; they were sturdy one-room buildings with close plank floors and good chimneys with open fireplaces. Two families lived in each cabin, sleeping in intimate confusion on piles of rags on the floor. There were nearly a hundred cabins forming two rows around the central square.

Every night, Goodpaster and Wayne himself and sometimes Ferret if he wanted the sport, as he called it, patrolled the pathways between the cabins. The Maddocks Negroes were considered tractable but, Goodpaster boasted, this was only because of his constant policing.

While they were walking along the path to the cabins, Wayne ventured to point out to Goodpaster that since the slaves knew they were coming to patrol they would surely be prepared for them. Any mischief they intended would be saved until after the patrol had passed.

'Exactly, boy!' sneered Goodpaster, keeping his voice low. 'They know we are coming but not at what hour. That keeps them in check, you see.'

'But if you only pass once a night, they can slip off after you have gone,' Wayne persisted.

'Aye!' Goodpaster was exasperated. 'So sometimes we patrol twice, or even three times. The nigra is a wily bastard, you have to surprise him all the time. Don't speak now, we're coming near.' He slowed his pace and shielded his lantern with his coat.

Wayne wondered why he bothered to take such elaborate precautions. The slaves, if they had any sense at all, would be asleep in their cabins waiting for the patrol to pass.

Goodpaster stopped suddenly. In the darkness, Wayne did not see and bumped into him. 'There's a trap,' he whispered in Wayne's ear. Wayne felt quickly for the pistol at his waist.

'See here.' Goodpaster caught Wayne's hand in his and guided it downward. He touched a vine stretched taut across the trail. 'Fortunate for us I found it.'

'What's it for?'

'That thing was set up so we'd walk right into it, boy. They wanted us to trip it and sound the alarm. That way the dam' nigras know we're coming to patrol.'

'What do you think they're doing?' Wayne whispered.

'Could be a prayer meeting or an agitator stirring them up with talk of freedom.' Goodpaster cursed under his breath. 'Come on.'

They stepped cautiously over the vine. Goodpaster doused his lamp and left it beside the trail. He drew his pistol. They came to the edge of the clump of trees outside the quarters and gazed in the darkness at the shadowy outlines of the cabins. Goodpaster nudged Wayne. He had spotted a thread of light at the base of the door of one of the cabins. They walked stealthily toward it and paused at the door.

Wayne pressed his ear to the wooden planks and listened. All he could hear was the drone of voices chanting uncertainly.

'Dam'me,' exclaimed Goodpaster. 'The bastards are learning to read.'

At his cry, the droning ceased. There was a scuffling sound, then the creak of a door being closed. Goodpaster hastily kicked open the door of the cabin and hurtled inside, yelling like a madman. A shadow emerging from under the cabin caught Wayne's attention before he rushed in after Goodpaster. There was something about that dark shape that stirred a flicker of memory in Wayne's mind.

Inside the cabin, a boy of sixteen and his mother crouched nervously in a corner. Two other blacks, tired old men, sat by the wall.

'Who was here, dam' you!' Goodpaster shrieked, waving his pistol. The slaves stared at him, rigid with fear.

'Get up!' he indicated the two old men sitting on their haunches on the floor. The men scrambled into a corner.

'Look what I've found!' Goodpaster crouched down where the two slaves had been sitting and pulled at a peg in the floorboards. It came up in his hands bringing a trap door with it. He peered into the darkness below.

'A trap door!' he muttered, his face reddening with anger. 'The dam' cabin is elevated off the ground. I should have spotted that. It's their favourite trick to get away.'

He glared around the tiny cabin again. Wayne's eye fell on a book lying open on the floor. He picked it up idly. 'This must have been what they were reading,' Wayne handed the book to Goodpaster.

He took the book with distaste looking first at it and then at the four blacks in the cabin. 'Yo' know it's forbidden for nigras to read!' he shouted. 'Who was here readin' to yo'?' Goodpaster strode over to the youth and clapped his ear soundly with the book. The boy tried to cover his face.

The remains of a small fire was burning in the fireplace, sending a sparse warmth around the cabin. Goodpaster threw the book back at Wayne, bent down quickly and snatched up an ember from the fire, holding the green end in his gloved hand. He lunged at the boy.

'Yo' know yo' ain' got no right to read, boy!' he roared.

The boy ducked in panic and his mother began to wail. The sound distracted the boy as Goodpaster leapt at him. The wood sank into the boy's eye and the sickly smell of burning flesh filled the cabin.

'I stumbled outside and puked,' Wayne concluded while I stared at him in horror.

'Wayne, that's awful!' I gasped. 'Why didn't you stop Goodpaster?'

'Me?' Wayne drew back. 'I'm not going to interfere. What chance would I have? Besides, there's likely to be more trouble.'

'What do you mean?'

'The book the boy was learning to read from, Fleur. I have it.'

'Really?' I was not interested. Wayne put his hand into the long pocket of his coat and withdrew a battered volume from its depths.

A sudden feeling of dismay swept over me as I stared at the book in his hand. I reached out slowly and Wayne thrust the book at me. 'Whose name is written inside, Fleur?'

I did not need to open the book to see. It was my own treasured volume of *Pilgrim's Progress*, one of the two books I had managed to bring with me from Savannah. 'Mine,' I whispered.

'Yes,' Wayne stood up and paced the floor of the parlour. 'Curious, don't you think? Why should an ignorant black boy be learning to read from a book belonging to his mistress?'

'I didn't give it to him!'

'Oh Fleur, no need to protest so much. I'm not your husband! Jem Hayard has that privilege. I'm merely the hired hand. It doesn't matter to me what you do. But your slaves, Fleur. Are they to be trusted? Someone was using your book to teach those nigras to read. Reading could be a lynching matter, Fleur.'

Wayne placed his hands on the arms of my chair and stared directly into my eyes. 'These are dangerous times, Fleur. Slaves are causing unrest and murders throughout the South. Do you want Maddocks to be burnt up and yourself sacrificed to a slave uprising?'

I paled, fear clutching my heart.

'I'm sorry if I've upset you, Fleur!' Wayne pulled

away from me and strode across the carpet to the parlour door. 'I wanted to make you realise that Maddocks is not Savannah. You can't be nice to nigras here or they'll rise up and kill you. They have support from the North.'

He paused at the door and turned as Garland opened it and peered in anxiously. He added bluntly, 'Jem will have to be firm to save Maddocks. And so will you, Fleur.'

CHAPTER EIGHTEEN

When Wayne had gone, Garland stepped into the parlour. Dusk was creeping through the house and I could hear Trott moving about the rooms lighting the lamps, accompanied by the whispers of the house maids who were helping him. Maddocks seemed to stir, as though changing its clothes at the end of the day and emerging in a twinkling evening gown for the night.

'What is it, Garland?'

'De marster, Mistis Fleur.'

'The master?'

'Yes, Mistress.' Garland grinned. His secret of being able to talk English like an educated man when he so wished was now a link between us.

I walked over to close the curtains on the back windows. Through the glass, I could see the compound outside where Mammy Mable was moving among the chickens and children who always clustered around the kitchen in search of food. I arranged the draperies carefully.

'He'll be here soon, Mistress,' Garland said.

'Tonight?' My voice wavered and I clutched hard at the drape.

'Yes.' He turned to go.

'Garland!' The strength of my cry surprised me as

well as him. I stepped over to the back of the couch and gripped the top of it. Garland looked at me curiously, waiting.

'Tell me, Garland. How do you know my husband will be here tonight? Did he send word he's coming?'

'No, Mistress. But he'll be here.'

'Indeed? You seem to know a great deal of what goes on here, Garland. What time is he going to arrive? What will he be wearing? Will he have a gift for me?'

Garland lowered his eyes in the face of my sarcasm. 'I was trying to help, Missy.'

'Oh, Garland, I'm sorry.' I hurried over to him and gently placed my hand on his arm. 'I didn't mean to offend you.'

He sighed, a shadow hanging over his eyes. His ebony face was serious and he turned to avoid me.

'Fie, Garland! Don't take on so.' I squeezed his arm and withdrew from him. 'I'm grateful for your information.' My smile made him respond and he grinned down at me.

'Shall I send Ladybelle to your chamber, Mistress?'

'Yes, Garland, please do. You're right, of course, I must prepare myself.'

Garland sidled from the room but when I raised my head unexpectedly I found him lingering in the doorway. He was watching me with a fervour I had never seen in any man's eyes before. He spun around and disappeared into the shadows of the corridor.

The passion in Garland's expression haunted me while I prepared myself for Jem's homecoming. Ladybelle chattered while she helped me dress, drawing my waist as tight as my body would allow. I ignored her flattering comments. A state of confusion nearly overwhelmed me. Garland's kindness, steadiness, and loyalty were what I needed in life. But it was Jem who brought me excitement. He was my husband, and though after his treatment of me, I should hate him, I did not. I was trembling with the desire to be with him.

Ladybelle caught my mood. 'Lor', Missy, ah declah yo' anxious fuh Marse Jem to return.'

Without answering, I arranged my ringlets to cascade over the revers of my rich plum-coloured silk dinner dress.

'Yo' gwine thrill him tonight, Missy.'

I stood up before the glass. My skirt was a double one, the lower part having two deep flounces trimmed with pleats of pearl coloured satin ribbon. The corsage was plain with the revers exposing my throat, opening waistcoat fashion. My sleeves were demi-long and full. I had even put on a tiny cap of the same plum-coloured silk to complete the effect. If clothes could win Jem's attention, I was ready.

'Marse Jem gwine hol' yo' an' never let yo' go, Missy!' crowed Ladybelle. 'When he see yo' he gwine regret he eber leab!'

If only Ladybelle was right! I stared at the glass and smiled. How I longed to see him! I dismissed Garland's strange expression from my mind and dreamed about the evening ahead. It amazed me that my reflection gave no indiction of the trembling I felt inside. My very heart seemed to be quivering as I thought of Jem.

My reverie was shattered by a noise from the piazza below. Ladybelle darted to the window, flung it open and leaned over the balustrade.

'For goodness sake!' I called, clasping my ears with my hands. 'Close the window, Ladybelle. The cold!'

Her face was flushed and her curls askew when she drew back her head and fastened the window. 'Marse Jem is here!' she called in excitement. 'I seen him on the piazza with Garland.'

Jem's bluff voice resounded in the hallway. How wonderful! He was home! I decided to descend the stairs to greet him instead of waiting in my chamber. We would have a fine supper in the elegance of our dining room. We would talk about our future together. We would laugh and be happy.

I hastened to the door of my boudoir, Ladybelle bustling behind me. I swept along the corridor and paused at the top of the stairs and gazed down at Jem.

Garland was aiding him to shrug off his cloak. Trott

hurried up with a jar of whiskey on a tray. Jem snatched the jar and spilled whiskey into a glass. He gulped it quickly and began to stamp his feet to warm himself.

'Take that cloak away, boy!' He growled at Garland. 'You have a fire in the parlour, Trott?'

'Ob course, sah!' Trott answered gravely.

'He be cold an' hungry, Mistis,' Ladybelle whispered. 'Go to he, see if don't warm heself in yuh arms!'

I gripped the banisters and descended the stairs, aware that Garland was watching me closely. His gaze made me falter when I reached the bottom step. I raised my head in his direction and my eyes met his. He smiled ruefully, and slipped into the darkness of the corridor behind him. I heard Jem pacing up and down in the parlour and hurried to meet him.

'Jem!' I swept over the floor ready to fall in his arms, my skirts swishing against my legs. He faced me rigidly, his back to the fire. I stopped abruptly in front of him and tilted my head up to be kissed. I waited for his arms to twine around me and clasp me to him.

'Bah!' he grunted, resuming his pacing across the floor in front of the fire.

'Jem, what's wrong?' I gasped in dismay.

'Questions! All you do is ask questions!' He continued pacing up and down.

'I'm sorry.' I bowed my head.

'It's a fine time to feel sorry.' He whipped around and faced me, wagging his finger in my face. 'The old man tricked me! You knew, didn't you? Oh, yes! You knew!'

'About what, Jem?' I grasped at his sleeve but he knocked my hand away. His sultry eyes were glaring at me and his handsome features were twisted in a snarl of hatred. 'Jem!' I cried, 'I don't know what you mean. Who tricked you? How?'

'Damn that innocent little face of yours, Fleur!' He spun around and flung himself into the chair at the side of the fire. 'When I remember how I fell for you the time I saw you at that inn in Milledgeville. Your uncle baited his hook and he caught me! Imagine that a mincing old fool like Leo Singer should be able to cheat me, Jem Hayard.' He clasped his forehead with his hand.

'What is it, Jem? I still don't understand. What's wrong?'

'When I gaze on your troubled countenance Fleur, I ask myself how you are so calm. In your heart, are you not exulting with victory? You have Jem Hayard as your husband, something countless Georgia ladies have longed to achieve. What a triumph, Fleur!'

'Jem.' I sat in the chair opposite him. 'There's some misunderstanding.' My voice was firm. I suddenly recalled how my mother sometimes spoke to my father. 'I married you because I love you, Jem, and to please Uncle Leo. I know nothing of what you speak.'

'Hah!' Jem slapped his hand down on his thigh. 'That's odd. I married you to please your uncle, too.' He chuckled but his laugh was dry and bitter. Trott sidled into the room and quietly placed the whiskey jar and a glass on the table beside Jem. He rolled his eyes at me and edged out of the room. I noticed that he closed the door deliberately behind him.

Jem splashed whiskey in his glass and sipped at it slowly. 'When I look at you, Fleur, I can't understand it. I could almost believe you knew nothing about this.'

'How can I know anything, Jem? I came here because my parents died. Uncle Leo asked you to escort me, you remember. But, of course, you had other things to do!' My vexed tone amazed me. Jem looked at me sharply.

'Singer promised me Maddocks when I married you, Fleur. He deceived me.'

'You mean Maddocks isn't yours?'

'No, Fleur.' Jem scowled but the heat was drained from his grimace. 'Maddocks is yours. Singer never changed his will.'

'I'm sure he meant to, Jem. His death was so unexpected.' A great worry had been settled by Jem's remark. If Maddocks was mine, Jem could not change it. I felt so loving and forgiving to Jem. I leaned forward. 'Jem,' I whispered. 'I married you to please Uncle Leo but I wanted to marry you anyway.'

'Dam' right you did!' Jem leapt up, shattering the tender moment growing between us. He gulped the whiskey down and poured another. 'A good-looking bachelor like me, eh Fleur? No woman can wait to get her legs wrapped around my waist.'

I paled at Jem's words. I gazed down at my beautiful plum-coloured dress and wondered how my husband could think of me in those crude terms.

'Old Singer was a wily bugger, Fleur. I declare you seem to be cast in the same mould.' He banged the whiskey jar down clumsily on the fragile side table. Jem's hair was dishevelled and dusty from his ride, and his face was pinched from the cold, a stubble of beard blue on his chin. He held his glass to his lips, watching me scornfully over the rim.

My heart thumped. In spite of his reckless bravado, I saw Jem as a disappointed man desperate for comfort. If only I could breach his tough façade, I knew Jem would be mine. I refused to be put off by his brutishness.

'Jem,' I whispered. 'Does it matter if you didn't get Maddocks and I did? If it's mine, it's yours. You're my husband.'

Jem drained the whiskey and snorted. 'Oh yes! And I have to ask your permission to drink on the piazza! I'm not going to be beholden to you for anything, Fleur. Singer fooled me. He said Maddocks was to be mine.' A sullen gleam entered his eye.

'Why should Uncle give you Maddocks, Jem? Am I so hideous I couldn't find a husband otherwise?'

'You needn't give yourself such importance, dear wife. Singer owed me Maddocks, after all I did for him!'

I sat forward in my seat. 'Did you do a lot for him, Jem? He seemed to be such a lonely man. I only wish I hadn't been so frightened of him. I should have spent more time with him. Maybe if I had, it wouldn't have happened.'

'What wouldn't have happened?' Jem's eyes narrowed.

'His death, Jem. I'll never forget what I saw that

night.' I felt my cheeks reddening. 'There must have been a reason for that.'

'What are you saying, Fleur?' Jem walked over to me and stood in front of where I sat, spreading his legs apart.

'Nothing, dearest.'

'Yes, you are. You're holding something against me, aren't you?'

'No, Jem. I've nothing against you. You are my husband. I've asked you to share Maddocks as though it were your own. That's what you want, isn't it?'

'But it isn't mine!'

'Oh, Jem!' I stood up so I faced Jem. 'You surely don't think I want to have anything to do with running a plantation, do you? What do I know about cotton and a herd of slaves? I'll tend the house, Jem, and you run the plantation. Isn't that how it should be?'

Jem whirled around and reached for the whiskey jar. He abandoned all pretence of gentility and lifted the neck of the jar to his lips, quaffing the contents rapidly. When he pulled the jar away from his mouth he glanced at me warily. 'You and your damned uncle planned this between you! You've got yourself a plantation manager without having to pay a stipend. I've been trapped.'

'Trapped!' My laugh was hollow. 'You, trapped? Surely I am the one who has been trapped.'

'You are indeed, Fleur.' Jem flung down the whiskey jar with a force which split the delicately fretted top of the table. He advanced toward me, his glazed eyes gleaming. 'You don't get the services of Jem Hayard free. There's a stipend to pay, Fleur, by the devil there is!'

His hands lashed out and seized me around my waist. 'I'll be your plantation manager, the best damn plantation manager Paxton County's ever seen. I'll make Maddocks flourish, Fleur.'

'Jem, you're hurting me!' I gripped his wrists trying to force his hands away from my waist. He took no notice. His whiskey laden breath assailed me as he focused his eyes on my face.

'Aha! Don't think you can trick me, Fleur, the way your uncle did. I'll work well for my wage, but you'll pay me well, too.'

'Let go! I beg you, Jem.'

'You beg me? You deny me my wages, Fleur?' Jem's charming smile had twisted into a sneer. I stumbled backward. My legs collided with the seat of the couch. I felt myself falling and screamed.

Jem's face hovered above my eyes and then he swooped down. His mouth snapped onto mine, crushing my lips against my teeth in a brutal parody of a kiss. I had fallen across the couch and lay sprawled along its length while Jem clambered on top of me.

'No!' I screamed again, tearing my mouth away from his. 'Jem, my dress! You're spoiling my dress!'

'What do I care for that?' He seized my hands as I tried to fend him off. 'Come, Fleur, come!' He pressed his body onto mine, forcing himself between my arms so that the coarse broadcloth of his coat rubbed against the bare skin at my throat. The silk pleats of my corsage were crushed under his weight. His boots jammed against my ankles, bruising them.

'Please, Jem!' I whimpered. 'You're hurting me.'

'And so I should! I should take the bullwhip to you and thrash these silks off you. You won't pay me my stipend, wench!' Jem paused and raised his head, his hair bedraggled and his face livid.

Suddenly he stood up, wrenching me away from the couch with his strong hands clamped firmly around my hips. I swung my feet to the floor sighing with relief. No sooner had I sighed than Jem was at me again, throwing his arms around my neck and forcing me to him. It was impossible to resist his brute strength. I kept my mouth closed tightly and twisted my head away from him. He muttered an oath, caught me up in his arms, and tumbled with me onto the floor in front of the fire.

'Jem!' I shrieked. 'Not here, Jem, not here!'

'Why the devil not? It's the warmest dam' place in Maddocks.'

To prove his point, Jem bent over my body, picked up a log from the pile beside the fire, and flung it onto the flames. Sparks scattered around us.

'Jem! You'll burn my dress.'

'I'll burn your backside, wench!' He was down on his knees beside me, pawing at the flounces of my skirt, drawing the dress up to expose my legs. I wriggled in vain under his hand, clamped across my waist. Abruptly he turned to face me.

'Lie still, wench!' His open palm descended on my cheek with a stinging blow which knocked the breath from my body. My eyes watered. I stopped struggling and pressed my hand gingerly against the inflamed spot. Tears trickled shamelessly down my face and onto the carpet.

I lay without resisting while Jem pulled my dress up to my thighs. He spread my legs apart and flung himself on me like a branding iron. His face pressed close to mine and his teeth gripped the lobe of my ear. I was sprawled under him being ravished like a slave, each thrust of his body against mine smashing into bits the love I had for him. My body was numb, my mind too. My hands lay limp as he plunged into me.

'Doesn't that move you, Fleur?' he panted. 'Why aren't you roused, wench?' He snatched my hand and thrust it behind his neck so I could entwine the locks of his hair in my fingers. 'Come, Fleur, come!'

The fire danced in time to Jem's assault. The log he had thrown onto the blaze was consumed by the fire, a warmth filling the room while the light from the flames played over our bodies.

I wept silently, praying for him to finish.

CHAPTER NINETEEN

I sat in the sewing room, my sampler balanced on my knees, gazing out of the window across the piazza and through Maddocks' magnificent white columns to the oaks swaying in the wind. Leaves flurried across the empty courtyard and the sky was heavy and dark with winter. It was the time on the plantation, so Jem claimed, when preparations had to be made for the cotton.

Jem was frequently absent from Maddocks and I had learned during the weeks of our marriage to expect neither consideration nor tenderness from my husband. He came and went as a guest and treated me with as much affection as he would a slave.

Marriage had changed Jem, but not the way I had hoped. His lusty laugh had cracked; the wild gleam in his eye which searched restlessly for a new burst of excitement had dimmed. He moved slowly, the lithe spring in his step replaced by a heavy tread. Where he once smiled, he scowled. His blustery manner had become embittered and the carefree tilt of his head as he flicked back his black locks had become an irritable quirk.

I tried to grow closer to Jem and to appreciate him. What he wanted from me I gave as my duty as his wife. Yet each time we were together, Jem tried to best me, plundering my body instead of sharing love. He showed no joy in being with me. Each time he held me in his arms I willed myself to respond the way he wanted, but instead we were prised farther apart.

Our marriage drifted into little more than a formal contract. Jem was true to his word about management of the plantation. He rose early to meet with Ferret and his men to supervise the slaves. At times he joined me for dinner, an occasion distinguished only by his snarls at the house slaves and sneers at me.

For my part, I assumed the duties of mistress of Maddocks as fully as possible. Mammy Mable was used to her role of managing the house so I was confined to sewing and reading and planning my summer dresses. I had no inclination to call on our neighbours and dreaded their visits, for then I was obliged to pretend to be a happy bride and engage in county small talk.

Jem was genuine in his vow that he would manage the Maddocks plantation successfully. If he had decided to continue his reckless ways as a young blade no one in the county would have been surprised. I heard enough tattle to know that most people had a poor opinion of his ability to work. It was common knowledge, even among the house slaves, that the planters of the county gave Jem only a season before he ruined Maddocks completely.

Perhaps he was inspired by their remarks to prove the county Cassandras wrong. It may have been his jealousy of his brother Forest who was going to inherit his father's plantation. It was certainly not through a desire to please me. But whatever was motivating him, Jem was determined to make Maddocks great. It was a challenge he had accepted and, reared as he was in the strict traditions of Southern honour, he could not back down from that challenge.

All at Maddocks felt the intensity of Jem's ambition as the chills of winter blossomed into spring and the beginning of the cotton sowing. Jem was preoccupied with his plans and – when he climbed wearily up the stairs at night – I imagined that he was the husband a planter's wife should expect. He came to me to fulfill a need within him and to seek solace. I never denied him and strove to glean what comfort I could from his brief, cold presence at my side.

His grouchiness while he considered the problems of raising a good cotton crop made all the slaves alert. Garland seemed to be fired with energy, escorting Jem onto the plantation during the day and helping Trott in the house in the evenings.

I kept to myself during Jem's preparations for cotton. He had taken over Uncle Leo's great mahogany plantation desk in the library and pored over the stock books in the dim light from his lamp late into the night. I wondered why he was doing it and decided that he was hoping to understand all the nuances of running Maddocks.

In spite of his expressed contempt for Uncle Leo, Jem did not seem ashamed to learn from Uncle's accounts and records. Had I been smarter at the time, I might have realised that Jem was trying to divert my inherited wealth to himself.

One evening, when I was tired of sewing with only Ladybelle to keep me company, I determined to find Jem and ask him to sit with me a while. We seldom exchanged more than a few words, but I could not resign myself to accepting the fact that I would never have the love and companionship a newly married woman was supposed to enjoy.

I pushed open the door to the smoking room and saw the streak of light from Jem's lantern seeping through the half-open door to the library. I slipped in and was about to call Jem when I heard him talking. His voice was somewhat slurred as it often was when he had been drinking, and he was speaking with the exaggerated county accent he was accustomed to employ when hobnobbing with cronies of whom he was secretly contemptuous.

'I hear how yo' put out a nigra's eye, Goodpaster!' Jem growled. 'Can't blame yo'. We can't have the nigras learnin' to read and fillin' their heads with stupid ideas. Got to stop stupid talk too. With those Free-Soilers rousing up the North and the talk of war, there's no knowin' what's goin' to happen if the slaves hear about it.'

'Nothin' to be alarmed at, Marse Jem.' Goodpaster drawled complacently. 'Maddocks nigras ain' got no incline to read. Not now.' He rubbed his belly happily.

I sank down on to the couch as a head peered around the library door and stared at me in surprise. It was Wayne. Quickly, I held my finger up to my lips to prevent him from speaking. He grinned, winked to show he understood, and withdrew his head, pulling the door behind him but leaving it unlatched so I could hear what was being said.

'Ain't no nigra there,' he announced to Jem.

'Good. I hear you have been patrolling with Goodpaster, Wayne. Pleased you've settled down. I knew I could trust you.' Jem's voice sounded so false to me, I wondered how Wayne could be fooled by it. Someone coughed.

There was the sound of a chair scraping across the floor before Jem continued.

'As y'all know, my wife and I have inherited Maddocks. And as you would expect, we shall continue to grow cotton on the plantation. That's why I've called the three of you here. I am quite content, Ferret, for you to oversee the cotton production and you to keep the nigras in check, Goodpaster. However, production must increase.'

There was a gasp of surprise. 'Increase?' Ferret exclaimed. 'We made more profit last season than any other plantation in Paxton County, including yuh father's!'

'I ain't accusin' y'all of anything Ferret,' Jem retorted. 'I know what you've done here for years, that's why I say I want you to keep your position. But I've been studying old Singer's stock books. We can do more! It stands to reason, don't it, that with five hundred nigras and all the acres we have at Maddocks, we can get more cotton out of a season.'

'More cotton! That's more work from the nigras,' whined Ferret. 'If we drive 'em too hard, they'll only malinger and bring down the production rate we got now.'

'I'll not have a malingerin' nigra at Maddocks!' Jem thundered.

'Ferret's right, Marse Jem,' a fruity voice added. 'A nigra's an ornery cuss. Sometimes ah lash a nigra to make him work and he'll flip over on his back, kick up his legs and die. New nigras cost a packet these days, too.'

'Dam'me Goodpaster, I never thought to hear these words from a man like you!'

'Don't take me wrong, Marse Jem. I know how to handle nigras better than any man in the county. I can get the most contrary runt to pick more baskets in a day than two mindless giants. But it's the way I do it. Mister Leo never let me beat them the way I should.'

'I don't care how you do it, Goodpaster, but I want you to do it.'

'The nigras might get troublesome if we try to push 'em further.' Ferret sounded thoughtful. 'I don't see no way we ain't pushin' them aplenty already.'

'Your presence on this plantation, Mister Ferret and Mister Goodpaster, will depend on an increase of twenty per cent in cotton production this season!' Jem snapped. He turned to his desk and opened a ledger to indicate that the interview was over.

Goodpaster coughed. 'Beggin' yuh pardon, suh,' he muttered, scratching his sparse hair unhappily. 'If we're to handle the nigras so they work harder, I've got to have a free hand, suh.'

'What do you mean?' Jem sounded bored.

'To do what I like with 'em suh.'

'You have that authority already.'

'I mean that some might be incapable of work after I've done with 'em. As an example to the others, y'understand,' he wheedled.

My stomach churned at the calm menace in Goodpaster's voice. I was relieved when I heard Wayne butt in on them.

'We ought to take care your example doesn't make the nigras insurrect. They ain't going to be pushed too far now, not with what's happening in the North. It's in the newspapers.'

'That's the sort of remark I'd expect from a lickspittle like you, Wayne Carter,' Jem sneered. 'Don't you concern yuh thick head with the North. The South will secede soon. Slavery is a legal right in the South and we aim to keep it that way. No pesky Free-Soilers and hot-headed nigras are going to stop us.'

'Dam' right!' echoed Goodpaster. 'Don't take no notice of the boy, Marse Jem.'

'Whoever heard of a blacksmith who can read?' Ferret chimed in.

'I do my job all right!' Wayne sounded cross. 'If you bought quality implements instead of cheap inferior tools I wouldn't have to do so much repairing. The nigras need good tools so they don't have to plough the soil with their bare hands.'

Jem grunted.

'What I mean, Jem,' Wayne persisted refusing to be silenced, 'is that it's not just the nigras. If they have proper tools, they'll do better work. They need a good meal in their bellies instead of a peck of corn and two ounces of bacon riddled with skippers every week.'

'Yo' sound like a dam' Northern Republican!' roared Goodpaster.

'Never call me that!' Wayne's voice cracked with anger. 'I'm Southern born and bred, Goodpaster, which is more than you can say.'

'Sit down, Wayne!' Jem shouted. 'I see what you mean, Wayne. Give the nigra better tools and more corn and you say they'll work better, eh?'

Wayne sniffed. 'I've been trading nigras with Ma Drax since I was eight. They ain't much different from horses. Give a horse enough feed and he'll go where you want. Same with nigras.'

'But yo' have to whip a horse, don't you, boy?'

Wayne was silent. Jem coughed. 'It makes no difference. We ain't got no means to give the nigras extra feed.'

'Then it's extra lashes!' Goodpaster gloated, scraping his chair on the floor.

I got up quickly from the couch and ran to the door of the smoking room to leave before I was discovered. I pushed open the door to feel it yield in front of me.

'Garland!' I exclaimed. 'What are you doing here? Were you listening?'

'No, Missy,' his eyes glittered shrewdly. 'I was looking for you.'

I coloured, knowing that he had caught me eavesdropping on my own husband. 'Well, here I am!'

'Yes, Missy. Marse Jem be comin'.' Garland held open the door of the ladies' parlour and I crossed the passage and stood in the doorway. It looked as though I was just leaving that room instead of the smoking room. Jem and the men had stopped at the door of the library and I could hear them laughing.

'Wives are peculiar,' Ferret chortled. 'Mistress Ferret was scared half-crazy to have her first born but now she's grown 'customed right enough. I reckon wives are like that.'

'Not nigras, anyhow. Eh, Wayne?' Goodpaster cackled.

'I'm not as well acquainted with nigras as you, Goodpaster,' Wayne replied.

'I've had a few brown skin wenches in my time!' I heard Jem say.

'The juiciest meat!' Goodpaster rubbed his crotch as he walked through the smoking room. 'I can round up some fine fillies for you out o' the Maddocks herd, Marse Jem.'

Ferret put his arm under Goodpaster's elbow. 'A married man oughtn't to pester his wife all the time, eh, Goodie? A Southern belle ain't built for that. Not like a nigra. Some of them slave wenches we got here is just dyin' for a taste of their master's rod, eh?'

Ferret and Goodpaster wheezed with excitement. 'There's that wench of Ma Sukey's,' Goodpaster sputtered, 'She's ripe with the roundest boobies I ever seen. Her ma asked me for a new smock for her only today. She said she's twelve now and too old to go walkin' around bare-assed in front the ol' nigras. I gave her a pinch or two me'self.'

'Ma Sukey?'

'No, Ferret, dam' you! The wench. She's got an ass like a watermelon and the brightest little hole you ever did see. My finger got near bit off!' The two men roared happily. Jem's eyes, I noticed, were gleaming. He leaned over to Goodpaster who stood in the doorway.

'Get her!' he whispered huskily. 'I'll walk to your cabin. Bring her there.'

Jem's laughter died when he observed me watching him from the other side of the hall. Goodpaster glanced around to see what was wrong and changed his guffaw to a violent attack of coughing. Ferret, already bent by the stoop of his shoulders, scuttled like a crab behind Goodpaster. Wayne's eyes sought mine. I drew myself up with as much dignity as I could and waited.

'Just going to walk home with the men, my dear,' Jem leered. The smell of whiskey wafted across the hall. 'Why don't you go to bed?' He clapped his arm around Goodpaster's shoulder. 'Come on, boys!'

Wayne looked back at me when they all reached the front door and stepped through onto the piazza. His blue eyes were grey with shame. I spun around quickly and found myself gazing up at Garland.

'Happy night rest, Missy,' he murmured, escorting me to the foot of the steps as though nothing had happened.

'Happy night rest,' I replied wryly.

With difficulty, I made my way up the stairs. The raucous shouts of Jem and his hirelings drifted in suddenly from the piazza. I glanced down in time to see Garland slipping stealthily out of the house. He closed the door carefully behind him and the gust of laughter died. I gripped the banister and continued upward, the flounces of my new apricot dinner-dress flapping forlornly around my legs.

'What be troublin' yo', Mistis?' Ladybelle questioned when I reached the corridor above. 'Yo' ain' feelin' sick?'

I shook my head miserably.

'If yo' be feelin' out of sorts, Mistis, maybe yo' be bigged!'

The shock of her remark shook the self-pity out of me. The thought that I might be carrying Jem's child was suddenly repugnant. 'That is my concern,' I retorted sharply, 'and none of yours!'

Ladybelle frowned and walked over to the bed. She picked up my nightdress and refolded it while I stared out of the window into the night. It looked cool and crisp in the courtyard with the moonglow dappling the moss hanging on the live oaks.

I was furious at the thought of Jem being out there, and Garland too. My husband should be with me. I had to know what Jem was really doing.

'Can you get a lantern, Ladybelle?'

'I suppose so, Mistis.'

'Get one. We're going for a walk.'

'Now?'

'Yes.' I hurried to my wardrobe and reached for my pardessus of black velvet. 'This will keep me warm and it's perfectly fine outside. I'll be quite all right.'

'I t'ought yo' was sickenin', Mistis.'

I wrapped the coat around me and quickly tied on a bonnet. If I stopped to contemplate what I was doing, I knew I would not succeed. Ladybelle's expression of incredulity goaded me on. I was out of the door and on my way downstairs before she roused herself to accompany me.

'You're a slow coach, Ladybelle,' I chided.

'But Mistis, yo' can't go out alone at night!' Her deep voice was frayed with panic.

'Not alone, Ladybelle. You'll come with me and hold the lantern.' I pulled open the porch door. The cold air made me more resolute. 'The lantern, Ladybelle. Go for it.'

A light suddenly detached itself from the corner of the piazza and swayed toward us. I put my hand out against one of the columns, wondering if Maddocks had developed a ghost. Ladybelle gasped. The light was followed by a familiar shape.

'Trott! What are you doing here?'

'Waitin' fuh de marster, Missy.'

'You shall accompany me then instead of Ladybelle. Where did Master Jem go?'

Trott's face gleamed with ardent disapproval and he muttered an unintelligible reply.

'Very well, then. Give me your lantern. I'll look for him myself.'

Trott clutched the handle and shook his head resolutely. 'Dis ain' Sabannah, Missy. De county ain' safe fuh young ladies.'

I sensed Trott was weakening. I linked my arm through his and guided him off the piazza and down the steps. He plodded reluctantly with me along the path.

As we neared the compound where Ferret and Goodpaster were housed, I paused and made Trott douse the lantern so that we would not be seen.

Jem sat on a bench on the porch of Goodpaster's cabin. The cabin door was open and a dim light flickered inside outlining Jem's head. He cradled a whiskey jar in his arm. Wayne sat beside him, his shoulders hunched and his head lolling forward with dejection.

Jem slurped whiskey from the jar, spilling it down his vest. 'Why ain't yo' like other folks, Wayne? Have a sip of this and join in the fun.'

The yelping of a girl being dragged down the track from the slave quarters grew louder. 'It fair makes me hard to hear that wench, boy,' Jem growled, his voice husky. 'Ain't had a nigra since the night I was married. Sprightly they are, real sprightly.'

Goodpaster and Ferret stumbled into the light and lifted up the frantic bundle of a female they were hauling between them and hurled her onto the porch. The thump as she fell made the lamp swing wildly, throwing grotesque shadows around the verandah. The girl slithered quickly across the floor and wrapped her arms around Jem's boots.

'Marsa, Marsa!' She whimpered, rolling her head anxiously.

'See the wench!' Goodpaster wheezed. 'Ain't she perfect! Get away from the master, gal, and stand up.'

The girl reacted immediately to the authority in Goodpaster's voice. She let go of Jem's boots and rose unsteadily to her feet. Despite the cold, she wore only a threadbare osnaburgh smock. It was too small for her and even in the shadowy light of the porch the fullness of her young breasts and thighs was obvious.

Goodpaster rubbed himself. 'She's prime and ripe.'

Jem's cheeks, already reddened by the whiskey and

the chill of the night, glowed brightly. His eyes swept over the girl's body and his mouth drooped open. He raised his hand and gestured to the men to take the girl inside.

'Wayne here don't approve,' he told the others. 'But wait till he tastes that black chit and then we'll see what he thinks.'

'I don't think I have any business here, Jem.'

'Course yo' do, Wayne. Yo' want your'n too, don't yo'?' Jem stood up and peered into the cabin. The door was open and I could see the girl inside from my hiding place. Goodpaster was standing in front of her, tugging at the top of her smock.

There was the sound of tearing and an exclamation from Goodpaster. He thrust the girl into the centre of the room with her smock hanging loosely about her waist. Her childlike breasts were taut.

I realised that the girl was more nervous than frightened. She sensed that she had impressed the men. Jem leered and stepped into the cabin. He had forgotten about Wayne on the porch and kicked the door shut behind him.

'She's mine first Goodpaster,' I heard him exclaim.

'Of course, Master Jem.' The slave breaker guffawed lewdly. 'I hope you ain' gonna be long, though. My pecker ain' going to hold back for ever.'

I heard the girl scream suddenly and then Jem cursed. 'For hog's sake, stop screamin', wench.' The girl whimpered into silence but there were sounds of a struggle as though she was trying to pitch Jem off.

'Give me your whip!' Jem said crossly. 'Got to open up the hole there somehow.'

The girl's screams of terror cut through the night air, making me flinch. I tensed, trying to close my mind to that wailing wave of horror. I knew that I should act but I was paralysed with fright. What could I do against three brutally aroused men?

The girl's screams were never those of pleasure, nor even those of a young slave being deflowered by her master. I could hear the dull notes of Jem grunting with exasperation and Goodpaster's wheezing laughter. Suddenly, Wayne rose from his seat on the bench on the porch. I watched him with bated breath. He drew his knife from his belt, and put his hand on the door latch.

As he pulled, another hand closed over the top of his and drew him away. Wayne was so surprised, it was a second before he resisted. In that time, his body was clutched in a hold against which he was powerless. His captor had his hand on his mouth, preventing him from crying out. I watched the silent struggle silhouetted by the moonglow, wondering who had prevented Wayne from entering the cabin.

Wayne was dragged off the porch and over to the shelter of his own cabin, only yards from where Trott and I were watching.

'Don' make no noise, Marse Wayne. Promise yo' won' make no noise an' ah gwine release yo'.'

The voice was familiar. It was Garland's. I strained to hear. The girl's screams had reached a searing pitch and I was sickened by her agony.

'Let me go!' Wayne whispered hoarsely. 'Give me my knife, I'll stop them.'

'No, Marse Wayne. It ain't no good.' Garland sounded stern. 'Collect yuhself, Marse Wayne.'

Wayne arched his back to shake off Garland's grip. 'Why are you stopping me? A nigra wench is being rogered to death. Listen!'

'Ah he'ah she.'

'You ain't protecting Jem, are you?' Wayne's shocked tones made me wonder if his accusation could be true.

Garland shook his head. 'Ah protectin' yo', Marse Wayne. Yo' ain' got no chance. Goodpaster will shoot yuh balls off an' then he still gwine jump de wench.'

The child's screams were breaking into cracked breathless sobs. Garland removed his hands from Wayne's shoulders.

'Ah be sorry, Marse Wayne.' His face was serious. 'Ah hope yo' understand?'

'You took me by surprise, Garland. I could beat you in a fair fight.'

Garland did not seem impressed. 'Dat could be, Marse Wayne.'

Wayne brushed down his coat, obviously baffled. What Garland said was right. Wayne's attempt to stop the rape would not only have been futile but it would have brought down vengeance against the girl, her mother, Wayne, and others. Perhaps it would have created a situation from which many of the slaves would suffer. But it was reprehensible for a slave to hold a white man the way Garland had done. Wayne knew that he could ask for Garland to be punished, but how foolish he would look in the eyes of the county whites when they heard about it! On the other hand, if Wayne did nothing he would be condoning Garland's behaviour.

'Come, Marse Wayne,' Garland urged.

'Where to?'

'Inside yuh cabin. De wench be all right. We nigras get 'customed to t'ings like dat, sah. She bleed tonight but tomorrow – ' He gave an elaborate shrug of his shoulders.

Garland held Wayne's elbow and guided him into the blackness of his cabin. He closed the door firmly so I could not even hear the whispering of the two men inside. Trott's hand was on my own elbow. I allowed him to guide me back along the track. When we reached the piazza, he steered me up the steps and into the hallway. My eyes blinked in the brightness of the light as I focused on him.

'Missy Fleur,' Trott announced gravely. 'Yo' don' wan' to follow yuh husband 'gain. Dere be matters on dis plantation dat ain' no concern ob yo'. Yo' stick to yuh readin' an' sewin', mah Missy, an' be t'ankful yo' does hab a husban' an' dis Maddocks house.'

I nodded tearfully and climbed the stairs once again to my room. Ladybelle tried to coax me to bed, but I did not go for a long time. I stood at the window that overlooked the kitchen. In the dim moonlight I saw a bent figure carrying a heavy burden. Mammy Mable! I had no doubt she was going to give what relief she could to the ravished child.

CHAPTER TWENTY

I was almost asleep when the heavy clump of Jem's boots on the stairs brought me back to full wakefulness. I gulped back my despair and listened anxiously. I prayed he would not invade my chamber tonight. Garland seemed to be having difficulty helping him up the stairs for I could hear his soft voice coaxing Jem as though he were a child.

'One muh step, Marster, an' yo' gwine be in yuh bed. Come on, Marster. Put yuh arm on mah shoulder.'

'Whoops!' Jem's voice bawled as he staggered.

'Yo' aimin' to break yuh neck, Marse Jem?' Garland steadied him. 'Don't let go de railin' or yo'll fall down de stairs and den' where we pore nigras gwine be?'

'Hah! You're a good boy, Garland.' Jem slurred. 'Lesh see, which is mah door?'

There was a crash as Jem fell against the door to my chamber. I sat up in bed and pulled the sheet around me. 'No!' I gasped quietly, fearing lest Jem should come in.

If only Jem would come to me at other times, I thought, in the morning to sit at the table for breakfast and discuss plantation business, or in the evenings by the parlour fire exchanging pleasantries – anything so long as he shared sensible thoughts with me. But Jem never did. He was completely insensitive to my needs.

Garland helped Jem. 'Not dat door. Marse Jem. Mistis Fleur be sleepin'.'

'What?' Jem sounded half-asleep himself. 'Let me be!'

'Yas, suh!' Garland answered obediently but I could hear the sound of him dragging Jem across the floor to his own chamber. Jem began to blubber like a child. Garland muttered. 'It's yuh bed for yo', Marse Jem. No pesterin' Mistis Fleur tonight.'

Jem's reply was incomprehensible. I heaved a sigh of relief when I heard his door open and Garland pick him up and deposit him noisily on his bed. Jem began to snore immediately. I listened while Garland moved around Jem's chamber.

There was a gentle tap on my own door. I tensed.

'Beg pardin, Mistis. Marse Jem be sleepin' nuh. He ain' gwine disturb yo' no more.'

I heard Garland's warm voice with amazement. 'Thank you, Garland!' I breathed more easily, sinking down comfortbly into the depths of the bed. 'You are so kind.'

'Yes, Miss.' There was sadness in his tone but I had scarcely a moment to consider it before sleep embraced me.

'Marse Wayne craves a word wid yo', Mistress,' Ladybelle announced from the parlour doorway.

I raised my eyes quickly to find Wayne watching me.

'Ladybelle said I could come.' His voice was gruff.

'Yes, yes, Wayne.' I remained in my seat and waved him into a chair opposite me. 'What do you want?'

'You sound weary. I'm sorry about last night, Fleur. I had no part in it.'

Wayne's intense eyes darted nervously about the room. He fidgeted uneasily. 'I tried to stop Jem, Fleur.'

'I know. I was watching outside the cabin. I saw Garland restrain you.'

Wayne seemed startled. He was about to protest but his eyes moistened and his tenseness evaporated. 'I didn't know how to tell you, Fleur.'

'There's nothing to tell. You surely don't think I'm not aware of Jem's character, Wayne? He's only acting the way planters in this part of the South are expected to behave.'

Wayne eyed me doubtfully. 'Marriage has changed you, Fleur.'

'I've accepted it. Not so long ago you said it suited me.'

'What do you know about Garland?'

His question surprised me. I raised my eyes to meet his, conscious of the bond of friendship between us. Was this his way of changing the conversation to matters less painful to me? I smiled. 'Hardly anything. He was Uncle's boy. He's kind and he works well.'

'I've been thinking about him, Fleur, since he held me last night. I'm not used to a slave besting me. Under that fancy livery he wears, he's pure muscle. Don't be misled by his meek appearance and dainty uniform.'

'I'm not, Wayne. He's most useful.'

Wayne ignored the remark and continued rapidly. 'There's something about him, Fleur, which you wouldn't have noticed because he is always polite to you and looks the perfect docile house nigra. But when he took me back to my cabin, I studied his eyes. They were filled with determination. He was appraising me and he made me feel somehow inferior.'

'Fiddlesticks, Wayne,' I laughed. 'You're cross because he was more sensible than you.'

'No, Fleur. I must warn you to be careful. The *Federal Union* newspaper that Jem gets from Milledgeville doesn't print reports of the attempted insurrections in the South, but they're taking place. My God! slaves have tried to slaughter their rightful owners and in this state too!'

'Hush, Wayne. Don't get so excited. You're surely not including Garland as one of your rebellious blacks?'

'It's not impossible that careless white talk has sown a seed of dissatisfaction in the boy's mind. He could overhear the matters you and Jem discuss here.'

My lips turned down in sorrow. 'Jem and I never discuss anything, Wayne.' The confession halted Wayne's chatter. His shoulders twitched and he shook his head. He must have decided I was ridiculing him because he went straight on with his story.

'I questioned Renty about it.'

'Who's Renty?'

'The head boy in the forge. We were having breakfast by the fire. I had two pieces of pork with my cowpeas so I gave one to Renty. He couldn't believe his good fortune.' Wayne paused to see if I was listening.

'Renty is a simple boy but learns easily. I chose him out of the field slaves myself. I liked the brightness of his eyes. It shows willingness. When he was half through the pork, I asked him about Garland. You should have seen him, Fleur! He stopped chewing, swallowed the meat down as though I was going to take it away from him, and stared at me. Then he began jabbering all kinds of nonsense, pretending he doesn't know Garland, how he ain't know nothin' and so forth!' Wayne rocked back in his seat and grimaced.

'What's that got to do with me, Wayne?'

'Don't you see, Fleur? Renty was lying; he was scared witless. I think that Garland has some kind of influence over the nigras. They look up to him. He could be their leader.'

'He is, Wayne.' I stood up. 'He is their leader! He's a house slave so your ignorant slaves in the fields respect and fear him. You're far too suspicious. Whatever happens in the rest of the State isn't going to happen here.'

Wayne leapt to his feet. 'I know nigras, Fleur,' he pleaded, bouncing at my side while I walked him to the parlour door. 'They can deceive! They may not even want to, but a Yankee can dupe them with talk of freedom. Even Paxton is rife with rumours about malcontents.'

'Uncle Leo never listened to gossip, Wayne, and neither shall I. Besides, I'm sure Jem knows what he's doing.'

Wayne stared at me. There was no way I could avoid his piercing gaze across the threshold of the parlour. His voice lost its excitement and became scarcely audible.

'You speak as though you're trying to convince *yourself*, Fleur!'

Jem's decree that cotton production at Maddocks was to increase soon shattered the orderly routine established in Uncle Leo's time. It was my first exposure to cotton growing, so I could only listen to the complaints of others to judge how things had been done in the past. With the weather warmer again, I delighted to sit on the piazza. I often heard the men talking to Jem in the library. Algernon Ferret, his grim face set in a dour frown, was particularly resentful.

'Them nigras seem like they're breaking them hoes deliberate!' he ranted, thumping his fist on Jem's desk one morning in early April. The cotton had long been sown and the first hoeing had begun. A pile of bent and broken hoes lay on the ground in front of the piazza.

'Look at 'em! They ain't never snarled up so many hoes before.'

Renty and the two boys who had been sent to help with the extra work were sorting through the hoes to see what could be repaired. Ferret stepped outside accompanied by Jem and Wayne. Ferret snorted with disgust.

'It's taken me and Goodpaster fifteen years to get the nigras to understand cotton. It's like a baby, you've got to nurse it. Yo' can't force cotton and yo' can't force nigras.'

Wayne leaned against the nearest coloumn, his eyes blinking in the sunlight. 'Ain't you forcin' nigras every time you lash 'em?'

Ferret's scowl deepened. 'Discipline, that's all. Ah mean there ain't no way we're gonna get a nigra to go beyond the point we got him at now. We got the lash flying from mornin' to night, every dam' day. How can we do more?'

Ferret poked his head up and glanced at Jem. He ignored the presence of Renty and the two boys and spoke as if they were not there. 'Nigras may be black raw heads but they're smart, Marse Jem. Cotton is the time when you see that, especially if you're trying to get more out of 'em than what they're accustomed to, like yo' want.'

From my seat in the shade at the other end of the piazza, I saw Jem's mouth twitch. I knew the signs well enough by now and wondered how long it would take him to lose his temper with the hunchbacked overseer.

'Marse Jem, we can lash 'em till they drop but if they have it in their minds, we got to watch out. They can slow up the work, they can break their tools,' he gestured toward the pile of broken hoes. 'Or they start to pretend they're sick or pregnant.' He sucked his teeth and delivered what he thought was the final threat. 'I've heard tell of nigras cutting off their own hands to stop havin' to work. Even killin' themselves!'

Jem picked up a damaged hoe and inspected it carefully. He handed it to Wayne. 'What do you think, boy?'

Wayne tossed the hoe back on the ground with a scowl. 'I ain't your boy, Jem, no more than that hoe is fit to work. It's from the north, it's a cheap product, and it's made of inferior steel. These hoes just ain' no dam' good.'

Ferret cursed. 'What do you know about it? It's the nigras, Jem.'

Wayne shrugged his shoulders. 'Them hoes are chipped too much for me to file down to use again. Anyone can see the poor quality, it's the kind of tool only crackers buy. How much commission did you make, Ferret? Can't think of any other reason you'd buy such shoddy trash.'

Ferret jacked his hump up and down, spitting with excitement. 'It ain't my fault what the Yankees send us, Marse Jem,' he spluttered.

Jem drawled laconically. 'Seems like Goodpaster's got his work cut out, Ferret. If you let them nigras get the better of you, we'll have no dam' cotton at all. I want that extra cotton. Perhaps you had it too easy under Leo Singer. Get me that cotton, Ferret. If you don't . . . !' Jem left the threat unspoken.

The overseer hurried down the piazza steps, muttering as he bobbed across the courtyard.

Wayne looked just as angry. 'The slaves are going to suffer to save that bastard's job!'

'That's right,' Jem gloated, whirling around and striding back into the library.

It was saddening to watch Wayne followed by his three helpers carrying the broken hoes across the courtyard. But it was too lovely a day for despair. Even the monotonous red-soiled fields beyond the paling of the pine trees surrounding Maddocks glistened. There was a zest in the air which thrilled me. I deluded myself into thinking I had found a modicum of contentment at Maddocks. The house was my greatest comfort. When Jem was bullying the slaves or soaking himself with whiskey in the privacy of the library, I wandered through the luxuriously furnished rooms with a sense of admiration.

The ornaments, the treasures, the delicate furnishings and drapes, the paintings, which Uncle Leo had collected over the twenty-five years he had made Maddocks his home, were exquisite. I imagined, as I strolled through the rooms, conscious only of the watchful servants in the shadows of the doorways, that Uncle Leo drew his strength from his fine possessions when the brutal realities of running his plantation tested his patience.

Jem took to his whiskey bottle, but Uncle Leo had demanded more from life. His influence remained in Maddocks. The walls seemed to speak to me, consoling me for Jem's insensitive ways, steeling me to be strong. Now that the blows of winter were past, I could sit out on the piazza and enjoy the bursting into life of the Maddocks landscape.

'Jem,' I called softly as he strode out of the library toward the steps between the centre pair of columns. He looked dashing, his hair rippling over his coat collar and his eyes sparking with the challenge of Maddocks.

'Yes?' He paused and gazed at me questioningly.

'Won't you sit a while, Jem?'

He shrugged indifferently but stepped over to the chair at my side. He threw himself in it with a grin, stuck out his long legs in front of him and turned to me.

'All right' he said. 'What is it, Fleur?'

I was lost for words. My book slipped from my fingers and fell to the floor. The thump as it landed startled me.

Jem bent down, retrieved it for me, and placed it on the table between us. 'Well?' he demanded, his voice brittle.

'Jem, I just want you to talk to me.'

'What should I say?'

'It's just that I see you so little. You take your dinner with the overseer and the hired hands. In the evening you confine yourself in the library with your whiskey bottle.'

'I do my duty by you, don't I, Fleur?'

I knew that I had gone too far but I couldn't stop. 'Duty? Is that all I am to you?'

Jem spoke arrogantly. 'You need a child, Fleur. When you have a family you'll not pine for me all the time. I don't shirk my responsibility to you. You know that. I come to your chamber frequently. A wife's duty is to bear children. If you don't have a child soon, the neighbours will say I'm neglecting you.' He guffawed. 'But I doubt anyone would believe that of Jem Hayard!'

'I'll have your child, Jem.'

'By the devil, are you in bloom, Fleur?' Jem leaned over to embrace me, his eyes gleaming with pleasure. He looked like the young carefree Jem I had fallen in love with.

'No Jem. Not yet.'

He scowled briefly and sank back in his chair, the air of indifference settling again on his shoulders. I studied him surreptitiously. His bold profile was chipped with furrows of meanness where before I had seen only wrinkles of laughter. His determined chin now seemed a sign of stubbornness and his fine, straight nose sought out a challenge to his authority. He sensed my eyes on him and jumped up abruptly.

'Be ready for me tonight, Fleur!' he ordered. 'If I don't big you tonight, I'll wager it's some trick you're playing on me. A child will rid you of this moping. A child will make a woman out of you!'

He clumped off the piazza with a shout at the boy who was running across the courtyard calling his name.

'What the devil's in you, boy?'

'Marster, Marster,' I heard the boy panting as he dropped on his knee in front of Jem. 'Marse Goodpaster say come quick, sah.'

'Indeed, boy. And why should I do that?' Jem cuffed the boy on the side of his head.

'Marse Goodpaster, sah. He say he gwine nut a nigra, sah.'

Jem grinned, nodding his head in apparent satisfaction. 'Indeed?' He turned toward me. 'Come Fleur. Would you like me to escort you? This should prove an amusing diversion.'

'What?' I gasped, clutching my bosom. 'Can't you stop it?'

'Don't be a prude, Fleur. If you want to share plantation life with me, let's go to the compound together. It seems the good Goodpaster is planning to castrate some worthless field nigra.'

'Oh, Jem, please – '

'Stop whining. Here's a chance to prove your mettle. If the nigras see us together, they'll know I mean what I say. A firm attitude is needed, Fleur, so come.'

I knew that I must go with Jem. If I simply remained in the house, hiding from the brutality of Maddocks, I would be forever lost. Somehow my words of protest must be heard. But at the moment I could say nothing.

Jem cursed under his breath and waved me into the house. 'Get a riding habit on, gal, and meet me at the compound. I'll send Garland to ride with you.'

Garland was waiting for me when I emerged from the house. His face was stern and I thought better than to question him.

I rode in silence beside Garland to the main field, about two miles away from the Maddocks house where the shoots of the young cotton plants were beginning to dot the furrowed sun-red fields.

Hundreds of slaves swarmed around the top end of the main field, their brown-black skins blending with the rusty hue of the ploughed soil. Drivers were whipping them into a crowd around Jem who stood in the centre with Goodpaster. Ferret, crouched astride his horse, was galloping fussily around the circle shouting at the drivers. Every slave on the plantation seemed to be gathered there, even Mammy Mable who stood proudly erect, her eyes straight ahead.

I reined in atop a mound at the edge of the field. I quailed at the thought of riding through all those slaves to join Jem. Garland sat uneasily on his horse behind me. Garland's impassive face contrasted with the deep rage burning in his eyes. Only a few of the slaves dared raise their heads to look at us.

Goodpaster had a young boy of sixteen lying on the soil at his feet. His ankles were shackled together and his hands were bound behind his back. Goodpaster placed his booted foot on the boy's neck.

'What has he done, Garland?'

Garland looked at me in surprise. He swallowed before answering. I turned back to the scene, my throat tightening with dread.

'Jem told Goodpaster to punish someone so the nigras will see what will happen to them if they don't work properly,' he said sullenly.

I mused aloud in horror. 'Is he really going to castrate that poor boy?'

Jem began to harangue the slaves, cursing them terribly for idleness. Ferret scowled, impatient for Jem to finish. Goodpaster was rubbing a bone-handled knife up and down his thigh, the blade glinting as it caught the sun. My attention was caught by the face of the boy under his foot.

He was russet-skinned but his sleek features were drained of blood and grey with fear. He was a youth so completely in his prime that he must surely have been one of the finest slaves at Maddocks. I remembered having seen him several times, stalking proudly around the plantation.

'Why is Jem letting Goodpaster do this to such a boy?' I gasped. 'If he wants to make an example, why spoil one of his best slaves? Why cut a slave at all!' I was crying in my agitation.

The boy wriggled. Goodpaster removed his foot from his neck. The boy slithered like a snake across the ground, dragging himself toward a throng of slaves. They pulled back in horror leaving the boy gazing mutely at them.

'Ho, me lad!' growled Goodpaster reaching down and

picking up the boy by the scruff of his neck, dangling him in his hands as though he were no more than a kitten, showing him off to the ring of frightened faces.

With a roar of disgust, Goodpaster hurled the boy to the ground. He glanced at Jem. Jem stared at the boy, his mouth twitching. He looked up, saw me watching, and waved. I caught my breath and turned my head away quickly.

'He gwine do it,' an old black woman close to me cried.

Goodpaster's knife flashed in the sun. À sudden shriek rose from the boy and a groan from the slaves ripped across the cotton geld. The drivers' whips lashed the slaves into silence. The knife carved a slit across the boy's belly. Blood spurted from the wound, staining the soil a deeper red.

'Stop!' I screamed. 'Stop!' I tried to urged my horse forward, but Garland held it firmly. I could not remove my eyes from Goodpaster. He dipped his hand in the gaping rent sliced in the boy's abdomen. He churned the flesh with his fingers and pulled, hauling out the boy's vitals. He held up the bleeding mess for all to see.

I slashed at my horse and broke away from Garland's restraining grasp, but I did not get far. Someone pulled at my leg and other hands reached to unseat me. I was falling. For a moment I saw the ring of black angry faces, then I sprawled on my face to the ground.

CHAPTER TWENTY-ONE

I did not faint but I was dazed by the fall. All around me rose a babble of voices. Someone struck me a blow, then another. There was the sound of withdrawal, followed by complete silence.

I rolled partly over and opened my eyes. A haze of

vivid yellow and red blinded me with its glare. I was conscious of someone kneeling close to me and the shadow of a man's face peering down at me.

My eyes drooped. A voice spoke, soft, kind, concerned. Not Jem.

'Fleur, are you hurt? Pray God, don't let her be hurt.'

I gasped for breath. 'The boy, what happened to him?'

I recognised Wayne's voice now. 'He's at peace, Fleur, do not doubt it. But you? Are you injured?'

I struggled to a sitting position, supported by Wayne's arm. I touched my cheek and my fingers came away bloody. Pain shot along my spine and my shoulder was numb.

Wayne cradled my head against his chest. Beyond him stood Garland but his back was to the sun and I could not see the expression on his face.

Wayne lifted me up, holding me tenderly, searching my face for signs of distress. I was amazed at his strength, for he looked so fragile beneath his blacksmith's apron and his loose-fitting chambray shirt.

I glanced about me. None of the slaves were watching us. They were being herded by their drivers back to the fields to work. Jem was at a distance, his head bowed in conversation with Goodpaster. Had he not seen me fall? Or was he indifferent?

Wayne was speaking excitedly. 'Why did you come here, Fleur? I saw you pass the forge, and I ran after you to try to stop you.'

'Stop me?'

'Of course, Fleur. This was no sight for you. I wanted to take you away. But I was too late.'

I began to tremble and to my dismay Wayne noticed. 'You must get to your chamber. Can you ride?'

'Yes, Wayne,' I answered too quickly. I put my hand on his arm as he steadied my mount. But I felt I had to explain. 'Jem commanded me to come. Why did he do this awful thing? Could no one prevent him?'

'I couldn't Fleur, if that's what you mean.' Wayne's voice grew cold. 'It wasn't my affair.'

I stared at him. His fair hair was longer and thicker

than when we had first met at Ma Drax's slave camp. He had lost that pinched, hunted look and even his rude toughness had mellowed to a compact strength. His blue eyes that had once darted from side to side now gazed boldly back at me. The moaning of the slaves in the background suddenly set off the frustration I felt inside me.

'Wayne' I exclaimed pulling at his sleeve. 'Not your affair, you say! Was I your affair long ago when you shot Brutus and rescued me and Trott from Ma Drax?'

A look of pain entered Wayne's eyes. 'That was different, Fleur.'

'How was it different? Because I was white and a woman and that boy Jem punished was black and a slave?'

Wayne's kind, friendly face tightened into a grimace of disdain. He snapped his arm away from me and held out the stirrup for me to mount my horse. 'Go back to your chamber, please, Fleur.' His voice was filled with anguish. 'Don't look for me to fight your battles.'

'My battles? What do you mean?'

'The solution is yours, Fleur, not mine. I know Maddocks is yours, not Jem's.' He waved his hand behind him. 'All these slaves are yours, including the one Goodpaster butchered. It is you who can stop it, not I. You must stand up to Jem, Fleur, if you do not like what he is doing in your name.'

I let Wayne help me on to my horse. When I glanced down at him there was no sympathy in his manner any more.

'Wayne, you know I'm helpless to interfere with what Jem does on the plantation.' He ignored my pleading and averted his face.

I gripped the reins firmly so that Wayne would not see my hands shaking. The animal moved forward and Wayne stood aside. I did not trust myself to look at him again. The picture of Goodpaster holding the entrails of the poor slave boy in his hands would never leave my mind. To imply that I could have prevented him was unreasonable. But did others think as Wayne did? I remembered the blows I had felt when I lay prone on the ground. Were these blacks venting their hate against the mistress of Maddocks? Did they, too, feel that I could have stopped the barbarous killing of the boy?

Garland rode at my side without speaking. I was glad for I was in no mood for conversation. When we reached Maddocks I dismounted quickly and ran up the stairs to my chamber, slamming the door and drawing the bolt to prevent Ladybelle from entering. I threw myself across the bed without pausing to remove my riding habit and let my bitterness burst forth in tears that no one else should see.

It was late when I roused myself. The night at my window was black and moonless and seemed to threaten Maddocks. Ladybelle lay across the threshold to my room when I opened the door and stepped into the corridor. She was sleeping. A candle in a glass shade burned on the table in the alcove beside her. I took it up in my hand and descended the stairs.

The hall was in darkness. One of the house boys stirred by the front door but my light did not wake him. His comforting presence made me think that Jem must have come home already. I expected him to be in the library. I pushed open the door to the smoking room carefully so as not to alert him.

There was a sliver of light under the heavy oak door to the library. I listened. Jem would be in there, hunched at Uncle Leo's desk, the whiskey jar at his elbow. He would look up in amazement when I entered, but before he could speak I would tell him I was determined not to suffer any more the insults and unhappiness I had known since marrying him.

The door handle yielded silently under my firm grip. I pulled the door open and marched in.

Jem was not at the desk.

'Mistis!' The startled gasp made me peer into the far corner of the book-lined room. A dark figure emerged from the shadows, a book held in his hand.

'Garland!' I exclaimed, catching my breath in surprise. He held up his finger quickly, pressing it against his own lips and pleading with his dark eyes for me to be silent. I watched him step quietly over to the door and close it softly behind me. He gestured politely, indicating for me to sit down on the couch. His astonishing behaviour silenced me and I found myself obeying him without question. He crouched down in front of me like a young boy. I noticed immediately how alert his face was, his eyes sparking in the candlelight.

'What are you doing here?' I whispered. 'Where's my husband?'

'Marse Jem is in Paxton with his cronies.' Garland's voice was husky. 'I don't want anyone to hear us, Mistress.'

I frowned. By engaging in this whispered conversation with Garland, I was becoming a fellow conspirator in whatever offence he was committing. I did not know what to do but I was more curious than concerned for myself.

'Tell me why you're here, Garland. You know you would be punished if my husband found you.'

Garland grinned. 'You're not aiming to tell him, are you?'

'That depends on the reasons for what you're doing.' I got the impression that Garland was testing me even while I tried to reassert my authority as his mistress. 'Perhaps you'd better tell me why you're in the house this time of night.'

'Why, to read, of course.'

'Read!' I sat up in alarm. 'Can you read?'

'Certainly.' Garland's eyes blazed proudly.

'Garland, that's nonsense. You're a slave. You're not permitted to read.' I was suspicious now as my composure returned. 'What did you really come here for? Tell me or I shall call Mammy Mable this instant!'

'Oh dear, will you, Miss?' Garland clasped his hands in front of him, feigning contrition. 'Why do you doubt my word, Miss Fleur? Doesn't a man visit a library to read?'

I was agitated, taken aback by his coolness. 'Don't

you know that slaves who can read can be sentenced to hang?'

'Oh yes, Miss. I often wonder why. Why is it so dangerous to be able to read? Are there things in books which we slaves are not supposed to know?'

'I won't argue with you, Garland. I demand you explain yourself.'

'I came here to read, Miss. Listen.' He held up a book in his hand so that the light from my candle fell on the open page. '"About five thousand, of nearly four hundred thousand slaves in Georgia",' he read in a careful tone, '"have been taught to read and write. These are generally owned by wealthy slave owners who have taught them in spite of laws forbidding it when it will better serve their own interest and convenience!"'

Garland raised his dark eyes and peered at me. I listened breathlessly. '"It is a fine of thirty dollars and thirty-nine lashes,"' he continued, '"to teach a slave to read in the city of Savannah. But wealthy slave holders are above all law, except the conventional code of their own caste, and when they want servants to go to market to transact business, to pass letters and papers from family to family, they teach them to read names, and to write simple directions, and reckon small sums."' Garland's eyes twinkled mischievously.

'Give me that book!' I was horror-struck. He handed it to me obediently. I opened the book at the title page. It was called *An Inside View of Slavery* and had been published four years earlier in Boston. 'This is Abolitionist propaganda!' I exclaimed.

'Do you agree I can read?'

'This is no grinning matter, Garland. Where did you get this book? Oh mercy, what am I to do?'

'Don't be worried, Miss Fleur. This book was here on the shelves. Your Uncle Leo had a great number of volumes on slavery. They are of abiding interest to me. I used to discuss their merits and flaws with him.'

'With Uncle Leo?' I sat back on the couch, no longer certain what to believe.

'Yes. Marse Leo taught me to read. Thirty-nine lashes

the book says he would get for that in Savannah!' Garland chuckled, then his smile faded as he grew serious. 'He was good to me. Many evenings I spent here while he coached me to speak correctly and to read and write. It was his aim, he said, that one day I should be free. He treated me more kindly than a father does a son.'

'I had no idea.'

'Of course not.' Garland smiled kindly. 'I tried to pass on what he taught me to others. Many of the Maddocks slaves can read now.'

I stared at him, my mind numb as a thought struck me.

'Yes,' Garland laughed, reading my expression. 'I was the one who took your book to the quarters. I liked that book very much.' His lips tightened. 'Goodpaster will pay for what he did to that boy, putting his eye out.'

I shuddered and my heart seemed to skip a beat. 'Garland,' I murmured, 'aren't you afraid that now that I know your secret I'll tell my husband?'

Garland looked incredulous. 'I don't believe you have in you the same evil that drives Marse Jem.'

'Oh, I don't, I don't,' I assured him. 'What a relief to find someone who understands, even though . . .' I paused, a tiny frown betraying me.

'Even though I'm a slave?' Garland shrugged his shoulders. 'I was born a slave and you were born my owner's niece. We're both human beings. What do you want me to understand, Miss Fleur?' Garland rose up from his crouching position and perched himself on the edge of the chair opposite me.

'Why, the way I feel! All this is so new to me! I didn't know anything of plantation life in Savannah. I never imagined slaves were beaten and butchered to death. That poor boy – ' My voice faltered.

Garland was patting my hand. 'It wasn't your fault.'

I choked. 'But I feel it was. I've been thinking about what Wayne said all evening. Uncle Leo left Maddocks and all the slaves to me. I don't want any part of it,

Garland.' I pressed the book back into his hands and drew myself up, my back straight. 'Maybe I'll just sign over Maddocks to my husband and let him run the plantation the way he will.'

There was silence in the room. The candle flickered. Suddenly a book dropped off the shelf with a crash. It seemed to be the house speaking in protest at my thought. Garland stared at me for several seconds, making me feel uncomfortable under his implacable gaze. He shrugged his shoulders.

'Yo' he'ah wha' Maddocks does say, Mistis?' he spoke gruffly.

'Garland!' I exclaimed without thinking. 'Why are you speaking in that ridiculous slave talk? I can't stand it!'

'Cuz ah does be yuh slabe, Mistis.' His teeth flashed mockingly.

'Don't do that, Garland!'

'No, Mistis.' He made no attempt to move.

'Garland, I really shall call Mammy Mable!' I was alarmed now. Garland's attitude had changed so quickly from being an intelligent and well-mannered friend to a fawning idiot.

'When yo' sign Maddocks to Marse Jem yo' sign de nigras to he, too, Mistis.' Garland scratched his neck, raking his nails until I thought he would draw blood. 'We does be better if we be dead.'

Outside the house, a dog barked once. It was a lonely sound echoing through the night from the slave quarters. In a few hours, the slaves would be roused from their sleep by the morning bell. Goodpaster would stalk through the quarters with his pistols and whips, prodding and lashing Negroes into line to tramp off to the fields.

I sighed. 'Please tell me in English, Garland.'

'You know what I'm saying, Miss Fleur.' His eyes peered into mine. 'Marse Leo willed Maddocks to you to prevent the house and plantation from being sold. If you give it all to Jem Hayard now, everything your uncle loved will be destroyed. Even me.'

'Destroyed?' Garland's words frightened and ashamed me.

'You're distressed, Miss Fleur, aren't you?' His voice was soothing.

'Yes, yes. The boy's terrible death this afternoon. It's unnerved me.'

'I know. You're young, Miss Fleur. It's hard for you to be strong. A slave has to be strong all the time.'

'You do understand?'

'I think so. I know I'm still ignorant, but I want to learn. Of course, one day I want to be free, but now I want to learn.' He waved his long-fingered hand at the books stacked on the shelves around us. 'There is so much to learn here. Will you please help me? Stay and help us all.'

The plea in Garland's eyes and the zeal in his voice, trapped me. 'Yes, Garland,' I whispered slowly so my voice would not dissolve in tears. 'I'll stay and I'll try to help. But don't expect too much of me.'

When Ladybelle called me the next morning, I was already awake. The sun was filtering through the side window of my chamber and I sensed it would be a beautiful day. Ladybelle set my ringlets, her deft fingers soothing me and helping me to control the passion which was raging within me. My eyes stared back at me from the glass and I observed how my intention to discuss plantation affairs with Jem had lent bright colour to my cheeks.

'Marse Jem done come home late las' night, Mistis,' Ladybelle remarked. 'I heard Garland greet him in de courtyard.'

'Indeed, Ladybelle?' I tried to appear unconcerned. I glanced at her face in the mirror to see if she intended any double meaning. Her bold eyes, Jem's eyes, held mine and her lips puckered inquisitively.

'I wish to take coffee on the piazza this morning with my husband, Ladybelle. It is such a beautiful day.'

Ladybelle's eyes widened till I thought they would pop. I swept up from the stool in front of the glass causing her to jump away quickly.

'Marse Jem be sleepin' still, Mistis.' Ladybelle hesitated. 'He had plenty whiskey las' nigh'.'

'I don't doubt it,' I sighed. 'I shall attend him downstairs.' Leaving Ladybelle to straighten the boudoir, I walked from the room along the corridor to the balcony. The door had been opened to let air enter the house, and I stepped through. The balcony was a tiny one above the front door of the house, sheltered by the main roof which spanned the expanse of the piazza. It afforded a view to the west of the plantation stretching out toward the highway.

In the bright light it was easy to see the long lines of slaves in the distance bent low while they struggled across the cotton fields with their hoes. Behind each line stalked a driver. The low moaning of the slaves and the regular snap of the whip were sharp on the morning air.

While I watched, Goodpaster and Ferret rode their horses across the cobbles of the courtyard in front of the house. They were engrossed in conversation and neither bothered to look up. Their raucous, callous laughter added to my disgust. Goodpaster, broiled red as a lobster by the sun, leaned over from his horse to slap Ferret on his hump. The two men chortled rudely and rode off down the drive to the highway.

It was difficult for me to grasp all that Garland had told me in the library. It was not so much what he had said but the recognition he had stirred in me of the slaves as people, as much a part of Maddocks as Jem and I.

They were my people! It was unnerving to think that I owned nearly five hundred black men and women and that they were my responsibility. I turned away from the vista and the slave hum and went back into the house. From the hawking sounds in Jem's room I knew he had awakened and I hurried down to the piazza, gave the astonished Trott my request for coffee for two, and waited.

Jem soon received word of my intention from the house slaves. He burst onto the piazza reeking of stale whiskey and a night spent in his clothes. His hair was uncombed, his eyes bloodshot and his chin grey with stubble. I wrinkled my nose when he threw himself down in the chair beside me.

He grabbed the coffee pot off the table and poured the heavy black liquid generously into his basin. He did not glance at me but continued to scowl ferociously, probably hoping to deter any attempt on my part to converse. He gripped the basin with a hand that trembled.

He shook himself, perhaps hoping to dislodge his hangover. Another plunge into the coffee basin and he glared at me. 'What's this "conference" about, Fleur?'

'Us.'

He banged the table with his hand so the crockery clattered in protest. 'Indeed? I trust you do not intend to scold me for not spending last evening in the parlour stabbing a sampler and chatting about our old age!'

'It would have been nice to have had your companionship, Jem. I so rarely see my husband.'

'Are you still wailing about that? I invited you to come to the nigra-breaking with me, and then you fell off your horse and had to be carried home by the blacksmith.'

'I fainted and you couldn't understand that?' I cried. 'How can you brutalise the Negroes, Jem? You even seem to enjoy it. It serves no useful purpose. I wish you'd stop.'

He broke into a cough, hawking phlegm up into his throat and gobbing carelessly into the yard, splattering the column with spittle. I remained calm although he was deliberately being crude to emphasise his disdain for me.

'You shrew!' he replied. 'I knew you'd start up sooner or later. How I run the plantation is my concern, not yours. Nigras need harsh treatment. Don't think of them, Fleur, you hear? You'll be happy enough at the end of the season when we have hundreds of bales for the factors in Savannah. That means money. Maddocks plantation is a business, not a rest house for nigras because you can't stand the sight of blood.'

'Do they have to be ill-treated? Uncle Leo managed without Goodpaster and Ferret carving them to suit his pleasure.'

'If they don't work, nigras have to be punished, Fleur. It ain't ill-treatment. It's persuasion.'

'I don't like it.'

'You ain't expected to, Fleur. No one is asking you to approve it. You don't ask my permission about household matters. I don't intend to seek yours about plantation matters.'

'How can you be so sure you're doing the right thing, Jem?'

'Because I know about nigras. They're an ignorant, stupid bunch of woolly-headed savages. The only thing they understand is the lash. That's how we teach the nigras to know their place.'

I tried to remain calm, feeling Jem's eyes on mine as he peered over his coffee. 'Teach?' I queried innocently. 'Surely you mean that you beat them into submission, Jem? What is there to be proud of in that?'

Jem flung his coffee dish to the floor and jumped to his feet, sending his chair crashing to the tiles. 'By old Horny, Fleur, what do you mean?' He bent down and swept the coffee things off the table with his arm. Our lovely silver coffee pot bounced on the piazza floor, showering my new silk dress with dark brown stains. I gasped as Jem leaned across the table and seized my chin in his hand.

'Fleur,' he spat, his eyes fierce with scorn. 'Listen to me!'

I felt his fingers scorching into my flesh as he tilted back my head forcing me to look into his face, ugly with rage.

'You are the chit your uncle used to snare me. The old bugger is dead now. I'll not have you whining and wheedling like him. Maddocks is mine by right, do you hear? I'm going to deal with nigras as I know best, and I'm going to get every ounce of cotton this soil will yield!' He relaxed his grip on my chin and slapped my cheek a blow so hard I thought he had dislocated my jaw. He turned his palm and hit me a blow on the other cheek. My head spun and I screamed.

Two dogs suddenly bounded out of the house and leapt at Jem, their fangs bared. Jem lashed out with his boot and cracked one on its skull. The other jumped at Jem and sank his teeth into his arm. Jem howled with pain and anger.

Garland poked his head around the door, and I noticed a flicker of triumph in his eye before his expression assumed his usual servile mask. Jem smashed the dog against the edge of the piazza until it released its grip and tumbled into the yard.

'Who the devil let those dogs loose?' Jem rubbed his arm. 'The bastard bit me. See, Fleur, he's drawn blood!'

My head was still ringing with the force of Jem's blows. My cheeks were puffing out and my eyes were swelling up. 'I hate you,' I cried. 'They should have killed you!'

'Go to your chamber, Fleur!' Jem roared. 'I'll deal with you when I come back. Garland, how did those dogs get here?'

'Ah doesn' know, Marse Jem, sah.' Garland stood meekly by the door. 'Dey 'scape de box, sah. Dey de guard dogs yo' keeps to hunt runaways sah. Dey t'ing some intruders be 'tacking de mistis, maybe.'

'Dammit, Garland, I'm bleeding. Saddle my horse at once. I must go to Paxton for Doc James to dress this. I could be poisoned!' Jem ran down the steps from the piazza without looking around to see if Garland was following. Garland glanced at me. I managed a smile. To my amazement, Garland closed his right eye and opened it quickly in a conspiratorial wink.

Thoughtfully, I stared after Garland as he swung down the steps. The pain in my cheek vanished and my heart soared. I was no longer alone.

CHAPTER TWENTY-TWO

At a little past noon I sauntered over to the stables. Even through my parasol the glare of the sun seared my skin. I had sent Ladybelle earlier to instruct Wayne to have horses in readiness. He was seated in the shade of a venerable oak tree. Upon my approach, he leapt to his feet.

Wayne squinted at my bruised face. 'Did Jem do that?'

I judged that Ladybelle had already told him about the scene at breakfast, so I simply nodded.

Wayne was white with anger. 'The man's a bounder. He should be horsewhipped. How badly did he hurt you?'

'No more than he hurts his slaves, Wayne. I know what it's like now to be defenceless while a man humiliates you.'

Wayne hurried to the stables and led out the horses.

'Where are we going, Fleur?'

'What happens to the slaves when they get beaten, Wayne?' I asked when I was comfortably mounted on my saddle.

'Nothing. They go on working.'

'Surely some of them don't. They need attention, don't they?' I urged my old horse forward and Wayne followed, bringing his mount to my side.

'There's the hothouse,' he said.

'Whatever is that? A jail?'

'Almost. Jem would call it a hospital but it's a hothouse just the same.'

'Then we'll go there.'

'Now?' Wayne looked worried.

'Why not?'

'Shouldn't you send word first? Ferret ought to know.'

'Really?' I rode on with my head in the air.

'It's only polite, Fleur.'

'Fiddlesticks, Wayne, who here is concerned with politeness?'

Wayne bowed his head but I noticed the flicker of a smirk on his face. His next remark surprised me.

'Fleur.' He guided his horse closer to mine while we trotted along the path to the slave quarters. 'You may not realise this but people like yourself could be in danger.'

'Danger? Whoever from?'

'The slaves, Fleur. From the same slaves you think are such pets.'

'Nonsense!' I retorted. 'Who would want to hurt me?' But all the same I remembered the hands that had pulled me from my mount and the blows on my body as I lay half-conscious in the cotton field after the boy had been killed.

Wayne's doubt nagged at my mind while we rode in silence in the cool of the pine trees. In the distance, the creek that cut the plantation in two and provided water for the cotton when rain was scarce, babbled soothingly.

Wayne rode closer to me again. 'Garland came to see me yesterday evening,' he said.

'He did?' I was puzzled. It must have been before I discovered him in the library.

'Fleur, your eyes give you away. They brighten when I talk about Garland. Are you being fooled by those ridiculous shoes, stockings, silk britches, and brocade vests he wears? He's black iron underneath.'

'Jem doesn't think so. Jem calls him a molly.'

'Then Jem Hayard is more doltish than I thought. I asked Garland why he tolerated what Jem and Goodpaster are doing to the slaves. I told him he could easily have stooped Goodie from slaughtering that boy. What chance would a handful of whites have against five hundred wild nigras?'

'It's you I should be wary of, Wayne. You're putting ideas into his head.'

'You know what he asked me?'

'No.' I was curious.

'He asked me what I thought of slavery,' Wayne contined. 'I told him I ain't really thought about it but if an owner treats his nigras bad he's bound to get his deserts. I'm sorry, Fleur, but I was trying to find out what he would say.' Wayne looked anxious.

'What did he say to that?'

'He said I was encouraging him to do a wicked thing. He demanded to know if I thought slavery was evil. I told him that was nonsense. How is the South going to survive without slaves to work on the plantations? That ain't evil,' I said, 'it's economics. It's the slave holder who might be evil.'

I sensed Wayne's embarrassment. He was confessing to a conversation with a slave about his owner. At an earlier time I might have asked him to leave Maddocks for such an act.

I stared at Wayne crossly. 'Why are you telling me this?'

'Because I want you to know the thoughts Garland has in his head. He knew I was trying to trick him but he revealed himself anyway. He's not afraid.'

We had reached a dilapidated building with a stone foundation and a wooden upper storey which Wayne said was the hospital. I dismounted quickly and looked around.

Wayne jumped down and took the horse's reins and fastened them to a tree. 'We should have told Ferret we were coming.'

'I don't have to consult Ferret when I want to visit somewhere on my own plantation, do I Wayne?'

He pulled the door and it creaked open. I peered into the gloom of the building and shuddered; the dark interior was fetid with the stench of death and echoed with the groans of the sick. The moans changed to pleas for help when the slaves recognised us.

'This is awful!' I whispered into Wayne's ear, as he steadied my arm. 'I had no idea.'

'You wanted to come.'

'Of course.' My back stiffened with resolution. 'The smell, Wayne! And I can hardly see.'

Wayne pushed his way through the gasping Negroes and flung open the windows so that we could see the state of misery the inmates were in. The sight was horrific.

Slaves lay everywhere, sprawling about the mud floor

like snakes in a pit. Some were comatose as though death had already seized them. Others crawled, clawed, and shrieked around us, begging for help. Flies filled the air, feasting on the open wounds of the injured and settling on the rheumy eyes of the sick.

'This is monstrous!' I tightened my grip on Wayne's arm.

'The responsibility is Jem's.'

'Jem's or mine?'

'Don't blame yourself, Fleur. Some slave owners don't care for their sick at all. They believe if they treat sick slaves kindly they'll encourage other slaves to pretend sickness.'

I snatched my arm away. 'What if an epidemic starts right here and kills off every slave on the plantation? Who's going to pick the cotton then?'

Wayne spread his hands in confusion. 'Don't ask me. That's Jem's affair.'

'Isn't Ferret the one who's in charge of this hospital? He must arrange some treatment for these poor people. The place is filthy. It should be opened up and cleaned out.'

'Are you going to tell him?' Wayne eyed me curiously. This was the challenge. What I did now would show if I was going to dispute Jem's authority or continue to accept meekly what Jem was doing to Maddocks in my name.

'Of course,' I snapped. 'These wretched creatures need care. Those wounds, they need to be rubbed. Mammy Mable will know what to do. I don't. We have cod liver oil and a small quantity of an arsenical solution in the house. I'll send that down, and some Seidlitz powders too.'

'There are more of them upstairs.' Wayne said, nervously. 'They've heard you're here.'

'Well, I can't start an insurrection of sick slaves, Wayne. A resurrection is what's needed.' I bent down to squeeze the hand of an old woman crawling across the floor to clutch the skirt of my riding costume.

'Don't touch her, Fleur!' Wayne pushed the woman

aside. 'Who knows what you might catch?'

When I returned to the entrance, I sighed. 'What can I do, Wayne? I don't know anything about sick people. But certainly they must be bathed and fed. They need beds to sleep on, too, instead of that damp mud floor. Is there no one to care for them?'

The tears gathered in my eyes at the spectacle of these people left to rot and die instead of being nursed. I stayed clinging to the doorway while the suffering and pleading of the sick slaves swelled around me. Suddenly I was conscious of a shadow falling across the sill and a deep voice asked what was wrong. I blinked at the newcomer. 'Garland!' I exclaimed. But no words could express what I felt. I pointed inside the building.

'Where is Marse Jem? I want him to explain this neglect to me immediately.'

Garland's face was expressionless but I knew the intelligence behind his mask of servility and was encouraged by his presence. 'Marse Jem done ride to Milledgeville, Mistis,' Garland replied solemnly. 'After Doc James treat he arm.'

'What!' Wayne grabbed Garland's sleeve to make the slave look at him. 'Milledgeville? Are you sure?'

'Yassah!'

'There might be trouble. Jem should be here.'

'Should he?' I queried. 'Jem's presence surely hasn't helped these sick slaves, has it, Wayne?'

'Yo' been in dere, Mistis?' Garland's voice betrayed his amazement, and I detected admiration in his glance.

'Why not, Garland? I'm going to return tomorrow, too. Wayne, I want you to find out who's in charge here. There must be a slave responsible for feeding these sick people. I want you to see that the place is swept and tidied. I'll have blankets sent down immediately and anything else we have that will make them more comfortable.'

Wayne was biting his lip. Even Garland seemed nervous.

'Fleur,' Wayne pleaded. 'It doesn't do to interfere in

plantation matters. Ferret will ride to Milledgeville after Jem if we start to meddle.'

'Fiddlesticks, Wayne Carter! Whatever happened to your gumption? If Ferret troubles you, knock him down! I'll not have a hothouse like this at Maddocks while we live in luxury in the big house.' My outburst surprised Wayne. I glanced at Garland, who was gaping at me.

'You, too, Garland. I'll expect you to help clean up this place.'

'Yas, Mistis.' His face split into a wide grin.

'Fleur!' Wayne called as I walked toward my horse. 'With Jem away you might need protection. Let me come and sleep downstairs in the parlour.'

I allowed him to help me onto my horse, then I smiled down at him. 'That would never do, Wayne! My husband would surely not approve!'

I jerked the reins so my horse moved forward. I waved at Wayne but he spun around with apparent anger and walked back to the hospital.

Garland glanced in my direction. He bowed his head and I rode off into the pine trees back to Maddocks.

That evening I dressed almost absent-mindedly. The ride through the vast acreage of Maddocks' lands had tired me. I was overwhelmed by the organisation which had developed over the years to establish Maddocks as a profitable business. I had the feeling that I was unprepared for the intricacies that I would uncover if I probed further. I lifted down the dinner dress of rich plum-coloured silk from my wardrobe. It was one of my favourites.

'Lor' Mistis!' exclaimed Ladybelle interrupting my thoughts. 'Why for yo' gwine wear dat lubly frock? Marse Jem ain' here.'

I faced her silently, handing the dress to her to help me. At least, I thought as Ladybelle fussed around and smoothed out my petticoats, I had discovered some means to alleviate the lot of the slaves who, according to the terms of Uncle's will, were owned by me. I would make the hospital into a place of solace for the infirm and of comfort and care for the sick. I would plead with Jem, when he returned, to stay the quick hand of the odius Goodpaster. I would leave all other plantation business to him.

'Yo' does be sulking like yo' be lovesick, Mistis,' cried Ladybelle, clumsily tightening my corsage. 'Why yo' be dressin' so fuh, I don't know.'

'For my pleasure, Ladybelle. My husband is away so I must cheer myself up.' Ladybelle's smirk of disbelief showed me that I could never fool her where my relationship with Jem was concerned.

'By the by, Ladybelle,' I countered. 'I shall not require you tonight.' Ladybelle eyed me suspiciously. 'After I've taken supper I shall read. Trott will be here should I need anything.' I sat down before the glass and began to arrange my hair myself.

Eventually Ladybelle was pursuaded to leave me alone. I did not descend for supper but sent for Trott to bring a tray of milk and biscuits. When the lamps in my room were lit, I sat by the window. It was a warm evening and I asked Trott to open the casement. As usual he cautioned me to be careful lest I fall out.

I settled down with my book in front of the open window, letting the silky softness of the night air caress my cheeks. I stared at the pages but did not read. I was waiting for Garland.

I must have been sitting motionless for a long time. His rapid knock on my door startled me and the book fell from my lap. I bent to retrieve it but Garland was already at my side, kneeling beside my chair to pick it up.

'Your book, Mistress,' he said, his dark eyes glowing. He pressed it into my hand. I stood up and closed the heavy velvet curtains which were quite inappropriate for my boudoir in summertime but which served a useful purpose in allowing Garland and me some degree of privacy.

Garland settled himself on a chair opposite mine and related the events of the day at the hospital. He spoke eloquently, his eyes, which seemed so mysterious and knowing, holding mine in their gaze. He was only two years or so older than I but I felt many years younger than he in experience and knowledge. I shuddered.

'You're cold,' he uttered instantly, interrupting himself and leaping to his feet. 'Let me shut the window.'

'No, no,' I stayed him with my hand. 'It's nothing. Tell me, do the slaves look better now?'

'Mistress, it's like a miracle. Their very countenances show it. The dinner you ordered for them included the first meat they'd had for weeks. Some of them are nearly fit for the field already.'

'And Wayne, he helped?'

'In his fashion,' Garland's voice faltered and his eyes flickered over me.

'Tell me everything, Garland. I'll find out.'

'Your friend Wayne fetched Ferret and Goodpaster to see what we were doing. I say "we" because Wayne brought down Renty and his boys from the forge to help.'

My spirits fell. 'What did Ferret do? Did he stop you?'

'No, Miss Fleur. He inspected the hospital, nodded his head, and told Wayne to continue.'

'Did he know it was I who had ordered the work?'

'Oh yes, but it seemed not to concern him. He and Goodpaster shrugged their shoulders and rode back to the fields.'

I sat in silence, Garland's eyes upon me. Maddocks was still; not even a board creaked in the corridor outside my room. Insane moths bobbed about the lamp glass and, from the back of the house, the snarling sound of two dogs tussling drifted up to us. It occurred to me that perhaps Jem planned to see what I would do in his absence and had instructed his overseers not to hinder me. I wondered what limits, if any, had been placed on my authority.

'Miss Fleur, you know this is a dangerous thing you're doing? You're not only flouting your husband when you champion slave welfare, but also the traditions of the South.'

'Hush, Garland. I'll hear no more of it. I'm capable of knowing my own mind. I am a married lady of property.'

'Yes, Miss.'

'Plese don't laugh at me, Garland! I don't think I could continue if I believed you were mocking me.'

'No, Miss Fleur, I'm not. When I smile it's with pleasure and surprise that you should care. You don't know what it means to me to have someone I can talk to, someone close to me in years who understands, especially someone who is as pretty as you, Mistress.'

Garland's hand hovered over mine like a humming-bird seeking water from a cactus flower. I removed my hand from my knee and sat back in my seat. Garland's remark had released a swarm of emotions buzzing through my mind and stinging me inside with vengeance which made me want to weep.

I rose quickly not to show my emotion. 'Garland, please do close the window. I'm afraid I may be getting cold after all.' I hurried to my vanity table, dabbed at my eyes, applied powder quickly and turned back to Garland. He was standing by the window.

'My uncle,' I said, hoping to return the conversation to normal, 'did you read to him at all?'

'Indeed I did.'

'Then you shall read to me, Garland. Hand me my book.' He returned the volume he had rescued from the floor.

It was a collection of Byron's poems, one of the two books that had been given me by my father that I had been able to bring with me from Savannah. I had seen it in Garland's hands before. Now I opened it to *Childe Harold*. He held out his tallow-white palm for the book and without looking up, read in a deep, mellifluous voice which gave the lines an added meaning.

Soon I was lost in reverie. Byron! It was strange what a part he had played in my life. He had been Daddy's idol and perhaps mine too. The portrait of Byron with his strong, bold features, his wavy hair, straight nose and wild deep-set eyes that was the frontispiece of the book, might almost have been a likeness of

Jem. Byron had been in revolt and his poetry exposed the follies of the various societies in which he lived. And that was the way I had wanted to see Jem. Not merely narrow, cruel and undisciplined, but an unconstrained rebel waging an idealistic struggle against artificial conventions. How I had deluded myself with my romantic fancies!

Garland's voice was rich and strong, capturing the music and the mood of *Childe Harold*, bringing out nuances I had never caught before.

At length he placed the book on the table. 'Garland,' I said, 'you read as though the words were your very own.'

'In a way they are. I agree with Byron that man is half dust and half deity.'

He stood up without warning. His eyes lost their brightness and he spoke in the black dialect. 'Yas, Mistis. I been tek yo' orders.' He pulled the door open. 'Good night, Mistis.' He stepped into the dark corridor and down the stairs before I could protest.

Another voice broke into my thoughts. Ladybelle stood at the rim of the light thrown by the candle.

'Garland be keepin' yo' comp'ny, Mistis?'

'Ladybelle!'

'Lor' yo' looks like yo' seen a spirit, Mistis. Sorry, I'm sure, Mistis.'

I led the way back into my chamber. Ladybelle cast a shrewd eye around the room. 'I done belieb I he'ah Garland recitin', Mistis.'

I tried to keep my voice calm. 'Garland tells me that he has cleaned up the hospital and the dinner we sent for those poor wretches was much appreciated.'

Ladybelle's look was bold. 'It ain' no concern ob me dat Garland be in yuh chamber wid de curtain close' an' de door lock'.'

I flushed with anger. Ladybelle would, without doubt, convey to Jem a highly coloured version of what had happened. A few minutes earlier I had felt so safe and secure while Garland read to me. Now I was being bullied by my own maid.

I turned away from her and sat on the edge of the bed. The words that Garland had chosen from Byron kept repeating themselves in my mind: 'Man is half dust, half deity.'

CHAPTER TWENTY-THREE

It was useless to think that I would be able to still Ladybelle's tongue. Her report to Trott and Mammy Mable of Garland's visit to my chamber must have sounded scandalous indeed. I saw nothing wrong in my attempt to help Garland, and told them both – Mammy Mable and Trott – so very forcibly, when they ventured to warn me of the dangers involved.

Garland became a regular visitor to my boudoir when he had finished his house and plantation duties. Such interesting evenings we spent together! Garland was limitless in his ideas and knowledge.

The kitchen was agog with gossip about these visits, but I ignored the furor. During the day, I worked in the hospital, visiting the sick and infirm. As hard as I worked, that pair of plantation tyrants, Ferret and Goodpaster, sent down more slaves, cut and bleeding with the slashes of the whip on their backs.

Garland was stoical when I related these cruelties to him. He seemed to accept the beatings as part of the lot of field slaves.

Two weeks passed before Jem returned to Maddocks. I was strolling across the yard with Ladybelle on my way to the hospital when I heard the clatter of a carriage racing up the drive. It came around the corner at such a speed, I dropped my parasol and took hasty refuge in the magnolias. Jem leaned out of the carriage window, his dark eyes glittering devilishly. He brushed his hair from his forehead with an arrogant grace.

'Hah, Fleur! Why are you skulking in the magnolias?' He shouted as the coach jerked to a stop at the piazza steps.

I was made speechless by this remark. Ladybelle picked up my parasol and I tried to compose myself. Jem leaped out of the carriage with a boyish zest. He looked different, more reckless, more carefree. He was dashing in a bottle green jacket and pants of light gold. His hair hung around his face like a halo; he was freshly shaved, looked young and handsome, and his eyes sparkled with excitement.

I rushed forward, calling his name as I crossed the yard.

He did not hear me. He was standing by the open door of the carriage, absorbed in helping a young lady to descend. I halted and stared in amazement. A flurry of petticoats, together with a burst of titillating laughter, marked her emergence. She accepted his hand as she daintily stepped to the lawn, then put her arm about him in a light embrace.

She was dressed in an exaggerated style which, I learned later, she claimed to be the latest in fashion from the North. Her costume was of black moiré with a skirt in three extremely full flounces and a basque trimmed with graduated bands of velvet ribbons. The sleeves were full puffs. But her most striking feature was her bright red hair that fell about her shoulders in perfect abandon.

She paused and cocked her head to gaze at Maddocks.

'Jem, only six columns?' Her voice was husky and crackled with a cynical laughter.

Jem threw up his hands in mock despair. 'If you want more, my dear, I'll have to sell some slaves to pay for them!'

His remark filled me with apprehension. I had no idea who this person could be. Why was Jem addressing her with such affection and speaking so lightly of Maddocks? His conduct was that of a man escorting a bride to her new home. Meanwhile he ignored me.

Trott threw open the front door and stepped onto the piazza. He looked with confusion from Jem to me, then at the woman.

'Whiskey! ' Jem snapped.

'Yassah!' Trott eased himself arthritically back into the house.

The woman gazed at Jem quizzically. He shrugged and led her over to a chair – the one I usually sat in. He plunked himself down in the chair opposite her. Hannibal led the carriage away. Jem was nodding with satisfaction still without looking in my direction.

'It feels strange coming back.'

'Why?' The woman's voice was intimate.

Jem gazed upward. 'All that I did while I was away to help me understand myself and Fleur, all those things that happened, and yet Maddocks is here still. It hasn't changed.'

'You speak as though it has a life of its own, Jem. You can change it anytime you want.'

'I knew you'd say that. You always understand.'

I could abide this familiarity no longer. I seized Ladybelle by the hand and stalked over to the steps. I addressed her loudly as she helped me up them. 'It appears that we shall be two extra for dinner, Ladybelle. Have the courtesy to inform Mammy Mable. Call Garland for me, please.'

Jem jumped up nervously from his seat. The woman smiled at him encouragingly and arranged her hands in the folds of her gown. They both stared at me while Ladybelle slipped past into the house.

Jem held me at arm's length, his eyes studying my face briefly. He frowned, perhaps noticed a change in me that I had missed. There was no embrace. Instead he released me and turned me toward the woman standing beside him. My eyes flickered over her resentfully.

'Fleur, this is my sister, Maxine.'

'Your sister!' I gasped with relief, and sank into a chair. Perhaps she did resemble Jem, I thought, watching her shyly. Trott arrived with the whiskey. To my astonishment, Maxine joined Jem in taking a measure of whiskey.

I was too upset to be polite. 'I thought you were married, Maxine. What happened to your husband?'

'Now don't start on Maxine, Fleur. She's had a terrible time.' Jem glanced at Ladybelle, who had returned, and the other servants hovering around the doorway. He waved for them to go away and they edged back inside the house, Ladybelle following at a slower pace.

Garland stepped through onto the piazza. He was almost as tall as the door itself. He wore a new livery which I had bought him. It made him appear more like a prosperous black banker than a houseboy. He stood at attention beside the door while Jem glared at him incredulously.

'You may leave us, Garland. You are not required.' Jem ordered.

Garland glanced at me for permission.

'Get out!' shouted Jem, suddenly angry. 'I'm your master, boy, and I'm here in my own house, so when I tell you to get out, get out fast.'

'Hush, Jem,' I said in an undertone. 'I sent for him to see if there is anything you and your guest need.'

'I'll hush when I want to, Fleur. Who gave that nigra that ridiculous raiment? He looks like a New Orleans pimp.'

'I did, Jem. I want our house slaves to look smart.'

'Huh!' Jem jerked his head back contemptuously and appealed to Maxine. 'You see?'

Maxine smiled sympathetically, perhaps hesitating to antagonise me. 'I've had an awful time, Fleur, so Jem very kindly invited me to stay here at Maddocks. My husband left me. I hope you don't mind my coming unannounced.'

'It's terrible when a husband leaves his wife,' I replied. 'Jem has been away two weeks and I've been distraught.' My smile felt false but I could not seem to let the matter be. 'Your husband must have been a perfect beast to treat you so.'

'Oh, he was, Fleur. I should never have married him. It's a relief for me to be without him.'

'But the disgrace, Maxine!'

'I know, Fleur. It's dreadful. I can't possibly stay at Hayard's Hall with my parents. They're so worried that Forest might not be able to marry his precious Miss

Vain because of the scandal. No one knows I'm here, Fleur.'

'Indeed?' I said and turned to Jem. 'Why didn't you tell me Maxine was in such trouble, Jem? You left without a word.'

'A fine thing!' Jem slapped his thigh with his hand. 'I bring home my sister and what gratitude do I get? She joins up with my wife to tear me to pieces.' He turned it into a joke, oblivious to the anger underlying my remark and to the real nature of my feeling for his sister. I was not surprised that she dared not go to Hayard's Hall. Instinct told me she was not to be trusted.

'You will want to see your chamber.' I rose from my chair and rustled off the piazza without waiting for Maxine. When I reached the door, Maxine jumped to her feet, smiled fleetingly to Jem, and glided after me, her heavy skirt dragging across the floor.

Inside the house, I told Ladybelle to show Maxine up to the guest chamber. I waited downstairs so I could watch what Jem would do. He leaned against the centre column and gazed out across the drive to the live oaks that shielded the house from the trail. There was a smile of contentment on his face.

He broke into a shout. 'Garland! Dam' Garland! Where's that fancy nigra?'

'Yassa.' Garland stood obediently behind him. Jem spun around. He glared at Garland briefly then put out his hand and plucked the stock out of his vest.

'You better get out o' that buckeroo's toggery, boy, before I tear off every shred with my own hands. You look better dressed than me!'

'Yassa.'

'And tell Ferret to come to me at once. I want to see how Maddocks functioned in my absence. Run now, boy, don't dawdle. If I catch you yapping to a wench I'll have you strung up and beaten, fancy house nigra or not.'

Ferret's report to Jem did not seem to disturb him for he made no reference to it during the uneasy dinner which he shared with Maxine and me. I was in a state of suspense awaiting his accusations about my interference in plantation affairs. Maxine and Jem laughed a lot about private incidents while I fumed inwardly at the attention Jem was giving her and which he had never shown me since we were married.

Jem's concern for his sister seemed to grow during the next few days and whenever he was in the house she sat with him. I chose to avoid her whenever possible and by mutual – and unspoken – agreement, we drew up areas of personal preserves. Maxine took over the ladies' parlour while I used the sewing room. I refused to enter her chamber and she stayed out of mine. When I sat on the piazza, she retreated to the main parlour. Even meals became exercises in discretion which set Mammy Mable to grumbling. If I found Maxine at the table when I descended, I would plead a headache and retreat upstairs to take my dinner in my boudoir. On the other hand, if I seated myself at the table first, Maxine sent word that she would not be taking dinner that day.

Jem hardly noticed the animosity between us. The cotton season was reaching its peak, which meant that he spent little time in the house.

One morning, I was moved by his neglect to ride out into the fields to find him. The plantation was transformed by the cotton in full bloom. Even the field slaves appeared livelier and appreciative of its beauty, greeting me with broad smiles. The cotton seemed to be purity itself, like a vast spread of light new-fallen snow. The Maddocks cotton was about four feet in height, each stalk burdened with a great many branches shooting out in all directions and overlapping each other above the furrows.

Jem seemed ecstatic with the prospect of a spectacular crop. I reined in my horse in the shadow of Ferret's house while Jem and Ferret talked. Jem saw I was there waiting for him, but he made no effort to finish his business and come to me.

'Get this crop in, Ferret,' he bellowed, gesturing at the field of swaying cotton behind the overseer's compound, 'and I'll wager we'll have the biggest crop of the county.'

Ferret nodded his head dourly. 'It depends on the weather now, Marse Jem. If it rains before we've picked it all, we're lost.'

'Rain? It ain't never rained in the cotton pickin' season.'

'Aye, but how we goin' pick all this cotton in the few weeks before it does rain?'

'You always managed it for Uncle Leo.'

' 'Tis true, sir. But this year we've more cotton and the same amount of nigras.'

'We ain't gettin' more nigras, Ferret.'

'No, sir.'

'You must make the ones we have work harder. They're too dam' lazy anyway. You're fortunate my wife's reform in the hothouse means you can send the sick nigras back to the fields quicker! Aye, send the whelps into the fields too. Any creature with two hands and two legs can pick cotton so long as you drive 'em proper.'

'We'll try, sir.'

'The devil you will! Get me a bonus crop, Ferret, and there'll be a bonus for you and Goodpaster and even Wayne.' Jem leaned across the neck of his horse and lowered his voice as he spoke to Ferret.

'I have, eh, well, you know, a number of commitments on this crop. It's spoken for already, you understand, and any extra we pick will be extra for me, and for you too, of course. I know you won't let me down. My position depends on it.'

'I won't sir, I won't.

Jem rode away from Ferret without a backward glance at me. I had wanted to talk to him about Maxine, to ask how long he intended to keep her at Maddocks, poisoning the calm of the house and shattering my security with her presence. I had no doubt Maxine meant mischief. The way she gloated when I passed her on the stairs and the questions she asked the house slaves about my habits indicated she had some malicious purpose. I sensed it, but did Jem?

The army of Maddocks slaves soon descended on the cotton to devour it, shredding the bushes like locusts.

An hour before dawn each day the horn was blown. The blacks dragged themselves out of their shacks, swilled down their coffee, and with one gourd filled with water and another with cold bacon and corn cake, plodded to the fields.

The pace of work Ferret and Goodpaster inflicted on them was merciless. Any slave who was idle for a moment was flogged. With the exception of a ten-minute break given to them at noon to gobble their allowances of cold bacon, the slaves were not permitted to rest until it was too dark to see. When the moon was full, picking continued until the middle of the night.

Each slave was given a sack which he fastened around his neck at chest height to hold the cotton. He was also given a large basket to leave at the end of his row of cotton for filling from his sack. Two slaves attacked either side of a row of cotton, gathering all that had blossomed and leaving the unopened bolls for the next picking. It was necessary for the slaves to exercise care going through the field because if they broke any branches, the remaining cotton would not bloom.

Wayne was enlisted to help Ferret and Goodpaster see that each slave picked his alloted amount. The fittest were expected to bring in two hundred pounds a day. If anyone brought less when the cotton was weighed, the unfortunate slave was stripped, made to lie on the ground with his face pressed into the soil, and lashed by his gang driver. Sometimes the driver himself had the ironic honour of being whipped by Goodpaster if his gang had performed badly.

To me it seemed that valuable time was being wasted on these whippings, but Ferret insisted that no work could be done without the lash as the reward for 'nigra contrariness,' as he called it. If a dry leaf or a piece of boll was found in a slave's cotton, or the slave broke a branch in the field, he was given twenty-five lashes. 'A mere brush' said Goodpaster. Fifty lashes went to slaves who were hesitant and a hundred lashes greeted the slave who was idle.

Even at nightfall, the day at Maddocks was not

finished. The whites had to supervise the ginning of the cotton. Maddocks had a gin machine but Ferret declared it could not work as fast as the fingers of a field nigra. Every one of them was compelled to gin a shoe full of cotton before going to bed. It was midnight before the slaves were herded back to their quarters.

We began to pray for rain. Not I alone, but the slaves as well. Jem was obsessed with gathering every ounce of cotton that could be plucked from the fields. He even worked alongside the slaves himself – if riding around on horseback shouting and slashing indiscriminately at them could be called working. Jem ordered Garland to follow him, thus denying me the only companion I had in the house. Sometimes, Garland had to pick in the fields himself if Jem thought the picking was not going fast enough.

I wondered how Garland would react to the pressure Jem began to put on him. It was unheard-of for a house slave to have to pick cotton with the field slaves, but Garland went about the task without a scowl. The house maids were sent to the fields as well and only Mammy Mable and Ladybelle remained with me and the vixen Maxine.

Over the weeks, there was no one at Maddocks who was not heartily sick of cotton. Jem's talk of a bonus for the whites began to lose appeal, even for Ferret. Every day, when we pried ourselves from our beds, our eyes gazed skyward. Would it never rain? Would the picking never end?

I was sitting alone on the piazza in the afternoon while the sun was poised behind the oaks ready to descend and set beyond the glistening fields, when a weary figure stumbled up the steps. His features were hardened and grimy and his mop of fair hair was thick with cotton dust. He flopped into the chair beside me without a greeting.

'Wayne! You look like death!'

He grunted and raised his glazed eyes toward my face. 'You see what I do for you, Fleur? Ah, your innocence is my reward.'

'Don't be silly, Wayne,' I murmured, feeling my spirit soar at what I assumed was a compliment. 'I'll call Trott to bring you a whiskey.'

He nodded without speaking and I ran inside the house for Trott. Wayne was dozing when I returned, his rugged face lolling forward on his chest. In spite of his tough exterior, he looked strangely vulnerable at that moment. He jerked his head back quickly when Trott called his name and proffered the whiskey jar.

I perched lightly on the edge of my chair. 'It's nice to see you, Wayne, even though you are so tired and workworn.'

'Where's Jem's sister?' he asked with apparent distaste.

'Why, if I'm here on the piazza, then she'll be in the parlour.'

'You don't relish her company?' Wayne raised his eyebrow and watched me mockingly.

'No, I don't. Jem adores her, of course, but she's not my choice for a sister-in-law.'

'Yes, Ladybelle told me.'

'Ladybelle! Do you discuss all my affairs with the servants?'

'I see Ladybelle from time to time. I have to if I'm to know what you're doing.'

'Me? I'm doing nothing but what a dutiful mistress of Maddocks should be doing.'

'And your husband?'

I frowned. 'My husband?' I repeated.

Wayne leaned forward and seized my hands, his weary eyes brightening with urgency. 'Fleur, don't you know what's going on in this house?'

'Of course I do, Wayne. Maddocks is mine.'

'Maddocks may be yours now, Fleur, but watch Jem. And his sister. Ladybelle has told me about them. Maxine spends hours with him, closeted in his chamber muttering and murmuring. Don't protest Fleur, listen to me.

'At Hayard's Hall, Ladybelle was Maxine's maid. They were as thick as thieves but Ladybelle tells me Maxine ignores her now. She says it's because Maxine is trying to hide something from her.'

'Ladybelle is such a gossip, I'm not surprised.'

'It's not that, Fleur,' Wayne squeezed my fingers. 'Tittle-tattle doesn't worry a woman like Maxine. She and Jem are up to something. You must beware of them Promise me, you'll take care.'

CHAPTER TWENTY-FOUR

A few days after Wayne accosted me on the piazza, I ventured into the backyard intending to plan the day's dinner with Mammy Mable. The dogs were tussling in the yard. Those Jem kept for hunting runaway slaves were leashed to stakes while the others, presumably more friendly, growled and roamed at will. Two of them jumped at me and I slapped them down quickly.

'Oh go away!' I cried, trying to fend off their dusty paws from soiling my dress. The dogs must have thought I was teasing them, for they leapt at me again. 'Mammy Mable!' I called, 'the dogs – ' I tried to dodge them, but more of them came. I suppose they found a lady in a flowing gown fine sport. I was getting nervous, clutching my skirt up with one hand and trying to brush off the dogs with the other.

'Mash!' The loud shout had a magical effect. The dogs suddenly fell to the ground and slunk away, whining and watching me anxiously.

I gazed at the kitchen. Garland was standing in the doorway, his huge frame blocking the entrance. He was naked to his waist, his chest glistening with perspiration like dew on polished mahogany. He wore tattered breeches and was barefoot. His crisp black hair was covered with a mist of cotton dust and his face showed the effects of his ceaseless toil in the fields. He was gnawing a smoked chicken and his eyes twinkled as he watched me.

'Thank you, Garland!' I sighed with relief.

Garland threw a bone to the ground and the dogs snatched it, watching him uneasily. He handed the rest of the chicken inside the kitchen where Mammy Mable took it. He stepped toward me and Mammy Mable joined him, smiling.

'Wha' de mistis wan' in de kitchen, Missy?' she asked.

'Mammy Mable,' I answered. 'There wasn't a maid in the house to send for you. There's a book I need on the highest shelf in the library, Garland will have to get it down for me.'

'He ain' gwine in de house lek dat!' Mammy Mable gawked. 'I gwine sen' Trott when he come from de chill house.'

'Very well,' I agreed. 'Then, Garland, you will escort me around the house to the shade of the piazza. I don't want to be set upon by those dreadful dogs again.'

Mammy wiped her hands on her apron. 'Yo' otten be scare' de dogs. Dey jus' playin'.' Her face was conspiratorial as she watched us.

I followed Garland out of the yard along the path beside the flower garden which Uncle had nurtured so lovingly. It was another day of blistering heat, and even in the shade from the house I could feel the perspiration beginning to flow under my basque. I dabbed my face with my kerchief. Garland ambled in front of me, his broad shoulders smooth as marble, his muscles rippling.

'Garland! It's so hot,' I panted. 'You walk too fast for me.'

He paused and stood to the side for me to catch up with him. His deep voice was like a caress. 'I'm sorry, Miss Fleur.'

We were in a cool spot, where a light breeze ruffled the vines and an oak tree threw a branch of shade across the path. 'Garland, I don't remember when I saw you last. That wretched cotton!'

'The picking's nearly done, Miss Fleur. Marse Jem sent me to tell Mammy Mable to send a jar of whiskey for the overseers this afternoon.'

'I'm so glad. You'll be able to visit me again soon. There's such a lot I want to ask you.' My heart seemed to lurch a little when I raised my eyes and saw Garland staring down at me. I lowered my head quickly, confused by the prickle of blood I felt rushing to my cheeks. 'Oh!' I gasped to hide my embarrassment. 'The heat!'

'I know, Miss Fleur.' His voice was so reassuring. It seemed he really did understand.

Perhaps the heat actually was affecting me, for I rambled on without thought of the consequences. 'Maxine's troubling me. I'm frightened of her, Garland, but I don't really know why. But sometimes her remarks are quite spiteful, and Wayne has warned me to beware of her.'

A frown shadowed Garland's face. 'Marse Wayne is probably right, Miss Fleur. Miss Maxine and Marse Jem are mighty close.'

I looked up at Garland curiously. His face was impassive but something in his voice hinted at a meaning I did not understand. I chased the thought from my mind and put my hand on his arm. I squeezed it. 'Garland, I've missed you these past few weeks.'

'Yas, Mistis!' He coughed loudly, startling me. I dropped my hand and looked at the piazza.

Maxine was standing at the end, leaning against the corner column and smiling provocatively. She brushed her hand through her bright red locks which shimmered in the sunlight. I heard Garland murmur and when I looked back at him he had turned and was hurrying back to the cotton fields.

Maxine's taunting voice jarred me. 'Strange company you keep, Fleur.' I gathered my skirt and bustled toward her, passing in front of the house and up the piazza steps. I approached her and faced her directly. She looked very cool in her robe of blue silk, her neck quite bare, shielded only by her red hair.

I said crossly. 'I am mistress here and must sometimes address my slaves.'

'Address, yes.' Maxine murmured with a leer. 'But not caress. You were stroking that nigra's arm!'

'Fiddlesticks, Maxine! I touched him to make him pay attention.'

'Oh, I'm sure.'

'I intend to ask Jem to encourage him. He wants to study.'

'They all do, Fleur. It's this wave of liberation breaking on the shores of the South. The nigras feel the vibrations and the next thing they want is education.' Maxine's husky voice dipped with scorn. 'I've seen them posturing in the North, Fleur. There is nothing more ridiculous than an educated nigra!'

'You find it ridiculous for a slave to want to improve himself?'

'Of course, Fleur.' Maxine's eyes glinted with malice. 'There's only one thing nigras are good for and it ain't book learning!'

I ran from the piazza and up the stairs to my room, my cheeks burning.

A ruckus on the piazza disturbed me as I was arranging flowers in the dining room later that day. I hurried outside to see what the commotion was about. Jem was standing in the centre surrounded by Goodpaster, Ferret, and Wayne. They had their hands clasped around one another's shoulders and all, except Wayne, were crowing drunkenly. A retinue of black slave drivers stood in the courtyard exchanging banter with them.

'Ah done dribe de hardes', Marse Jem, sah!' cried one burly fellow with the scars of the lash etched into his fleshy shoulders.

'Nossah! Yuh buck Gray done get yo' mo' cotton from dem nigras!' The driver pushed the other away and pranced in front of the piazza like a child.

Jem and Ferret bellowed with laughter. 'Come boy!' Jem called, crouching at the edge of the verandah with the whiskey jar in his hand. The Negro ran over and stood with his head tilted back and his mouth open while Jem tipped whiskey down his throat.

'Me sah, me sah!' shouted the rest of the drivers, all naked except for their breechcloths. They jostled one another for a turn at Jem's whiskey fountain while Jem shook with mirth.

'Dam'me, if I ain't got the fastes' cotton-pickin' nigras in the whole county!' He jerked back the whiskey jar and thrust it at Wayne. With a shout, he tugged off his hat and sent it spinning into the air, whooping like a child. Ferret, not to be outdone, started bobbing and weaving in excitement. A grin of triumph was fixed on his lean face. Goodpaster mopped his brick-red brow while I stared, stunned by the realisation that we had at last reached the end of the cotton picking.

'Y'all done well, Ferret!' Jem clasped his arm around the overseer's grotesque shoulder. 'I knew you were the best dam' overseer in the county. Forest at Hayard's Hall ain't even half way through his pickin' yet, and he ain't got as much as we.'

Ferret stopped jigging. 'Y'all be payin' the bonus yo' spoke of, Mister Jem?' His tired eyes watched Jem closely.

'Bonus?' Jem paused and glanced quickly at the others before gazing out across the courtyard to the shorn fields. 'Bonus? Why yes, of course. As soon as I've sold the crop. How many bales do we have, Ferret?'

'Nigh on seven hundred.'

'Seven hundred!' Jem frowned, obviously trying to calculate the value of the crop.

'That's two hundred more than last year.' Ferret's wheedling tone passed over Jem's head.

'And we only lost six nigras,' gloated Goodpaster.

'Six!' I exclaimed. 'That's six lives! And how many sick and dying because of the lashes you gave them? Just to pick seven hundred bales of cotton to pay Jem's debts!'

All the men spun around to face me, expressions of disbelief shattering their good humour. Out of the corner of my eye, I saw Wayne frowning furiously, shaking his head to discourage me from saying anything further.

Jem regarded me as though seeing me for the first time. 'That's right, Fleur,' he sneered. 'I'm glad you understand.' He spat on the ground in front of me, then clattered down the piazza steps, beckoning the others to follow.

Ferret and Goodpaster chased after him like frightened slaves; only Wayne hesitated, supporting himself on the column at the top of the steps while he gazed at me.

'Wayne, you're just like Ferret and the rest. Jem has you hanging on his coat tails for the sake of a few dollars.'

'No, Fleur – '

'Go to him, Wayne. What's the use?'

A flicker of anger shone in Wayne's eyes. His upper lip curled in a scornful smirk. 'Very well, Fleur, I will!' He lurched away from the column and down the steps running across the courtyard after the others.

With the cotton harvested, Jem wasted no time in leaving Maddocks. He told Trott, who relayed the news to me, that he was going to Savannah to arrange the sale of the cotton. I was not surprised that he hadn't bothered to tell me face to face. From the day he'd brought Maxine to Maddocks, he had almost ceased speaking to me at all.

With the frenzy of the cotton picking over, I drifted in a daze through each day awaiting only the visit of Garland to my boudoir at night. In my euphoria, I was lax with the house slaves and declined to be irked by the heat, the flies, or even Maxine.

Maxine and I continued to avoid each other; but when we were unable to do so, I tried to be polite and considerate. She watched me strangely, as though waiting for me to lash out at her and tear her red hair from its roots. I ignored her and dwelt on my plans for my evenings with Garland.

One night after I encountered Maxine returning from the kitchen compound, an odd look of guilt crossed her face. Then Garland's usual hour for visiting me came and went without a sign of him.

I cried myself to sleep that night, feeling more lonely than at any other time since I had come to Maddocks.

In the morning, I rose early. I knew that Garland had many duties to attend to on the plantation as well as in the house. I hoped to be able to send him a message before he left the kitchen compound.

I roused Ladybelle, watching her with exasperation as she dawdled over her toilet.

'Wha' yo' wan' me do, Mistis?' she pouted.

'Do you know where Garland sleeps?'

'Yas, Mistis.' Ladybelle rolled her eyes.

'Good, I want you to take him a letter.'

'A letter?' Ladybelle was aghast.

'Oh, don't worry, child.' I walked over to my writing desk and quickly penned a note. 'It is nothing of importance. But you must not show it to anyone but Garland. Do you understand?'

Ladybelle nodded, accepting the letter relucantly.

'If you deliver it safely, Ladybelle, I'll give you a petticoat.'

Ladybelle relaxed and hurried out of the room. She herself could not read but had enormous respect for the power of the written word. She held my note cautiously in case its contents might have some effect on her.

Perhaps her excitement at the nature of her errand made Ladybelle careless. I stood at the door of my room and watched her blunder down the staircase. To my horror the menacing figure of Maxine awaited her in the hall below.

'Ladybelle!' I called. 'Come back.'

Maxine put out her hand and grasped Ladybelle's wrist. 'Where are you hurrying to, wench?'

Ladybelle tried to hide the note in her skirt but Maxine's hand closed round it and plucked it from her.

'What is this?' She unfolded the paper quickly.

'Mistis Fleur sen' it for Garland! Give it back!' Ladybelle snatched at the note.

'Why, you little hussy!' cried Maxine. Unaware that I was watching, she moved over to the open door to read my letter by the morning light.

I started down the steps to comfort Ladybelle, who

had buried her face in her hands and was sobbing pitifully, her body partly on the floor, partly on the stairs. I did not look up until I crouched beside her. Maxine was still at the piazza door, staring at me boldly. Her lips quirked in a defiant smile. Without a word she slipped the letter into her corsage and turned away, her heels clicking on the tiles of the piazza.

For the whole morning, I fumed in my chamber. I vowed that when Jem came home I was going to discuss his sister's presence at Maddocks with him. Either Maxine must stop interfering in my affairs or she must go! My friendship with Garland was no concern of hers.

I was roused from my speculation by the sound of a horse pounding up the drive. Jem galloped into the courtyard. He shouted with glee at Maxine who was ensconced on the piazza. I gathered my skirts about me and hastened down the stairs to greet him.

Garland held open the door onto the piazza. There was no opportunity for me to speak to him but I gazed quickly into his eyes. They were dark and expressionless. He wore an old livery bursting at the seams and his face seemed haggard. I realised that he had dressed this way to avoid arousing Jem's ire.

Jem was in high spirits. He was joking with Maxine when I swept onto the piazza. I tried to embrace him but he fended me off and turned to Maxine with a laugh.

Winking at Maxine, Jem said, 'Anxious for news from Savannah, Fleur?'

'Of course.' I sat down trying to make the best of a bad situation. 'Did you get a good sale for the cotton?'

'A fair one!' Jem took a glass of whiskey from Garland without glancing at him. 'Not quite as good as I expected. But it's in cash.'

'I hope it's enough to buy tools. You need more plows and hoes, better quality than last year.'

There was a pause as Jem watched me curiously. 'Such matters shouldn't concern you, Fleur.'

'Oh, but they do. Wayne has been telling me how Ferret wasted money buying inferior tools that made it difficult for the slaves to work. If you buy better equipment won't they work better?'

Jem coughed impatiently. 'I'll worry about that, Fleur. I'm to deliver the cotton in two weeks and will collect the cash on delivery.'

'You're going away again?'

'I have to, my dear.' Jem paced the piazza restlessly. 'I've had an offer for some slaves as well. Imagine, two thousand dollars for a nigra!'

'Two thousand!' It was Maxine who exclaimed, sitting forward on the edge of her chair. 'How I wish I had some to sell!'

'That's for a skilled boy, of course, like the one Wayne has with him in the forge.'

'I don't think I want to sell any slaves, Jem,' I said coolly.

'What!' Jem halted in his circuit of the piazza and stared at me, his eyes blistered with resentment.

'The slaves, Jem, we don't need to sell them do we? Won't the cotton give us enough money?'

'Fleur!' Jem strode quickly across the piazza and stood in front of my chair, resting the palms of his hands on its arms and glaring into my eyes.

'Perhaps you don't understand. I could only get a modest price for the cotton, barely enough to support Maddocks for the year. We must sell some slaves to raise more money. Besides, we've too many dam' nigras to feed.' He stood up decisively, appearing to have closed the matter in his own mind.

My lips tightened with determination. 'No, Jem. A few weeks ago, I heard Ferret tell you we don't have enough hands for the cotton; now you say we have too many. Uncle Leo didn't like selling his slaves; he said they belonged here at Maddocks. That's what I think, too.'

Jem grimaced at Maxine, not realising that I saw him. He turned back to me and flashed a shallow smile. 'Very well, Fleur. As you say, we'll discuss it another time.'

'We certainly shall. I'm adamant.' I surprised myself by the forceful tone of my voice. I doubted if Jem was telling the truth. I knew that cotton was fetching an all-time high price in Savannah. Ferret and Goodpaster had checked for themselves through friends in Milledgeville because they were concerned about their bonus.

'I want to see you later, Jem. Alone.'

'By the devil, Fleur, that's the stuff!' Jem bounded to my side and perched himself on the arm of my chair, wrapping his arm around my shoulders. 'Whatever you say, my dear!' He squeezed me, but his blatant attempt to charm away my objections to his scheme did not fool me.

I struggled. 'Do stop it, Jem. Maxine – '

'Maxine ain't shocked, Fleur. Come on, where is my welcome home?'

'Jem, you'll break the chair.' I didn't know what to do under Jem's assault. Maxine rose and walked to the edge of the piazza, leaning against a column and gazing out at the grey skies which hung over the plantation.

'Ain't you pleased to have me back at Maddocks?' Jem teased.

'Oh yes, I am.'

'Fine. I've arranged a little diversion, Fleur. To celebrate our first cotton crop.'

Jem's humour in contrast to the meanness of his usual mood troubled me. I knew his display of affection was only to fool me. 'What diversion?' I asked cautiously.

'A real bust, Fleur. A gander pulling.'

'A gander pulling!' Maxine squealed and clapped her hands with excitement, turning away from the columns. 'Oh, when, when? Do tell me.'

'Whatever is it?' I was intrigued.

'Ha! You'll see my dear. A county sport! I've arranged it with Ferret already. For tomorrow.'

'Oh!' Maxine gasped, her hand flying to her hair. 'Where will it be?'

'Why here, of course. At Maddocks. In the overseer's compound.'

As Jem whirled and clattered down the steps I called to him. 'Will I see you tonight?'

'Maybe,' he retorted grouchily. 'Maybe.'

Jem did not return for dinner or for supper. Garland had disappeared too, but I assumed he was with Jem. Maxine retreated to her own territory and remained in her chamber so I was not worried about bumping into her. The evening darkness cast vast shadows in the corridors and the lonely rooms but I drew comfort from them as I wandered about with my solitary candle flickering before me.

The slaves were in awe of Maddocks at night but the house made me brave, not frightened, and its very existence gave me strength. I loved Maddocks when it was overwhelmed with darkness. An aura of half-forgotten memories, the smells of polished mahogany and sandalwood, and the trapped warmth from the sun in summer, and the log fires in the winter. For me, Uncle Leo still lived in the clocks, paintings, and ornaments with which he had endowed the house. His presence was a friendly one which brought me comfort and consolation.

I sat down in the sewing room to listen for Jem. The candle was my only companion. I stared at the dim flame that barely broke the curtain of darkness in the room. The door opened and I looked up expectantly.

'You have no lanterns burning. Are you all right?'

'Oh!' My eyes clouded over. 'Wayne! I thought you were my husband.'

'Your husband!' Wayne spat out the words with disgust and flung them back in my face. 'You know nothing about your husband, Fleur. Your marriage is a mockery and your husband is swindling you!'

Wayne glared at me from the doorway and I watched him without speaking, unable to grasp what he was saying.

'Oh, you may sit there as pretty as a night sprite, Fleur, seeking solace from loneliness in Maddocks. But I care what he's doing even if you don't. Jem isn't going to gyp me out of what is mine.'

Wayne came close until his face was lit by the candle.

I remembered how I had first seen him in Ma Drax's slave camp, reflected in the light of the campfire. He had looked young and hopeful then, his eyes bright with confidence. The face that watched me now was riddled with bitterness and disillusionment.

'What did Jem tell you about his trip to Savannah?' Wayne persisted. 'That he got a low price for the cotton, right? You know that's a lie, I can see it in your eyes.'

Wayne spread his hands and walked quickly around the sewing room, moving in and out of the candle glow like a captive moth. 'The cotton house is packed to overflowin' with bales. You know what Jem told his precious sister Maxine. No, you wouldn't know, would you? Ladybelle knows. She heard him say that Maddocks had saved him and made him a fortune.'

'If it has made a fortune, Wayne, it's not Jem's. The cotton belongs to Maddocks. I intend to use some of that money to build a proper hospital. I'll talk to Jem about it.'

Wayne twisted about in exasperation. 'You're deceived, Fleur!' His voice grated harshly in the gentle atmosphere of the darkened sewing room. 'You know Jem doesn't love you. He only humours you to get Maddocks. He steals from you, Fleur. Don't you understand? He wants to steal from me too by not paying me my bonus! I won't tolerate that even if it means nothing to you that he plans to swindle you and keep all the cotton money for himself!'

Wayne's face was flushed with anger as he stared down at me. 'It's true, dam'me, it's true,' he shouted when he saw how calm I remained. I held up my hand to quiet him. 'I know Jem doesn't love me, Wayne, but he *is* my husband.'

'Oh Fleur!' Wayne suddenly toppled to his knees and placed his hands on the arms of my chair, trapping me. 'How can you live like this when I love you!'

I tilted my head to one side, looking straight through him but seeing nothing.

'Do you hear me, Fleur? I love you!'

'It's a love I can't accept when I have a husband, Wayne.'

'Your husband! Do you know where he is now?'

'No.' I stared at him anxiously. I had been awaiting Jem the whole evening. I was sure he had not come into the house without my noticing.

'You'll find your precious Jem in Maxine's boudoir. In her bed, Fleur!'

'No! That's impossible. How can you say such a thing! Get out! Get out!' My mind reeled at Wayne's remark. 'I hate you. You're mean and sly. Go on! Get out!'

I jumped out of my seat in a rage. Wayne fell backward to the floor. 'It's not true! I'll show you it's not true!' I rushed out of the room, my wide skirt brushing against the occasional table knocking the candle onto Wayne's face. He shouted as the hot wax scorched his cheek.

I fumbled my way through the ladies' parlour, ignoring Wayne's shouts. Another trip-table crashed to the floor. I flung open the door to the corridor and groped my way to the stairs. 'No! No!' I was muttering to myself with fright.

There was a lamp burning in the alcove at the top of the stairs. I seized it and threw open the door to Jem's room. It was empty. I bit my lip with relief. No! No! I reflected trembling as I turned away from Jem's door and raced to Maxine's chamber.

The door was open. I stared in amazement. Maxine was standing in the doorway, her face impassive. Her only clothing was her cambric and lace *robe de nuit.* Her red hair fell loosely over her shoulders. Her eyes blazed with contempt. She stepped aside and I peered into the room. Jem, utterly naked, lay on top of her bed.

I plunged my face into my hands, squeezing the palms in my eyes, trying to obliterate the ugly scene from my mind.

'Please don't get overwrought, dear Fleur!' Maxine crooned with menace. 'I heard what Wayne was shouting. It's quite true. You would have discovered it long before this if you hadn't been mooning over your nigra paramour all the time.'

'I don't believe it,' I muttered. 'You're his sister!'

'Oh yes, I am. It helps build a much stronger relationship don't you think? You see, Jem and I are the same class, the plantocracy. You're a slut from the Savannah waterfront, giving yourself airs. You could never understand Jem, nor really love him.'

I felt something deep within me flicker and die. I staggered away from Maxine as if felled by a blow. I leaned against her boudoir table and stared speechless. Jem, on the bed, smiled nervously.

'Accept it, Fleur, you can't do anything to stop us. Jem and I will stay here and you can do what you like, leave or die for all I care.'

I shook my head to clear it. 'No! No! You're going to leave here, Maxine. At once, tonight. You shan't have Jem, you shan't have Maddocks.' I was too angry for tears.

'You want to send me away, Fleur? Are you so blameless, yourself? Do you think you're fit to remain in Maddocks?' She plucked a piece of paper from the bosom of her night robe and brandished it in front of my nose. 'What about this?'

I was puzzled. 'What is it?'

'Do you forget, Fleur?' Maxine waved the paper at me like a swordsman in a duel.

'What is it?' I gasped.

'Now you're curious?' Maxine gloated. 'If you want me to leave Maddocks, Fleur, think what the county will say when they hear what is written on this paper.' She waved it again in my direction. 'It's your letter, Fleur. From a lady to her slave. From you to Garland.'

'There's nothing wrong in that!' I snapped.

'No? What do you think, Jem? Have you ever heard of a mistress writing to her slave? Writing! A slave who can read is very dangerous in these times. Slaves have been put to death for less.'

'You wouldn't touch Garland!' I countered.

Maxine grinned at Jem, arching her eyebrow. 'You see, Jem? I don't think I'm to leave Maddocks, do you?'

'What does the letter say?' Jem drawled, flaunting

his nakedness at me. I blanched and turned away.

Maxine shrugged her shoulders. 'It's of small consequence, Jem. But it exists, and in *such* tones! "I yearn for your company, Garland!" Your pretty innocent wife writes to a nigra. A mistress – your wife – yearning for her slave, Jem? What does it mean?'

'It's perfectly innocent!' My voice gained strength as I turned to Jem. 'Garland must not be harmed. He has done nothing, I swear it. You can have Maxine at Maddocks and I'll say nothing. But you must never do anything to harm Garland.'

Maxine exulted with mock kindness. She folded the letter carefully and poked it back into the folds of her night dress. 'How sweet you are Fleur! It's touching to see you want to protect a nigra. Although I suppose you have your reasons?'

She glided over to the bed and sat down beside Jem. 'I was giving Jem a massage, Fleur. He is so tired after his journey. Do you want to watch?' Maxine's hands touched Jem's waist, her long red hair brushing his chest as she leaned over him.

I hurried from the room.

Book Three

'THE SOUTH HAS ONLY TRADITION'

Winter 1859–Fall 1860

CHAPTER TWENTY-FIVE

The gander pulling began at dusk the next day. Crackers from the whole neighbourhood were crammed into the yard in front of Ferret's cabin. Jem sent down a cask of whiskey and Goodpaster sat himself beside it, ladling out the liquor like a bloated patriarch. From his florid cheeks it was obvious he had already sampled the whiskey's quality and found it satisfactory.

'Ain't no one here gonna shay Jem Hayard ain't the best planter in the whole of Pashton County!' he challenged. 'Y'all know that, eh Ferret?'

'Sure do, Goodie!' Ferret swayed on the verandah and clutched the railing for support.

I stood by the side of Ferret's cabin in the shadows, smiling bitterly to myself. Goodpaster and Ferret would have more to think about when they discovered Jem was cheating them and had no intention of paying the bonus they expected.

I had left the house to avoid Jem and Maxine. They were whispering together in front of the fire in the parlour and it was too cold for me to sit on the piazza. I was desperate to see Garland. Ladybelle reported she could not find him. Mammy Mable preserved a dignified silence, making me feel I had somehow offended her. I was desolate. It seemed that no one cared about me.

I glanced at the crowd, hoping to find Garland there. A slave was walking over to the tree in the centre of the yard with a wild goose tucked under his arm. This was the gander, the excuse for the festivity Jem had arranged. The bird had a very long neck, broad where it rose above the breast but tapering gradually until it became small and serpent-like with a slim head and peaked bill. The head and neck were lubricated with oil.

Lanterns and flambeaux were lit around the yard. It was quite dark now, so I knew no one would see me. I watched as the Negro, one of Ferret's drivers, climbed on a bench and fastened the gander from a limb of the tree by a cord which secured its legs. Finding itself suspended ten feet from the ground the poor gander flapped its wings in surprise and raised its long neck to see what was in store. The crowd bawled with anticipation. The driver removed his bench to the side of the tree where a boy stood with a long whip in his hand.

'I'm the first' shouted Ferret, capering off his verandah and leaping for the horse which Hannibal was holding. He mounted safely and the crowd fell back so he had a clear run up to the tree. Ferret dug in his heels and raced at the spinning bird, holding out his hand to grasp it.

'Now! ' yelled the driver.

The boy cut down with his whip on the rump of Ferret's horse. The animal bolted at the moment Ferret grabbed for the gander. He seized the neck but the horse galloped on and the bird, being well oiled and with so small a head, slipped out of Ferret's reach. The crackers howled with delight.

'Jem, yo' sure have the best busts in the county,' crowed a cracker. I caught sight of Jem riding into the yard, surrounded by a host of lickspittles, as Uncle called them, drooling with too much whiskey.

Jem waved. 'The one who pulls his neck off gets the gander!' he shouted. 'And as much whiskey as he can drink!'

The men pushed around Jem, laughing and calling out his name. His face flushed and he allowed himself to be dragged off his horse. As he fell into the arms of the crackers, his eyes suddenly latched onto mine. I turned away quickly as another man grappled the neck of the gander and let it slip through his fingers.

'Fleur,' a voice called to me softly from the magnolias behind the cabin.

'Who's there?' I whispered, peering into the leaves.

'Wayne,' the voice replied. 'Come, Fleur, quickly! Before Jem gets here.'

I frowned at the magnolias. I was wondering how I could face Wayne again. There was a chill wind blowing up and I fastened my cloak around me and walked slowly toward the bushes.

Wayne emerged and stood in front of me, blocking the path. Behind me I could hear the shouts from the crowd but otherwise the night was strangely quiet.

'Don't speak, Wayne. You were right, I was wrong. I'm sorry.'

'Send her away, Fleur.'

'I can't.'

Wayne didn't ask why. His eyes were staring at me in the darkness. 'Come with me then, Fleur. We'll go away together.'

'Oh no!' I took a step backward. 'That's what they want! I won't do that. I won't leave Maddocks and Gar – ' I stopped, but it was too late.

'Garland!' Wayne spat on the ground close to my foot. 'You're in love with him!' he growled contemptuously.

'No!' My voice was sad.

'Say yes, Fleur. That's the only way you'll know what you're doing.'

'Doing?'

'Loving a slave, Fleur. Is that right?'

'I don't have to answer you, Wayne. I respect Garland, yes. He's more of a man than you or Jem. He has pride, grace, strength, and keen intelligence. If he weren't black and a slave, he could be a great man.'

'But he is black and a slave, Fleur!' Wayne tried to control his temper. 'And he is servile and gutless.'

'Wayne! I won't listen to anything against Garland. I've put him in danger by trying to help him. I must stay now to protect him.'

'You owe him nothing, Fleur.'

I raised my hand slowly and waved him into silence. 'Wayne, do you think you should stay at Maddocks? You aren't bonded. If you want to go I can give you money.'

'Are you trying to buy me off, Fleur?'

His words stunned me. I stared at him, biting my lip anxiously.

'I'm sorry, Fleur. Perhaps you're right. I'll only cause you unhappiness if I stay.'

'I'm not thinking about myself, Wayne. I ceased to do that last night. It's you. Jem will get revenge if he can.'

'I can look after myself!' Wayne clenched his fists. A shout behind us indicated that someone had succeeded in wresting the neck off the gander. 'Ain't nothing Jem going to do to hurt me, Fleur!'

'Wayne!' I turned away from him. 'I'm sorry.' My voice choked with tears. He made no move to stop me. I hastened along the path back to the house. The columns loomed in front of me. They reminded me of giant bars imprisoning the inhabitants in the traditions those columns represented. Uncle Leo had built Maddocks as he had modelled his life, in a fashionable style embracing the customs of the Georgia plantocracy as his own. Suddenly, I thought that by adopting me to succeed him. Uncle Leo had sentenced me; Maddocks was my jail.

The shock of the idea made me stop abruptly and gaze at the house. The moon hung in the night, a huge disc spilling its brilliant glow over the live oaks and onto the piazza. I withdrew into the shadows. Trott ambled onto the piazza and peered out into the night. Was Trott my jailor? Was Jem the judge and Maxine the executioner? My mind raced. If I entered Maddocks again would I ever escape from the convention which governed the South?

I hesitated only a moment before plunging into the undergrowth, ignoring the paths and oblivious to the brambles snagging my stockings and ripping my dress. My thoughts were confused. I knew only an overpowering desire to run from Jem Hayard and his sister and the misery they were bringing to me and Maddocks.

'Wayne! Wayne!' I cried when I reached the place where Wayne had asked me to flee with him. 'Wayne?'

My cries were swallowed up by the raucous shouts from the drunken crackers outside Ferret's cabin. I ran down the path toward the cotton house.

There was a lantern shining on the ground in front of the cotton store. I stopped at the edge of the coppice and peered at it. Two figures were crouched beside the lantern arguing softly. I sank to my knees, exhausted, my face scratched and my hair raddled. I had lost my bonnet and my dress was ripped and torn beyond repair.

I stared in dismay at the two shapes outlined by the light. One was Wayne; the other was Ladybelle.

Wayne was squatting on his haunches. He picked up the lantern and swung it toward the cotton house. Ladybelle grabbed his arm.

'Stop dat, Wayne. Come back to yuh cabin.'

'I ain't never goin' back. Jem tricked me. He tricked Fleur. It'll teach him a lesson.'

'No, Wayne!'

'No? Dam' you, Ladybelle. Take your hands off me.' He flailed at Ladybelle with his free arm. She dived for him, knocking the lantern out of his hand. It rolled away, spilling flames on the ground.

Ladybelle screamed. 'Out it, Wayne. Quick!'

I leaned back against a tree and watched the fire racing toward the cotton house door. Wayne had only to stamp on the flames to smother them before they did any damage.

I smiled to myself. Behind the door were the seven

hundred bales of cotton on which Jem and his sister had pinned their hopes of swindling me.

Wayne rose slowly to his feet and gripped Ladybelle by her shoulders. 'No, wench. Let it burn.'

Ladybelle struggled in his arms. 'Wayne – yo' be mad! Ah gwine call Jem!'

'No, you ain't!' Wayne cuffed her viciously across her mouth. 'You ain't callin' no one.'

Wayne hit Ladybelle again and hurled her to the ground. He fell on top of her. The flames began to leap higher, licking the old wooden boards of the store house door. Ladybelle began to scream but Wayne stuffed the hem of her dress in her mouth.

'No, Ladybelle.' I heard him mutter. 'Not a word from you till the cotton burns.'

The fire was creeping under the door. There was a roar as it tasted the dry cotton and leaped from bale to bale. The fire spread rapidly.

I was unable to move as the heat of the flames scorched my face and Wayne, in front of the burning door, plunged himself mercilessly into Ladybelle's writhing body.

'Mistis! Mistis!' Mammy Mable burst into my boudoir. I was staring at myself in the glass, puzzled why my face showed no sign of the terrible events I had witnessed. True, it was scratched and smeared with soot from the fire, but my eyes did not look harder nor my smile less innocent.

'Missy Fleur!' She flung her arms around me and looked down at my face. 'De cotton burning, de cotton burning!'

When she saw the cuts and bruises, she screamed. 'Mah Gawd! Wha' happened to you? Yuh face! Yuh robe, Missy! Yo' does look lek yo' be hurt bad, bad.'

I looked back at the glass and down at my hands and arms. Now, suddenly, I began to feel the pain of those last few moments. The shock of seeing Wayne and Ladybelle together had banished the foolish notion of my fleeing with Wayne. I wanted to be in the secure bosom of Maddocks again. I had rushed back to the house, my hair catching the leaves and twigs as I ran through the undergrowth, my dress and arms ripped by thorns and branches. Thank heaven, no one had seen me!

'Please help me clean up, Mammy Mable,' I urged, 'I must make myself presentable.'

'But de cotton house, Mistis Fleur. It a-burnin' one big hole in de sky. Don't you care, Mistis?'

'I know, Mammy. I was there.'

Mammy Mable stared at me for a moment but she was too concerned for my welfare to digest the meaning of my remark. 'So help me now, please.'

She fussed around, bathing my face, laying out a fresh gown, babbling comforting words all the time.

It was I who became impatient. I hurried out into the corridor and she followed me to the window at the back of the house. I threw it open defiantly and put my arm about her waist as we looked out together. The quick chill of the night air gripped my cheeks and I shivered, but whether it was from the cold or delayed shock, I didn't know. Flames lit up the horizon, throwing the live oaks which shielded the house into grotesque dancing silhouettes.

'Yo' wan' go out dere?' Mammy Mable's voice held a hint of excitement. 'Trott an' me will 'company yo', Missy. Garland does be wid de field slaves, dem runnin' to de creek fuh watah!'

I shook my head hopelessly. Leaving Mammy at the window, I returned to my boudoir, closed the door, latched it carefully, threw myself down on the bed and gazed in despair at the damask ceiling of the four-poster.

'Whom can I trust?' I muttered aloud. I had no friends left. I could depend only on Garland. He would never treat me the way I had been used by my husband. In every way he was the opposite to Jem.

The thought disturbed me. What had happened to me, I wondered – to be thinking of a Negro like this! I rolled my head from side to side on the bed. Garland's image would not fade from my mind. He was such a comfort when he was with me.

I grasped my pillow lying at the top of the bed. 'Garland.' I whispered. My body weakened when I pronounced his name. It was wrong, I knew, for me to consider a black man in such a passionate manner. Had not enough scandal invaded Maddocks without my contributing more?

I closed my eyes, giving way to the feeling of lonely desolation sweeping through me. I tried to think of Jem as I had first known him when he had seemed so fearless and charming. But all I could picture was Jem's smug smile as Maxine leaned over him the night before when he lay naked on her bed.

It was Garland's face I saw as I drifted off to sleep.

Maddocks was in an uproar the next morning. Jem's voice as he berated the slaves and even shouted at Maxine reverberated through the corridors of the house. Mammy Mable sent a girl up to help me dress and I hurried to prepare myself. I wanted to find Garland.

I was watching the slaves dolefully crossing the front drive on their way to work hoping to see Garland when Jem's voice suddenly sounded outside my door. I quickly composed myself and signaled to the girl to let him in.

'We'll have to sell the animals, the slaves, the furniture, Fleur!' he shouted at me as he strode into the room. I turned to him trying to appear indifferent, as though it were no concern of mine.

'Whatever for?'

'To live, of course! We have to pay for all this year's expenses and for next year's as well. We'll be forever in debt if we don't do something. It was bad enough before the cotton burned. Now we have nothing.'

'Please don't bother me with such things, Jem,' I said. 'You can ask Maxine to help you, but not me.'

Jem stared. 'That's fine coming from you! At least Maxine is white!'

'You misjudge me, Jem, but I do not misjudge you.'

'Fie!' Jem slapped his thigh. 'You say you care for Maddocks, Fleur. If you do, then agree to my selling the furniture and slaves to pay our debts.'

'I'm sure credit can be arranged through the bank in Milledgeville,' I snapped. 'Uncle Leo left enough security.'

'But that's all in your name, Fleur.'

'Yes, so it is.'

'Dam' me, Fleur! Am I to be forever shackled to your petticoats?'

'Perhaps you should have considered me before you invited Maxine back into your life!' I spoke brutally but the words brought tears to my eyes. I had loved Jem once and seeing him now so much in need of me stung my heart.

'You won't help?'

'I've told you, Jem. Management of the plantation is your concern. That agreement still stands.'

'Someone started the fire,' said Jem watching me strangely. 'It wasn't an accident.'

'You don't think I had anything to do with it, do you?'

'Wayne is missing.'

I shrugged. 'He wasn't bonded to Maddocks so he was free to go.'

'Where's Ladybelle?'

'I really don't know.' I stared at Jem defiantly. 'Mammy Mable hasn't been here today. She sent another girl to attend me this morning.'

'I see,' Jem paused to consider something. 'Wayne is gone and so is Ladybelle. She was his wench, or so I've heard. Doesn't that seem odd to you?'

'I hope they'll be happy!' I turned away from him, disgusted.

When I heard Jem's footsteps and the angry crunch of the door as he slammed it shut, I put my head in my hands and slumped in front of my mirror, the horrors of the past few days overwhelming me. I did not hear the door open, nor the footfall on the floor. A hand rested on my shoulder.

'Stop your crying, Miss Fleur. You're not really alone,' a deep tender voice assured me. 'I'll always take care of you.'

The face that swam into focus when I blinked was Garland's. His hand tightened its grip on my heaving shoulders. My misery shifted into suspense and I quivered at his touch. I knew it was wrong to encourage him, but I felt alone and helpless.

'Garland,' I breathed huskily. 'I'm so glad. I need you, Garland. I really do.'

'Then we can solve your problems, Missy Fleur,' he answered calmly, his eyes soft with compassion. 'I'm yours by the bond of slavery; I would also be yours by choice, if I were free to choose. If you have need of me. I'm here.'

'By choice?' I studied his face leaning over me. It was young and proud, like an African prince perhaps, but his eyes were sad and concerned. I reached up to touch his cheek.

'How soft your skin is!'

Garland looked puzzled. 'You're surprised?'

'I thought your skin would be hard to touch. Your face is as soft as mine.'

Garland grinned. 'Not like yours, Miss Fleur. Yours has the softness of cotton in bloom.'

'And if you touch it you'll find it's on fire like our own cotton. Garland, so much has happened! Where have you been?'

He suddenly turned his head away, avoiding my eyes.

'Garland, what is it?'

'I wanted to come before, Miss Fleur, I really did. I thought you didn't want to see me again.'

'You thought what!'

'That's why I came here now, to ask you why. I've never done anything to you which I shouldn't. Haven't I always respected you?'

'Yes, Garland, of course you have. I don't understand. Where did you get this idea from? I've wanted to see you so much. Sit down.'

'No, I can't Miss. Marse Jem has gone to look for Ferret and Goodpaster. I must go to see what he intends to do about the fire. He'll punish some of us for it, for sure.'

'You haven't told me, Garland. Look at me.' I put my hand up to touch his arm. 'What did I say to make you think I didn't want you to come again?'

'Nothing to me, that's why I found it strange. Why did you tell Miss Maxine that I must keep away from you? Why did you send her instead of telling me yourself?'

'Maxine!' I could not conceal my dismay.

'Yes, Miss Fleur. Is something wrong?'

'What did Maxine say?' I gasped.

'She told me that you had forbidden me to come to your boudoir again. She said it was a scandalous thing to do and that she would tell Marse Jem herself if I saw you again.'

'Garland, that's not true!' I gripped him around his waist and rested my head against his hard stomach. 'Maxine is a monster, Garland. She's trying to prevent my seeing you.'

Garland caressed my ringlets, his long fingers gently tracing the curves of my neck. 'Missy, I know about her and Marse Jem. I heard everything.'

'Oh Garland, what shall I do?'

'Be brave, Missy. Don't let Marse Jem and Miss Maxine rob you. You can fight them, Missy. I can't.'

'Yes, you can, Garland.'

'No. I feel for you, Missy, I do.' He wrenched his eyes from my gaze and wrung his hands in a futile gesture. 'But I'm not free, Missy. I must do what Marse Jem and Miss Maxine tell me.'

'Miss Maxine! Is it her commands you obey now, Garland?'

'She is persistent, Missy. She watches me more closely than Goodpaster guards his field slaves.'

I was surprised. 'Why? Jem promised me no harm will come to you.'

Garland snorted with scorn. 'A slave never trusts his master's word, Missy. It's Miss Maxine herself. She has some scheme for me, I think. She is forever ogling me with those large green eyes and fluttering her eyelashes and smiling at me, Missy.'

'Fiddlesticks, Garland. That's Maxine's nature, she's a wanton baggage. Take no notice of her, and don't believe anything she tells you.'

'I must go now, Missy.' He laid his hand on my arm, smiling broadly. 'Missy, you aren't sorry for yourself any more?'

'No, Garland. How can I be when you're with me? Won't you stay longer? I'm so confused!' I stood up facing him and laid my head on his chest. He did not move.

'I'll help you with Marse Jem and Missy Maxine,' he sighed. 'But remember, Missy, I'm a man just as you're a woman. I'm a Negro, but a Negro man. I have feelings like other men. I'm not a black stallion, Missy.'

'A stallion!' I dropped my hands quickly and stepped back from him. 'A stallion!' I gasped again. 'I don't understand.'

'I hope you don't, Missy. That's what Miss Maxine called me, a pedigree black stallion!'

'Oh, Garland!' My hands crept to his arms.

Garland smiled. 'A time will come when we can hold each other as equals.'

'Equals!' I shuddered and let my hands drop again to my side.

'Only when we are equal can I tell you the truth, Missy. Only then can I say how my heart aches whenever I think of you. Oh, so many things!' He stepped back and hung his head. 'But you are you and I am me,' he murmured so softly I could hardly hear. 'I am your slave, Missy Fleur, and you are my mistress. I do not own my body, even that is yours.'

His eyes were filled with sadness when he raised his face to gaze at me. 'Missy Fleur, I beg of you. Don't take me! You will destroy me.'

'No Garland, never.' I answered hastily, not understanding what he meant. My answer reassured him for the sadness vanished and his eyes flashed.

'Missy Fleur?' he held his hands out.

'Marse Jem says he is going to sell some slaves so that he can raise money. Is it true?'

'I really don't know what he plans to do, Garland.' I turned away and walked toward the window.

'Surely he can't sell slaves without your consent?'

'Oh, I do wish I had nothing more to do with Jem and Maxine!'

'You must do plenty with them! If you allow them to do as they please, you'll lose Maddocks.' He paused. 'And me.'

'Garland, is that a threat?' I was cross. 'Will you run away?'

He laughed.

'No Missy. Marse Jem says I'll be the first slave he'll sell.'

'He dare not!'

'Who will stop him, Missy?'

'I will of course!'

Garland frowned at the authority in my voice, then his face broadened until he was beaming proudly. He held his arms open again and I ran to him. I nestled against his massive chest.

'Now there is hope, Missy Fleur!'

I could feel Garland's heart thumping through the coarse shirt he was wearing. I raised my head to kiss his neck but his strong hands held me off.

'No, Missy. Let us wait. Let us wait until we are equal.'

CHAPTER TWENTY-SIX

I stared at the trees opposite the window for a long time after Garland had left me. The sky was overcast and its colour matched my melancholy. Garland filled my mind. He understood me better than anyone else. He knew how to get me to do what was best for me. He had manoeuvred me skilfully, playing on my emotions to get me to defy Jem and Maxine.

The squeal of carriage wheels below the window snapped me back to reality. I waited nervously.

'Mistis Fleur!' Mammy Mable's voice was firm. 'Marse Jem done send for yo'.'

'Indeed?' I swung around to face Mammy Mable and she smiled with pleasure at my appearance. I had brushed my hair and put rouge on my cheeks. My eyes sparkled with the assurance Garland's concern had given me.

Mammy's kind old eyes studied me and a slow smile widened her lips. She said, 'Lor' bless you', Miss. Ah sure does be happy seein' yo' look so good. Ah t'ought yo' was sick'nin' sittin' up here alone all mawnin'.' Her gentle fingertips caressed my face.

'Thank you, Mammy Mable. How could I ever get along without you! But who's our visitor?'

'Marse Granger, Mistis.'

Granger Hayard was sitting in the parlour. He scrambled to his feet and gave a courtly bow when I hurried into the room. Jem remained in his chair, scowling darkly. Maxine averted her eyes. They were red, but I was not certain whether she had been crying, or imbibing too freely from the whiskey jar. Her face was drawn and pale, her complexion made more sickly by the contrast with her bright red hair.

'Mister Granger, how nice of you to visit.' I was genuinely pleased to see him and hoped that it showed in my voice.

Granger Hayard sank back in his seat and stared at me. His white hair tumbled about his neck. There was a red mark etched into his forehead by the brim of his hat. He looked old and frail. Is this what Jem would look like in thirty years? Would Jem ever develop the kindly tolerance of his father?

'Would you care for a drink, Mister Granger?' I asked, taking a chair close to him.

'Jem's already sent for whiskey.' Granger's voice possessed a certain wry humour and the somewhat exaggerated charm of the Southern gentleman.

'Pa's here because of the fire,' Jem growled.

'I'm sorry it takes a misfortune to bring you to Maddocks, Mister Granger.'

'Humph!' he snorted. 'Seems like it will take a death for mah daughter-in-law to call on us at Hayard's Hall.'

'I rarely go out. There is so much to do here, especially with Jem away so often.'

Granger's eyes narrowed. 'You ain't neglectin' your wife, are you boy? I don't see no sign of a baby yet, Jem.'

'Oh, I'm not having a baby, Mister Granger.'

'Whyever not? Is Jem tom-cattin' around?' A lopsided smile took the sting from the words.

'I really don't know. Are you tom-cattin', Jem?' I smiled in Jem's direction but he was saved the embarrassment of a reply by Trott's loud entrance with the whiskey decanter.

Granger and Jem served themselves quickly. Maxine looked doubtfully at her father then reached for a glass and poured herself a measure. Granger appeared not to notice.

'Dammit,' he muttered, addressing Jem. 'You've been married long enough for Fleur to be in bloom by now.'

Jem shifted uneasily in his seat. Normally I would have blushed at such a remark, but it was said with too much humour to offend. Granger continued to rail at Jem.

'I aim to see mah grandsons before I die. Forest ain't got himself wed to Miss Vain yet and Maxine's got no chance of children now she's left her Yankee husband. It's up to you and Fleur to get on with it, Jem.'

'Mister Granger!' I exclaimed, alarmed at the old man's persistence. 'Please!'

'I know mah Jem's hot, young Fleur. He takes after his Pa. And I'm not so senile I don't know when a young miss has that light in her eyes. You had it for Jem, gal, and he for you.' Granger paused casting his eyes over me quickly.

'What happened, gal? That light's gone. Why ain't you bearin' me mah grandson?'

'You should ask your son, Mister Granger,' I retorted.

'Eh, Jem? Dam' me, you ain't foolin' around with the nigras, are you? Plenty of time for that when you've done your duty by your wife.'

'Pa! By the devil, why don't you shut up! You said you'd come about the fire.'

The old man shook his head, scratching his ear. 'Shut up? Is that how you speak to your own father?' He coughed softly. 'I saw your cotton house, or what's left of it. You're plumb cleaned out, ain't you?'

Jem nodded his head.

'Slaves can be mighty troublesome these days, boy. You don't know what they're going to do next.' The old man sucked his gums thoughtfully. 'I saw those men of yours, the red-faced baboon and the pickle-faced one. They were cuttin' up your nigras sump'n terrible.'

'You mean Ferret and Goodpaster.'

'You knows who I mean, Jem, I ask mahself, is it wise?'

'Wise, Pa? Dammit, all the cotton's gone.'

'Exactly, son. Carvin' up your nigras like those two men are doing ain't goin' to get the cotton back, is it? I say, is it wise?'

'They might tell us who did it.'

The old man shook his head. 'None of 'em know. If they did, they would've run. You should call your slave breakers off, Jem. You'll only get more trouble. It's in the air.'

'I don't think so. A good thrashing will teach them not to start anything for themselves.'

'Your men ain't thrashin' them, Jem. They're cuttin'. A tongue here, an ear there. That's butchery, and it'll bring you problems. I'm tellin' you.'

I cried out in dismay. 'No, Jem! Don't do that to the slaves. It's not their fault.'

'How do you know?' he snapped.

'I just know. The slaves will die if they're treated cruelly. We need every one we can get to plant next year's crop.'

'Gadzooks! Your wife is right, Jem. Take heed of what she tells you, boy. She has sense.'

'Pa, you were never accustomed to concern yourself with the nigras' welfare before!' Jem scowled.

'It's the times, son. I'm old, I've seen it all before. Nigras get uppity when they get pushed too far. An uppity nigra is a dangerous one.'

'That's Yankee twaddle! I never thought I'd hear that from you, Pa.'

'Maybe it is. But I tell you, boy, you've got to sway with the times. The South can't live without slavery. If we want to keep our nigras we got to treat them better, Jem. Like human beings.'

'You sound like Maxine's husband!'

'That varmint was a rogue and a thief, Jem. I ain't a Free-Soiler. I'm aimin' to keep Hayard Hall and if you've got any sense, you'll call off your pair of blood-letters and let your nigras be, before you have an insurrection on your hands.'

I stared at Granger Hayard with new respect.

'I don't understand you, Pa!' Jem was stalking across the floor, his face livid.

'No? Look at Kansas. Fightin' over slavery. I don't believe them Northerners worry about slavery for itself, Jem. It's the abuses that unsettles them. Make your nigras happy and where are you going to get criticism?'

I slipped out of the room before Jem answered. I ran upstairs, took my cape from my wardrobe, tightened my bonnet and headed downstairs for the door to the piazza.

I rushed down the steps and into the courtyard, clutching my skirt above my knees so that I could hurry more. I was almost running when I reached the overseer's yard.

I squinted at the sight in front of me and had to clutch at a sapling to stop from stumbling. Two blacks with blood drooling from their mouths were lying on the ground in front of Goodpaster. Another slave, a boy not more than sixteen, was running around the yard squealing, his hands clasped to his head to stanch the blood spurting from the gap where his ear had once been. A young girl stripped of her clothes was pegged out on the ground. Ferret knelt beside her, jabbing a burning log at her breasts. The air was sickly with the smell of charred flesh.

'Julie!' I cried in amazement when I saw Ferret's wife standing over another slave, stabbing him with a pitchfork. My cry made all three of them look up.

'Good afternoon, Mistress Fleur!' Goodpaster crooned sarcastically. 'Have you come to help?'

'Stop this outrage at once, do you hear?'

'Outrage, Mistress?' Ferret got to his feet, leaving the burning wood lying on the slave's stomach. 'Outrage? A year's work's been lost and my bonus stolen from me by that fire. That's the outrage, Mistress. The nigras did it.'

I hurried over to him and bent down and grabbed the charred log from the girl's stomach. The smell nearly made me choke. I waved the wood at Ferret.

'You stop this at once, do you hear? I'll not have any more of it.'

'You won't have no more of it?' Ferret's wife advanced on me. 'And who are you, pray? Some orphan brat Marse Jem brought here from Savannah!' She pointed her pitchfork at me. 'Get back to your boudoir, you fancy Mistress! This is plantation business and it ain't no concern of yer'n.'

'It's my plantation, Julie Ferret. I'll see you dismissed for this!' I waved the fire brand at her in my astonishment at her words.

'Hear the grand lady! I ain't one of yore fancy house nigras you can do what you like with. I was born right here in Paxton County not a mile from this plantation. I belong here!'

The woman lunged at me with the pitchfork. 'It does be you an' yore kind what makes a misery for us poor whites!' I stepped aside as she lunged again. Goodpaster drew his pistol and pointed it at me.

'You've all gone mad!' I screamed. The pitchfork plunged toward me again. 'I'll not tolerate this!'

'Oh, you won't, my fine lady? What are you going to do about it, eh?'

My foot caught in the hem of my dress as I tried to avoid the pitchfork. I toppled backward. I heard Julie Ferret's cackle of triumph and saw the prongs of the fork descending to skewer me to the ground. There was a shout and a shot rang out.

I rolled over in terror until I came to rest against the Negro girl staked to the ground. She was whimpering softly, numb with the pain from her burns. Cautiously, I lifted my head.

Granger Hayard was stalking over the grass toward me, a smoking pistol in his hand. Jem, Maxine, and Garland trotted behind him. I looked around, Julie Ferret was glaring wildly at me while Ferret crouched over Goodpaster who was stretched out on the ground, his bloated belly pointing upward.

'He's dead!' I heard Ferret mutter.

'You killed my nigra breaker, Pa!'

'Sorry about that, Jem,' Granger growled, stuffing his pistol back in his belt. 'He was aimin' to shoot your wife. Don't that mean nothin' to you?' Granger strode over to me and helped me to my feet. 'You're a brave woman, Fleur.'

Granger looked around the compound at the injured slaves and the overseer and his wife clasping each other and glowering defiantly at him. He barked orders quickly. The drivers moved forward cautiously to release the bound slaves.

'You, boy!' Granger shouted at Garland. 'Escort Miss Maxine to the house. Jem, I'll leave you to decide what you do with your overseer. Fleur, can you walk?' He grasped me roughly around my waist.

'Of course.'

'Come, we'll go to the house.'

'Wait,' I said. 'Let me help these poor tortured slaves first. They must be in agony.'

Granger let me slip out of his grasp, a rugged smile on his face. 'Jem, boy,' I heard him mutter. 'If you had sense enough to bide by your wife –'

Darkness had fallen by the time I finished. I comforted

the poor girl who was burned like a hoe cake, and dressed the wounds of the boy whose ears had been severed. Granger Hayard waited patiently for me on the verandah of Wayne's old cabin. He sipped from the whiskey jar which Rollo brought out for him.

'I'm ready now, Mister Granger. It was kind of you to wait for me.'

He looked at me quizzically. 'For a lass who was about to be skewered to death by a mad cracker wench not long ago you're remarkably unruffled, Fleur!'

I tightened my bonnet, waiting for him to descend from the verandah. 'Maddocks has taught me how to survive in difficult circumstances, Mister Granger. I'm grateful to the slaves. They've given me strength.'

'The slaves?' He rumbled off the verandah and gripped my elbow. 'What do you know about nigras?'

'They've an inner strength, Mister Granger. How else could they tolerate the barbarities inflicted on them by their masters?' Through the pine trees we could see the distant lights of Maddocks glowing reassuringly in the dark. I linked my arm under Granger's elbow and directed him along the path. We had not seen Jem since he had escorted Ferret and his wife back into their own cabin. We were alone.

'Don't let nigras fool you, Fleur. They are duplicitous creatures. Believe me, Fleur, I know. I have gets by some.' The darkness was making him bold. 'The wenches are adorable when they want but it's for their own gain.' He chuckled gruffly.

'White people can be the same.'

'How now, Fleur!' Granger sounded shocked. 'Are you so cynical at such a tender age?' He tried to see my face but the moon was weak and the night's heavy shadows protected me.

'I know,' he growled. 'It's Jem. He's always been an uncontrollable lout. I'm sorry if I offend you, but it's a fact. His mother spoilt him, and Maxine too. They were as thick as thieves when they were small. Always stealin' off together and doing the most terrible things to the slaves. I thought you'd tame him. Give him a child, Fleur. Maybe that will do it.'

Granger pulled me close to him. I remembered how, when I first saw him on Factors Wharf in Savannah, I had instinctively trusted him. I trusted him still. He was a leathery old codger, steeped in the traditions of the South and used to having his own way, but I sensed he was just and would help me, even if it involved his own son and daughter. We were walking in a comfortable silence while I resolved to tell Granger about Jem and Maxine and the hold they had over me.

'Mister Granger – '

'Hush Fleur!' he said roughly. He stopped, cocking his rugged grey head on one side. 'You hear that?'

'What – '

He jerked my arm. 'What's through them trees?'

I peered into the bush. Maddocks was ahead of us, silent, even ghostly, in the moonlight. There were lights in the parlour and the back windows but no sound. Granger was pointing to the right of the trail at the kitchen compound.

'That's where the house slaves have their cabins,' I whispered. 'What's wrong?'

He turned to face me. 'I don't know, Fleur, but I'm going to find out. You didn't hear that laughter?'

'No.' I was amused. 'Sometimes our slaves do laugh, Mister Granger. Uncle Leo insisted on happy people in the house.'

'That weren't no nigra laughter, Fleur. Let me take you to the house and then I'll come and see what's going on.'

I resisted his attempt to start me along the path again. 'Mister Granger, I'm supposed to be mistress of Maddocks. If there's something untoward, why, I'm going to come with you to uncover it!'

'You're a spunky lass, Fleur, eh? No simperin' and tattlin' with the county cabals for you, eh?' He put his arm around my shoulders and hugged me proudly. We stepped off the trail and pushed our way through the undergrowth to the cabins.

There were four slave huts in the kitchen compound together with the kitchen itself, the smoke house, and other buildings used for stores. The girls who served in the house lodged in one of the cabins, the boys in another, while the other two were for Trott and Mammy Mable. We approached close to the cabins when Granger halted, sniffing the air.

He clutched my arm to prevent my speaking. 'I smell a woman's perfume. Don't you?'

There were odours but they were quite indistinct to me. I glanced at Granger in wonder.

'Quiet now,' he warned, crouching down and beckoning me to follow him to the wall of one of the cabins. I stood behind him as he put his ear to the back of the hut and listened. There was a sudden burst of high-pitched laughter.

My skin prickled. I recognised that laughter.

I put my head forward to listen to the cabin's occupants. Granger gestured me away, frowning furiously. I pretended not to notice him.

At first I could not understand the voices muffled by the boards of the cabin wall. It was not a conversation I was overhearing but a series of grunts and protests. I pressed my ear closer.

It was Maxine's voice which shrilled with an ugly laugh of triumph. 'Yes! Yes!' she was saying. 'Now you are safe, now you are safe!'

Garland's anguished groan was unmistakble. 'No, no, Miss Maxine. It ain't right. Don't, don't.' He uttered a long moan, as though life were being drained from him.

My heart quickened and I fell back from the cabin wall gasping for breath. Granger Hayard held me in his strong arms and kept me on my feet. His eyes were blazing with a wild anger. Without speaking, he propelled me around to the front of the cabin. He glanced around the compound. There was a lantern burning in the kitchen and its glow fell across the yard to the door of Garland's cabin.

'Wait here!' he ordered gruffly, withdrawing his pistol from his belt.

'What are you going to – '

I was still speaking when Granger put his shoulder to

the door and heaved his way into the cabin. 'Don't move!' he shouted, brandishing his pistol.

'Pa!' Maxine shrieked hysterically.

I peered into the dark depths of the cabin, ashamed of myself but determined to see if what I had heard was the truth. Garland was lying on his bed board, his breeches bunched around his knees. Maxine was on top of him, astride him like a man riding a horse. I shut my eyes and gripped the cabin door for support.

'Pa!' Maxine's shriek changed to a sob. 'Thank God you came. This nigra – he was – he was – raping me!' She choked, her shoulders shaking with dry tears.

'Get up, Maxine!' Granger still held his pistol covering the two of them.

Maxine held down her skirt as she eased herself off Garland and dismounted slowly. She staggered onto the floor and eyed Granger with loathing. Garland snapped to his feet and pulled up his breeches.

'Shoot him, Pa! Shoot him! You saw what he was doing. He's a vile, rotten nigra – he forced me in here – he forced me to do it, Pa!'

Granger's lip curled. His mouth opened and he hawked a stream of spittle into Maxine's face 'You're trash, Maxine! Worse than trash. I should shoot you down like a lame horse.'

Maxine wiped the phlegm from her cheek. 'Have you gone crazy, Pa! The nigra must be lynched. Jem will lynch him! He's Fleur's favourite but she'll lynch him herself when she knows he rogered me.'

'No, I won't!' I stepped into the cabin. Garland faltered. His frightened face dissolved into utter dejection. I longed to put my hand out to comfort him. Instead, I drew myself up to my full height and thrust my face an inch away from Maxine's.

'I heard what you were doing, Maxine.' My voice shook and I was quivering like a hummingbird. 'It's – it's despicable! Garland's told me how you have been pursuing him. You forced him to do this – this shameful thing.'

'That's enough, Fleur.' Granger brushed me aside.

'You, boy, what d'you have to say?'

Garland hung his head.

'Speak, Garland!' I whispered. 'Mister Granger will listen.'

'The nigra can't speak!' Maxine gloated. 'He wouldn't lie, he's too well trained for that. What you heard Pa, means nothing. It's what you saw. You wouldn't let a nigra pester your own daughter, Pa?' Maxine seized Granger's arm. He raised it quickly, catching her under the chin with the butt of his pistol. She tottered back and collapsed on the bed board.

'You ain't no daughter of mine, gal!' snarled Granger. 'First a Yankee and now this nigra! You don't have to speak, boy. Ain't no one gonna lynch you, not while I'm alive. I know this bitch. It ain't the first time!'

He turned to me. 'She was always in our nigras' britches at home, since she was twelve.' He coughed quickly. 'I'm sorry, Fleur. Let me take you inside. I forgot. You must be distressed.'

'Hah! Distressed. She certainly is!' Maxine shouted from the bed. 'She dotes on that nigra herself.'

'Indeed?' Granger swung out of the cabin, grasping me around my waist and almost lifting me off my feet. Garland followed us.

'I'm sorry, Miss Fleur. I couldn't help it. She, she just bewitched me.'

'Go about your business, boy!' Granger's voice was gruff but kind. 'Miss Fleur will see you in the morning.'

Granger Hayard stayed at Maddocks for a week. His bluff banter kept us all on our toes. Many times he gazed at me with an avuncular expression and I was deeply touched by his concern. Jem and Maxine, however, took elaborate steps to avoid prolonged contact with their father.

One day there was a heated session between Jem and Granger which the drapes and hangings of the house failed to deaden. Their voices drifted through to me in the sewing room. I hurried out into the hall and met Maxine stealing down the stairs. She glared at me.

'What is it?' I gasped, shocked at the noise.

'Wouldn't you like to know!' she snapped. She opened the door to the dining room and stepped in quickly.

I sighed and went to the smoking room which adjoined the library so I could hear better.

'Mammy Mable!'

The old housekeeper jumped away from the library door in surprise. She gave a little guilty titter that changed to a laugh.

'Ah ain' able to shut mah ears to dat noise, Mistis.'

There was a loud thump as someone struck a table top. 'Oh, Mammy! They're not going to fight, are they?'

'No, Mistis, dey does talk too much fuh blows.'

I gripped the back of a chair, listening with anguish in case Jem told his father lies to put me in a bad light with the old man.

'In God's name!' thundered Granger. 'How have I been cursed with such an ass for a son? Will you do nothin' your father tells you?'

'I ain't a nigra, Pa! Dammit, you treat your nigras better than me.'

'That's because you're ruder than any nigra would ever dare to be. Where is your respect?'

'Respect!' Jem hawked loudly, spitting on the library floor. 'You ask for respect from me when you don't give me none. Who asked you to push your way into this house and start running it like it's your own? You shot my nigra breaker dead and you won't let me punish a nigra who raped my sister.'

'It wasn't rape, Jem, and you know it yo'self. You already agreed with me on that point. If I didn't shoot your slave beater you would've had a dead wife.'

'Hah! You want to interfere in everything! When I was a child you ignored me and now you won't let me alone. I believe you're jealous of me, Pa! You're jealous that I have Fleur as my wife and Maddocks as my home. You've always wanted Maddocks, haven't you? Maybe you want Fleur too? Well, Fleur and Maddocks are mine, Pa! I got them myself without any help from you.'

Oh, how he lies, I muttered to myself, grasping the chair for support.

'What would you have given me, eh, Pa? Your plantation will go to Forest. You ain't never cared a damn about me until I proved I could raise the best dam' cotton this county ever saw. Then you ride in here and shoot my whip master dead. That's murder, Pa!'

'I saved your wife, Jem! She doesn't concern you no more? You've got to cherish her, Jem.'

'You see! You see! Why should I? So you can get a grandson to dance on your bony knee? What's wrong, Pa? Are you afraid Forest ain't never going to wed Miss Vain? Are you scared I'll get into some scandal that will make her call off the engagement? Miss Vain's so dam' well-connected in Milledgeville. What will she say when she hears her future father-in-law killed a man?'

Granger roared with exaggerated laughter. She'll know I'm a man in the old tradition, Jem. Protecting a lady. She'll treat me properly and be proud of me. So will her father and his colleagues in the Assembly.'

'Well, I ain't Miss Vain, Pa! I want you to get out o' Maddocks and stop your interferin'!'

'Are you tellin' me to leave, son?'

'Dam' right I am. I had to fire Ferret and his wife because of you. Where am I ever going to get an overseer like Ferret again?'

'I did right, Jem. You couldn't keep a man like him at Maddocks. Not after what he and his wife did to Fleur.'

'Fleur! Fleur! It's always Fleur.' Jem's voice was scornful. 'If you're so concerned about Fleur, you can have her!'

There was a slap followed by a startled cry from Jem.

'Mah Gawd!' muttered Mammy Mable, backing away from the door.

A chair crashed to the floor. Granger's gruff voice cut through the air with icy authority.

'Don't move, boy. Ah ain't worried about shootin'

you if I have to. I should have licked your hide with a bullwhip when you was a whelp. How'd you like it if I started to cut you like your men cut your nigras, eh? I got a right to slice that tongue out of your mouth for the things you've been sayin'.'

'You wouldn't shoot me, Pa!' The fear in Jem's voice surprised me. 'Pa!' he squealed in panic.

'You ain't worth the cussin' boy!' Granger's voice was filled with contempt.

The door of the smoking room flew open and Granger strode out. His face was mottled red with anger. His white hair bristled as he marched through the room. He stopped when he saw me and his face softened.

'Fleur,' he spoke calmly but seriously. 'I'm goin' home. But anytime you need help, you come to me, you he'ah?'

I kissed him quickly, not daring to speak lest the tears begin to flow. I turned abruptly and made my way along the hall and up the stairs to my chamber.

CHAPTER TWENTY-SEVEN

Christmas was a joyless occasion at Maddocks. The tension that stalked the house seemed to communicate itself to the slaves. Mammy Mable made an attempt to follow the traditions but, defeated by our combined lack of interest, she gave up.

Maxine and I refused to eat in the dining room together and, as neither of us knew when the other would be at the table, we both ate in our rooms. Jem sat in lonely splendour for his dinner when he bothered to come in from the plantation. With Goodpaster dead and Ferret and his wife gone, Jem was supervising the slaves himself.

Sometimes from my window I watched Jem ride off in the early morning on his rounds. He slumped in his saddle now, no longer riding with the carefree arrogance of our early days together. He was still accompanied by Garland and this worried me. I knew Jem hated Garland and might even kill him. I had not realised that Jem was feeling a depth of loneliness perhaps as great as mine. Maxine could not help him with the plantation. He needed Garland.

I used to stand at my window as night fell, anxiously awaiting their return. It was not Jem's haggard figure that drew me there, but Garland's. Garland would stand below my window – I'm sure he did it deliberately – and help Jem off his horse. Poor Jem! After a day in the fields he could hardly stand.

I guessed that he had jars of whiskey stashed in various hiding places on the plantation, for he usually reeled onto the piazza, crashed through the door and flung himself wearily into a chair. Sometimes, Maxine ran to him, chiding him to take better care of himself, and her.

Over the weeks, I observed that Jem had cooled in his feelings for Maxine. Sometimes, I overheard Maxine begging him to embrace her. Jem, perhaps through fatigue or his preoccupation with drinking, refused. He would shout at Maxine until she left him alone.

After helping Jem off his horse, it was Garland's custom to walk the animal out onto the drive and look up at my window. His smile was the only thing that gave me comfort during those difficult weeks. That smile began as a rueful grin then spread across his face until all his teeth shone with the brilliant promise that we would soon be together. I used to wave back happily, like an imprisoned princess in a turret, until he had ridden out of sight around the corner of the house to the stables.

Generally one of the kitchen girls brought a tray with my supper on it. One evening I had just turned away from my lonely vigil at the window, sighing with pleasure at the sight of Garland astride his horse, when the door banged open and Mammy Mable stomped in bearing the supper tray in her gnarled hands.

'Mammy Mable! What's happened?'

'Lor' in heaven, Mistis Fleur!' Mammy stood with her arms akimbo. 'How long yo' gwine waste yo'self in dis boudoir?'

'Waste myself?'

'Yo' know exagly what ah mean, Mistis. It ain' no good you' turnin' yuh eyes on me like ah be stupid. Ah plumb tuckered ou' takin' care Maddocks fuh yo'.'

I blinked in surprise. Mammy Mable advanced into the centre of the room, wagging her finger at me. With her cloth cap and drag floor-length gown, and a fierce expression on her face, she looked formidable. I sank back in the chair, intimidated.

'Yo' t'ink dis house an' plantation take care itself, Mistis? Uh, uh! It need a mistis an 'a marster. Garland be wid Marse Jem so de plantation ain' neglec', but de house! It does need a white mistis touch. Tell yuh Mammy Mable what yo' does be dwine all day in dis chamber. Is yo' sick? Is yo' bigged?'

'Heavens no, I hope not.'

'Hah!' she exclaimed in triumph. 'You t'ink yo' be de only Mistis' wid a no-good marriage? Ain't one Mistis ah ever know whose man be good fuh she. Yo' got to get out yuh boudoir an' down on yuh piazza, Mistis Fleur. Ah ain' gwine take care Maddocks no mo', an' dat be final!'

I raised my head and looked at Mammy Mable uncomfortably. The flesh hung loosely on her tired face, outlining the bones below her sunken eyes. She had been at Maddocks since the day Uncle Leo had laid the first stone. She was part of the house.

Suddenly I understood. I rose from my chair and ran to her.

'Oh, Mammy!' I cried. 'You're right. I'm not helping anybody just sitting here. Not even myself.' I wrapped my arms around the old lady and felt her hands holding me tightly.

'Well, get started doin'!' Her voice was soft once more. 'Ah know yo' gwine shake yuhself ou' dis mess o' self-pity an' give Maddocks yuh love.' She released me and held me at arms' length, her face made beautiful by the kindness in her eyes.

'Yo' be such a pretty gal, Mistis Fleur. Yuh hair shine when de sunlight dance on it an' ah see yuh eyes sparkle wid joy jus' to be alive. Ah gwine see dat again, Mistis, ain' I?'

I nodded ruefully, thinking of Garland's smiles. 'I'll try, Mammy Mable, I'll try.'

'Good, Mistis. Ah sure need yuh help! Marse Jem does get so 'toxicated at night, ah ain' got no one to turn to.' Mammy paused and watched me shrewdly. 'Seems like he not payin' much 'tention to Miss Maxine no more, Mistis. Missy Maxine done ax Garland 'company she fuh she walks.'

'Garland?' I gasped.

'De bery same, Mistis. Mah boy, Garland. Yo' ain' speak to him fuh weeks, Mistis. He be sad, Mistis Fleur, cuz he don' know if yo' be vex wid he.'

'Oh no!' I blurted out. 'I could never be vexed with Garland.' I ran to the window and peered out. It was dark and I could see nothing.

'Ah tell he dat yo' ain' be vex, but Garland be los' widou' yuh kindness to guide him like yo' done befuh.'

I turned away from the window unhappily. True, I had not spoken to Garland in weeks. He was always with Jem and there had been no opportunity. Besides, I needed time to understand my feelings for him. Every time I saw Garland striding across the courtyard with his long limbs and proud body, my heart faltered and I was assailed by a feeling of melancholy.

'Mammy Mable,' I said, my face flushed, my voice low, 'Master Jem, where is he?'

'He be snorin' in de smokin' room, Mistis.'

'And Garland?'

'Garland, Mistis?' Mammy Mable's face was a mass of happy wrinkles. 'He in de kitchen gettin' he vittles.'

'Tell him to meet me on the piazza, Mammy. I'll get my cape. I want to go for a ride.'

'Yas, Mistis. Yas, Yas!'

Garland rode quietly by my side. Neither of us had

spoken since Hannibal had saddled my horse and we had left the stable. The night was chilly but not cold. A bright moon threw life into the heavy boughs of the trees, making them dance with shadows when the breeze stirred them. The sky was clear and the stars had a gemlike brilliance.

Garland was riding proudly, his back straight and his head erect, alert to catch any unexplicable noise ahead of us on the path. His large hand grasped the reins easily and he seemed completely relaxed.

He wore the coat I had had made for him months before. It fit him snugly over his cotton shirt with its ruffled collar open at his throat. He felt my eyes on him and turned and smiled.

'Garland,' I whispered, reining in my horse when we reached the creek. He bent across and took the reins from my grip. I withdrew my hand quickly so as not to touch him but he pulled my horse closer until I was directly opposite him. Our eyes met.

He leaped from his mount and helped me gently until my feet were on the ground, his strong arms clasping me close to his body. I inhaled the night air deeply. My senses soared and I was unable to speak. Instead, I tilted back my head and closed my eyes.

Garland's face hovered above my cheeks, his gentle breath tingling my skin. His lips descended onto mine. I clung to him passionately as his mouth began to explore mine. The months of tension, teasing, and despair vanished. My heart, my brain, and my soul were all responding recklessly to Garland's kiss.

I opened my eyes. The stars flickered above Garland's halo of hair, lit his fine, delicately carved features. His face shone with undisguised love. We were standing in a glade in the pine trees. The creek was a few yards from us, burbling where the water, dark with red mud from the upper fields, tumbled over stones. I closed my eyes again and abandoned myself to Garland. His arms twined even tighter around me and his hands caressed my back. I knew I was poised at a threshold. I tore my mouth away from his and beat his chest with my fists.

'What is it, Missy?' Garland's deep voice sounded anxious.

'Garland. I want you so. It's been so long, waiting, wondering. Now finally we're together and I'm afraid.'

'Hush, Missy.' Garland bent his head low and placed his mouth over mine. The kiss was different. It instilled strength in me that I did not know I had. I clung to him. He raised his head and gathered me close to his body, guiding me toward the gently sloping bank of the creek. I sat beside him and gazed into the dark water as the moonlight flooded the glare.

Garland removed his coat and placed it on the grass behind me. In the ivory light, with his ruffled shirt open to his waist, he was a tawny Greek god. I sighed as he held me in his powerful hands and drew me back on the coat.

Garland's eyes were only inches from mine, they were peering into my very depths. I could hardly breathe.

'Garland, I've longed for you to hold me. But now –'

He rested his body on his elbow. 'You're not sure?'

'It's difficult for me, Garland. My heart says yes, but my head, Garland, my head.'

'It says no.' He sat up, his voice deep with regret.

'I don't know why, Garland. It's so strange. I suppose I – I don't feel right about it, Garland. Do you?'

He rose slowly, held out his hand and pulled me to my feet. His eyes were moist.

'Missy Fleur, I'm sorry. Please forgive me.'

'Sorry? No, no Garland. I am the one who should beg forgiveness. Do you understand?'

'You think too much, Missy.' Garland spoke softly, stroking my hair. 'You have such lovely hair. I shall remember it always.'

'You speak as though you are going away!'

'Don't fret, Missy!' he spoke softly. 'A slave never knows his future.'

'Don't think of yourself as a slave.'

'I was born one, Missy.'

'Well, you aren't going to die one!' I gasped, surprised at the words which tumbled out of my mouth.

Garland bent down for his coat, slung it over his shoulders and gently urged me to the path.

'Granger Hayard told me that in the North many blacks are free.'

Garland uttered a suppressed laugh. 'In the North? Of course, Miss. But what about here in the South? I was born at Maddocks, Missy, and you can't free me, even if you own me.' He held his fingers to my lips. 'That's for me to do for myself.'

I was puzzled by the look that flickered across his face.

'Jem?' I blurted out suddenly. 'Does he make life hard for you?'

Garland's eyes narrowed. He seemed relieved to talk of something else. 'Now that Marse Jem is the overseer he rides behind the field nigras, lashing them himself like cattle. I don't know why he lashes them so, Missy. If he leaves them be, they're going to do more work than when he troubles them. They're proud of Maddocks, Missy. We all want to have the best cotton crop in the county the same as he does.'

'If you promise to help me, Garland, I will see Maddocks run the way it should be. Granger is right. If we must have slaves, let's make it bearable slavery.'

'Did he say that?'

'Yes.'

'Then we've got hope!'

'Of course you have.'

'No Missy. Not the way you think. We've got hope because Marse Granger is a wise buckree. If he's thinking to make a slave's lot more bearable it's because he's scared that we slaves are going to rise up and finish with slavery ourselves. Yes,' Garland beamed, 'We have hope.'

I wondered if he could be right and how long he would have to hope. I wound my arm around his sturdy waist and we walked in close embrace to the horses. Garland helped me mount.

'It's so late,' I gasped as I looked up at the sky. 'Everyone will know I've been out riding with you.'

'Why shouldn't you, Missy? You're mistress of Maddocks.'

I shook my head doubtfully. 'Sometimes the mistress is a slave too.'

'Only if she wants to be!'

Garland slapped my horse and the animal carried me off in the direction of the house. He galloped behind. We made no attempt at secrecy. My bonnet flew back and my hair soared out behind me in the breeze.

Garland escorted me with correct formality to the steps of the house. I appreciated his caution. He opened the door for me, gave me a lantern, and then bowed his way out of my presence.

I stared at the darkened hallway; shadows danced when I raised the lamp to the heavy furniture. I smiled happily. Uncle Leo had made Maddocks his sanctuary. With its books and paintings, it was a house for people who could find joy in life. I had discovered a real friend in Garland. I was content.

My heart was singing joyously as I began to ascend the stairs to the comfort of my chamber. Suddenly I reeled back and clutched my breast. The crack of a floorboard snapped through the stillness of the house like a pistol shot.

'Who's there?' I croaked in fright raising the lantern and peering into the shadows. The door to the ladies' parlour opened slowly.

'So, you've been consorting with your nigra!' Maxine's spiteful voice wrecked my contentment. I took a deep breath.

'What are you doing here? Has Jem thrown you out of his bed?'

Maxine's tired eyes flickered with surprise at my retort. 'Fancy, Fleur! You've found your tongue.'

'Perhaps.' I gathered strength from the memory of Garland's strong hands around me. 'I don't intend to lose it, Maxine.' I replied coolly, my voice stronger. I stared at Maxine. 'I sometimes wondered what Jem saw in you. Now I think I know. He loves you because he loves himself. You look just like him, Maxine. Jem must think he is lying with himself when he beds with you. He's incapable of loving anybody but himself.'

I was amazed at my boldness in uttering such words. Maxine was shocked. She clutched the door jamb and stared at me, blood draining from her already pale face. She opened her mouth to speak but no sound came. She tried again.

'How dare you speak to me like that, Fleur. After what Jem has done for you.'

'What has Jem done for me?' I uttered a hollow laugh. 'He may have saved me from a New Orleans whore-house by shooting my uncle in a duel, but it was Wayne Carter who brought me here, not Jem. Jem married me, but for what? To get his hands on Maddocks.'

'Do you forget how he has turned a blind eye on your behaviour with that nigra?'

'What behaviour?' I bridled. 'I've done nothing I should be ashamed of.'

'Hah!'

'Tell me, Maxine,' I challenged. 'Where would you and Jem be but for me? Certainly not standing in my hall disgracing all that Maddocks represents.'

'Maddocks! What do you care about Maddocks?' Maxine's pallor had given way to a mottled flush. 'You've closeted yourself in your chamber like a sulking novitiate these past weeks. Suddenly you sneak out for a moonlight ride with that wretched house boy. Isn't that disgracing Maddocks?'

'If I want to ride I can only do so with a servant because my husband is either drunk or bedding his own image.' I drew back my shoulders. 'I'll thank you not to spy on me, Maxine Hayard. Maddocks, at least, is still mine even if my husband is not. I can do as I please here.'

Maxine gave a tight-lipped smile. 'One day you won't be so proud, Fleur.'

'Proud? Of a husband who is a scoundrel and a sister-in-law who stole him!'

'I didn't steal Jem. He was mine before he ever saw you.'

'Then I owe you gratitude for the loan, I suppose?'

My brain raced. Maxine had something brewing in her mind, I was sure. This was not like our occasional exchange of remarks in the past. She seemed oddly vulnerable tonight.

'Why are you spying on me, Maxine? Do you want to trap me for some reason?'

Maxine seemed to crumble before my eyes. She gasped for breath, retreating slowly. 'Fleur, won't you come in here? I was waiting for you, yes. I want to speak to you.' Her bloodshot stare was a sickly appeal for help. I frowned with suspicion.

'Bring the lamp, Fleur. We can sit down.'

'You invite me into my own parlour, Maxine?' I was unable to suppress my sarcasm.

'You have been avoiding Jem and me for so long, Fleur. We don't know what you want.' Maxine walked unsteadily into the parlour. Curiosity made me follow.

She sat, with obvious relief, on the couch and gazed at me as I placed my lamp on the occasional table. Her eyes flickered to the chair opposite her. I pursed my lips in annoyance and sat down but I refused to make it easier for her. I waited.

'Fleur, I don't know how to begin.'

'That hasn't worried you in the past!' I said without hesitation. 'Don't break down in tears and tell me you're sorry and, because Jem doesn't want you anymore, I can have him back.'

'You aren't making it easy for me, Fleur.' Maxine's veneer of superiority cracked. Her voice was hushed, quite unlike the strident tones I was used to. She looked frail and tired. If she had been my friend I would have clasped her to my bosom so we could cry together. But I refused to feel sorry.

'I suppose I shouldn't expect you to,' she coughed.

'Don't cry, Maxine,' I replied. 'It won't help you with me. I've cried myself to sleep every night for weeks because of what you've done. You stole my husband and then that awful incident with Garland. If you let one tear fall out of those whiskey-soaked eyes of yours, I'll go out of here immediately, I swear.'

Maxine jerked back her head as though I had lashed her. 'Whiskey? Fleur, how do you know? Does it show?'

'Show? Have you looked at yourself in the glass, Maxine? Maybe that's why Jem doesn't want you anymore. You have the eyes of an old drunkard, red and bleary with liquor.'

'Oh!' She gave a little cry of dismay, brushing at her hair instinctively. The strands falling on her forehead refused to settle back but formed cobweb patterns across her face. Then she rallied to return insult for insult.

'So,' she screamed at me. 'You think you're so much better than I. You pretend you're innocent. But tell me what were you doing tonight? I've been waiting to catch you like this, just waiting for you to go to your black paramour. I knew you would!' She laughed dryly. 'Now I've got you.'

'If that's what you want to tell me, then I'm going.' I stood up. How dare she defile my friendship with Garland in such a manner. 'My conscience is clear!'

'No! Don't go!' Maxine's voice changed to a whine.

I peered at her more closely. I had been right about the whiskey. For the first time I noticed the empty decanter on the carpet behind the couch. She was quite drunk.

'You crave my company, Maxine?' I was astonished. 'What evil plan do you have in your mind now? You'll never trap me with Garland.'

'I hadn't expected you to be like this, Fleur.'

'I know! You thought I would weep and swoon and beg you to keep my secret and avoid a scandal. Well, I haven't any secret. You can't drive me from Maddocks by your tales.'

'I don't want you to leave Maddocks, Fleur!' Maxine's voice dropped to a whisper. I was so surprised by the change in her tactics that I sat down again.

'You don't? Well, I'm not going to, so you've got your wish.' There was something wrong with Maxine. The hostility seemed to be drained out of her. 'Are you trying to make it up, Maxine?' I was sceptical. 'You can't blackmail me so are you trying to win my sympathy instead? Give up, Maxine, all you can win from me is my hatred.'

She sniffed. Hate was a word she seemed to understand. She hunted in her gown for a handkerchief and dabbed at her eyes. 'Fleur, I know how you must feel – '

I cut her short. 'No apology, Maxine. Nothing will undo what has happened here.' Was this really me speaking?

'Fleur, won't you give me a chance? This is to help you as well as me.'

'Help me? What do you care about me?'

'I have to tell you, Fleur, even if you don't want to hear. Jem and I thought that as you were confining yourself to your boudoir you would agree. But now that you have come out of your boudoir and have been seen by the slaves, we have to tell you. We have to make sure, for your sake as well as ours.'

'I can't believe you're looking out for my welfare,' I shook my head in amazement.

'Oh dear, please listen.' Maxine dabbed her handkerchief at her face again. 'You mustn't go out of the house, Fleur. You mustn't go riding on the plantation, even with Garland. You mustn't receive any visitors. You must stay in your chamber!'

'A prisoner? In my own house!' My mocking laughter surprised us both.

'It's to help you, Fleur!' Maxine cried in despair.

'Fiddlesticks! You don't want to help me! You just want to help yourself. Why must I stay in my chamber?'

'I'm pregnant.' Maxine was watching my face as she spoke. I managed to control myself and raised an eyebrow.

'Indeed?'

'Don't you see, Fleur? If people know I'm pregnant they'll know about Jem and me. He's the only man at Maddocks. They'll know that you have acquiesced. You'll be disgraced as well as Jem and me. But if we both stay in the house incommunicado until after the child is born, we can say it's yours!' She paused, watching me anxiously.

'No one will know!' she added when I didn't reply.

'No one?' I was suddenly weary. Why had this confrontation happened at the moment when I thought I had discovered my freedom? I gazed blankly at the haggard woman sitting opposite me.

'I suppose' – I muttered as the thought struck me – 'I suppose that the fact that Granger Hayard will leave his fortune to his grandson has nothing to do with it? It would suit Jem's purpose. He can say the child is mine and return to his father's favour.'

Maxine wrung her hands. 'If you won't think of me or Jem, Fleur, then think of yourself. You'll never be able to remain at Maddocks if this scandal gets out.'

'No? Why not? Uncle Leo was no paragon of virtue by all accounts. He managed quite well. Maddocks was his refuge from the pettiness of the crackers and the gossip of the plantocracy. I think Maddocks will protect me. It's you who will have no place here – you and your child!'

'Then you won't help us?'

'No, I won't.' I got up and swept to the door carrying the lamp with me, leaving Maxine cradling herself in the dark.

'Fleur – ' she wailed pathetically.

I didn't answer.

'Garland – '

I halted angrily. 'Don't mention Garland's name!' I lost my temper. 'You're not fit even to think of him!'

'Aha! Am I fit to bear his child?'

'His child?' The lamp flickered as a fit of trembling seized me.

'Yes, Fleur.' Maxine gloated. 'I'm in bloom but I don't know if the father is Jem. Or Garland!'

CHAPTER TWENTY-EIGHT

In the months of Maxine's pregnancy, I watched Jem grow old. His flowing black locks which had attracted me so much when he galloped along the plantation paths thinned out and lost their youthful lustre. His eyes, once bright and dark, grew dull and resentful. Even his lips seemed to be twisted into a permanent scowl. The only remaining feature of the Jem I married was the defiant set of his jaw. As the birth of Maxine's child grew nearer, that jaw hardened with a bitter determination.

When Jem spoke to me he seemed to be addressing a tiresome younger sister. Beyond essential matters, we had no contact at all. We received our guests separately. Jem's cronies drank with him on the piazza or in the library while I received neighbours in the parlour, pantomiming a genteel respectability.

Of course, there was no way we could still the talk of the slaves. Gossip and rumours flourished in Paxton County, and Maddocks was the main topic of conversation whenever the planters and their wives gathered together. Slaves talked to each other and the housekeepers and maids carried wildly exaggerated stories to their mistresses. As a result, hardly a day passed without a carriage drawing up in front of the house to disgorge a bevy of bonneted and chattering females.

I quite enjoyed the popularity, although doubtless, if I had known some of the rumours, I would have been abashed. Anyone who asked for Maxine was told politely that she had a headache and was staying in her chamber. Those who insisted on seeing her were firmly refused entry. Gifts and letters arrived daily from solicitous neighbours trying to worm their way into Maxine's boudoir.

I became Maxine's only contact with the outside world, apart from the slaves. My loathing for her mellowed until I felt only disdain. She wallowed in self-pity, doing everything possible to win my sympathy. But, each day that I observed her stomach grow rounder, I hardened. If it was Jem's child she was carrying, it should have been mine. If it was Garland's? The likelihood of that was beyond consideration!

'How can you look so serene?' Maxine demanded sulkily after I told her who the latest visitors were to inquire about her health. 'These dreadful people smell out a scandal from across the length of the county. You refuse to help me so I must hide here pretending I'm ailing. What's going to happen when my baby is born?'

I could find no satisfactory answer, so I shrugged.

'The baby, Fleur! What will become of it?'

'I dare say Jem will find a wet nurse.'

'Will it stay here, Fleur?'

'You mean that you haven't discussed all that with Jem?'

Maxine pouted. 'No. You know he's avoiding me as though I had the plague.'

I was not surprised that Jem stayed away. Pregnancy did not suit Maxine. Her face had blown up and her flawless complexion was permanently veined by the whiskey which she demanded of Mammy Mable each day.

'What does Jem say, Fleur?' Maxine pleaded.

'You ask me?' I exclaimed. 'I barely see him.'

'It's due in four weeks. Imagine, Fleur, that my baby must have a nigra mid-wife. If I have a doctor, the whole county will know.'

'Does it really matter, Maxine?' I asked, exasperated by her perpetual complaints. 'You're a married woman. No one would know that Jem is the father.'

'Fleur! How could you! It's a scandal. I haven't seen my husband for more than a year. Everyone knows that. They might think I took a cracker for a lover.'

I paused at the door and nodded sadly. Why should this be worse in her own mind than bearing a child by her brother? Or Garland? I watched her reach for the decanter, wanting to snatch it away from her, but realising it would only lead to a tantrum. At this rate the child would be born with liquor in its veins, not blood.

Maxiine had seen her relationship with Jem as a means to an end: to drive me from Maddocks. Now her scheme was awry. What might she and Jem try next? Would they really do something to deprive me of my heritage? I shuddered. I was prepared to go to any lengths to keep Maddocks.

My demeanor was serene, according to Maxine. But she did not know that within me there now stood an alert and strong-willed woman who was a stranger even to me. It was Garland who had roused that woman in my soul.

Garland was now the overseer of Maddocks in all but name. Jem could not call him such for he would become the laughing stock of the county if it was known that his overseer was a slave and not a white man. But cotton governed plantation life.

After Ferret left, it was time to sow the next crop. There being no one to supervise the workers, Garland, as the only slave with a sense of authority, took charge. He was a natural leader and the slaves worked better for him than they had ever done for Ferret and Goodpaster. Jem was pleased, probably because Garland's efficiency saved him from having to pay a white overseer. Jem gave Garland a cabin in the overseer's compound in which to live.

With Garland no longer attached to the house as Jem's boy, my opportunities for seeing him were limited. We could meet only when Jem was out of the house or rendered incapable of noticing by drink.

When it was safe for Garland to come to me, I lit the lamp in my room and closed the curtains on one of the windows on the side of the house, leaving the other window shining out into the night. I used to descend the stairs and wait on the piazza for his whistle.

In this fashion, we were able to manage a tryst once or twice month. How I longed for Jem to drink himself stupid or gallop off to Milledgeville and join his cronies in a bust! I lived for my meetings with Garland. We would sit in the pine forest while the night wrapped Maddocks in shadows and talk in soft, intimate whispers.

Garland was constantly worried about me; my welfare and happiness seemed his major concern. He made me tell him exactly what had occurred in the house since our previous meeting, who our visitors were, what they said, and what I told them.

Garland plied me with questions about the gossip my neighbours brought to Maddocks. Because of this, I listened more carefully to their conversations. He liked news about politics, of which I was ignorant, and about the activities of slaves in other parts of the state.

'That garrulous Mistress Runacres was here today,' I told Garland one evening when we sat together in the gloom of the live oaks, our eyes on Maddocks. 'She was full of news from the North. Her son was a medical student there but he's come home.'

'Why?' Garland tugged my arm. 'Did she say why?'

'Because he fears trouble in the North. He says hundreds of Southern students are withdrawing.'

'Secession!' breathed Garland happily.

I sniffed. 'I don't know why you're so interested in what the politicians are saying. But here, look, I kept this for you. It's a clipping from *Harper's Weekly*, quoting from President Buchanan's third annual message to Congress last December.' I took the crumpled paper from my purse and spread it on my lap. 'He speaks of some trouble at a place called Harper's Ferry. He says "it's a symptom of an uncurable disease in the public mind, which may break out in still more dangerous outrages and terminate at last in an open war by the North to abolish slavery in the South." How could he say such a thing? The north would never wage war against the South!'

He took the clipping from me, reading it carefully. 'People in Milledgeville agree with this, Fleur.' His face was grave. 'You don't know what's going on. Maddocks is too isolated. The South and the North are split.'

'But war, Garland? Over slavery. I don't believe it.'

Garland shook his head. 'What does the grand Runacres lady say?' he asked, as though humouring me.

'She was vexed!' I laughed as I remembered her indignation. 'She said that a justice in the North itself had declared slaves were property so couldn't be free and what right had the North to interfere with the South.'

Garland stared at me without speaking. His hand clenched mine until the pain made me cry out.

'I'm sorry, Fleur,' he apologised. 'I sometimes wonder if we will ever be free.'

'I'm not staying, Garland. I didn't know my news would distress you. Mistress Runacres said a war couldn't last long. The North would be defeated in a matter of weeks.'

Garland smiled derisively. 'The North has the votes, the power, and the will to survive. The South has only tradition and the personal courage of its defenders.'

'But Mistress Runacres said – '

'Mistress Runacres has one hundred and thirty Negroes and a mortgage no cotton can pay off. She doesn't have a chance.'

'What do you mean?' I was alarmed by the flash of anger in his eyes. 'She has a beautiful house and the most respectful house slaves I've ever seen.'

'Forget what I said! It doesn't concern you.'

I was anxious now. 'How do you know all these things about the slaves, Garland? What interest is it of yours?'

'I listen. I like to know what people are thinking in my county.'

'Your county? Garland, you must be careful to whom you speak like this. Some people would have you punished immediately.' I suddenly thought of something I had heard.

'Garland, you don't go off the Maddocks plantation at night, do you? The patrollers are being increased. They say they have orders to shoot any black they meet out at night who doesn't have a pass.'

Garland frowned, his eyes narrowing thoughtfully. 'Why are they doing that?'

'It's the planters, Garland. Jem has agreed as well. I think they had a meeting in Paxton last week. One of Mistress Runacres' companions said that the planters fear insurrection and that there have been several uprisings by slaves in the state which the newspapers haven't reported. They say that some slaves are planning mischief and that patrollers will stop them going from plantation to plantation at night spreading their plan.'

Garland looked serious. 'Why do you think the planters are so afraid of their slaves?'

'I've no idea, Garland. Perhaps they don't treat them right. You know, the way Ferret and Goodpaster were.'

'Marse Jem is afraid too?'

'I've really no idea. Why should he be? You keep the slaves working hard, don't you?'

Garland was concerned. 'Marse Jem has his pistols, hasn't he, Fleur? I hear that some plantation wives in the county sleep with firearms by their beds. You have yours?'

I laughed aloud, forgetful that someone in the house might hear. 'Whatever for? That's a strange idea, Garland. Maddocks slaves would never harm me. You know that yourself. You're with them every day.'

'Yes, that's right.' Garland bent his head to meet mine and tried to kiss my neck. I brushed him away and stood up so he could escort me back to the piazza.

Even when I did not see Garland, my days and nights were filled with happiness. The thought that he was at Maddocks pleased me. I lost my fear of giving way to my feelings for him. I began to forget he was a slave and saw him instead as a kind, tender human being from a different background.

We were in the middle of the relentless cycle when everyone on the plantation was committed to cotton. The crop was even more important this year because Jem had the loss of last year's crop to make up. Maxine, stuck in her chamber and swollen like a dead cow, was neglected by us all.

Garland was curious about Maxine when we met by the magnolias a week before the child was due, 'I wanted to come earlier but Maxine was troublesome,' I told him. 'I've got one of the girls sleeping in her room now. She's getting so frightened not even the whiskey is comforting her.'

'Frightened? Why?' Garland held me away from him

and watched my eyes in the glow of the lanterns from the piazza.

'She's afraid the baby might be black, Garland. After all, that night Granger and I came upon the two of you in the cabin . . .'

'Yes,' he said, 'and if it isn't mine, almost any of the others could be its father. I didn't want to tell you this, but Miss Maxine's been prowling around. She's been with more than one.'

Suddenly Maxine's attempt to arrange matters so that the baby would appear to be mine grew even more diabolical. If the baby were black and had been passed off as mine, she and Jem would have Garland lynched and me sent off in disgrace. Then she and Jem could have Maddocks all to themselves.

'Garland!' I gasped. 'Thank God you told me this!' Quickly, I reviewed for him Maxine's attempt to trap me into going into seclusion so that the baby would appear to be mine.

Garland was dumbfounded, but another question occurred to him. 'If that was her plan, what is she going to do with the child now?'

'I don't know, but she and Jem must have worked out another scheme. Perhaps they have some other arrangement to get me to leave Maddocks. But they won't steal Maddocks from me! I'm not going to let them.'

Garland grinned and I allowed him to pull me to his side, drawing comfort from his touch.

CHAPTER TWENTY-NINE

The chaos of cotton picking caught Maddocks firmly in its confusion once again. Everyone on the plantation was forced to work beyond endurance, the whites as well as the blacks. Because Jem had sold slaves earlier that year, when I was going through the period of not caring what he did, the plantation was short of hands.

The bookkeepers patrolled the fields and Jem even hired some crackers to help as supervisors. Poor Garland was up from dawn until after midnight. Jem scarcely came back to the house to sleep. He claimed to be in Ferret's old cabin. If he was, I was sure he had his slave wench with him.

For most of the time, I was alone in the house with Maxine, her maid, Mammy Mable and Trott. It was an opportunity for me to go through Jem's papers in the library. There was nothing extraordinary that I could discover, I knew about the mortgages on the crop and on the slaves. Jem appeared to have debts of his own but his figures were so confusing, I could not understand them. The Maddocks records seemed to be in good order.

I was rummaging through a pile of routine plantation correspondence late one afternoon when I became aware of someone watching me. Both doors into the library were closed. I glanced up quickly at the window.

'Maxine!' My heart lurched at the sight of her ravaged face pressed to the thick windowpane. I leaped up from my seat, scattering papers on the floor, and dashed out onto the piazza.

Maxine looked dreadfully pale. 'I saw you!' she croaked triumphantly. She stared at me, tottering dangerously on her tiny feet. She was wrapped in a voluminous cloak and seemed to have made an attempt to brush her straggling red hair. The door of the house banged and her maid hurried out.

'Ah beg excuse, Mistis,' she whimpered when she saw me. 'It ain' mah fault, Mistis. Missy Maxine slip ou' when ah go to de kitchen fuh de whiskey.' To support her story, the girl held up the whiskey crock.

'I saw you!' Maxine's voice rose to a screech and she pointed a shaky finger at me.

'Very well, girl. Put the crock on the table in the hall and help me get Miss Maxine back to her chamber.' I tutted with dismay. 'You should be more discreet,

Maxine. If someone comes to call, you'll be discovered. Why have you left your room?'

The girl retreated into the house, deposited the whiskey jar, and emerged almost immediately. She stood behind me while I advanced on Maxine.

'I saw you, Fleur!' Maxine shrieked again.

'I'm sure you did, Maxine. Now come along, let's go back to your room.'

'No!' She pulled her arm away from me. 'I've caught you now. I won't go back to my room. Where's Jem?'

'Jem is in the cotton fields, Maxine. Do be a good girl and return to your room. You don't know who will see you.' I glanced quickly through the columns at the wide sweep of the driveway. Fortunately, it would soon be dark, and too late for unexpected visitors. All the crackers were working in the fields about a mile away. I prayed that none of them would choose this moment to come to the house.

Maxine continued to lean uncertainly by the window with one hand clutching the cloak over her bloated stomach. I marvelled that she had swollen so big. Her eyes were glazed and her breath was heavy with the stench of whiskey.

'Help me with her, girl.' I stepped over to Maxine's side and took her arm firmly. The slave girl hesitated before taking the arm Maxine was using to support herself against the wall of the house. Maxine relaxed suddenly and would have toppled but for my firm grip under her arm. We edged her over to the open door.

'You! You were looking in Jem's papers!' Maxine stared at me, her eyes suddenly clear.

Her unexpected coherence made me ease my hold on her. She slipped out of my grip with drunken agility. The slave girl let go and dropped back in fright.

'What if I was?' I challenged, piqued by Maxine's obstinacy. 'I have a perfect right to do so. Please don't be silly, Maxine. You'll catch your death of cold out here on the piazza, even if you don't care who sees you.'

'Hah! You'd like that, wouldn't you?' Maxine sneered

and thrust her face close to mine. I noticed how her skin was grimy with neglect, her once attractive features turned coarse and puffy.

'Maxine!' I said between clenched teeth. 'Get inside the house.'

'No.'

Her eyes watched me sulkily and I sensed that she wanted me to lose my temper.

'You'll have to force me, Fleur!' Maxine grinned.

I backed away from her foul breath.

'Or you can call your nigra pup, Garland, to do the job.'

'Maxine! I'm beginning to lose patience with you,' I muttered. 'You're sick. The baby is overdue! For God's sake, get inside and go to your chamber.'

'No!'

She goaded me and I snapped. I raised my hand to her shoulder and pushed. There was no resistance in her. She fell immediately, toppling backward and making no attempt to save herself. I watched with horror as her head cracked against the door jamb.

'Oh Mistis Fleur!' wailed the maid, edging away from Maxine as she lay motionless.

'Oh dear!' I muttered, annoyed with myself for allowing Maxine to taunt me and fearful that she might be hurt. I knelt down by her side quickly and touched her face. Her eyes opened.

'Fleur!' she moaned. 'The baby!'

I glanced down at her stomach. Maxine's hands were pressed between her thighs.

'Are the pains coming?'

'Yes, Fleur. All afternoon,' she gasped. 'That's why I came down. I was so scared.' She squeezed her eyes shut, moaning loudly.

I spoke to the slave. 'Run down to the fields and find Marse Jem. Tell him to come at once. And call Garland, too. He may have to go to Paxton for a doctor. Hurry now.'

'Yas, mistis,' thc girl answered.

Maxine's fingers were gripping my wrist. I pulled

myself free and shouted down the hall for Mammy Mable.

I was never so relieved as when she bustled down the corridor wiping her hands on her apron. 'Oh mah Lor'!' she said, taking one look at Maxine. 'Wha' she doin' down here?'

'The baby, Mammy. I think it's coming.'

Mammy threw her hands in the air. 'Come, Mistis, she ain' goin' have no whelp on de Maddocks piazza. Help me tote her inside.'

With Mammy Mable gripping Maxine by her arms and me struggling to lift her feet, we carried Maxine over the threshold and into the house. She moaned and howled pitifully. Mammy Mable pushed open the door to the smoking room and we eased her in.

'She gwine birth de chil' right here, Mistis! Stay wid her.'

'Where are you going?' I sank into one of the leather chairs and gazed at Mammy helplessly. Maybe she knew what to do for Maxine, but I knew nothing about birthing a baby.

'Ah go fuh hot water!' Mammy dashed from the room.

Maxine cried out and clutched herself.

'Oh dear, Maxine, please wait until Mammy Mable comes back! I don't know what to do!' I felt so helpless.

Maxine writhed on the floor, her body twisting under her cloak. Her hands stretched back above her head to reach toward me. She grasped the leg of the chair and her body began a sequence of thrustings. Maxine heaved her body upward, uttering the most frightful groan. The cloak fell open around her. She was completely naked underneath. Mammy Mable bustled into the room carrying cloths and an enormous cauldron of boiling water. She knelt down briskly beside Maxine, dipped a cloth and began to bathe her with the nearly scalding water.

'Mistis Fleur, if yo' ain' gwine be no use in here, an' ah don' believe yo' is, ah t'ank yo' to go ou' de kitchin an' carry me de nex' kettle of watah when it bile.'

I glanced down at Maxine before I dashed from the room. She looked deathly pale but there was a weird smile of triumph on her face in spite of the dreadful pain she must have been feeling. I muttered to myself as I rushed across the yard to the kitchen. The dogs hanging around the compound looked startled when I plunged through them.

The kitchen was dark inside, only the flames from the hearth throwing a light around the shack. There were two babies crawling over the floor. They gurgled happily when they saw me. A chicken squawked in alarm and jumped off the table and a goat ran out, bleating. I found a towel to wrap around the handle of the kettle and lifted it off the fire. I hurried out into the yard. The dogs jumped around me, snapping at my ankles in excitement and making me spill some of the water.

I was nearly crying when a black hand closed over mine and took the kettle from me. 'Garland! Thank God you're here!' He helped me up the back steps into the house.

'Marse Jem's coming. I rode faster than he.'

Garland carried the water down the passage. He paused outside the door to the smoking room. His eyes held mine as I put my hand on the door handle. 'The baby – ' he asked huskily.

'Garland, what shall we do?'

'Who's there with Maxine?'

'Only Mammy Mable.'

Garland's face relaxed. His eyes fell on the whiskey crock. 'Is Maxine soaked?'

I nodded and opened the door. Maxine screamed in agony. Mammy Mable was crouched over her, peering between her thighs. She put her hands under Maxine's knees and eased her legs up. 'It don't be long nuh, Mistis.'

'Poor Maxine,' I said, pouring the water from the kettle into the cauldron.

'Yo got more towels, Mistis? An' a piller fuh her head?'

I nodded and stepped out of the room again. Garland

had the whiskey crock in his hand and put it down quickly when I called him.

'Yes, Missy?' His face assumed the blank expression of the docile house slave.

'You look so silly like that, Garland. Like the cat caught with its paw in the cream! Please go to the kitchen and bring another kettle of water. I declare I'm run off my feet already.'

'Yas, Mistis!' He took the kettle from me and hurried off down the corridor.

There was another appalling scream from behind the closed parlour door. The whiskey would keep her quiet, I thought as I glanced at the jar on the table.

A few minutes later, when Maxine's screams were dropping to wild yelps, Garland returned with the kettle. He stood uncertainly outside the door.

'I'll take it,' I told him.

'You ain't nervous no more, Missy?'

'No, Garland. I'll go in.'

Mammy Mable's face was tense when she saw me enter. She was holding the kitchen knife in her hand. My eyes dropped to Maxine who lay so open on the floor.

'It ain' born yet, Mistis. But it comin'.'

'Fleur!' It was Jem's voice outside the door. I put down the kettle and darted out of the room.

'You mustn't go in there!' I told him.

'Humph!' he grunted, glancing around the hall. He sat down on the tiny chair by the table. 'Whose dam' whiskey is this?'

'Maxine's, of course. You don't think it's mine, do you?'

'You might be less of a pain in the neck if you did take a snort now and then!' Jem glared at me. 'Garland, there ain't no cause for you to stay here. Go and stable my horse.'

'Yas, Marse Jem.' Garland strode to the front door. Turning his head quickly so that Jem could not see him, he gave me an encouraging glance.

'Oh dear, I've just remembered that Mammy Mable asked me for a pillow.'

'Well, get it then!' Jem snapped, fingering the neck of the whiskey jar. 'Go on, I won't go in. I'll pour myself a drink.'

When I came down the stairs a little while later, Jem was nowhere around. The whiskey crock was still on the table. I put my ear to the door and listened. There was no sound from the parlour. Cautiously, I pushed open the door and peered in. Maxine lay on the floor, her body very still. There was a pool of blood between her legs, and blood smeared across her thighs and stomach.

I stepped into the parlour just as the door which led to the dining room closed softly. That's odd, I remember thinking as I looked around. Mammy Mable wasn't there and neither was the baby.

I listened. I was sure I heard a baby crying. I rushed across the parlour and was just about to open the door into the dining room when Maxine stirred.

'Fleur!' she called, so weakly I could barely hear her. 'Fleur, are you there? Please, Fleur, please.'

'Poor Maxine!'

I released the door handle and returned to Maxine. She was trying to sit up so I placed the pillow under her head. I reached down and covered her body with the cloak.

'Mammy Mable might have cleaned you better than that! All that hot water I brought her. It's gone cold now.'

'Did you see my baby, Fleur?'

'Not yet, Maxine. Mammy Mable must be bathing it. Lie still, you'll see it soon.'

The library door burst open and Jem stalked in. Garland was behind him. 'Have you had it?' Jem asked hoarsely of Maxine.

'Yes, she's had it.' I answered for her.

'Garland, bring that whiskey jar here. She needs a drink.'

'I'll get a glass,' I said, rising from Maxine's side and taking one from the cabinet.

Garland brought in the jar and I held the glass while he poured the whiskey into it. He avoided my eyes as

Jem watched us carefully. I knelt down and held the glass to Maxine's lips.

She sipped slowly at first then gradually drained the contents of the glass. She smiled, her eyes opening wide and focusing on Jem.

'My baby, Jem? Where is he?'

'Ain't got no idea, Maxine.'

The door opened and Mammy Mable entered. She had a cup in her hand. There was a commotion down the corridor as some of the kitchen dogs growled. Mammy Mable saw the crock of whiskey in Garland's hands and her eyes flickered quickly at Jem.

'Yes, yes!' Jem muttered. 'Give her a tot, Garland.'

Garland poured whiskey from the jar into Mammy Mable's cup. She raised it to her lips and began to drink. After a few sips, she gazed first at Jem, then me and finally at Garland.

Maxine gasped 'Where's my bab – ?' Her eyes began to bulge and her hands clawed at her stomach. The cloak fell away from her and she arched her body off the floor.

'My God!'

A strange gurgle escaped from Maxine's throat. She tried to rise up but fell back, her head rolling off the pillow onto the floor. A spasm shook her whole body and then suddenly she lay still. The four of us glanced at one another.

Jem knelt down quickly and lifted her head back onto the pillow. 'She's dead,' he said.

Mammy Mable screeched. Her hands flew to her throat as though she was strangling herself. She staggered back against the wall.

'Mistis,' she gasped. 'De baby – !' She slowly slid down the wall, tearing a painting from its hook so it came crashing down with her. She slumped forward in an inert heap.

Garland stared in horror. He held the whiskey jar limply in his hand. It slipped from his fingers and shattered on the floor.

I clasped my hands together and sank into a chair. I was unable to think.

Jem stepped over Maxine and grabbed Mammy Mable by the wrist, trying to pull her up but she only crumpled over on her side 'Dam' you! Where's the baby? The baby!'

'I think she faint, Marse Jem.'

Garland spoke softly but his words helped rouse me. It was almost dark in the room. I listened carefully to see if I could hear the child crying.

'Mammy Mable must have put him somewhere. Go for a lamp, Garland. We must look.'

Garland ducked out quickly.

'Did you see the child?' Jem turned on me angrily.

'No, Jem. Did you?'

'Me? I was getting a drink in the library. You told me not to come in here, you remember.'

Garland stepped into the room, the lamp in his hand throwing an eerie light on Maxine. Her lips were drawn back over her teeth so she seemed to be smiling, mocking me, even in death.

'Dere ain' no baby up stair,' Garland announced gruffly. 'Ah search all de rooms.'

'Where the devil did Mammy Mable put it?' Jem grabbed the lamp from Garland's hand.

'I know!' I exclaimed. 'The kitchen. That's probably where she went.'

We hurried down the corridor to the back door, Jem leading the way. The dogs, tearing at some meat, growled at us as we tried to pass.

'Get away!' Jem kicked at them hurriedly, but the dogs snarled and drove him back.

Jem raised the lamp above his head and filled the yard with light. There was blood smeared across the paving stones. The dogs watched us warily as they gnawed at bits of flesh.

'My God!'

Suddenly, I knew what had happened to the baby.

I wanted to faint but I knew I must not do so. I rushed back to the smoking room. Mammy Mable had not stirred. I knelt down beside her. She was breathing, a deep rasping sound. I drew her to my breast, not knowing what to do, only knowing I must not lose her.

Garland loomed in back of me, swooping Mammy Mable up in his arms, his face gentle. I heard his heavy footsteps as he carried her along the corridor. I looked around. There was no doubt that Máxine was dead. But where was Jem? There was no sign of him. I called his name. There was no answer.

CHAPTER THIRTY

A pistol shot roused me from a troubled sleep. I was lying on my bed; a lamp burned dimly by the window. I was alone. There was a murmur of agitated voices from the parlour below me. My door was ajar, the way Mammy Mable always used to leave it. I hugged myself, trying to digest the horror of Maxine's death, the baby's destruction, and Mammy Mable's collapse.

'Seize him!' Jem's shout penetrated my worry. Another shot cracked out, thudding into the ceiling of the room below mine. Jem sounded wild, urged on by the craziness which used to drive him into his senseless shoot-ups of the Savannah taverns.

'Shackle him, dam' you!' he cried out again. 'The next bullet goes clean through you.'

I heard the anxious voices of the slaves who were gathered in the parlour. They seemed reluctant to do what Jem ordered. 'Where you want us to take he, Marse Jem?' I recognised the excited tones of Gray, one of Jem's favourite drivers.

'Take the bastard to the smokehouse.' Jem shouted. 'Make sure he's shackled good.'

I heard the clink of chains being dragged across the floor and then Jem's exclamation. 'That should hold you good for the night! At dawn we're going to lynch you, boy. There ain't no way you can escape. Gray, take two boys and guard the smokehouse tonight. If this nigra escapes, I swear I'm gonna string up every one of you. Now get!'

There was a murmur of resistance from the slaves gathered in the parlour. I listened in astonishment. Suddenly. Garland's dignified voice echoed up to me. 'Sah,' he said slowly. 'Ah ain' done nothin'!'

There was the slap of Jem's fist smacking into Garland's face. 'It was you that gave Maxine the whiskey, boy! Now shut up before I put this pistol to your head and blast it off.'

I leaped off my bed and rushed to the window in time to see the group of slaves tramping sullenly down the steps of the piazza with Garland in the centre. His arms were bound behind him and a chain trailed from his wrist to his ankles. Jem was stalking after the group with two pistols pointing at Garland. His bullwhip was stuck under his arm.

I looked around my bedroom quickly, half-expecting that Mammy Mable would come bursting through my door to tell me what was going on. Suddenly, I even missed Maxine. I was completely alone.

Glancing out of the window again, I caught sight of a shadow flitting across the light shining out from the open porch door. I frowned, wondering who it could be. There was a nervous footfall in the hall. Someone had entered the house. I listened carefully.

There were the sounds of a man bumping into the furniture as he groped his way through the unfamiliar terrain of the house. The noise increased when the intruder began a clumsy ascent up the stairs. I hurried over to my door and closed it quickly.

'Mistis, Mistis!' A voice hissed nervously in the corridor. My heart raced with fear.

'Mistis, Mistis!' The voice whispered again. 'Dey take Garland 'way, Mistis.'

I relaxed, opening the door a few inches and peering out into the dark of the landing. 'Who's there?'

'Renty, Mistis.' The voice sounded relieved. 'De blacksmit', Mistis.'

I opened the door a little wider. 'What do you want?'

'Mistis, it be 'bout Marse Garland.'

I let Renty enter my room. He was a tall boy with a pleasant face. The unmistakable odour of sweat and horses hung about him like a cloak he could not remove. I backed away and watched him anxiously. I remembered seeing him in the forge with Wayne.

'What about Garland?' I demanded sharply.

'Marse Jem done chain him, Mistis. He say he gwine lynch him tomorrow.' Renty squeezed his powerful hands together in front of him, uncertain what to say.

'Yes?' I was impatient. I had to think how to deal with this development.

'Forgive me, Mistis, but ah know yo' be partial to Marse Garland, Mistis.' I swung around to stare at him. He continued to speak.

'We nigras does respec' Marse Garland, Mistis. We don' wanna' see nutin' happen to he, Mistis.'

'I see.' A plan began to form in my mind. 'You did right to come to me, Renty. Can you ride?'

'Ob co's, Mistis.'

I walked over to my tiny secretary, sat down, and quickly wrote two letters. I knew that Jem might return at any minute. When I finished, beckoned Renty to me, trying to keep myself calm.

'This is your pass, Renty.' I handed him one piece of paper. 'If the patrollers stop you, be polite to them and show them this. Tell them it's urgent.'

I handed him the second letter and gave him instructions on its delivery. He seemed to understand.

'Tell Hannibal you have my permission to take the fastest horse from the stables. Ride quickly, Renty, and Garland will be safe.'

'Yas, he gwine be safe, Mistis.' Renty's eyes held mine with a look I did not understand at first. He was not agreeing with me, he was threatening.

He turned abruptly and strode out of the room before I could speak. His words hung in my ears. They were menacing words but they were all the comfort I had.

As soon as he was gone, I went in search of Mammy Mable. I found her lying on a cot in the hall. I touched her and she stirred away from my hand, but, though I called her name several times, she could not open her eyes. I drew up a chair and sat beside her motionless figure. I was still there when the ceaseless tolling of the bells outside the overseer's cabin drew me back to the window overlooking the piazza.

There was a bawling of voices in the driveway and the shuffling of feet. When I looked out I saw that the slaves were being herded in front of Maddocks by their drivers and some crackers. It was not even dawn.

I heard Jem stomping through the house in his heavy riding boots. The crash of a cabinet toppling to the floor when he collided with it showed he had spent the night drinking. Any minute I expected him to appear and order me to descend to the piazza and watch his bizarre revenge for Maxine's death.

Light filtered across the sky, lifting the black pall of shadows from the oaks which reared above the lawn. The slaves were clustered together in swaying groups facing the piazza. I gasped when I saw Gray and two others slinging a rope over a branch of the tree nearest the house. A noose had been fastened at the end of the rope and it dangled at the right height to slip over the neck of a man on horseback. Gray tested the rope. It held securely.

I could not believe that this was happening and I was powerless to stop it. Jem was determined to hang Garland. There was murmur of smouldering anger from the crowd. I peered out of my window and saw Garland being marched over from the smokehouse. He was not resisting his escort but walked with his head raised proudly, as though utterly unconcerned by what was going on.

'Garland!' I cried, but no one heard me.

The crackers moved back from herding the slaves together and formed a circle around Garland. Each of them was armed and eyed the slaves viciously, daring them to make a move. Garland was marched up to the front of the piazza steps. I ran down the stairs as fast as I could.

The door was open and Jem stood at the top of the steps with his back to me, framed against a background of Negroes by the white columns on either side of him.

I stared in dismay at the sullen black faces filling the drive; an ominous sea of slaves which seemed set to surge over Maddocks and destroy it. Jem must have felt the tension for he spread his feet and braced his back against the wall.

'Jem!' I called urgently from the safety of the doorway. 'Come here, come here!'

He ignored me. One of the drunken white crackers he had bribed to protect him glared at me, waving his shotgun menacingly.

My temper flared. 'You threaten me, young man.' I snapped, 'and I'll have you horsewhipped off my plantation. Jem!' I stepped out onto the piazza. The muttering of the slaves changed key. I saw Garland frowning at me as though begging me to stay away.

'Jem Hayard! What are you doing?' I cried, sweeping across the piazza and laying my hand on his shoulder.

Jem jumped at my touch. He swung around before I could dodge away from him and lashed at me with his pistol. The blow struck me on the side of my head. I fell down more from surprise than pain. The low murmur of the slaves swelled to an angry roar. The crackers walked backward to the portico, their pistols pointing at the slaves.

'Jem!' I shrieked from the floor, not bothering to protect myself. 'If you lynch Garland, you'll lose Maddocks! Don't you see the blacks will kill you?'

He swung his foot back to kick me. I braced myself. A shot rang out instead of the blow I was expecting. I opened my eyes quickly. Jem was staring in surprise over the head of the slaves.

I raised myself off the ground. Galloping through the herd of Negroes, waving his pistol above his head, was Granger Hayard. Renty rode at his side and behind came five white men all heavily armed. I recognised them as Jem's brother, Forest, and some of the Hayard overseers.

'Thank God,' I whispered, sinking back against the columns. 'Thank God he came in time.'

Granger took charge immediately. The house girls,

my feet. The Hayard overseers began to chivvy the slaves to the fields while Forest attended to Jem. frightened out of their wits, poor things, helped me to Granger ordered Garland to be unshackled.

'The rope,' I cried before being helped into the house. 'Oh God! Remove it, please.'

'Why yes, lass!' Granger smiled sympathetically. 'Come inside and let us get to the knuckle of this affair. I'm glad you sent for me.'

'Garland? Is he all right?' I was on the verge of hysteria by now and didn't care who knew my feelings.

'The boy?' Granger's voice was kind. 'Yes, Forest will bring him in. Come, Fleur, everything is under control.'

We assembled in the main parlour at the rear of the house. Jem, his hands trembling with the need for a drink, sat on the couch with Granger at his side. Garland stood at the other side of the room where Forest kept a wary eye on him. I sat by myself, dabbing at my face with my handkerchief, trying to restore some dignity.

Granger brushed back his hair and stared around the room without speaking. From outside we could hear the voices of the slaves being hustled to the fields by his men.

'Forgive me,' I said, making an effort to do the correct thing. 'We're in such confusion, Mister Granger, I've quite forgotten my manners. Can I get you something?'

'There's no need for that, Fleur. Mah men will take care of everything. Now, are you ready to tell me what happened here?' Granger turned to Jem.

'I was going to send for you, Pa!' Jem blurted out. 'Just as soon as I had lynched that nigra.'

'Were you now? That's mighty decent of you. But you didn't think it necessary to notify me when mah own daughter died. Your mother is in a terrible state. Miss Vain is with her.' Granger's voice dropped. 'Jem, will you never learn to respect your parents? Must you always be a young hothead?'

'Pa! I ain't your brat no more. I'm of age and I'm capable of looking after myself without you interfering.'

'Indeed, son? Do you know what you were doin' out there, boy? You were asking your nigras to insurrect, boy.'

'I don't care!'

'Maybe you don't, but I do. Paxton County has been peaceful so far but once one plantation goes, we all go, including me. You ain't got the right to ask your nigras to kill you and Fleur and burn Maddocks. It's the whole county you'll destroy if you do.'

'Pa!' Forest jerked his thumb at Garland. 'Pa, this nigra can hear all you're saying!'

'Sure he can, but if he is going to be hung it don't matter.' Granger scratched his chest under his coat and peered at Garland. 'It's true what I'm sayin', ain't it, boy? Tell your master what he don't want to know. If he strung you up like he wanted, he'd be dead too, eh?'

Garland stared at Granger. I knew that look. He was weighing the man's character in his mind. His lips twitched, then he grinned affably.

'Sure 'nough, Marse Granger, sah. De nigras ain' be please if ah be punish fuh somet'in ah ain' do!'

'Boy, you have a fresh tongue in your head!' Granger sucked in his cheeks as though considering the matter, then turned back to Jem. 'What happened, son?'

I listened carefully as Jem explained the events of the night before.

'That nigra gave Maxine the whiskey, Pa, and then he served Mammy Mable. He poisoned them both! Why did you stop my lynchin' him, Pa?' Jem glowered sulkily as he sank back on the couch and waited for Granger to speak.

'If it's how you say, Jem, then the blighter must go to Paxton for trial and be hung proper. That way you ain't gonna start an uprising right here and spoil the cotton.'

'Ah ain' gib no one no pison, Marse Granger.'

Granger looked at Garland in surprise.

'You're lyin, nigra!' Jem exploded.

'Wait, Jem.' Granger put his hand on his son's knee. 'I know this boy, don't I?'

Jem shrugged his shoulders.

'What d'you do at Maddocks, boy?'

'Ah be de oberseer, sah. Marse Jem put me ober all de field nigras.'

'Indeed?' Granger raised his eyebrows. 'You surely trusted this boy, Jem. And ain't he the one I caught Maxine messin' around with?'

'Ah neber rape Mistress Maxine, sah, and ah be de bes' overseer Maddocks eber hab, Marse Granger. Marse Jem say dat we gwine get mo' cotton dis year dan Ferret an' Goodpaster harves' las' year.'

'That's enough!' snapped Granger. He turned to Jem. 'Why do you think this boy poisoned Maxine and the old woman?'

'It's like you say, Pa.' Jem was sounding more coherent. 'The slaves are being stirred up by the Free-Soilers. Don't be fooled by this nigra's slave talk. He has a quick brain and he's smart. That's why I've been using him over the field nigras. And I was dam' right. Ain't going to find no white man around here what can get the nigras working like this buck does. He's their leader, you see, so they do what he tells 'em.'

I tried to keep my gasp of surprise to myself but Jem noticed.

'Fleur thought I didn't know about Garland. I made some inquiries. A jar of whiskey can make most nigras talk. This one's been teaching the slaves to read and write. He's been telling them that the day will come when they're going to be free and equal to you and me, Pa!'

Granger snorted. 'If you knew this, Jem, you should have reported it.'

'I tell you, Pa, I sure was going to when the cotton was picked. Cotton's more important right now.'

'Is it true, boy? Can you read?' There was silence as we all looked at Garland. 'Is it true what Master Jem is telling me?'

'Yes, sir!' Garland snapped back his shoulders

proudly. Forest, who kept his pistol pointing at his chest, edged closer.

Granger frowned. 'Well, that might be a hanging offence, make no mistake about it.'

'You see!' Jem turned to me, a complacent smirk on his face.

'But you connived with him, Jem,' Granger frowned. 'The authorities ain't going to like that and I don't believe they would hang a nigra right now. Times are changing.'

'You can hang me for my reading, Mister Granger, sir, but not for poisoning Missy Maxine. As for Mammy Mable, she's my own mother. I would never have poisoned her or anyone else, sir. I'm a peaceable man.'

There was a hush of astonishment at Garland's words, spoken in clear English. I raised my finger to my lips, warning him to keep quiet.

'Don't listen to him, Pa!' Jem railed. 'It's obvious he killed Maxine. He hates whites, just like all nigras. We've got to lynch him.'

'We haven't got to do anything of the kind, Jem. We'll take him to Paxton so he can stand trial.'

'Trial!' It was Forest who spoke, his high pitched whine rasping at my nerves. 'Do you mean that? You know Miss Vain has agreed to be my wife. If there's a court case about Maxine, it'll mean more scandal than her family will tolerate.'

Granger nodded his head. 'That's true, Forest.' He rubbed his hands together. 'Miss Vain's father is running for office. Any suspicion of a scandal would finish him.'

'You mean you'll hang Garland without a trial?' I jumped to my feet, speaking for the first time.

'No. Not that. We're civilised men, Fleur. But we're boxed in. No matter what we do someone will be unfairly hurt.'

Forest rose quickly, his pistol pointed at Garland's chest. He advanced a step. 'Maybe you don't know what to do, Pa. But I do.'

I threw myself in front of Garland, shielding him

from Forest's pistol. My chin tilted upward in defiance.

'I refuse to let you kill Garland,' I said steadily. 'He didn't do it.'

'Oh? He didn't?' Granger was trying to humour me. 'How do you know that?'

'How do I know? I'll tell you how,' I watched them warily. 'I know Garland didn't kill Maxine, because I did! I put poison in the whiskey jar when I sent Garland off to get water for Maxine. I didn't know Mammy Mable would drink it too. I'm sorry about that.'

'No, Missy! No, Missy!' Garland stretched his hands out toward me. Forest jabbed the pistol at him, forcing him back. 'No Missy!' Garland repeated, shaking his head.

'It's true, it's true!' I stamped my foot. 'Send me for a trial, Mister Granger. Then you'll hear scandal!' I laughed dryly. 'Unless you want your men to string me up in front of Maddocks. I wouldn't want to inconvenience you.'

From behind me, I heard Garland's muffled sob.

Forest was the first to react. 'You can't do that, Pa. It would ruin us. Miss Vain – '

'Hold your tongue, boy!' Granger's face was red and the kindness had drained from his voice. 'Fleur!' he snapped. 'I don't believe you. What did you have against Maxine?'

'You don't believe me! Ask your precious son, Jem, what Maxine and he did to me.'

'Fleur!' Jem jumped up and lunged at me. Garland was quicker. He clamped his powerful hands around Jem's shoulders, pinning his arms to his side in a bear hug.

'Let him go, boy!' Granger said wearily, lifting his pistol. 'Sit down, both of you.'

Jem glared at me, shook his shoulders free of Garland's grasp, and returned to his seat.

'I don't know what's been going on in this house, Jem. I'll never understand you. Your wife says she killed Maxine. What do you want to do?'

Jem peered at me; he looked baffled.

'She can't stand trial!' Forest said in a defeated voice.

I smiled. 'I've nothing more to say, Jem. Unless you want me to tell your father about Maxine – '

'No!' His shout cut into mine. 'Pa! I need your help. I know I've been foolhardy and reckless in the past. Look where it's got me!' He buried his head in his hands. 'I'm sorry, Pa! I really am.'

I doubt if Granger was fooled by Jem's performance. His tears sounded quite unreal.

'Help me, Pa!'

Forest tucked his pistol in his belt. 'You've got to help him, Pa,' he wheedled. 'If no one knows about all this then I can go ahead and marry Miss Vain and you'll get – '

'Damn it, shut up, both of you! Let me think.'

I glanced in triumph at Garland.

'The whole county will be here soon. Maxine cut quite a figure in these parts.' Granger was thinking aloud. 'Forest, I want you to ride to Paxton and get Doc James here.'

'Doc James!' Forest laughed. 'I'll never get him to come. He's always to drunk to stand. You want the new doctor, Doc Felix!'

'I want Doc James, boy! Won't you sons of mine ever do what I tell you? Doc James is goin' to come here and say Maxine died from a fall down the stairs, right? For a cask of the best whiskey you have at Maddocks, he'll sign the certificate and we can bury poor Maxine today.'

He raised his face to look at me, a deep loathing spreading across his features. 'You'll never say anything of this to anybody, Fleur!'

'What about Garland?' I demanded.

'Garland?' Granger turned to Jem. 'You've got the cotton to bring in, haven't you, Jem? You ought to tell your nigras to get back to work instead of wasting our time here!'

Jem scowled and nodded his head. He seemed relieved that the matter was temporarily ended. With a slight bow, he said softly, 'Yes, Pa, whatever you say.'

CHAPTER THIRTY-ONE

I sat motionless in the sewing room, staring through the window into the weak sunshine of the fall afternoon. The sampler on which I had intended to work lay untouched on the table by my side. Only birds moved, their aimless flight emphasising the isolation which seemed to be my destiny at Maddocks. There were four hundred people living on the plantation, but not one of them was to be seen from my lonely perch. There was an ominous silence as I watched the sad dying of the day.

The blacks and Jem's hired crackers were in the cotton fields. I dreaded what would happen at the end of the cotton picking. Jem was not stupid. He knew that if he laid a finger on Garland, there would be no cotton. Jem needed that cotton, but I knew Jem. He would not forget the injury to his pride inflicted by his father. Jem was waiting for the cotton to be picked, ginned, and baled and then he would unleash the hatred coiled in his heart. I feared for Garland.

There were only a few days to go before all the cotton would be stored and the numbing routine of picking would be over. The lashes of the crackers' whips would be stilled, the slaves would be given other tasks and Jem would have time to plan his revenge.

I was sure he planned something. In the weeks which had passed since Maxine's death, I had no opportunity to speak more than briefly to either Garland or Jem. Both of them seemed to be avoiding me. Trott said that Jem was living in the overseer's house soaking himself in whiskey day and night. I longed to see Garland. Trott took several messages pleading with him to visit me, but always the reply was the same – he must remain in the cotton.

The sun was diluted as it slipped behind the magnolias leaving the sky a watery light blue. I recalled how Uncle Leo had tended to the flowers at Maddocks with an erratic determination. In his moments of stress, he drew comfort from their beauty. I thought, perhaps, that I should take more interest in the garden. I would ask Garland for a pair of tractable boys to assist me. Garland! There – the more I resolved not to think of him, the more he entered my mind.

I peered in astonishment at the drive. A branch of a magnolia shrub silhouetted against the sunset detached itself and advanced toward the house. I blinked the sun-stars away from my eyes and peered again. I was right, but it was a man, not a magnolia branch, riding out of the sunset and up to the portico. There was something oddly familiar about him.

I jumped up from my seat and ran to the front door. Trott was grumbling as he opened it. I paused, settled my skirts around me, and made my way onto the piazza.

'Wayne!'

'Hah, that's the greeting I dreamed of.' Wayne raised his hat and smiled broadly. His tousled hair flopped over his brow and his soft eyes gleamed.

'You look like a slave stealer!' I exclaimed, taking in his torn coat, dirty breeches, and mud-encrusted boots. His horse steamed.

'You aim to shame me, Fleur?' He jammed his hat jauntily on the back of his head and swung out of the saddle. He eyed me cautiously. 'Is it permitted for a trader to relax himself on milady's piazza?'

'Why, of course, Wayne. Do come in. I'm delighted to see you.'

'I never thought I'd be hearing such sweet words from you, Fleur. You sent me away with a flea in my ear twelve months ago.'

I shivered in the crisp chill of the twilight. 'Come in,' I repeated, leading the way into the house. 'There's a fire in the parlour.'

'I'm honoured!' Wayne laughed, a self-disparaging sound which grated on my ears. He sat opposite me and stared.

'You make me nervous with such a look, Wayne. Am I changed?'

'In looks, more lovely than I ever remembered, Fleur. In heart, only you can say.'

'Oh, fie, Wayne!' I wished I could still blush.

'You asked for that, Fleur.'

'So I did. I've been lonely these past weeks. All the slaves are in the field, no neighbours call now that the funeral's over, and Jem, well Jem is busy too.' I twisted the wedding ring on my finger.

'I've heard about Maxine,' Wayne said harshly.

'You offer no sympathy?'

'To you, Fleur? Her death could not have been a happier accident. Such a convenient fall.'

This time I did blush. I raised my hand to my breast hoping to hide the pounding of my heart. 'Wayne,' I whispered. 'You haven't learned tact while you've been away, have you?'

'No,' he said boldly. 'And I'm happier for it.'

'Why have you come here?'

He gave a wry smile. 'Your spontaneous welcome for an old friend has disappeared quick enough, eh? Are you worried, Fleur? Anxious in case I discover things best not known outside Maddocks?'

'You're hateful!' I stamped my foot but not with real anger. I watched Wayne slyly. He was the opposite of Jem, blond where Jem was dark, short where Jem was tall, cheerful where Jem glowered.

'Am I hateful, Fleur?' His eyes held mine in blunt appraisal. 'I hoped you'd find me otherwise.'

I gasped.

'Do I find you receptive, Fleur?' His voice quavered.

'No, Wayne, you do not! You've come at a strange time. I was feeling lonely. Please don't take advantage of me in my grief.'

'In your grief!' Wayne laughed aloud. 'What grief do you know about, Fleur? "In your relief" would be a better choice of words.'

'Don't taunt me, Wayne,' I snapped crossly. 'Maxine's death wasn't easy to bear.'

'For someone other than you, Fleur, it would have been a tragedy. I have no doubt you had Garland to console you.'

'Garland!' I flushed angrily. 'Why do you mention him? Garland is the overseer now. He's supervising the cotton. I haven't seen him for days, not since Maxine died.'

'So the black giant still attracts you, does he, Fleur?' Wayne sounded regretful. 'I had hoped your feelings would have strengthened for me, not for him.'

'Wayne, you've said enough! I'll have to call Trott to show you the door.'

'But I've only this minute arrived!' Wayne spread his legs and smiled easily. 'I'm in no hurry to start travelling again. Do you know, Fleur, what I said to myself as I rode up the drive and saw the tall columns of Maddocks ahead of me? I said, "So this is what it's like to come home!" I really did. I look on Maddocks as my home.'

'Your home!' I was touched.

'Yes, Fleur. All those months I was travelling, it was the thought of one day being able to see Maddocks again which kept me going.'

'Maddocks! Not me?'

'Ah, Fleur, disappointed? There is hope for me, is there? Maddocks has the same hold on me as you have, Fleur. Together, you are irresistible!'

'Fiddlesticks, Wayne Carter! You're a good-for-nothing vagabond and you've come back here to see what you can get because no one else will have you.'

'Exactly! Isn't that one reason why I like you? You have none of the false gentility of our Southern belles. Your guts are made of sterner stuff.'

'Wayne! Look to your language!'

'And you to yours, Fleur! Such a way to treat a guest. I'm a vagabond but what right have you to tell me so? I'm not in your employ.' He paused. 'Am I?'

'Heavens, no. I expect Jem will chase you off with the dogs as soon as he sees you.'

'I think not.' Wayne stuck his legs out in front of him. 'I hear he has need of good overseer. What better man can he find than me?'

'He has Garland!'

'Oh yes, your precious Garland. It was Granger Hayard himself who suggested I approach Jem. From what I understand, Jem would quickly see the merits of having me in Garland's place. What do you think, Fleur?'

'It makes no difference to me.' I was considering what this would mean to Garland. If Wayne stayed, Garland would lose his use to Jem but, with the picking coming to an end, he would lose that anyway. I smiled.

'Yes, perhaps it would be pleasant to have you here, Wayne.'

'There is a glint in your eyes, Fleur. What makes you think I'm to be trusted now where I wasn't before?'

'Because' – I hesitated meaningfully – 'I know that you burned the cotton house.'

Wayne gripped the arm of his chair and glared at me as I rose and swept across the floor. I closed the door properly so that we could not be overheard.

'I saw you do it, Wayne, so there's no need to deny it. I was looking for you that night. It was silly of me, I know, but I thought I would run away with you. I suppose I was ashamed of myself.' I paused. 'Fortunately, before I threw myself at you, I saw you with Ladybelle. I realised then that Maddocks is more important – whatever happens.'

I peered out of the back window at the flambeaux of the slaves as they marched in the distance from the fields to the gin houses. My voice was husky when I turned and faced Wayne. 'By the way, what happened to Ladybelle? Did you sell her when you got tired of her?'

'Fleur, don't judge all men by your husband! Since you know, there's no point in pretending. Ladybelle died, in New Orleans. A fever. I miss her.'

'You've known the love of a slave, Wayne. We have that in common.'

Wayne gazed at me without speaking. There was a look of bewilderment in his eyes. He brushed back his hair quickly, and his features brightened, 'It's a good beginning, Fleur,' he said hopefully.

'Perhaps. I'm going to my chamber now, Wayne.

Trott will bring you a lamp. You must see Jem. Arrange with him what you want.'

Within days of Wayne's arrival, the cotton picking was over and he was installed as the overseer. The matter was arranged speedily over whiskey, and Wayne and Jem emerged from the library with their arms clasped around each other's shoulders. Jem managed a smile.

'I'm going to Savannah,' he told me curtly. 'Wayne here will be in charge of the nigras. All of them!'

'I'm pleased to hear it.' I looked up innocently from my sewing.

'Shall I buy you a bauble from Savannah, my dear?' Jem's voice was slurred.

'You needn't bother.'

'A drop of poison perhaps!' He roared with laughter and stumbled out onto the piazza with Wayne. I listened to the two of them descending the steps and making their way drunkenly to the overseer's compound.

It was night and my eyes hurt from the strain of sewing. I called Trott to close up the shutters and walked wearily up the stairs. When I reached the darkened alcove on the landing opposite my room, I paused. I lifted my head and listened carefully. I sniffed. There was the unmistakable musky odour of cotton hanging in the air.

'Garland!' I exclaimed, pushing open the door to my chamber and hurrying inside. He stood in the centre of the room, his tall shadow rearing out of the darkness. I placed the lamp down on the table and ran to him.

'Garland!' My legs weakened and tears filled my eyes.

He didn't move. I stood on the tips of my toes to kiss him but his body was unyielding. He was staring over my head at the door.

'Garland, what is it?' I glanced behind me anxiously. The door was closed. 'There's no one there, silly.' I wound my hands around his waist.

'I thought I saw Mammy Mable.'

'Mammy Mable? Oh Garland, she's been too sick to climb the stairs.'

'I know, Fleur. You said you poisoned her and Maxine. You saved me from hanging when you said that. Why did you do it?'

I released Garland and walked over to my chair by the window. I sat down and gazed at him. His worn chambray shirt clung tightly to his torso, his broad back rippled with muscles. He had toughened in the fields, his youthful grace replaced by an appealing ruggedness.

'For you, of course.'

'No, Fleur. Don't play with me. Why did you kill Maxine? Was that for me?'

'Kill her?' I must have looked appalled. 'I didn't kill her, Garland! I only said that I did to stop Granger and Jem from hanging you.'

Garland frowned, his dark eyes misting with anxiety.

'I believed *you* did it to rid me of Maxine,' I told him.

'No!' Garland flopped onto the edge of my bed, staring at me. 'No!' he croaked.

I was puzzled.

Garland swallowed thickly. 'It's been haunting my mind all the time, Fleur. I wanted to come to you but I had to wait until the cotton was over. I didn't kill Maxine. I really believed you did. If you didn't put the poison in her whiskey and I didn't, it must have been –'

'Jem!' I snapped.

Garland nodded his head, peering unseeing out of the window. The blackness of the night mirrored his face. He felt me gazing at him and turned slowly to face me.

'It's all over now, Garland! The picking is finished and Jem is going to Savannah to sell the cotton. We can be together again. You can come here and read. We can talk. We can plan.'

'No! We're not the same, Fleur!'

'I know that, Garland. But, don't you see, it doesn't matter to me one bit.'

'Not to you perhaps. But what about me? Do you ever trouble to think of me, Fleur?'

'Why of course I do!' I walked over to stand in front of him as he sat on the bed. 'I've thought of you the whole time while you've been picking that silly cotton.'

'That silly cotton killed one nigra this season, Fleur. He was too sick to work so the crackers lashed him until he died. It's the same every day, Fleur. There's nothing I can do to stop Marse Jem from striking them when he –'

'That's over now, Garland. Wayne is going to be the overseer. You've always respected him. He'll be kinder to the slaves.'

'Fleur!' Garland raised his voice. 'I'm not a child.' He pounded his fist into the palm of his hand. 'When Marse Jem comes back from Savannah, he's going to come for me. You know that yourself and all the blacks know it. He doesn't need me so he's bound to try to break me. He and the crackers.'

'Oh Garland!' I began to tremble with fear.

'I'm not scared for me, Fleur. I'm scared for you.'

'Me?' I stopped trembling.

'Fleur, don't you understand what's happening? The days of bondage are drawing to an end. The time is swiftly coming when we blacks are going to be free. We're going to take that freedom even if we have to fight for it.'

He stood up and advanced toward me, his fists clenched. 'If we have to fight, Fleur, we must kill.' He raised his fists in front of his face, clenching them until they shook.

My eyes widened in consternation. 'Garland! What foolish talk have you been listening to?'

'Foolish talk?' His eyes blazed. 'There's a gentleman called Lincoln campaigning for President, Fleur. If he wins, then slavery is going to end.'

'If that is so, why are you talking about fighting?'

'Can you see the South freeing its slaves because a Republican president tells it to?'

'Heavens, no!'

Garland shook his head sadly. 'I'm telling you how it will be, Fleur. If Jem harms me, Maddocks will be lost, burned to the ground. The slaves are only waiting for the moment. There's nothing I can do to stop it now. You must go away, go back to Savannah where you belong. Where you'll be safe.'

Garland spun around and stamped from the room. I gazed after him, gritting my teeth with-determination. No one, not even Garland with his band of slaves, was going to drive me from Maddocks.

CHAPTER THIRTY-TWO

Garland stayed away from me while Jem was absent. I missed his companionship for I had looked forward to the time when we would be able to share moments together again. I realised he was torn between his feelings for me and the loyalty he felt for his slave compatriots. If only he would return to me, I was sure that I could convince him that he had been misled.

I was musing before my glass one morning when the sound of a horseman galloping up the drive disturbed me. I listened carefully as Trott greeted the rider. I shuddered. It was Jem.

'Mistress about?' I heard his loud question.

'She be in she chamber, sah.' Trott pondered. 'She say she ain' wan' to see no one –'

Jem was already running up the stairs, taking them two at a time while Trott's frail voice drifted up behind him. I had time only to pass my hand over my hair before Jem was at my door. He pushed it open without knocking.

'Jem!' I dug my fingernails into my palms mustering courage for whatever evil he was going to let loose around me.

'Am I to be admonished for entering my wife's chamber?' he asked, his face twisted with grim mockery.

'What do you want?' I sat nervously on the edge of my stool.

'Maddocks!'

I was incredulous. 'Well, at last you have the courage to utter your intentions aloud instead of scheming behind my back.'

'How like a woman! I want Maddocks, of course. I want Maddocks preserved, Fleur, not a charred ruin.' He paced across the floor and I noticed how his eyes were bright with excitement.

'There is evil afoot sure enough, Fleur, but not on my part.'

'On mine then?' I straightened my back.

'Hell, no. You are just a spoiled hussy. The slaves, Fleur.' He threw himself into my favourite chair by the window. The chair seemed to shudder under his weight.

'You haven't thought to ask why I've returned so quickly from Savannah.'

I raised my eyebrow. This Jem straddling my chair and reeking of excitement and action quite unnerved me. I had steeled myself to a coldness whenever he was close but seeing him outlined against the window, his dark hair falling across his forehead and his jaw set defiantly, made me falter.

'Why the haste indeed, Jem? It was surely not concern for me.'

'You can be as spiteful as you like, Fleur. I told you, it's Maddocks. The nigras can have you, for all I care.'

I was bursting with curiosity. 'What have you heard?'

'Aha, now you're worried! The county is under siege, Fleur. Those Northern seducers have been prowling through the plantations like patrollers, only they're a lot more efficient. The nigras, Fleur, every one of 'em, is scheming insurrection.'

I gasped. Garland was right.

Jem took my startled expression as one of fear at his news. He smirked. 'What do you think of that, Fleur?'

'Why Maddocks?' I whispered suddenly aware that I might lose my beautiful home after all.

'Maddocks? Oh yes. My pals in Milledgeville say that they've heard Maddocks will be the first house in the county to burn. Pa should have let me hang Garland that first day when he pestered Maxine.'

'Your father was right!' I stood up and stamped my foot. 'Garland has done no wrong. You wouldn't have any cotton at all without him, and you know it. He's the one who has kept the slaves in check while you've been mistreating them!'

'Me? Ill-treat a nigra? It's impossible! But it's not nigras alone. There are whites behind them. Nigras ain't got no brains to think of uprising by themselves. They'll work slow or pretend they're sick to inconvenience us, but they wouldn't try to destroy us, Fleur.' Jem looked indignant.

'They could have heard about the sympathy people have for them in the North. They could plan their own destiny, Jem.'

'You're right, Fleur! But they got their news from the Free-Soilers swarming through the county. Every white man is suspect unless he's a slave-holder himself.'

'The crackers are white. I can't see them causing any trouble.'

'Crackers! The factor in Savannah told me to watch the crackers. They hate the nigras because they're doing the work and there's nothing left for them. He said they want the nigras to be free so that planters have to employ crackers instead.'

I couldn't help laughing.

'It won't be ridiculous when Maddocks is burnt to the ground. Like the cotton house was!'

I gasped, staring at Jem in alarm. Wayne! Was he here to stir the blacks up?

Jem stood up. 'I don't know who burnt that cotton but I'll wager it was a dam' Republican. We have to be on our guard, Fleur.'

'What are you going to do?' I tried to sound light-hearted so Jem wouldn't notice my concern.

'I'm going to keep Garland under my eye for a start,' growled Jem, his hand on the door. 'I'll thank you not to write any notes of passion to him, Fleur. This could be a matter of life or death.'

Jem was true to his word. He brought Garland in from the fields and forced him to trail after him like a pet dog. He made him don the livery of a house boy again which must have been humiliating to Garland after being accustomed to having control of the slaves. Garland said nothing and was correct in his conduct. But it was the way he hunched his massive shoulders or flexed his muscles contemptuously when he thought Jem was not watching, that revealed his true feelings.

Garland was cold and arrogant whenever he carried a tray to my chamber or held the lamp for me to read by. I tried to break through his façade, with a whispered word of endearment but he always turned away.

Jem watched Garland carefully. He refused to let him out of the house by himself and even made him sleep on the floor of his chamber at night. It was tantalising to know that Garland was lying in the next room but I could not speak to him. I was worried by the tension between Jem and Garland. It seemed that each was waiting to see who would break first.

I expected Jem to escort the cotton to Savannah. It was the best crop ever raised at Maddocks and Jem was proud of it. He had been offered a price which would pay off the debts from the previous season and provide funds for new seed and tools. Jem took no chances that it would be burnt again. He put some of the drivers to guard the cotton house and hired crackers to watch the guards. It came as a surprise and disappointment when Jem told me he would not be going to Savannah himself.

'You shouldn't be surprised, Fleur!' he grinned. And the grin implied that he knew the reason for my disappointment.

'But who will take the cotton to the factors?'

'I'm touched by your concern, Fleur,' he said blandly. 'I thought you found such matters of no interest.'

'I'm wondering whom you can trust to deliver the cotton safely. After what you've told me about danger.'

'Wayne, of course.'

'Wayne?' I gasped, wondering how Jem could be so insensitive to Wayne's real character. 'You're not going with him?'

'Now that would be foolish, Fleur. You ask me to leave Maddocks in your care? For you and Garland for a month?'

'It seems no more foolish than leaving the cotton in Wayne's care.'

'I think not, Fleur. You see, Wayne is like all men. The promise of a reward and a pleasant occupation when he returns here will buy his loyalty. He can't swindle me. I've arranged for the money to be paid to our bankers as soon as Wayne delivers the cotton.' He grinned slyly. 'I'll remain to protect you and Maddocks, Fleur.'

Jem's mocking sealed my silence. But I was certain that we should never see Wayne again. It would be simple for him to sell the cotton to another factor and disappear with the money. In a way I was pleased. Jem would be forced to reinstate Garland as overseer if Wayne did not return. It would give Garland his self-respect so he would respond to me again.

I smiled knowingly and returned to the book I had been reading.

There was a lull at Maddocks, an air of suspense. With Wayne away, Jem patrolled the plantation with more arms than a buccaneer. His cracker cronies and other planters rode over in the afternoons and held long sessions in the library and smoking room, keeping Trott and Garland darting backward and forth with jars of whiskey for them. I could make no sense of their talk of secession and war. It seemed like the foolish ranting of spoiled children.

Instead, I usually retired early to my boudoir. I would read a little or sit at my window gazing out at the moon over the live oaks. One night the raucous sound of Jem's voice as he stumbled up the stairs broke into my reverie. He was drunk every night and depended on Garland to get him to his room.

'You're the most elegant nigra, Garland. You know that? I swear I could get over two thousand dollars for you in Milledgeville.'

I caught my breath. So that was his plan: to sell Garland! I gripped the side of my chair, listening carefully. Jem crashed into the wall of the chamber. Garland opened the door and manoeuvred him through.

'Cuz if I took you to Natchez, I gonna get more than that!' he slurred. 'Don't need no papers in Natchez. I'll write the bill of sale mahself!'

There was a loud thud which must have been Jem falling against his bed. I rose quietly from my chair and tiptoed over to the door which joined our rooms. It was locked from Jem's side but I could hear him muttering drunkenly.

'Pull the dam' boot, dam' you!'

Garland was helping him undress.

'Where's the 'tensil?' Jem demanded. There was a sudden exclamation. 'Boy, you shit in that?'

'Nossah!' Garland's voice was edged with anger.

'But it's full! You didn't empty it this mornin', boy.'

'Nossah.' Garland sounded defiant.

'Why not, boy?' The drunken meandering of Jem's voice changed to tones that were menacing and controlled.

'We was busy, sah. Yo' take me wid yo' to de fiel's sah. Ah ain' have no time, sah,' Garland drawled.

'No time, eh?' Jem chuckled. I heard him unbuckle his belt and imagined him standing up to face Garland, his ever present pistol in his hand.

'Well, you have time now. I give you one minute to drink all the piss and shit in that pot. One minute from now.'

There was silence. I knelt down quickly and peered through the keyhole. Jem was holding the pot in one hand and his pistol in the other. Garland stared at him, his pink tongue running swiftly over his lips, like a snake's.

'Take it boy. Go on!'

'Ah ain' drinkin' yuh piss, Marse Jem.'

'You refuse?'

'Yassah!' Garland seemed to swell as he stood in front of Jem. His chest ballooned out, his shirt ripping as he tightened his muscles.

Jem watched curiously then jerked his hand upwards. 'If you won't drink it, try bathin' in it, you ornery bastard!'

The urine in the pot splashed into Garland's face, drenching him. Garland stood motionless letting the stinking mess drain off his face onto his chest.

Jem fell back on to the bed, chortling to himself, his pistol hanging loosely in his hand.

Slowly, Garland raised his right arm and wiped his eyes on his sleeve. He blinked them open and sneered at Jem. 'Is dere anyt'ing' else, sah?'

'No, boy, no.' Jem sounded mellow. 'Lie down an' sleep.'

'Yassah.' Garland walked backward away from the bed.

Jem barely watched him. Too late, he realised that Garland was by the door. 'Hey! Where you going?' Jem shouted. 'I said lie down an' sleep.'

Garland stepped out of the room and closed the door behind him. Jem fumbled with his pistol and aimed. The shot slammed into the door and Jem cursed. He rolled off the bed groping around for his boots.

I ran over to my own door and opened it as Garland was walking slowly to the stairs. 'Garland!' I cautioned. 'Run! He'll kill you.'

'Yas, Mistis.' Garland paused and bowed his head.

'Have you gone crazy, Garland? Don't try to be smart.'

'No, Mistis. Good night.' He continued to glide toward the stairs like a stately butler. I ran to him and seized him by his arm.

'Quick,' I whispered. 'Come into my chamber. Jem will think you've gone down stairs.'

We heard Jem fumbling to unlatch his door. Garland's face, still dripping with the mess from Jem's pot, quivered. I pulled him across the floor. He was in a daze, struggling to control himself. I was terrified that he might ignore Jem's pistols and try to fight him.

I got him into my room and shut the door as Jem opened his.

'Where'sh de nigra?' we heard him mumble.

'There.' I pointed out my wardrobe to Garland. He stood in the centre of the chamber unable to move. 'Oh, get in it, Garland.' I pushed him toward the closet and opened the door. 'Get in before he comes!'

Garland sighed heavily and stepped into the wardrobe like a gentleman of leisure entering his coach for an afternoon drive. I smothered him with dresses, ignoring the stinking mess dripping down his face. I shut the door.

My heart was thumping so loudly, I expected Jem to hear it. I tiptoed to my door and stood quietly behind it. Jem was groping his way along the landing, mumbling to himself. 'I'm gonna get that nigra! Once and for all!'

Jem reached the stairs and began a lumbering descent to the passage below. There was a crash as he threw open the piazza door and lurched into the night.

CHAPTER THIRTY-THREE

Garland sat in a confusion of flounces, frills and ribbons. His damp brown face glowered at me under brows heavy with anger. I put my hand on his shoulder.

'You can come out now. Jem has gone off into the plantation to find you. He'll be hours.'

Garland shrugged my fingers off his shoulders and emerged slowly from the wardrobe, parting the dresses hanging around his head with annoyance. He stared at me sullenly.

'Why did you involve yourself, Fleur?' His lower lip hung open and he gripped the corner of the wardrobe in his huge hand.

'What a funny question!' I moved over to the open window and pulled the heavy curtain across it. I had slept alone ever since Ladybelle's departure a year before, so there was no maid who could interrupt us. I stepped silently over to the door to lock it.

'Leave it!'

Garland's face shook off its sulkiness and his eyes

followed me with calculated determination. I hesitated.

'He might come back,' I crooned.

'Of course he'll come back. I want to be ready for him.'

'What are you going to do?' The hard glint in his eyes unnerved me. I sat at the foot of my bed.

'You know, Fleur. The slaves have wanted me to lead them for weeks. I always said no. I can't stop them any more. We have to destroy Jem. And Maddocks. We must be free.'

'Fiddlesticks, Garland! What is this freedom? If you and the others rebel you'll be hunted down by the crackers and their dogs and lynched from the nearest bough. You won't have a chance.'

'We have a chance, Fleur. You've stopped me in the past but you won't stop me again. Why didn't you leave Maddocks and go back to Savannah when I told you?'

'Because I won't let you do this, Garland! Don't you see I can help you! I can help you run away, now, before Jem comes back. I can give you money, and a pass. You can go to the North and be educated. You'll be free then, Garland, not wasting the last minutes of your life skulking in ditches while the patrollers hunt you.'

'Fleur!' Garland advanced toward the bed. 'Aren't you frightened? Don't you know what we're going to do to Jem? Don't you understand what will happen to Maddocks and to you? You're the one who must run away.' He towered over me.

I looked up at him with my heart breaking. He was still thinking of my safety. I walked over to the washstand in the corner of the room and carried the basin of water back. 'Sit here,' I said. 'Let me wash your face.' Wordlessly, he dropped into the chair and I drew the washcloth across his face with a caressing movement. 'If it's really I who must run,' I whispered, 'then at last we are equal.'

Garland's face was close to mine. I could feel his breath on my cheek. I tilted back my head so that my hair tumbled over my bare shoulders, the white tarlatan of my night dress shimmering before his eyes. His breathing increased until I could see the rise and fall of his chest under ruffles of his open shirt.

He sighed. 'Fleur.' The determination had slipped from his voice and he uttered my name with a passion which set me trembling. I raised my hands to touch him. He seized them in his palms and lifted them to his lips, smothering my fingers with kisses.

'Garland! Stop! Stop!'

'No, Missy.' His voice was deep and anguished. 'You're not going to tell me when to stop any more.' His mouth fastened on the inside of my left wrist and slipped up my bare arm to my elbow, nibbling the flesh with kisses of exquisite gentleness.

'Garland!' I moaned, overwhelmed by the tremors soaring through me. I was limp, all strength drained out of my body by his touch. My lips, guided by a will of their own, parted slowly. Garland's cheek brushed against mine, tingling my flesh. I shuddered and his strong arms snaked around my waist and clasped me to him. My eyes closed as his lips found mine. I surrendered to his embrace.

There were no doubts for us now. He laid me tenderly on the bed and spread my skirts under me with elaborate care. His kisses explored me, each caress shivering through my body until I lay writhing beneath him, fluttering with a fever which only he could still. I clutched his broad shoulders desperately, running my hands under his shirt and twining the tight whorls of hair at the nape of his neck around my fingers.

Garland entered me slowly. His whole body blended into mine. His gentle, graceful loving touched a deep sensation in me which Jem's brutal thrusting had never stirred. I clung to Garland and flowed with him. I became part of him, and he part of me. We were more than equal, we were one.

The door crashed open and a whip slashed into Garland's shoulder tearing his shirt to shreds. As it withdrew the tongue sliced across my bare breast drawing a thin line of blood above my nipples. Garland leaped off me and stumbled to his feet. Jem furled the whip for another strike, clenching his fingers around the leather shaft with a snarl of grim satisfaction.

The bullwhip is the master of all whips. Its stock is loaded with lead to give it force. The thong does not bruise, it cuts. I screamed as Jem's arm snapped back and the whip scorched through the air and hacked into Garland's back again. He was fumbling on the floor to pull up his breeches which were bunched around his ankles. The blow toppled him over.

'No, Jem!' I screamed. 'No.'

Jem turned a baleful eye on me and grinned. The whip spun through the posts of the bed and tore at the soft flesh of my breasts. Blood seeped out of the stripes and oozed onto my fingers when I clutched myself to staunch the pain.

'Jem!' I screamed as the lash descended again.

The tongue caught around the post of the bed. Jem tugged at it quickly but he was too late. Garland seized the whip and pulled. Jem was dragged into the room, struggling to keep the stock in his hand. Garland was on his feet facing him. Jem glared at him and flung the stock at his face, drawing his pistols and pointing them at Garland.

'I can shoot now,' drawled Jem, 'or sling up a rope and hang you so the nigras can see.'

'Don't shoot him, Jem. Shoot me instead.'

My cry distracted Jem and he turned to glare at me. Garland snatched up the stock and flicked the bullwhip into Jem's face. The lash carved a line across his eyes. Jem gasped, dropping a pistol on the floor and discharging the other as he staggered back. The ball singed the damask top of my bed and lodged in the ceiling.

Garland crouched low on his haunches waiting for Jem to move into the centre of the room. He dropped the whip by his side and sprang at Jem like a cougar. His fist smashed into Jem's face.

Jem rolled with the blow, lifting his pistol and smacking it down on Garland's head with a crack. Both of them fell to the floor, stunned.

Jem rolled onto Garland, using his pistol as a club

and raining down blows on Garland's face. Garland twisted out of the way, grabbing the leg of the bed to haul himself to his feet. Jem continued to pound him with his pistol.

I was standing in the centre of the bed, my night dress hanging in tatters around me. I was too frightened to scream for help. Suddenly I had an idea. I tugged at the coverlet of the bed, gathered it in my hands and threw it over Jem. It settled on his head, falling over his eyes and blinding him. He tore it from him with an oath but Garland was on his feet again.

Garland charged like a bull, knocking Jem over as his shoulder thudded into his stomach. Jem clutched at the air for support and tumbled backward. He fell against the curtain in front of the balustrade. The curtain parted and the balustrade splintered with a loud crack. Jem grasped at the curtain but it slipped through his fingers. His eyes vivid with fear, he hurtled through the window into the dark night.

'Fleur –'

Jem cried out my name before his voice was cut off by the slap of his body crashing into the hard stone floor of the piazza.

Garland helped me down the stairs. Neither of us spoke but we kept our arms wrapped around each other saying more by this gesture than by any words. Slaves were rushing toward the house from the quarters. I wondered if this was the beginning of the insurrection.

Trott stood anxiously by the open door to the piazza. He threw up his hands with despair. 'Oh Mistis, oh Mistis –' he began, hobbling toward me.

Before he could continue, a figure emerged from behind the centre column, two pistols pointed straight at us. The figure beckoned Garland and me out onto the piazza. I gripped Garland's hand and he tightened his hold on my waist.

'It's all right,' Garland whispered, tapping Jem's pistols which he had stuck into his own belt. 'I'll protect you.'

'Come on, Garland, step lively now!' The figure advanced out of the shadows into the faint glow of the lamp.

'Wayne!'

'Yes, Fleur. You sound surprised. I arrived in time, it seems.'

'I thought you'd gone to Savannah with the cotton.'

'I did Fleur, sold it too, as directed. Step over there, Garland.' Wayne waved with his pistol to where Jem's body was lying. I averted my eyes.

'No, Fleur, you, too. Take a look. See!'

Jem lay face down, his body shattered and his head twisted under his arm. His face was rigid with terror. I began to weep, recalling how, at the end, he had called my name.

'Who killed him, Fleur? He didn't jump from the window, I suppose?'

'I.' Garland glared defiantly across Jem's body at Wayne.

'Indeed?' Wayne grinned. 'I didn't think you'd let me down, Garland.'

I turned on Garland with dismay, remembering what Jem had told me about whites helping the slaves to revolt.

'Did Wayne tell you to kill Jem?'

Wayne prevented Garland from replying. 'Heavens no, Fleur. Garland can manage his own insurrection without any order from me, can't you, Garland?' Wayne lowered his pistols and looked directly at us both.

'Jem's dead. You're free, Fleur. And so is Garland, I suppose.'

Garland sat down suddenly on Jem's chair and cradled his head in his hand.

'Go to your quarters!' Wayne shouted at the slaves who had gathered in the courtyard. 'You, there,' he identified some of the drivers in the crowd. 'Get them back to their cabins.'

No one moved. A mass of black faces stared at us. I put my hand on Garland's shoulder, squeezing it tenderly. He raised his eyes to meet mine, a look of regret smothering his bitter smile. He shrugged his shoulders.

'You've saved Maddocks, Fleur. You and Wayne. You've beaten me, but I'll always love you, Fleur. You've made me become a man.' He stood up and moved to the edge of the piazza.

'Where are you going?'

'North!'

'No, Garland.' I shrieked. 'Stay. I'll give you your freedom. Anything. Only stay, please! Stay!'

'I'm bound to go now, Fleur. You showed me that. I'm going to study, to be worthy of you.'

'Yes, you should go.' Wayne's interruption surprised me. I had forgotten he was there.

'Hold your tongue, Wayne Carter.' I snapped crossly. 'Maddocks is my plantation and I'll thank you to keep your nose out of my business.'

Wayne scowled and stuck his pistols back in his belt.

'One day I'll come back, Fleur, I promise.' Garland's eyes were moist. 'Maddocks is my home, too, you see.'

Renty led Wayne's horse up to the steps and Garland bounded off the piazza and leaped quickly on to its back. He glanced at Wayne who was watching him with a sour smile of triumph on his face.

'I ain't stopping you, Garland. I aim to look after Fleur.' He chuckled.

'I'm Mistress Fleur to you, Wayne Carter!' I snapped.

There was a whip on the chair. I snatched it up and held it nervously in my fingers, twisting the stock and staring first at Wayne, then at Garland. Garland looked at me and sighed.

Quickly he turned the horse and jabbed his heels into its flanks. The horse trotted away from the piazza, the slaves falling back to make a path for him to pass.

I wanted to beg him to stay, but the words hung unsaid in the air. Garland did not falter. He pushed his way through the throng of blacks without glancing back. His proud head towered above the slaves as he rode briskly around the bend in the carriageway and the night swallowed him up.

I gasped, tears clouding my eyes.

He was gone.

My fist clenched around the stock of the rawhide whip. Behind me, I heard Wayne snort with contempt at my foolishness. The slaves, too, seemed to sense my weakness, sniggering among themselves.

I spun around, raising the whip above my head so quickly that Wayne had no time to scramble out of the way. I slammed down my arm with a strength I never knew I had, shocked into action by my shame and frustration.

Wayne blanched when the leather thong sliced into his unshaven cheek. His eyes flared at the insult. Before he had a chance to protest, I pushed past him and stood on the threshold of the front door. My face was twisted with determination and my voice rasped angrily.

'I may be a woman, Wayne,' I glared at him. 'But I am not your prize. Maddocks is mine, and so are these slaves. You're the overseer, aren't you? Well, oversee! Get them back to the quarters dam' you!' I tossed the whip at him.

A gleam entered Wayne's eye. He strode down the steps, the whip clenched in his fist, his pistols in his belt. He struck out, the whip slashing across the naked chests of the slaves grouped around Maddocks. They fell back instantly, anxious to avoid the gleeful fury blazing in his eyes.

I peered over the heads of the slaves into the darkness where the carriageway disappeared from view behind the magnolias. I gazed down again at the piazza floor where Trott bent over Jem's broken body.

A tottering step sounded beside me and a gnarled old hand slipped into mine. I sighed and walked past Mammy Mable to the edge of the piazza and stared once more into the empty night.

I had lost the only man I loved.

RICH

BY GRAHAM MASTERTON

RICH IS POWER!

RICH IS PASSION!

RICH IS PRIVILEGE!

RICH IS EXPLOSIVE!

RICH is the story of a family that grew from poverty and innocence . . . to become wealthy, beautiful – and damned.

Follow their incredible ascent through seven sprawling decades, in a thrilling saga that springs to life from the pen of Graham Masterton, the most exciting new storyteller since Harold Robbins!

Get RICH quick . . . read Graham Masterton's blockbusting new novel RICH

FICTION 0 7221 5988 9 £1.95

Bare Essence

BY MEREDITH RICH

TYGER HAYES IS ON HER WAY TO THE TOP!

In the glossy world of high fashion, perfume is big business. Each year conglomerates spend millions in the eternal search for the sweet scent of success . . . the ultimate fragrance.

Then a multi-national decided to go one better. And hired a stunning jet-set beauty to create a scent that would capture the imagination of the dazzling élite. Heading a team picked from the cream of the world's leading designers and perfumers, Tyger Hayes was determined to make 'Jazz' the most irresistible and exclusive aroma ever launched. An ambition equalled only by a burning desire that drove her from lover to lover until she found one man who would fulfil her impossible dream and share her need for love.

BARE ESSENCE – the sensational story of a woman determined to fight her way to the top of the fabulous world of high-fashion fragrance. A world of sensual sophistication, make-or-break intrigue, and ultra-chic luxury . . .

GENERAL FICTION 0 7221 7333 4 £1.35